To: Tay

So great to meet you!

# TAKEN BY THE FAE

Tristan ♥'s you!

*Jess Elliott (signature)*

# JESS ELLIOTT

*Taken by the Fae*

Published by Jessi Elliott

Copyright © 2023 by Jessi Elliott

All rights reserved.

eBook ISBN: 978-1-990056-21-5

Print ISBN: 978-1-990056-18-5 (character)

Print ISBN: 978-1-990056-19-2 (alternate)

Visit my website at www.jessielliott.com

Cover Design: Keylin Rivers

All rights reserved. Without limiting the rights under copyright reserved above, no part of this publication may be reproduced, stored in or introduced into retrieval system, or transmitted, in any form, or by any means (electronic, mechanical, photocopying, recording, or otherwise) without the prior written permission of both the copyright owner and the above publisher of this book.

This is a work of fiction. Names, characters, places, brands, media, and incidents are either the products of the author's imagination or are used fictitiously. The author acknowledges the trademarked status and trademark owners of various products referenced in this work of fiction, which have been used without permission. The publication/use of these trademarks is not authorized, associated with, or sponsored by the trademark owners.

# Also by Jessi Elliott

*These Wicked Delights*

# DEDICATION

*For the readers who love when he falls first.
This one is for you.*

# PLAYLIST

DO I WANNA KNOW - ARCTIC MONKEYS
POISON - FELICITY
THOUSAND MILES - TOVE LO
THE OTHER SIDE - RUELLE
I FEEL LIKE I'M DROWNING - TWO FEET
CONTROL - ZOE WEES
EMERALD - LYRA
HELIUM - SIA
HAUNTED - MATY NOYES
WAR OF HEARTS - RUELLE
DON'T BLAME ME - TAYLOR SWIFT
ASHES - CLAIRE GUERRESO
NEED THE SUN TO BREAK - JAMES BAY
DARLING - ROTHWELL
TICK-TOCK - HANS ZIMMER
TRUTH - 5 SECONDS OF SUMMER
EXODUS - RUELLE
I MISS YOU, I'M SORRY - GRACIE ABRAMS
I GET TO LOVE YOU - RUELLE
HOLDING ON TO YOU - ADAM FRENCH
EAT YOUR YOUNG - HOZIER

# PART ONE

So she sat on with closed eyes, and half believed herself in Wonderland, though she knew she had but to open them again, and all would change to dull reality.

— LEWIS CARROLL, *THROUGH THE LOOKING GLASS*

# CHAPTER ONE

Historically, the first week of the fall semester of college is one giant party filled with unhealthy amounts of alcohol and takeout, staying up all night, and trudging through lectures grossly hungover.

Which is why I find myself squished between my best friends, Allison and Oliver, in the back of an Uber, heading to my first—and last, if I can help it—party of senior year.

We're dropped off outside a student rental in one of the nicer neighborhoods in the city where music vibrates from the three-story gray stone house.

Allison is already swaying her curvy, jean short-clad hips to Arctic Monkeys's "Do I Wanna Know" that's blaring inside as we make our way across the lawn, the trees we pass strung with twinkling lights, casting a soft glow across the property.

An empty beer can crunches under my ankle boot before Allison loops her arm through mine, her floral perfume tickling my nostrils as we walk toward the house. She runs her free hand through her shoulder-length golden blond waves and shoots me a smile. Oliver, who's dressed in a gray T-shirt and black jeans with his favorite loafers, walks ahead of us and opens the door. Students pack the house; no one will notice a few more coming in, but it's still weird walking into a stranger's place without knocking. Evidently, I'm not well-versed in house party etiquette.

We make our way through the foyer, and my eyes lift to the vaulted ceiling while I follow the others, with an inward cringe at the overwhelming stench of body spray and weed. Oliver leads us into an open-concept kitchen with stainless-steel appliances and granite countertops—most of which are covered with empty beer bottles and pizza boxes.

A small group of people have gathered in here, away from the aggressive volume of the music. Oliver hollers at the guy manning the keg, throwing his arm around his shoulders before he grabs two Solo cups, filling them with beer, and handing them to Allison and me. The guys spark a conversation about a new album from some band I've never heard of, while Allison and I exchange a glance, her tawny eyes reflecting the boredom I'm sure is in mine.

Allison leans up and pushes the russet curls out of Oliver's face, kissing his cheek—more than their typical PDA. I think they're worried about making me feel like a third wheel, but I really don't mind. "Ro and I are going to dance," she announces, and then we're moving again, this time into the living room where people are singing and dancing.

I gulp down the beer, cringing at the bitter aftertaste, and follow Allison's lead, moving to the beat of the music by shifting the weight between my feet. She grins at me, throwing her head back to belt out the words as her merlot corset top rides up, exposing a sliver of her stomach. I laugh at her dramatic display, joining in when the only part of the song I know comes.

Allison and I have been friends since freshman year, when we ended up roommates. While we look similar enough to be sisters—though my blond hair is longer and more white than golden—our personalities are total opposites. Allison is an outgoing, carefree English major who loves to party, whereas I'd be just as content to spend my Friday night in the library. My education is the most important thing to me; I know what I want for my future, and I'll do whatever it takes to get it. Right now, that's a bachelor's degree in business management. And this party is supposed to act as a distraction from my nerves over my upcoming internship interview. I have to nail it. To impress my mentor and increase my chances of receiving an offer of employment straight out of college. I need an income to pay my parents back for helping with my tuition over the last four years.

"Aurora, hey! I thought I saw you guys come in!"

I swallow the last of my beer, turning toward the voice and smiling at Danielle, who lives on the same floor of the dorm as us. She's also in my program, so we've had several classes together over the years. I've told her on multiple occasions she should've majored in fashion, and her stunning pastel violet cocktail dress that she no doubt sewed herself is only further testament to that. It makes me feel slightly underdressed with my beige cardigan, black tank top, and high-waisted jean shorts, but we can't all be fashionistas.

She grins at us, her smile bright against the crimson lipstick she's wearing; based on the flush in her cheeks and alcohol on her breath, she's been here a while. "If I knew you were coming, we could've shared a ride!"

Allison offers a brief smile before grabbing my empty cup. "We need a refill. Be right back." She's weaving through the crowd before I can open my mouth. I frown at her abrupt exit, wondering what the hell that was about.

"Are you having fun?"

My attention returns to Danielle. "Time of my life," I remark dryly. "Can't you tell?"

She laughs, tossing her straight chestnut hair over her shoulder. "Funny." Glancing past me, her cobalt-blue eyes light up. "I'll catch you later, okay?"

"Sounds good."

An hour passes in a blur of drinking and dancing. My hair clings to the back of my neck and my cheeks are warm. I break away from the crowd and leave Allison chatting with a group of girls from her program while I search for the bathroom.

"Upstairs," a deep, unfamiliar voice says. I turn toward it, my stomach dipping at his deep, grass-green eyes as they roam over me. He has dark lashes, sharp cheekbones, and a charming smile... that I'm totally staring at.

I force my gaze back to his. "Huh?"

He chuckles, tipping his head back against the wall so the sandy brown hair shifts away from his face. It's perfectly tousled, shorter on the sides and longer on top. "The bathroom. It's upstairs. You're the third person to come by here looking for one in the last half hour." He points to a set of stairs a few feet away. "There's one on this level, but someone clogged it hours ago."

I wrinkle my nose at the last part. "Gross. Thanks."

"Sure." He wipes his palm on his jeans before sticking it out to me. "I'm Grant."

"Aurora," I offer, shaking it. His grip is firm, cool from holding the glass bottle of beer.

"I know." His lips quirk. "We've had a few classes together."

I pull back, my cheeks heating. "I... That's right. Sorry." He seems vaguely familiar; I've probably seen him in passing more than once.

Grant's grin widens and his voice is light with humor when he says, "Don't worry about it. I'm not very memorable."

It's my turn to laugh, because Grant is easily the hottest guy here. "Right. Have you looked in a mirror, like, ever?" *Fuck me. Did I just say that out loud?*

He presses his lips together against a smile, then takes a drink of his beer. "I'll see you around, Aurora." He touches my shoulder briefly as he walks away, and the butterflies in my stomach give a healthy flutter, my head spinning. I'm not sure if it's from Grant's attention or the beer sloshing around my stomach as I climb the stairs, but I have to grip the railing to keep my balance. I go with the latter, because I've always been a lightweight.

The second floor is ridiculously massive, and I suddenly wish I could hold it long enough to order an Uber and go back to campus. "I'm going to get fucking lost in this place," I mutter to myself, trailing my fingers along some fancy art print hung on the wall as I pass. There are so many hallways and doors, but I follow the sound of voices, groaning when I round a corner and find a line for the bathroom. I stand at the back and pull my phone out, scrolling through my photos from this summer to pass the time: visiting family in Michigan with my parents and little brother, Elijah, the weekend my mom and I spent at a cottage with her sisters, and a few outdoor concerts with Allison and Oliver.

Once I've gone through them all, I can't help my thoughts from going back to Grant. My stomach tightens, remembering how nice it felt when he smiled at me. I hope I'll see him again before the party's over; I'm just the right amount of tipsy to be confident enough to ask for his number.

Finally, the line moves, and it's my turn. When I'm done, I attempt to retrace my steps, slipping through a group of girls laughing drunkenly on their way to the bathroom line.

I must've taken a left when I should've gone right, because I end up in a hallway I don't recognize, the back of my neck tingling when I find it more difficult than it should be to find my way. I didn't drink *that* much...

Without warning, the door to my left opens, sending me stumbling back as a guy steps into the hallway. He can't be much older than me, though the scowl on his face ages him. As does his neatly styled black hair. Not to mention his dress shirt and slacks ensemble; he looks out of place at a college party. And paired with the sharpness in his eyes that almost seem to glow, the chiseled line of his jaw... He doesn't look *human*.

"My bad." His voice is unapologetic. If anything, he's annoyed. His voice is unapologetic. If anything, he's annoyed. His blue eyes narrow when I don't respond, and my stomach sinks when his lips curl into a faint grin. "Nothing to say? Come on. You made this too easy."

*Why is he talking as if he knows me?* My thoughts freeze and my heart pounds so hard I feel it in my throat as I shake my head. "Do I know you?"

He smirks, his teeth straight and white—too perfect not to be veneers. "You should."

I steal a glance around the empty hallway, far more sober than I was a few minutes ago. Voices shout over the music downstairs, but there's no one in sight. The pit in my stomach tells me this is someone I shouldn't spend another second with. "I need to get back," I say in a forced level tone as my body temperature rises. "My friends are waiting for me."

"Your boyfriend?" My pulse jackhammers, and he tilts his head to the side. His irritated gaze follows me, and the curve of his lips as he stares at my throat makes me think he *heard* my pulse race, which doesn't make sense.

I take a step back at the same moment he steps forward. "What the fuck are you doing?" My voice cracks as tightness clamps down on my chest.

"You're in a lot of trouble, blondie." He moves in a blur, grabbing me by my throat. My eyes pop wide, and when I open my mouth to scream, nothing comes out. I can't make a sound. I can't move. My arms are weighed down and my feet are blocks of cement. Black dots swim across my vision, and my ears ring over the pounding of my heart. Then my legs give out, and I collapse onto the floor, the music and voices fading into nothingness.

## CHAPTER TWO

Silence surrounds me as I blink my eyes open for what feels like the first time in days, squinting at the sparkling chandelier hanging from the ceiling. My neck hurts from sitting with my chin against my chest and my head is so fuzzy it takes a few seconds for my vision to clear. Once it does, it becomes apparent I'm in a luxury hotel suite. It's filled with neutral colors and furnished with a king-size bed, blackout curtains that block my view, and a massive TV hung on the wall near where I'm seated. The soft hum of air conditioning is the only sound, and the room smells freshly cleaned.

I take a slow, deep breath, trying to halt the panic creeping up my throat. It doesn't do much good, especially when I glance down and find my wrists tied to the chair. Heavy rope bites into my skin when I try to move, making my heart lurch as I double my efforts to no avail, and I wince before I stop fighting.

There's a soft *beep* before the door across the room opens, and my breath catches, my throat thick with unshed tears. I go rigid as the guy I ran into at the party steps inside and closes the door behind him, pocketing a keycard as he approaches. Those same sharp blue eyes slice right through me. He's wearing a navy dress shirt now, which makes me think it's the next day.

"You're awake."

I blink at him, my head still fuzzy. *Did someone spike my drink at the party? Would I know if they drugged me? Oh god... Did he touch me?*

"And you're observant," I shoot back through my teeth, clenching my hands into fists to hide how they shake. *Don't show him weakness.*

I blink, and he's in front of me, glaring viciously. *How did he move so fast?* "You've got a mouth on you, blondie." He yanks the rope off the chair and forces me to stand, leaving my arms tied together. *How is he so fucking strong?*

I gasp as the light from the chandelier above catches his face in such a way it appears almost translucent with a slight bluish silver tint. I immediately try to pull away, but his grip is solid. "Who are you?"

"Doesn't matter."

"Where am I?"

"Chuck E. Cheese," he deadpans.

I nearly scowl at that, but the panic clawing at my chest is making my throat dry. "Why did you bring me here?"

He sighs heavily, and I swear the blue of his eyes darkens. "You ask a lot of questions."

I swallow the lump in my throat, blinking back tears. "I think there's been some mistake—"

He pulls me forward by the rope, licking his lips as he inhales. "Your fear is sweet like candy."

My eyes pop wide, and I lean as far away as I can, my

stomach twisting with nausea. "What?" I squeak, because *what the fuck* does that even mean?

"There's never much to feed on around here. Nothing I'm allowed to, anyway."

"Try a McDonald's drive thru," I remark bitterly, even as my voice shakes.

He laughs. "You're funny, too. Good to know." He reaches out and grasps my chin. Panic floods through me, and I attempt to rip his hand away, lifting both my arms and digging my fingernails into his skin as hard as I can.

He reels back momentarily, hissing, "You stupid girl." His hand shoots toward me, wickedly fast, and he wraps his fingers around my throat. The subtle scent of his cologne hits me, along with the coffee on his breath. "Forgive me," he mutters with fake sincerity. "I get irritable when I'm hungry." Black dots dance across my vision, my heart slamming against my chest as I struggle to breathe. My eyes roll back, but he scoffs and releases my throat before I pass out. While I cough and wheeze, he takes a step back, his face contorted with annoyance. "Try anything, and I don't care what my orders are. I will drain you."

I suck in a breath, greedily filling my lungs with air as he removes the rope from my wrists. "Please," I force out as the rope hits the floor. "Let me go. I won't—"

"Tell anyone?" He barks out a laugh. "Of course you will."

When he steps forward again, I act without thinking, driving my knee up and catching him in the groin. He doubles over, growling loudly as he clutches himself, and I bolt for the door, yanking it open and throwing myself into the hallway. My ankle boots echo against the marble floor like thunder as I run with my heart in my throat, too afraid to look behind me. As I round a corner, I'm grabbed from behind and thrown against the wall, the edge of an art print slicing into my forehead. My head throbs as I turn away from the wall, and I reach up and touch my forehead with a shaky hand. I'm unsurprised to find blood when I pull it away. A trail of warmth trickles down my face, dripping onto the floor at my feet.

"I've decided that I don't like you," he hisses in my ear, and I shudder. He grabs my face, forcing me to look at him. "Your fear..." He slams my back into the wall, and I cry out. "It's stronger now. Lucky me." He grins, but all I can focus on is the darkness in his eyes as he leans in, his unforgiving glare dropping to my mouth as my breath hitches.

"Seriously, Max?" a sharp, female voice says. "You can't follow the simplest directions, can you?"

Max scowls, turning to look at the tall Asian woman coming toward us with her brows raised. She stops off to the side, radiating elegance in a plum dress and heels that have to be at least six inches high, though I didn't hear her approach because Max was about to... I'm not even sure. Kiss me? My gut tells me that was definitely *not* what he was going to do, but I can't rationalize anything else.

"Back off, Skylar. This has nothing to do with you."

She rolls her dark brown eyes, sparing me a brief glance before returning her attention to Max. "I'm looking out for *you*, asshat."

Max pulls his hand back, shifting his body away from mine to face the woman.

"What would you have me do? Let her go?"

"That's not my call," she says. "Or yours."

*How is she being so casual about this?* I shake my head,

then bolt again. I need to get the hell out of here and... do what? Call the police and report my kidnapping by whoever these people are? I can't think about that now. It's something to figure out once I escape them.

I have no idea where I'm going, but when an elevator comes into view, my heart nearly trips over itself with relief as I sprint toward it, slamming my fist against the call button.

"You're going to let her get away?" Max hollers, making the panic in my chest dig its claws deeper.

There's a delicate chuckle and then: "Let her try."

With a faint *ding*, the elevator slides open, and I throw myself forward—into a solid wall of muscle. I reel back as my eyes meet a pair of lapis lazuli irises. They're like the darkest parts of a lake, woven with lighter hues, and dangerously captivating; it's hard to look away.

Relief pours into me, but before I can tell this guy about the psycho who knocked me out and brought me here, the aforementioned grabs me again, pulling me back as the new arrival steps off the elevator and it slides shut behind him. The stranger in front of me is tall—at least a foot taller than I am—and built. I think he's older than me based on his expensive-looking dark gray suit. He exudes power and control, and if I wasn't battling the fear and anger in my chest, I might think he was even attractive. Who am I kidding? They're all impossibly stunning in an almost creepy, ethereal way, which leads me to believe there's a good chance I'm hallucinating this entire ordeal.

"Max," Blue Eyes says in a measured voice, "remove your hands from our guest. Now."

My stomach drops; this guy knows the one who took me, which means he isn't here to help. And he has the audacity to call me a guest. I clench my jaw and press my lips into a thin line. *Guest* implies I chose to be here, which couldn't be further from the truth.

Max huffs under his breath before letting me go, and I realize Skylar isn't anywhere in sight. Maybe she didn't want to be an accomplice to whatever the hell these guys are up to, which only fuels the fear raging in my chest.

Those blue eyes hold mine as he says, "Leave us," effectively dismissing Max.

The heat of him at my back disappears, and when I turn, expecting to find him walking away, I frown at the empty hallway. *What the*—

The man clears his throat, and my gaze whips back to him. He focuses his attention on my forehead, and a muscle feathers along his defined, stubble-shadowed jaw when he sees the gash there. My face stings where blood continues to trickle from it. I touch it again and wince at the sharp pain that follows. My eyes flit to the closed elevator, narrowing at what's between me and my freedom.

"Move," I demand, surprising myself with the harsh tone of my voice.

The man raises his brows; I've surprised him as well. "And where exactly are you going to go?" He sounds curious, amused. "Do you know where you are?"

I ignore that and say, "I don't know what the hell you've got going on in this place, but I'm not going to die here." Despite the shallow quality of my breathing, the determination is clear in my voice.

"I'm glad to hear that." He steps forward, bringing his hand toward my face, and frowns when I inhale sharply, balling my hands into fists. His gaze drops to them for a second before returning to mine. "You're going to fight me?"

"Don't fucking touch me. Who *are* you?"

"That doesn't matter right now." He lifts his hand to my face before I can move away and holds me in place. His fingers brush along my jaw and the throbbing slowly fades, leaving a warm, tingling sensation as he moves them over the sharp pain radiating from my forehead, wiping it away with a simple touch.

My eyes widen, and I turn my face away from his hand as I stumble back a step. "Wh-what the hell was that?" My heart pounds as I reach up once more and find the gash in my forehead completely healed.

"You're welcome," he says with no explanation.

My brows pinch together, and I all but whisper, "Are you going to tell me who you are now?"

"Tristan, there are more important things to deal with right now." Skylar is back with a tablet in her hand. She taps a few times on the screen before glancing between us.

"I'll deal with what I decide needs to be dealt with, Skylar."

"Or just let me go," I suggest. "No need to deal with me at all."

"The human makes an excellent suggestion, and that's coming from me."

*Human?*

"Skylar," Tristan says, and there's a warning in his voice that makes the hair on the back of my neck stand straight.

"Fine. Want me to handle this?" she asks Tristan, pointing a manicured finger in my direction.

Now both sets of eyes are on me, and Tristan sighs. "No. I think this requires my attention. Perhaps you should speak with Max and remind him how things work around here. I will deal with him later."

"Very well," she says, and I expect her to walk away, so imagine my surprise when she vanishes in the time I take to blink. She was standing only four feet from me, and now she's gone.

My hand flies to my mouth as I suck in a sharp breath. "What just..." I trail off, unable to finish my sentence as my head spins.

Tristan glances at me as if he's waiting for me to find my words, his eyes roaming over my face, calculating but not unkindly.

I jerk my fingers through my hair, pressing them into my scalp, urging myself to wake up from this horrifically realistic nightmare. When Tristan steps forward, I reel back, bumping into the doorframe to another room in the hallway.

"Aurora, I need you to listen to me," he says in a calm voice. *How does he know my name?*

I shake my head adamantly. "Stay away from me!"

"I'm afraid that's not going to work." He advances once more, and my back collides with the wall; I have nowhere to go. In an instant, I lose it. I try to push him away, slamming my hands against his solid chest, but he doesn't move an inch. "What the hell are you?" I demand through chattering teeth, fighting to keep tears back. None of this makes any sense.

His eyes flick across my face, and he sighs. "Calm down. Take a deep breath." He waits until I exhale before he continues. "I'm a fae knight, Aurora, though I imagine that means nothing to you." My brows shoot up, and he adds, "I thought not."

"Why am I here?" I ask, forcing myself to hold his steely gaze.

"That is the eternal question, isn't it?"

I close my eyes, letting out a shaky breath. "Fae," I whisper in disbelief.

"Yes."

Forcing my eyes open, I study him closely. *Fae aren't real*, I tell myself. They are mythical, *fictional* creatures with sharp teeth and pointy ears and—He's lying. He must be. But then, what explanation is there for his ability to heal my injuries? For Max moving so fast and Skylar disappearing into thin air?

As much as I want to deny everything, what I saw with my own eyes is making it difficult to discredit. It's possible I'm suffering from some wicked, drug-induced hallucinations. I can't count that out yet.

"I suppose you're in shock," Tristan offers, cocking his head to the side, and a bit of his light brown, almost blond hair falls across his forehead.

I lick the dryness from my lips. "You—you look human," I attempt to rationalize aloud. "I don't... This doesn't make sense."

He regards me closely, and there's a hint of suspicion in his eyes, which makes absolutely no sense considering the role he's in here. "What is it you believe you know about my kind?"

*Why the hell does he care about what I know, and why is he so casually discussing it with me?* I press my lips together, considering it for a beat. Maybe I can use this to get information that'll help me get out of here. "I'll tell you what I believe if you tell me why I'm here."

"You wish to trade information?" He rubs his hand along his jaw. "Fine. You're up first."

I stare at him for a moment. *Oh, he's serious.* "You're

immortal," I say, recalling the basics of most inhuman creatures, which until now I believed to be purely fictional.

He offers a charming grin. "Mostly."

"You can't lie."

"True," he says, "though we are masters at evading."

"Iron is poisonous to you."

His grin slips, and he hesitates—which is answer enough—before the word leaves his lips. "Yes."

"How did you heal me?" The pain in my temples is completely gone.

Tristan shrugs. "Magic." When my eyes narrow, he offers a thin smile. "My kind can heal living things."

"Oh, so vampires and zombies are on their own?" I have no idea where that quip came from, but Tristan exhales a surprised laugh.

"Vampires can heal themselves and zombies aren't real."

I shake my head at his response, because there's no way I have the brain capacity to consider the existence of vampires right now.

"While we're at it, I can only heal things I understand and have knowledge of. I can't heal incurable illnesses like cancer or dementia. Magic doesn't work like that—it has to have a balance with nature, because that's what it's rooted in."

"Right," I respond, the pressure in my chest making my voice lower than normal. I ask for what feels like the millionth time, "Why am I here?"

An unreadable expression paints his features. "You don't wish to offer more of your knowledge of the fae? You were doing quite well."

"What I *wish* is to go home and pretend I wasn't

abducted and tormented by someone who got all up in my personal space and tried to, I don't know, fucking kiss me?" The doubt and confusion deepen my voice.

Tristan's jaw works. "He was going to feed from you." My stomach plummets, and he continues, "Fae survive on human emotions and energy."

"How?" The question leaves my lips before I can clamp my mouth shut.

"By physical contact," he answers. "So long as we don't take too much, the humans rarely notice anything besides slight fatigue."

"Oh." My head is damn close to exploding, and I don't know why he's being so open with information. Unless—

"It's how the immortal stay immortal, Aurora."

My stomach roils. He's being so forthcoming because I'm not getting out of this place. "I... I'm here to be fed on?" The race of my pulse sends my head spinning again. "Are you—" My voice breaks, cutting off before I can force the words out.

He frowns briefly. "I'm not going to feed on you."

Something like relief flickers through my chest, but I'm still stuck here with Tristan standing between me and the exit. "If I wasn't brought here to be a human vending machine, why *am* I here?" I'm still in denial, but the words tumble out of my mouth as if I believe what he's been saying. What other choice do I have?

"It was an honest mistake."

"Of course it was *honest*. You can't be untruthful."

Tristan smirks. "It was a case of mistaken identity," he explains. "I sent Max to retrieve someone, and he mistook you for her."

Confusion knits my brows. "If I'm not who you want, why am I still here? And how did you know my name?"

"There is a certain protocol to be followed when something like this happens. Keeping you wasn't a decision Max made. I did. As for your name, we found you in your school's database."

My eyes widen, and I shake my head at the complete insanity of this exchange. "I have a family, you know. And I'm no criminology major, but even I know kidnapping is a felony."

"You'll find your laws mean nothing to us. We have our own laws—our own moral code."

"Neither of which frown upon kidnapping, apparently," I mutter. "Do you plan on keeping me here?"

"No, Aurora, I don't. But as for the family you mentioned... It seems they are partly to blame for the unfortunate mix-up last night."

"What the hell are you talking about?"

His eyes take on a curious light as they flicker across my face. "You truly have no idea, do you?"

I glare at him. "Does this look like the face of someone in the know?"

"You have fae ancestors. I'd guess hundreds of years back. None related closely enough to make you fae, but close enough that a small remnant of their magic lies dormant in you. That's why Max thought you were the one he was sent to collect."

I blink at him, then burst out laughing. "I don't think you understand how crazy you sound." The throbbing behind my eyes is coming back, making me squint as tension pulses in my temples.

The corner of his mouth kicks up. "You don't believe me." It's not a question.

I exhale a humorless laugh. "You almost had me. But

trying to bring my family into this?" I shake my head. "Absolutely not."

*Fae can't lie.*

No. No. No.

Fae are *not* real. I want to deny it, but the longer I spend here, the more difficult it becomes. It's hard to ignore what's happening right in front of me.

Tristan shrugs, as if this doesn't really matter to him. It probably doesn't. He steps closer and places a finger under my chin, tilting it upward. I freeze as his eyes dance across my face, studying every inch meticulously. He traces the line of my jaw, brushing my hair back and tucking it behind my ear. "Are you hurt anywhere else?" he asks, his voice low.

I swallow and shake my head.

"Aurora."

"Tristan," I level.

He smiles. "You're not afraid of me."

I consider that and decide he's right. As much as I probably should fear him—an alleged fae knight, whatever that means—I don't. Because as crazy as this entire ordeal has been, Tristan hasn't hurt me. He *healed* me.

"You silly, silly human." He shakes his head in exasperation, his fingers lingering against my cheek. "It's a good thing you won't remember any of this." His fingers warm against my skin, and his eyes capture mine in a gaze that goes on too long. Then, his eyebrows lift, and he adjusts his hand, squinting as he peers into my eyes.

I blink at him. "What are you doing?"

He drops his hand and lets loose a surprised laugh. "This is going to be a problem."

It takes a second for my head to catch up. "What did you mean by 'you won't remember any of this?'" I gape at him. "Holy shit, were you trying to give me some freaky ass fae amnesia?"

He offers me a thoughtful look. "It seems my manipulation doesn't work on you."

Despite the pounding of my heart, I smile. He can't control me.

# CHAPTER
# THREE

Tristan is quiet as we step onto the elevator, though he doesn't need to make a sound for me to feel him all over. His presence alone is overwhelming. Despite appearing deceptively human, the more I look at him—his measured, graceful movements, his vivid eyes and perfect smile—the harder it is to ignore the voice in my head telling me this could be *real*.

I press against the wall of the elevator, keeping as much distance between us as possible, and ignore the way Tristan's lips twitch. I stare at the panel of buttons, holding my breath when he leans over and scans a keycard before pressing the one marked PH—the penthouse. There are forty floors; the thirty-ninth floor has a small black placard next to it labeled WESTBROOK INC. OFFICES, and the penthouse is the only level above it.

Tristan trains his gaze on me when he says, "You'll have to forgive me for Max's behavior."

I press my lips into a tight line, avoiding his eyes. "Forgive *you*?" I fold my arms over my chest, slowly forcing my gaze over to him. "Max's actions are on him," I say in a low voice. "I blame you for the fact I'm still here."

He crosses one ankle over the other, sliding his hands into his pockets and leaning against the wall as the numbers on the panel beside me continue to climb. "I see."

I swallow hard. "You can't keep me here." My voice comes out quieter than I want. It lacks assurance, and I hate that. Allison and Oliver are going to wonder where I am, why I disappeared from the party and didn't come home last night.

"I had no intention of keeping you here once I adjusted your memory. This may come as a surprise, but I don't particularly enjoy forcing the company of someone."

I exhale through my nose, loathing the next words to come out of my mouth and for how little control I have over the situation. "What happens now?"

"I'm still figuring that out. I can't let you go knowing what you do about the fae."

I grip the handrail until the hard metal bites into my palms. "How is that my fault? I didn't ask for this!"

"I understand that," he says, his voice strained.

I shake my head and lower my voice despite the privacy of the elevator. "I won't tell anyone what happened or about you, okay? You don't have to be concerned about me running my mouth. Trust me, I'd like nothing more than to forget this entire experience, but since that isn't an option, you'll just have to take my word for it." I would've preferred my memories to be wiped at this point. I don't *want* to know the things I've learned, but I wasn't lying—I would keep them to myself. No one would believe me if I told them what happened, anyway.

Tristan's chest rises as he takes a deep breath. "This

isn't an ideal situation for me either, but I put my people above all else."

The pressure in my chest grows. Trying to wrap my head around the existence of the supernatural is moving me dangerously closer to hyperventilating. *How many fae are there?* I'm assuming less than there are humans, but maybe I shouldn't be. "I can't—You *can't* keep me here. Find some way to convince your people I'm not a threat."

His expression remains impassive as he watches me, tapping his shiny black dress shoe idly against the floor. "Aren't you?"

At the burn of tears in my eyes, I want to turn away, but I force myself to hold his gaze. "Tristan, *your* guy kidnapped *me*. I don't have the upper hand here."

His brows tug closer. Silence lingers, and it makes me shift my weight back and forth. Finally, he says, "I'm going to offer you a deal."

My breath hitches at the same moment my eyes widen. "What kind of deal?"

"There's a fae on your campus I need located."

"Why?" I ask without a second thought.

"Not your concern. Locate the fae and contact me to collect her. End of story."

"And that would make you trust me?" I ask as we glide closer to the top floor.

Tristan smiles, almost as if to himself, as the elevator slows to a stop. "That's the idea." He steps forward as the door slides open to reveal a large entryway and gestures for me to walk ahead of him. My eyes narrow, and I make no move to push away from the wall. With a faint smirk, Tristan exits before I follow reluctantly.

"How do you expect me to do this, anyway?" I ask as

we walk across the black marble floor from the elevator to a set of solid white double doors.

He pulls his keycard out. "I'm going to provide you with a charm that will allow you to identify the fae." He taps the keycard against a panel on the door, and it makes a soft *beep*.

"I don't..." I shake my head, then my eyes widen. "Magic?"

He glances at me over his shoulder and nods, then opens one door and steps inside. I follow him, taking in my surroundings as I walk farther into the lavish apartment suite. A golden sunset beams through expansive windows that overlook a cluster of skyscrapers and some green space and illuminates the living room. *Sunset. Fuck, how long did Max have me knocked out?* I shove that thought away with a shiver as my eyes roam around the room. Plush black furnishings frame a glass coffee table, and a TV hangs on the wall above a fireplace with floor-to-ceiling black brick. The suite smells fresh and a bit like lemons, as if it's just been cleaned. It also smells like *him*. A crisp, alluring scent I haven't quite figured out, and one I'm fighting not to like.

"Of course you're rich," I mutter, unable to stop my gaze from wandering around the space.

He faces me, shrugging. "I'm a successful businessman."

My cheeks burn. "So what? You use your fae... whatever, and trick people into giving you money?"

His expression darkens, his eyes narrowing. "I have earned my wealth here honestly."

I walk past him and stand against the wall. That way, I can't be surprised from behind. I prop my foot against it, trying to look casual despite my uneven pulse. "Where is *here?*" My gaze flits toward the window again. "Earth? Narnia? Wonderland?"

Tristan presses his lips together against a smile, sliding his hands into his pockets, completely at ease. "We reside in the human world. The fae can exist here because we glamour ourselves to appear human."

I nearly roll my eyes, because he looks far too perfect to be human. "Do I even want to ask what glamour is?"

"It's exactly what it sounds like. We aren't physically altering our appearance to be human, but projecting normal features to hide the ones that would expose us."

"Like?"

His brows lift. "Curious about what I truly look like behind this mortal mask?"

I freeze, suddenly worried he's going to show me. That's not something I think I can handle on top of everything else. I shake my head, hoping to shift the subject. "You said, 'human world' before. Is there a *different* world?"

He nods tightly. Huh. So he's less forthcoming with the information now that he knows he can't make me forget.

My brows draw closer, and I fold my arms over my chest. "And you chose this one?"

He almost smiles. "*Chose* is a strong word." The edge in his voice clarifies that's all I'm going to get, and that's fine with me. Honestly, the less I know, the better.

"Fair enough. Can we please get back to me going home? Because I'd like to. Now."

Tristan steps closer, and my back stiffens automatically. "You're uncomfortable," he says, watching me with a spark of curiosity in his eyes, which seem several shades lighter now. "This has been inconvenient for everyone involved." He moves past me, shrugging off his suit jacket, and drapes it over a nearby chair before rolling up the sleeves of his white dress shirt as if he's trying to make himself more comfortable. Or maybe it's an attempt at appearing casual to make *me* feel better. Either way, my eyes follow the movement a little too closely.

I shake my head to clear it and force myself to focus. "Inconvenient?" I remark incredulously, pushing away from the wall. "You think this was some minor blip in my weekend plans? Your guy kidnapped me—and now you want me to help you kidnap someone else!" My bottom lip is trembling, and I blink quickly to keep the tears back. I can't break down. Not here. Not in front of *him*.

He waits until I've finished shouting, then says, "You are not the only one at a disadvantage. You were taken by accident, Aurora, but now you know about us. The fae magic in you prevents me from removing your memories, which makes you a liability."

"I'm not—"

He continues as if I didn't speak. "My people expect me to protect their existence—that's what being a fae knight means. I have no desire to kill a woman over a mistake, let alone one who is part fae. Work with me on this. It will help me sell my decision to... spare you."

My next breath gets stuck, and I sink my teeth into my lip to keep it from quivering. "If you're some powerful fae knight," I say in a low voice, "why do you need me for this? Don't you have, like, an army to go after your enemies? She's one fae. I don't get it." The words just keep tumbling out of my mouth.

A muscle feathers along his jaw. "This matter isn't one I'd like known on a large scale." He walks to a row of black bookshelves built into the wall next to the fireplace, retrieving a small box which he brings to me. "As for the fae in question—dealing with her is more of a preventative measure."

My gaze lifts to his as my brows tug together. "Meaning?"

"Again, not your concern. Now, there are many fae on your campus. To ensure you identify the correct one, I'll send you her photo."

I blink at him, stuck on the whole 'many fae' thing. I probably sit next to them in lectures, pass them on campus, even live in the same dorm as some of them. *Focus.* I snap myself back; I can freak out once I'm free of this place. "Fine." I nod to the box in his hand. "What's that?"

He opens it, and sitting inside is a bracelet with a circular turquoise charm set around a dainty silver band crafted to look like tree branches. "Put this on," he instructs.

Eyeing it warily, I pick it up from the box, holding it flat in my palm. It's ice cold, as if he just pulled it out of a freezer. "What the—"

"That's how you know you're in the presence of my kind," he explains. "The metal drops in temperature."

I peer at it suspiciously. "How do I know it won't do anything to me?"

Tristan chuckles. "Guess you'll just have to trust me."

My eyes snap to his and narrow. "Yeah, that's going to be a giant fuck no."

"It won't harm you, Aurora," he says, his eyes glimmering with amusement. "If I wanted to kill you, we wouldn't be having this conversation."

"That's reassuring," I mutter, hesitating a few moments longer before slipping the bracelet onto my wrist. Nothing happens while I stand there staring at it, so I force myself to relax. "Can I go now?"

"You don't want to stay for dinner?" He gestures to the spotless, near-sparkling kitchen across the suite. It's decked out with stainless-steel appliances, a massive island, and a professional grade espresso machine that would have me drooling if the circumstances weren't... well, what they are.

My lips smack as I gape at him. "That's funny. You're really funny."

His expression turns serious, his features hardening. "You will keep this bracelet on no matter what. Understood?"

I want to take it off and throw the damn thing at him, but I nod. My teeth hurt from keeping my jaw locked, and I'm pretty sure I look feral.

He reaches into his pocket again and pulls out a business card. "Call me directly when you find her and be discreet."

I take his card, slipping it into my pocket, then lift my wrist, inspecting the bracelet again. "You said I had fae magic in me. Won't that complicate things?"

Tristan shakes his head, walking past one couch, and runs his fingers along the back. "It's too minimal to trigger the magic in the charm."

"And what happens if I find this fae you're looking for and she catches on?"

He doesn't miss a beat. "It's a simple task, Aurora."

"Is that what you told Max?" I remark, my voice dripping with sarcasm. Call it a momentary lapse in judgment —or a brave flare of defiance toward this entire situation— but I can't stop myself from adding, "What's to keep me from bailing on this 'simple task' at the first opportunity?"

He pauses, taking his time meeting my gaze, sizing me up like an animal surveying its prey. "You'd like to test me?"

I force a neutral expression even as he closes the distance between us in a single stride. "It doesn't seem like many do."

A dark look passes over his face as he dips his chin and lowers his voice. "There's a reason for that."

My heartbeat rattles the cage of my ribs. The weight of Tristan's gaze makes me feel as if I'm wide awake and dreaming at the same time. As if none of this is even real, which I'm still not entirely convinced it is. And yet, I don't back down. I don't cower away.

His eyes narrow. "Who *are* you?"

It takes me a second to find my voice. "I guess you should've done your research before you abducted me."

"Had it been my intention to bring you here, I would have."

I shrug. "Oh well. Now do I get to go home?"

He offers a tight-lipped smile as he unrolls his sleeves and picks up his jacket, pulling it on and buttoning the front. When he inclines his head toward the front door, I follow him back to the elevator, again standing on the opposite side, and we ride in silence to the lobby.

It's quickly apparent I'm in one of the fanciest hotels in the city. The white marble floor and sparkling crystal chandeliers are a dead giveaway.

"This... is yours?" I ask, unable to hide my surprise.

"Yes," he answers.

The lobby has a subdued atmosphere that comes with wealth. I've never considered a career in hotel management, but I feel an uncomfortable sliver of respect for Tristan. I immediately want to slap myself and insist it's strictly professional interest.

Or Stockholm Syndrome.

Tristan walks me to the front of the building, where a black town car is waiting at the curb. "My driver will take you home." He opens the backseat door for me and stands behind it, waiting for me to get in. I slip into the car, buckling my belt, and Tristan leans inside. "Remember our deal, Aurora."

I force my lips to curl. "Has anyone ever told you how much of an ass you are?"

He mirrors my smile. "No one alive."

I roll my eyes. "Good one."

He closes the door and steps back onto the sidewalk. Keeping my eyes on Tristan, I tell the driver where to go. As we pull away, I watch Tristan stand at the curb until we turn a corner out of sight.

I stare out the window for a while before I realize I'm crying and quickly wipe the tears away. I'm no longer running on adrenaline. Glimpsing myself in the rearview mirror, I cringe. I look, well, like someone who was kidnapped and held captive for hours. My hair is in a tangle of messy waves, and both my eyeliner and mascara have smudged almost all the way off since the party last night. I glance at the clock on the dash; it's almost six in the evening. Last night feels like a long time ago.

*I was taken by the fae.*

The driver clears his throat, and I startle from my reverie to realize the car has stopped moving. I glance at him for a moment and then go through the motions of unbuckling and opening the door to get out.

I wrap my arms around my waist and hug my cardigan

closer as the car pulls away. It's September, and the weather is still warm, but I can't stop shivering.

---

My dorm is exactly as I left it last night, yet nothing feels the same. Allison isn't here, and when I reach for my phone to text her, my stomach sinks. I don't *have* my phone. It could be several places at this point: the house the party was at, Tristan's hotel, or anywhere in between. I groan, sinking onto the end of my bed and making a mental note to order a new one at some point this weekend.

My eyes keep going back to the bracelet around my wrist. The charm stares back at me, making my skin tingle with nerves. This entire situation is insane; I'm still struggling to wrap my head around it. And the thought of telling anyone, besides promising Tristan I wouldn't, shoots icy panic through my veins.

I lose track of time, pacing the room, raking my fingers through my hair too many times as I try to come up with a solution to this mess. Any option requires leaving my dorm, which I have no desire to do. I don't want to walk around campus and find out I'm surrounded by fae. So I keep pacing. My stomach grumbles, reminding me I haven't eaten since yesterday. I grab a protein bar out of the snack drawer in my desk, chewing on it as I replay everything since the party in my head. At some point, I collapse onto the bed and stare at the ceiling, too restless to fall asleep despite the exhaustion that clings to my muscles. After an hour, I give up trying to sleep and force myself out of bed to the bathroom.

After a shower that I had hoped would calm my nerves —it doesn't—I tug on a pair of leggings and a plain black tank top. I'm battling the knots in my hair with a comb when the door to our room shuts. Peeking through the half-open door, I find Allison tossing her bag onto her desk and flopping onto her bed. Her eyes lift to me when I step out of the bathroom, lighting up as a grin touches her lips. "Where'd you disappear to last night? Oliver said he saw you talking to some guy." She shoots me a suggestive look, wiggling her eyebrows.

Oh, right. Grant. Talking to him, the butterflies in my stomach, that feels like forever ago. Given what actually happened—and because Grant is undeniably attractive—I *wish* I'd disappeared with him.

I step out of the bathroom, slamming into an invisible wall. Chills spread through my arm, and my gaze drops to my wrist.

*No...*

The charm in the bracelet Tristan gave me is ice cold.

## CHAPTER
# FOUR

"What the fuck?" I breathe, my gaze lifting to look at my best friend.

"What's wrong?" She sits up, her expression filled with concern that makes my chest tighten.

My movements are robotic as I pull the bracelet off my wrist. "You..." My voice cracks, and I swallow hard.

Allison scrambles off her bed, her eyes locked on the bracelet. "Aurora, where did you get that?" Her hazel eyes are wide, her cheeks flushed.

This is *not* happening. Not after all the shit I went through.

I shake my head. "Um..." I shift my hand behind my back as I fumble over what to say. I want to climb out the window and escape this moment, but I don't think I'll fit. We're also not on the ground floor.

She steps toward me, her chest rising and falling quicker than a moment ago. "Aurora..."

"You're fae." The words spill out, barely above a whisper.

The color drains from her face. Between one moment and the next, she's in front of me, grabbing the bracelet. It hits the carpet between us, and Allison grits her teeth, lifting her foot and bringing it down hard, over and over, until the charm cracks.

"Allison—"

"I'm so sorry," she says, desperation creeping into her voice as her brows tug closer. "You were never supposed to find out." Her eyes search mine. "How *did* you?"

A rush of emotion hits me, filling my eyes with tears. I can't pin it on something specific, not fear or anger, but a general overwhelm of the whole thing. "Some fae named Max took me from the party last night. He thought I was someone else, so he knocked me out and brought me to some fancy hotel where I met another fae —Tristan. That's when I found out about the fae, which I'm still trying to wrap my head around. So if you want to chime in anytime with the punchline to this joke or reveal it was all an elaborate prank you and Oliver are playing on me, please do, because I am freaking the fuck out."

She frowns. "How are you here now? How did you escape Tristan?"

"I didn't. He let me go under the condition that I track down the fae he was actually looking for. Though that's going to be difficult, considering he was going to send me a photo of her, and there's a good chance my phone is somewhere at his hotel."

Allison wrings her hands in front of her, pressing her lips into a tight line. "Son of a—" She shakes her head. "I'm so sorry, Ro."

I exhale a heavy breath. "It's not your fault."

Her brows pinch, and she looks as if she's fighting back

tears. "I think it is. I'm pretty sure I'm the one Max was after."

I step back instinctively, wincing when the corner of my desk jabs the back of my thigh. "Why?"

"I'll tell you everything, but not here. There isn't time. We have to go."

"*We*? No—"

Allison steps forward faster than I've ever seen her move and grabs my hands. "Come with me." Her plea is desperate.

"What?" I squeak, trying to pull free of her grasp. She's unrelenting, and her effortless strength is a pulse-pounding reminder of how crazy the last twelve hours have been. My best friend being fae is the tip of the fucking iceberg. *How the hell didn't I notice anything before?* I feel more and more ridiculous about missing it the longer I look at her. The girl has never had a bad skin day; her complexion is blemish-free, her face chiseled and appealing, though she, like Tristan, appears otherwise human.

She must see something in my expression, because she lets go, her voice rough with unshed tears when she says, "I never wanted you to find out what I am. You didn't need to know."

"Didn't need to know?" I echo, shaking my head. "Like I didn't need to know about my fae ancestors? Did you keep that from me, too?" I don't entirely trust what Tristan told me—okay, *trust* is probably the wrong word, considering he can't lie, but seeking answers elsewhere seems like a better bet.

She freezes. "You're part of a fae bloodline?" Something like recognition passes over her face. "That's why—I've always sensed *something* on you, but I never knew what, and I couldn't bring myself to say anything. It was clear you didn't know or you would've known about me, so I ignored it."

I stare at her silently, still trying to figure out how I missed it.

Her eyes bounce across my face. "I'm sure you have a lot of questions, but we can't stay here, Aurora." She grabs her bag, shouldering it and shoving her feet into the shoes she left by the door. She stops and looks at me over her shoulder. "Please, I'll explain everything. Just come with me."

I hesitate. "Where?"

"My cousin Theo owns a nightclub across town. We can go there and figure things out."

I bite the inside of my cheek, glancing between her and the door. "Your cousin—"

"Is also fae," she interjects, "and he's always looked out for me."

Raking my fingers through my hair, I exhale a heavy breath. "I don't know, Al." I have a lot of questions, but I'm not sure I'm ready to hear the answers. I trust Allison far more than Tristan, but this whole thing... It's too much.

"You're scared," she says, walking back to me. "I understand. You have every right to be scared and confused and angry. I didn't want to suck you into this world. I thought I was doing everything necessary to keep you out of it, to keep you safe, but I fucked up and I am so sorry."

My eyes sting, and I blink quickly, forcing the tears back. There's a nagging voice in my head telling me I should be more insistent she tells me why Tristan is trying to track her down, but I shove it aside for now. Allison is my best friend, and I sure as hell trust her more than the fae who held me captive. "Okay," I finally say. "Let's go."

She starts toward the door again before pausing. "I'd

normally shift there, but I don't think that's something I should put you through today."

*Shift?* That must be what Skylar did at the hotel to disappear seemingly into thin air. There's not a chance in hell I'm going to do that. "Fae can teleport anywhere?"

"Uh, not really." She walks to her desk, grabbing the jacket on the back of her chair, and shrugs it on. "We can move locations with an ability called shifting, but there are limitations in terms of distance. I haven't tested it, but the farthest I've gone is across the city, which would typically take half an hour driving." She pulls her hair out of her jacket before zipping it up, then wets her lips. "We also can't shift somewhere we've never been."

"Right." I nod along, as if my best friend isn't telling me about her supernatural abilities. "How does it work?"

She shrugs. "I've been doing it for as long as I can remember, so it's second nature. I just visualize where I want to go, focus on it, and I shift there."

"Oh. Cool?" I offer weakly.

She almost cracks a smile. "For new fae, I'd imagine it would take a lot of concentration and practice."

"New fae?" I echo. "Wait. How long have *you* been fae?"

Allison purses her lips. "Almost twenty-three years. I was born fae, like Tristan, though not all are."

"How does someone who wasn't born fae become one?" I ask before I can stop myself.

"It's an involved process. A fae needs to feed on them while transferring their own energy into the human. They both need to be equals in that sense. It's dangerous because their energy levels become extremely low during the process. Once that equal level is reached, the fae will drain the remaining human energy, so only the fae energy remains."

"That doesn't kill them?"

She shakes her head. "The human exists in a sort of in-between state. They need to feed on human emotions to complete the transition. Once that is done, a fae is made."

"Oh. You were born fae, so does that mean—"

"Both my parents are fae. My mom was born fae, and she changed my dad."

I've only seen them a handful of times over the few years I've known Allison, but come to think of it, they struck me as impossibly attractive when we met the day Al and I moved into the dorm.

"How old is Tristan?"

"I'm not sure exactly, but it's under a hundred."

"Oh-kay." My voice is low, and panic creeps into the tone.

"We can also shift into dreams," she adds. "Though most fae call it dream walking."

My breath hitches, and I rake my fingers through my hair, pressing them against my scalp as my mind races. "Have you ever done it?"

"A few times, just to see what it was like," she admits.

"Have you ever done it to *me*?" The question tumbles from my lips, though I'm not convinced I really want the answer.

She shakes her head. "Absolutely not. I'd never do anything to risk you finding out about me."

That eases a bit of the tension in my muscles, and I sigh wearily.

"Listen, I know this is a lot. I can't imagine what you must be thinking and feeling right now, but we really need to get out of here."

I'm officially overloaded with information. All I can do

is follow Allison out of the dorm toward the campus bus stop.

---

Sweaty, dancing bodies fill the club, and it's so loud the building is vibrating. It's also about ten degrees too warm to be comfortable, but that comes with the crowd.

Allison pulls me closer and says into my ear, "Wait here. I'm going to find Theo, then we can go somewhere quiet and talk, okay?"

I don't know what else to do but nod. In the time I take to blink, she's gone, weaving through the dancing bodies faster than my gaze can follow.

I wait a few minutes, then make my way through the crowd to the bar and order a ginger ale. It likely won't settle the unease in my stomach, but it doesn't hurt to try.

When Allison isn't back by the time I finish my drink, I scan the crowd, squinting at the darkness and flashing lights. I lean back over the bar, catching the bartender's attention. "Where can I find Theo?" I shout over the music.

She points in the direction Allison went before returning to the patrons waiting for drinks. I can barely make out a hallway across the room, but I make my way toward it, squeezing through the crowd as I hold my breath against the heavy smell of liquor and body odor mixed with cologne and perfume. I try not to shove anyone; it's difficult with all the flailing arms and grinding hips everywhere. The front of the hall is congested with people waiting to use the bathrooms, but I break through it and find the rest of the hall empty. The fluorescent lights flicker and there's a door at the end of the hall marked

EMERGENCY EXIT. There are a few doors before it, and I start toward the first one.

Before I can reach for the handle, an arm wraps around my waist and hauls me toward the other side of the hall. It happens too fast for me to react until I'm in another room, pressed against the closed door.

I try to scream, but a firm hand covers my mouth and muffles the sound. My pulse surges, and when the single lightbulb in the middle of the small room flicks on, I recognize my captor immediately, and annoyance ripples through me. I try to shove him away, but he pushes back, grabbing my wrists in his other hand and pinning them against the door above my head with ease.

There's a moment when his eyes narrow that tells me he's noticed I'm not wearing the bracelet.

My chest heaves as I fight with every ounce of strength I have to break free from his grasp. I make a sound faintly resembling a growl against his palm when he doesn't budge a damn inch. Those dark blue eyes flash with amusement as Tristan finally moves his hand away from my mouth.

"What the fuck are you doing here?" I seethe, quickly taking in what appears to be a storage room behind him. It's a dark, windowless space that clearly isn't meant to be one people spend much time in. It's tidy enough, but the air is stale. Three out of four walls are lined with metal shelves that are filled with boxes and bottles of liquor. The fourth wall has the only way out of here—the one I'm currently trapped against.

"I could ask you the same question," Tristan says, and his proximity paired with his scent—an inviting combination of sandalwood and citrus—makes it difficult to think clearly. And the curve of his lips makes me think he fucking knows it.

The music from the club is much quieter in here, but the bass still vibrates the shelves of liquor enough they clink together. If I could just break free of Tristan's grasp, I could grab one of them and smash it against his head. That's if I could move fast enough, which the pit in my stomach says is unlikely.

I try to pull my wrists free again and fail. "Did you follow me?" I ask as my eyes travel across his face and drop to his chest, where a landscape of hard muscle pulls at his black T-shirt. It hits me then that if Tristan followed *me*, he followed Allison and knows where she is. I should've thought of that sooner, but I'm struggling to keep my head on straight as it is.

"An interesting idea, but no. I was informed that the fae I'm looking for is here."

"That's weird," I mutter. "I don't remember calling you." I see no point in telling him my phone is gone. Even if it's at his hotel, I don't expect to get it back, and I'm sure as hell not going there to get it.

A hint of a smile plays on Tristan's lips, and he finally releases my wrists. "The man who owns this club contacted me," he says.

I frown. Allison's cousin sold her out? *So much for looking out for her...* What could she have done to warrant that? "Oh? I hope I'm not hindering another kidnapping attempt right now." My voice is soft, laced with false sweetness. "Maybe you should find another hobby? Perhaps a less creepy one?"

He reaches forward, quick and graceful, and snags my chin. "Would you like to tell me why *you* are here? And while we're sharing, perhaps you can tell me where the bracelet is? You know, it's rude to discard a gift from a gentleman."

My eyes narrow, and I smack his hand away. "You are no gentleman."

His eyes seem bluer somehow. "I can be."

"Great, so you'll let me out of this stuffy storage room, then."

"Hmm, in a moment. I'm not quite done here."

I press my lips together, my stomach dipping. It's not an entirely unwelcome sensation, which is why I grit my teeth against it. "What do you want from me?"

Something I can't decipher passes over his face. He hesitates before settling on: "Did you find her?"

I stand straighter, forcing myself to meet his gaze. "I won't let you hurt her," I say fiercely.

"It sounds like you know this girl," he muses.

"It doesn't matter if I do or not," I shoot back, shifting my gaze past him to the row of a few kegs on the floor near the back row of shelves.

"Come on, now," he says mildly. "Mysteries have never been my thing."

"Being held against my will isn't my thing, and yet, here we are. Again."

"Answer my question, and I'll be happy to step aside and let you leave. Though I enjoy your sharp wit."

My gaze snaps back to his. "You are one twisted son of—"

He tuts his tongue, shaking his head. "There's no need for that."

"She's my best friend," I snap.

He has the decency to look surprised, though he

recovers quickly, his expression smoothing as he pulls at the cuff of his jacket sleeve. "I see. Of course you want to protect her. You're loyal to her—that's admirable." He inhales slowly, taking a moment to consider his next words. "I'll make you another deal."

"Oh no," I cut in before he can elaborate, "we already did that. We're done."

His smirk is a flash of perfect white teeth. "I think you'll find this more agreeable, considering how strongly you feel about protecting your friend. If you get to her first, I'll ensure she doesn't face punishment. However, if I find her before you do, she's mine to hand over to the court."

*Punishment for what?*

*Court?*

My thoughts trip over themselves as my heart slams against my rib cage, trying to escape my chest as I'd like to this room. "Why—"

"Not only is she mine," he interrupts, his eyes twinkling. "As are you—at least for dinner. You are still a bit of a puzzle."

An exasperated laugh escapes my lips. "And you are absolutely insane if you think I'm going to agree to that." My tone is firm, and yet, the image of sitting across from Tristan at a restaurant flashes through my head.

"Are you doubting yourself?" He's mocking me, and I want to slap the smug grin off his face.

I lean in despite my uneven pulse. "You think I'm going to agree to something like this? On the off chance you find her before I do, I've not only sealed her fate, but my own as well? You're out of your mind."

"Yet you've made a deal with me once before."

"I didn't have a choice then," I remind him sharply.

His jaw tightens, and he schools his features into an expression of indifference. "You can agree, or I can use you to get to her."

I pull back, hitting the door with a faint *thud*. My breath catches as I glare at him, the temperature of my body increasing steadily. "Why are you doing this?"

Tristan flicks his tongue across his bottom lip, and I hate the way it makes my stomach dip. "Immortality can get a little dull. I like to keep things interesting." He steals the distance between us again, brushing his fingers over my cheek as he snares my gaze, tilting my chin up. "And you, Aurora, are most certainly interesting."

I fight to ignore the way my skin warms and tingles under his touch. "Why does it matter so much?" I force out. "What did Allison do that has her in so much trouble?"

"Perhaps you should ask your friend."

*I plan to just as soon as I can find her.*

I swallow hard, my heart in my throat. "I'm going to find her."

His eyes hold a challenge in their dark blue depths. "We have a deal, then?"

"Fine," I snap. The word is out of my mouth before I can stop myself; I need this to be over. I grab his wrist and pull his hand away from my face. "Now back off."

He raises his hands in front of him in mock surrender and steps back. I'm out the door in a second without looking back as I race toward the dance floor. I have to find Allison and make sure she's safe. That, and if I don't find her before Tristan does... Nope. Not going there.

I'm less polite this time as I make my way through the crowd of gyrating bodies. More than once, I think I see her, but when I approach, it's always a stranger. My heart is pounding so hard I can feel it in my throat and my palms are sweating. I catch the top of a blond head walking toward the bar, and I follow. My pace quickens when I recognize Allison's shirt. I grab the back of it, and she whips around, her eyes wide.

"Where the hell have you been? I checked the office and upstairs. I don't think Theo's here." She frowns. "I texted him, but—"

"We have to go!" I yell over the music. I found her first, but I'm not taking any chances. I'm not trusting Tristan to keep his word. Though there's a small part of me that wants to rub it in his face.

She reaches for my hand, pulling me through a mass of writhing dancers. I squeeze between two people, cringing at the damp warmth of their bodies, and push a few more out of my way. Finally, we make it out the door and stand in an alley beside the building.

"Your cousin called Tristan," I pant in between shallow breaths.

She freezes, her eyes welling. "Shit." She rakes her fingers through her hair, pacing across the width of the alley. "Shit, shit, shit."

I've never seen her this panicked. *What did she do?*

Before I can open my mouth to question her, the back door swings open with a loud smack against the brick. Four people stumble out of the club, laughing and smelling of booze. They look at Allison, recognition narrowing their eyes before they turn their attention to me, and my throat goes dry.

"Whoa," the redhead says with a breathy laugh as her bright green eyes snare my gaze. "I can practically taste your fear."

Fucking fae. I've known about them for a day and I'm

already sick of their shit. How does one say *"bitch, I'm not food"* relatively politely?

Allison reaches for me, but the other fae is faster, dragging me toward her as two of the others block Allison from getting to me. In the time I take to blink, I'm against the cold brick of the building. I whimper involuntarily, then gasp when she cuts off my oxygen, gripping my throat. Panic clamps down on my chest, filling my veins with ice. The fae leans in, filling my entire world with those hungry emerald eyes.

"Don't touch her," Allison screams, and the sounds of her struggling against the other fae fill the alley.

I choke on the dryness in my throat as the fae feeds on me. Only seconds pass before dizziness floods in, and I can't move. Black spots dot my vision, and I can't fight her off. I can't make a sound.

Allison's voice cracks when she hollers, "Let go of her!"

The woman doesn't stop. My knees shake as my ears ring and things start to feel fuzzy.

The door we came through swings open again, slamming against the brick, the harsh sound reverberating off the buildings.

"Fuck!" shouts one guy, and the sound is muffled, as if cotton fills my ears.

The woman feeding from me turns her head, and her eyes widen before she wrenches her hand away from my throat as if my skin burned her. She vanishes a moment later, dematerializing right in front of me.

With the fae no longer holding me by my throat, I sway on my feet. The pavement rushes to meet me as if we're old friends. I close my eyes to prepare for the impact, but it doesn't come.

It takes me a few long seconds to realize someone is

holding me. I pry my eyes open to find Tristan. My vision ebbs in and out, but his wild expression is unmistakable. He's glaring at me, his jaw sharp and his lips pressed into a thin line.

Tristan snarls, a beast in a pretty package, and then the darkness swallows me whole.

## CHAPTER
# FIVE

There are jackhammers in my head, chipping away at my temples. I blink several times before I realize I'm squinting at the familiar ceiling above my bed. I'm back in my dorm and I'm alone. *How the hell did I get here?*

Visions of yesterday fill my head. The club, trying to find Allison's cousin, Tristan showing up... being fae food. Nausea rolls through me, and I sit up in a flash, wincing at the lingering dizziness. What I wouldn't give to forget that whole scenario. I shudder at the memory that refuses to dissipate and struggle to shove it away.

Swinging my legs over the side of the bed, I use the nightstand to stay upright. I'm surprised to find my phone sitting on top, and I snatch it up, immediately calling Allison. My stomach sinks as it goes straight to voicemail. Next, my finger hovers over Oliver's number. If he doesn't know about Allison, calling him about her being missing might not be the best course of action. Unless... What if Oliver is fae too? If Allison kept it from me, surely Oliver could too. The pressure building behind my eyes makes me squeeze them shut for a minute. I can't think about this right now. One impossible problem at a time.

I blow out a harsh breath, because fucking hell, I have approximately zero other options here. Walking across the room, I grab yesterday's shorts out of my hamper, shoving my hand into the pocket and pulling out the business card. I grit my teeth as I flip the card over and dial the number on the back. My pulse ticks faster with each ring, and I pace the small space between my bed and desk.

"Tristan Westbrook." His voice is clipped, professional.

"You lied," I say.

His response is a brief chuckle and then: "We both know that isn't true."

"You're telling me Allison isn't with you?"

"I'm telling you I didn't lie." The amusement in his voice has me balling my free hand into a fist and hitting it against my thigh so I don't scream through the phone. Having him in my ear like this does weird things to my stomach, and I hate that I don't hate it.

"You lost our deal, Tristan."

"Hmm," he hums.

"*What?*"

"I enjoy when you say my name, even when your voice is dripping with venom."

I ignore that, mainly because I have no clue how to respond to it. "I found her before you did."

"Are you sure?"

"I'm not playing this game with you," I shoot back.

"No?" he challenges, his voice annoyingly arrogant. "What exactly *are* you going to do then, Aurora?"

I bite back a string of expletives, my face burning as I grip the phone so tightly my fingers spasm and I nearly drop it. "You sent me to find her to prove you could trust me. What about my trust in you?" I'm not sure this is the best angle to play, but I'm out of ideas.

Tristan chuckles. "As much as I'd like to continue this conversation, I'm walking into a meeting, so we'll have to put a pin in it for now. Oh, and you're welcome for returning your phone. Max brought it to me yesterday—figured you'd want it back."

"Wait—"

"Always a pleasure, Aurora."

The line disconnects before I can respond, and I throw my phone onto the bed, my entire body flushing with heat as I stomp toward the door.

---

I'm on my way to the Westbrook Hotel before I can talk myself out of it.

I charge up the marble stairs that lead to the building and fly through the open door. My footsteps echo on the ornate lobby floor as I approach the reception desk, where I slam my fist against the dark wood counter.

"I need to see Tristan," I demand.

The young blond receptionist offers a polite smile. "My apologies, Mr. Westbrook isn't in his office at the moment. Would you like to wait?"

"No," I snap. "I need to see him now."

"I'm sorry, that's not possible."

"I don't have time for this. You seem like a lovely person, so I'm sorry." Before she can respond, I sprint toward the elevator. Jamming the button as if my life depends on it, I look over my shoulder in time to see her lift the phone, presumably to call security.

Once inside, I press the button for the penthouse and blow out a frustrated breath when it doesn't illuminate.

"You came back?"

I jump at the sound of Skylar's voice, and whip my head toward her, not sure how I missed her when I got on; she must be coming from a level below the lobby. Today her knee-high dress is bright red, matching the matte color on her lips.

"I had to." I lean back against the wall and watch the numbers tick by as the elevator ascends.

Her laugh is a tinkling sound, like raindrops on a window. "What for? To make sure it was real?"

I shake my head. "To make sure he doesn't hurt my best friend."

Realization flickers across her features. "You figured out who he was looking for."

My jaw clenches. "He sent me to look for her."

"And you found her. Obviously."

I nod.

Her lips curl. "You didn't know your best friend was fae?"

I bite back a scowl. "I didn't know the fae existed until a few days ago, so no, I didn't know my best friend was one. How many of you are there?"

Skylar shrugs, and even that looks graceful. "A lot."

*Super helpful.* The elevator stops, and Skylar steps toward the door as it opens. "Coming back here was stupid. He let you go once. I don't see him doing it again."

I stuff my trembling hands into my pockets. "She's my best friend."

Skylar sighs, as if my decision to put myself in danger is annoying. "You won't be able to get to the penthouse." My stomach sinks, but before I can say anything, she pulls out a keycard and taps it against the panel on the wall, then presses the button for the penthouse. "Good luck," she mutters in a voice dripping with sarcasm before the door shuts and I'm alone again. I don't know why Skylar helped me, though there's a good chance she didn't see it that way. She's probably hoping Tristan will throw me out himself—or kill me.

My heart hammers in my chest, and my nerves sing with coiled energy as the elevator reaches the penthouse level. I step off and through the foyer to his door and bang my fist against it several times. As I'm getting ready to kick the damn thing in, it opens to reveal an annoyed looking Tristan. His casual attire catches me off guard, and I stare too long at his dark jeans and black T-shirt.

"Where the hell is she?" I growl, pushing my way inside.

He glances between the empty hallway and where I'm standing in his suite. "You are persistent, aren't you?" he murmurs.

"Where is Allison?" I push.

Tristan closes the door and walks toward me. "Aren't you going to thank me?"

I blink at him, my pulse kicking up as heat fills my cheeks. "What?"

"For saving your life last night."

"You're giving yourself too much credit."

He cocks his head to the side, his eyes dancing over my face. "You think so?" He offers a soft chuckle. "Did you become a fae expert since yesterday?"

"I—"

"If I hadn't showed up, you would be dead."

My eyes narrow. "Allison—"

"Couldn't help you. Clearly."

I exhale through my nose. "Tell me where she is." I'm done talking about last night. I'd love to forget the sickening feeling of being trapped against a wall and fed on while they forced my best friend to watch.

"She's here awaiting my orders."

"What the hell does that mean?"

Tristan wets his lips, and I have to stop myself from letting my gaze drop to his mouth. "You really shouldn't know any more than you already do, but I suspect you won't leave well enough alone and return to your life like you should. Just know, this world you've stumbled into is dangerous, Aurora. The less you know, the better. Knowledge may be powerful, but it'll also thrust you deeper into a world that could easily tear you apart."

My heart beats like the wings of a hummingbird, but I hold his gaze. "You really don't know me at all."

The corner of his mouth pulls up slightly, and he exhales a short laugh. "Fae laws are much like your own," he continues. "Actions have consequences and there are punishments for misconduct."

I frown. "What misconduct are you talking about?"

He says nothing.

"What did she do?" I push, though I'm not sure why. It's something I should ask Allison. I trust her answer over Tristan's, anyway. "What are *you* going to do?" I amend.

"I'll treat the situation as I see fit." His voice is firm, unforgiving, and his response is utterly useless. "It's time for you to leave."

"I'm not leaving without her," I say. "You lost our deal. I found her first."

Tristan arches a brow, a faint smirk on his lips, and glances over his shoulder when there's a knock at the door. When it opens, I stiffen, and Max steps into the suite, his eyes landing on me immediately. A potent mixture of fear and disgust goes to war inside me, and I step closer to Tristan without thinking, as if some part of me feels he's safe—at least safer than Max.

"Back for more fun, blondie?" he taunts.

I recoil, revulsion twisting my expression as my last encounter with him plays on a loop in my head.

"Miss Marshall was just on her way out," Tristan says smoothly.

"You're letting the human go? Again?" Max questions. "She could open her mouth and put us all in danger. Wipe her memory. We've got the one we were after."

I look between them and take a couple of steps away from them both, my heart rate kicking up as they turn to watch me.

"I'm handling it," Tristan says in a firm tone, flicking his eyes to me. Evidently, he isn't going to tell Max he tried and *couldn't* use his freaky fae manipulation on me.

"Fine," Max mutters, his teeth flashing in a snarl when he glances at me. His eyes quickly return to Tristan. "We need to talk. I'll be in your study when you're done with this."

I can't help the small gasp that escapes my lips when he shifts out of the room. That's definitely not something I'm going to get used to anytime soon. "What about *his* misconduct?" I ask. "Shouldn't he receive punishment for his actions against me? Or does it not matter because I'm not fae?"

His jaw works. "There are no laws to prevent fae from taking humans."

My brows tug closer as I glare at him. "I don't have the mental capacity to get into how fucked up that is. So just let Allison go, and we'll be on our way."

"I don't see that happening," he says mildly.

I grind my molars, my muscles tensing as I fight the urge to take a swing at him. I'm not a particularly violent person, but Tristan knows just the right thing to say to get my blood boiling. "You don't think people will wonder where Allison is? She has friends and a boyfriend. People will question her whereabouts."

Tristan sighs, pinching the bridge of his nose. "She will return to her life soon enough."

Some of the tension in my chest releases, and my lips part in surprise. At least he said he'll let her go. "After you're done with her? Because she answers to you?"

"Yes. Just as you do. That's how it works when you choose to return to a world that wasn't meant for you."

"I do *not* answer to you."

Tristan moves closer, faster than my eyes can register the movement. "I saved your life. Twice."

"My life was in danger twice *because* of you!" I wait for him to respond with some high-handed remark, but he stands there with a stoic expression.

"How unusual," he says thoughtfully, licking his bottom lip.

"*What?*"

"You're so responsive. It's refreshing. Most people I encounter have a healthy fear of me or a high level of respect. It's clear you have neither."

I stifle my laugh and arch a brow instead, because something tells me if Tristan wanted me dead, I wouldn't be standing here. "You want me to fear you? Too bad. I don't. As for the respect? That's earned. You don't magically get it because you're some fae knight—whatever that even means."

"How do you think I became a knight?" he challenges.

I shrug. "I'm guessing some seriously dodgy politics."

His laugh is a rich sound that makes him seem dangerously human. "You have no idea."

"True, but I have been paying attention, so I know you're into deals. Let me make you one this time. If you let Allison go, I'll... have dinner with you." The words taste bitter on my tongue, but if it means getting Allison away from here, I'll do whatever it takes—including subjecting myself to more time with Tristan.

He blinks, his brows lifting, and scratches the hint of stubble along his jaw. "As tempting as your offer is, I'm afraid I have to decline."

"What the hell? Isn't that what you wanted?"

"The choices I make aren't often the result of what I want, Aurora. Now, if you'll excuse me..." He trails off, walking to the door and opening it, clearly dismissing me.

I grit my teeth, crossing the room toward him. "If you hurt her," I say in a firm, low voice, "I will make you regret Max's mistake on an entirely new level."

Despite the sharp edge to my voice and the threat I gave, Tristan's lips twitch. "Duly noted."

I'm not completely sure what gripped me to mouth off to a creature who could easily kill me and, I'm sure, get away with it. But something—a weird, nonsensical gut feeling—tells me Tristan won't hurt me. At the very least, because I've captured his interest. And as much as I hate it, he's caught mine, too.

## CHAPTER SIX

Back on campus, with a pit in my stomach and frustration making my skin itch, I attempt to distract myself by prepping for my upcoming internship interview. I review and tweak my resume and cover letter until my eyes burn, and I jump when my phone buzzes on the desk beside me. Oliver's number illuminates the screen, and I hesitate, biting the inside of my cheek before picking it up.

"Hey, what's up?"

"I'm starving, and Allison isn't answering her phone. Pretty sure she went to visit her parents today. I can't remember if she said she was going home this weekend or next," he rambles on. "Anyway, want to get lunch?"

"Uh..." My stomach grumbles, reminding me I still haven't had a proper meal since Friday. "Yeah, I could eat. Where should I meet you?"

"The Iron Lounge? I'm craving their deep-fried pickles."

"Sounds good. I'll head over there now."

"I'm coming from the library, so I'll probably beat you there. I'll grab us a table."

"Great. See you in a few," I say, then end the call and exhale a deep sigh, deciding I can use this opportunity to see if Oliver knows about the fae—if he is one. I just have to be careful with the way I go about it.

---

The Iron Lounge is a casual pub in the middle of campus. It's an old church building with indoor seating and a covered patio, which has soft music playing and twinkling lights hung from the awning and lattice encompassing the space. Their food is amazing, their drinks are cheap, and they often have live music, making it an ideal atmosphere for college students.

Before learning of the fae, I wouldn't have thought twice about the name. Now, though, I consider it must be owned by a fae—or at the very least, someone who knows about them.

I pull open the repurposed stained-glass door and step inside, immediately enveloped by the aroma of alcohol and fried food. There's a three-hundred-sixty-degree bar in the center of the room, with a dance floor and stage on the left and a seating area with cocktail tables and booths on the right.

Spotting Oliver near the wall of floor to ceiling windows, I start toward him, coming up short when Grant slides off a bar stool into my path.

"You disappeared the other night," he says with a charming grin that makes my stomach dip. He's wearing a burgundy hoodie and jeans and his hair is unrulier than it was on Friday night. It suits him, the casual model look. "I was hoping to see you again."

I exhale a shaky breath that sounds somewhere between a laugh and a sigh. "Yeah, it was kind of crazy." My jaw clenches; I need to be careful about what I say.

"Join me for a drink?"

Heat fills my cheeks, and my pulse picks up at his offer. "I'm meeting a friend." I point toward the booth Oliver's in.

"No worries." Grant pulls out his phone. "Let's plan to hang sometime." He holds it out, open to a new message. "Text yourself so you have my number."

My pulse ticks faster as I take his phone and type in my number, then add a quick *hey* and send it. My phone vibrates from my pocket.

"I'll let you get to your friend," he says as I hand his phone back. "It was nice to see you, Aurora."

"You too." I smile before continuing to where Oliver is waiting, sliding into the booth across from him. "Hey."

"I saw you getting your flirt on with that guy from the party." He wiggles his brows, and I roll my eyes. "You gave him your number?" Oliver asks, flipping his navy ball cap around, making his hair stick out the front.

I shrug, scanning Oliver's face while trying to be subtle about searching for any hints that he's fae. "Maybe. I kind of like him."

"Good. It's about time you got laid."

I scoff half-heartedly. "Thank you so much for being concerned about my sex life. I really appreciate it."

He grins at me over the menu. "I ordered you an iced coffee."

"Now *that's* what I like to hear."

Oliver and I chat about classes after we order—him,

the fried pickles and a caesar salad with steak, and me, a giant bowl of bowtie pasta with tomato sauce and grilled chicken. I let him do most of the talking, using that opportunity to inspect him. Oliver isn't unattractive, but his complexion isn't flawless like the fae I've met. His skin has texture and blemishes in spots, and his eyes are a dull brown and have darkness and lines beneath them, normal for any college senior—any *human*. If the fae can alter their appearances to look human, surely they can create flaws to help sell their disguise.

*I need him to lie*, I decide, dropping my gaze momentarily. My eyes land on the utensils on the table, and I press my lips together. *Or maybe I don't*. They're likely made of stainless steel, which means there's iron in them. I continue listening to Oliver go on about how many assignments his marketing class has as I pick up my bundle of utensils as if I'm getting ready to eat. I purposely fumble it, letting the knife slide out and clatter against the old hardwood floor. "Shit," I mutter.

Oliver laughs. "Nice one." He shifts to the end of the booth, and my breath halts. He swipes it off the floor and sets it back on the table with no reaction to touching it.

I let out a breath, reaching for my iced coffee. "Thanks."

With that out of the way, I'm able to enjoy the rest of our meal—the first real one I've had in a couple of days. I scarf it down along with my iced coffee, then sit back and groan, because I ate way too much, but it was a-fucking-mazing.

We walk back across campus, Oliver pausing outside my dorm. "When you see Allison, will you tell her to give me a shout?"

"I will," I tell him. "Thanks for lunch."

"Of course," he echoes before waving goodbye and continuing to his dorm building next door.

Instead of going inside, I head for the bus stop. I'm not entirely sure what possesses me to get on the bus and ride several blocks to the nearest hardware store, but I stand in front of a selection of fencing materials—including iron stakes. I walk down a few of the other aisles, stalling. Whether I'm trying to talk myself into or out of buying them isn't all that clear, but after ten minutes of pacing, I finally blow out a breath and grab half a dozen of them, carrying them to the cashier. Sure, I get an interesting look from the teenager behind the counter, but I don't really care. Not if having these is going to give me a sense of control over the crazy that has become my life in the last two days.

Choosing to walk back to campus, the stakes clink around in the canvas bag I bought to carry them in. Once I get back to my room, I store the bag in the bottom drawer of my desk and flop onto my bed, pulling my laptop out.

An internet search for *fae* leads absolutely nowhere. I've been sitting on my bed for over an hour pouring over articles of mythology and the different origins of fae, and all it's done is make my head pound.

Pacing the minuscule square footage of our room, I come up with a list of what I think I know about them. I fist my hair, groaning as I shuffle over to my bed and flop onto it, throwing my arm over my eyes as I focus on slowing my breathing.

"Aurora?"

I sit up in a flash and find Allison standing in the doorway. She looks fine, not a hair out of place, no wrinkles on her clothes. Her face is free of makeup, which is unusual for her; otherwise, she looks normal. "Are you really here?" I ask.

She takes a moment to smile. "I'm here."

I launch myself off the bed and throw my arms around her.

She pulls back and stares at me for a moment and then hugs me tighter. "I am so sorry about everything. Are you okay?"

I step back. "Are *you*?"

"I'm not the one who was attacked and fed on, Ro." She surveys my face, studying me as if checking herself to make sure I'm not hurt. The guilt in her eyes makes my chest ache.

"Besides not having any idea what happened between the time I passed out in that alley and waking up here, I'm fine. I was mostly worried about you, and when I tried to talk to Tristan, well, I'm sure you can imagine how that went. You know him better than I do."

Allison nods. "Tristan brought you back here last night while Max and I shifted to the hotel."

My pulse jumps at the thought of Tristan being in here. Of putting me to bed. Heat flares in my cheeks, and I glance away. At least I was unconscious; otherwise, I probably would've puked on him during the shift. "What happened at the hotel?"

"Nothing you're probably worried about. He didn't hurt me."

"Good," I say, then lower my voice and add, "because I sort of threatened him."

Her eyes pop wide. "You *what?*"

I offer a humorless laugh. "I, uh, just made it clear that if he hurt you, there would be consequences for his actions."

Her brows draw together, concern filling her eyes. "Aurora."

I bite the inside of my cheek, then say, "I told him I'd make sure he would regret abducting me."

She closes her eyes, letting out a slow breath as she runs her fingers through her hair. "I love you for being protective of me, but that was so incredibly stupid, I want to shake you."

"It's fine," I tell her. "You're back now, and it's fine."

She shakes her head. "Fine? Aurora, with the news of your fae lineage, Tristan won't let Max's mistake go so easily. He can't. Which means he isn't finished with you."

The panic that's been living on the surface rears its unforgiving head.

*He isn't finished with you.*

And it all goes back to why this happened.

I clear my throat. "What did you do? Why did Tristan send Max after you?"

Her gaze lowers, and she scratches the back of her neck. "Fae living in the human world are required to follow certain rules. One of which has to do with who we associate with, um, romantically."

My forehead creases. "Are you kidding me? Fae aren't allowed to be with humans? That's the most ridiculous thing I've heard since I found out about all of this."

She pauses, offering a tight-lipped smile. "You don't know the half of it."

"No kidding. So what? You have to break up with Oliver?"

"It's not safe for him to know about the fae, same as it isn't for you. Part of Tristan's position means protecting his people against threats, including exposure."

"How noble," I deadpan.

Allison frowns. "I may not like the guy—in fact, he scares the shit out of me sometimes—but I respect him. He has worked hard for years protecting us from the unseelie court."

"I'm going to need more than that." This is the second time *court* has come up without an explanation.

She blinks at me. "Right. Sorry. I'm not sure how much you know." Lowering herself to the end of her bed, she clasps her hands in her lap, focusing her attention on me. "There are two fae courts—the seelie court and the unseelie court. Tristan is a knight of the seelie court and the king's right hand."

"Of course there's a fae king," I mutter.

Allison pulls her bottom lip between her teeth for a moment, as if she's worried about overwhelming me. *That crazy train has left the station.* "There's also a fae queen who rules the unseelie court."

I drop onto my bed before my legs give out. "Tristan works for the seelie king?"

"Yeah. In business terms, Tristan is a manager, and the king is the CEO." Weirdly enough, that helps me make sense of it.

I almost laugh. "Manager of the seelie fae."

"At least in this area."

"Right... How many knights are there?"

"Twelve in each court, spread out over the world."

*The world.* Of course, the fae are everywhere. "How many *fae* are there?"

"I can't give you an exact number, but around ten percent of the population."

I nod robotically. "I tried searching for information. It was wildly unhelpful."

She almost laughs. "Were you looking for something in particular?"

"Weaknesses," I admit.

Allison pulls back a bit. "I shouldn't share that information with you." She pauses, tugging at the corner of the blanket across the end of her bed. "But I understand why you want to know so I'll tell you. Iron is poisonous to us."

"I knew that part." My gaze automatically flits toward my desk drawer before moving back to Allison.

"If we don't feed, our abilities can become practically useless. Shifting quickly becomes impossible, and manipulation is out of the question. It's extremely dangerous to go without feeding because it's the only way for us to glamour our appearances to blend in with the humans."

"Do the courts have different abilities?"

She shakes her head. "Physically, we are the same. Our beliefs and way of living are what differentiate us."

"Oh." I'm not sure that's something I want to touch right now.

"Is there anything else you want to know?"

I press my lips together, considering it. I probably have a million questions that I'm too scared to get answers for, terrified I'll be pushed further into the fae world. "My fae ancestors... Is there any chance you could find information on them?"

Her eyes widen slightly, then fill with compassion. "I'll ask around."

"I'd appreciate that. I don't know what answers I'm looking for exactly, but whatever you can find out would be a start."

She smiles. "Of course. Do you want to know more?"

I rake my fingers through my hair, exhaling a heavy breath that does nothing to ease the pressure living in my chest. "I probably should hear it, considering there doesn't seem to be a way out of this world for me, but my head feels like it's going to explode, so can we maybe put a pin in it for today?"

Allison nods before she stands, then sits next to me on my bed, wrapping her arm around my shoulders and hugging me against her side. "I know this is a lot. Why don't we take a break from the fae stuff and do something normal? It's Sunday night—let's order takeout and watch a movie. Sound good?"

I force a smile, though I'm not sure I remember what normal feels like anymore.

---

Thursday is my internship interview, and I sleep through my alarm. Or it doesn't go off, which means I forgot to set it last night. Doesn't really matter—I'm late.

I throw myself out of bed and into the bathroom to put myself together as fast as I can. Once my hair looks decent, twisted into a quick French braid, I apply a few swipes of light makeup so I look alive. I get dressed in a formal black jumpsuit and shrug on a matching blazer. Grabbing my bag off the dresser, I shove my portfolio inside before I slide my feet into some heels and rush out the door.

I've never run across campus, but there's a first for everything. My stomach is twisted with nerves and my palms are sweaty. I can't remember ever being this anxious. If I'd had time for breakfast, I'm not sure I would've been able to stomach it.

I burst through the conference hall doors, speed-walk to the check-in desk, and hand over my student ID.

"You're late," the older gentleman behind the desk says, typing on his computer.

"I'm aware," I say, still trying to catch my breath. "Sorry."

He lifts his gaze and hands back my ID. "Your interview is in room 109."

"Thanks." I rush toward the room, but when I reach the door, my hand freezes halfway to the doorknob. Closing my eyes, I take a deep breath, letting it out slowly. *I've got this.* Straightening, I knock before walking into the room.

We all have moments in our lives where we reflect on every bad thing we've done to comprehend why a terrible thing is happening to us. To determine why we deserve something so awful. As I approach the table and lock eyes with Tristan as he closes his laptop, I'm sucked into one of those moments. *What did I do to deserve this?*

He rises from his chair at the head of the table and buttons his black suit jacket, offering me a downright wicked smile. "Good morning, Miss Marshall," he says as I stand there, screaming profanities in my head.

"This isn't... You can't... What the hell are you doing here?"

The corner of his mouth kicks up. "An interesting way to introduce yourself to a potential boss."

My jaw clenches, and I glance around the windowless meeting room, despite Tristan being the only other person here. It's not an immense space; there's enough room for the eight-person mahogany table with rolling chairs around it and a projector screen at the front. "I am *not* working for you." I step back toward the door. "There must be some mistake. I'll interview for someone—*anyone*—else."

"I figured you'd say that." He lifts his shoulders in a shrug. "I'm the only mentor available for you."

I stand frozen, glaring at him in silence as I try to come up with an alternative. I need a completed internship to graduate, which means I have to do this if I want to stay on track with my degree.

With a sigh, I approach the table separating us. "My education is the most important thing to me." I don't elaborate. Tristan doesn't need to know my parents took out a second mortgage to put me through school, and I need to graduate on time so I can start paying them back.

"Clearly," he offers with a glint in his eyes.

My eyes narrow. "Are you capable of pretending this is something more than some temporary entertainment for you?"

"You can unclench, Aurora," he says mildly, the curve of his lips making my blood boil.

"No," I snap, "I can't. This is my future, and I'm pissed you're screwing with it, so I'm telling you how this is going to go."

"Are you?" he asks. "Please continue."

I step forward, gripping the back of the closest chair. "You ask me questions, and I answer them. You're impressed, and then I leave. Got it?"

"I thought I was supposed to ask the questions."

"Tristan!" I shout without thinking. It's unprofessional, sure, but nothing about this situation is normal, and he has been nothing close to professional either.

He chuckles. "Why don't we start?"

I stare at him for a moment longer. *He's enjoying this.* Bastard. And of course, he looks like a goddamn GQ model in a three-piece suit, the blue of his tie bringing out his eyes and—oh my god, I hate him. "No. No, I'm not doing this."

Tristan nods. "That's unfortunate. I'm sorry you won't graduate until next semester then."

My chest tightens, and I grit my teeth. "Why are you doing this?"

He brushes his thumb over his lower lip, and I can't help but track the movement way too close to feign indifference when it makes my stomach warm and flutter. "Consider it an insurance policy."

I cross my arms. "Insurance for what?"

"You."

"What is that supposed to mean? Tristan, I'm not—"

"This is the *least* invasive option to ensure my concerns about you don't happen. Would you prefer I keep you at the hotel?"

"That's not what you're doing?" I challenge. "What do you call this, then?"

"Doing you a favor," he replies, his jaw ticking.

My grip on the back of the chair tightens, and I look around the plain room as my heart races and my thoughts spiral, trying to decipher his motivations. My gaze catches on the mural on the wall next to where I'm standing. It's filled with soft blues and purples. "If you think this somehow means I owe you," I say in a low voice, "you are very incorrect."

Tristan chuckles, stealing my attention once more. "If you stop for a moment and think about the opportunities this internship provides you, perhaps you'd be more grateful. Forget the otherworldly reasons for this arrangement. You are a business major, and I am a successful business owner. Any of your classmates would kill to be in your position."

"They're welcome to it," I shoot back.

Tristan slides his hands into his pockets. "The alternative internships were three different law firms that all specialize in personal injury, several apartment leasing offices, two veterinary clinics, and a country club. Do any of those sound appealing to you, Aurora?"

I hate the way my stomach dips when he says my name.

*No. I hate that I don't hate it.*

I bite the inside of my cheek as I consider lying.

"Go for it," he says with a glimmer in his eyes. "I can hear your heart beating erratically and feel every emotion passing through you."

*Fuck. Me.*

"Fine. I'll do the interview," I snap, exhaling through my nose as I try not to panic at the idea of Tristan knowing exactly what I'm feeling. It makes sense, considering he survives on human energy, but it's incredibly inconvenient. As if I needed more of a disadvantage here.

I walk closer, selecting the chair that keeps one between us. I pull it out and set my bag on the table. When the sandalwood and citrus smell of him reaches me, I suddenly wish I'd taken the seat at the other end of the table.

"Ready?" he asks, his eyes shifting between mine.

*Not even remotely close.* "Yes."

He offers me his hand. "Good morning. I'm Tristan Westbrook."

I hesitate, but place my hand in his and shake it. "Aurora Marshall."

"Come on. You can do better than that." His tone is light as he adds, "Do I make you that nervous?"

I snatch my hand back. "No." My response is too quick as I drop into the chair. "Let's just do this."

"Very well," he says before he returns to his seat, shooting an amused glance at the chair I've kept between us as he unbuttons his jacket and sits.

I pull my portfolio out of my bag. Opening it, I slide my resume out and set it on the table. I flick a glance up to find him watching me, and I push the paper toward him. He picks it up and reads it over before setting it back down, then says, "Your volunteer work is impressive."

I blink at him. I wasn't expecting a compliment. "Thank you."

He meets my gaze. "What are you aiming to gain from this internship?"

"Experience, of course. That's what anyone in my position would say. This isn't for me to get a taste of what my career might be to see whether I like it. I'm in my final year of this program. I don't have time to change my mind. Before walking into this interview, I would've said this might lead to full-time employment after I impressed my mentor, but circumstances shape my answers, so I'm going to stick with experience."

There's a hint of a smile on his lips as he nods. "Have you been in positions of power in the past?"

"Yes. I've led several school events, and over the past few years, I've been one of the head members of the student union."

"Do you seek these positions of power?"

"If you're asking if I like control, I think you—" I stop myself as Tristan sits there with an annoyingly impassive expression, just listening. Having his undivided attention is equal parts nerve wracking and heady. "Yes, I do," I finish, folding my hands on the table.

"You seem quite driven."

"I like to think so," I say. "I know what I want, and I plan to do whatever it takes to achieve it."

He clicks the pen in his hand, and the smile that touches his lips makes me want to look away as it warms my cheeks. "That doesn't surprise me."

"Any other questions?" I need to keep this meeting on a narrow path, wrap it up, and get out of this room before I suffocate. Because annoyance isn't the only thing racing through my veins right now. As I fight to hold his gaze, I can't help the unexplainable sense of... safety in his presence. There's a part of me, one I don't understand in the least, that believes I'm not in danger with him. In danger of running my mouth and getting in trouble, though, that's another story.

There's a flicker of surprise in the fae knight's gaze before his expression smooths. I have to think he notices or feels the anxiety pouring off me, because instead of taunting me some more, he asks, "Do you have a copy of your class schedule?"

Handing it to him from my portfolio, I cringe at the way my hand shakes. I knew this interview would make me nervous, regardless of the mentor, but Tristan holding that position is heightening that tenfold. *I just need to get through this.* Folding my hands in my lap, I sit straighter, breathing in through my nose and out through my mouth to calm my uneven pulse.

"You have Mondays off," he observes.

"Yes," I say, though I don't think he was actually asking.

"Excellent. I'll see you every Monday, nine o'clock sharp."

My stomach flips at the burst of anxious excitement in my chest. "I... Hold on. That's it?"

He leans back in his chair. "That's it."

"What if I don't want to work under you?" I can't help it. Despite the alternative internships, I'm not sure I can do this one. With *him*.

"I don't think I've ever had anyone say that to me," he says with a twist of his lips, and before I can scowl, he continues, "As I said, I'm the last mentor available, so it's me or nothing. Your choice. But as I recall, you need this to graduate. And as you said, your education is the most important thing to you."

"I'm going to—"

"What? Tell your program coordinator that I manipulated her mind to ensure she placed you with my company?"

Shaking my head as I step away from the table, I turn my back on this fucked-up interview and head for the door. I'm reaching for the handle when I make the snap decision to decline the internship—I'll figure something else out. I turn around quickly, only to find myself face to chest with Tristan. His presence overwhelms me all at once. Heat radiates from him, warming my cheeks as I fight to not inhale his scent. I need to keep my thoughts clear.

"What are you doing?" I breathe.

He steals my gaze. "You turned around," he says, a challenge in his tone.

"You were following me," I counter, unable to force my eyes away from him.

"And soon you'll be following me." He flashes a grin. "Lighten up, Aurora. Your negative energy is ruining this moment. Try to see it as a unique learning opportunity."

I glare at him. "Are you kidding?"

He raises a brow. "What would you like me to say?" He dips his face closer, and I have to remind myself to breathe. "You're not making this little situation of ours any easier."

"You're the one who waltzed into my life all tall, dark, and... *you*." I want to kick myself for letting his proximity cloud my head for even a second.

He leans forward, and I step back until I'm against the door. "I'm almost glad my manipulation doesn't work on you," he says in a voice so quiet I barely catch it. "I think that would eliminate all the fun we have."

I try to shove him back, but it's pointless. Instead, he ends up closer. "What part of this do you think is *fun* for me? You think I go home laughing to myself at how much *fun* I've had dealing with an arrogant, egocentric fae who could ruin my entire life if he chooses?" My hands are still pressed against his chest. *Why* are my hands still pressed against his chest?

Tristan tilts his head to the side, watching me with interest. My chest swirls with nervous energy as my eyes flick across his face.

"I'm not afraid of you. I'm concerned why you're paying me so much attention. Max was right. If only you could make me forget, then I wouldn't have the knowledge of your kind, regardless of whatever creepy connection my family has to the fae."

Tristan seems to consider this for a moment before he says, "If it were possible, would you want to forget?"

"That's not what I'm saying," I mutter, finally finding the will to pull my hands away and let them fall to my sides.

"I'm asking you."

"I don't see that it matters now," I say.

"Answer the question."

"Why?" I snap.

He's quick in sliding a finger under my chin and tilting it until our eyes meet, and my heart slams against my chest. His eyes flit back and forth across my face as I stand there, frozen. The wildness of his irises calms for a moment. There's a shift, almost too insignificant to notice, but I catch it. For a split second, a pained expression darkens his features. It's gone before I can understand what it means, and he steps away, dropping his hand and giving me room to breathe.

"I think that answers my question."

My throat is too dry to speak; my voice will crack if I try, so I stay silent—aside from the pounding of my heart. This interview is over. I reach for the door and step into the hallway, feeling Tristan's gaze on my back. My feet carry me toward the exit, but my mind is elsewhere. I'm almost far enough away to let myself relax when I hear his send-off.

"Good to see you, Miss Marshall. Until next week."

# CHAPTER SEVEN

Allison jumps when I return to our room and slam the door shut, throwing my bag onto my bed. My mind is still going a million miles an hour with no end in sight.

"Aurora—"

"Tristan hijacked my internship."

She stiffens, her eyes widening. "What the hell? How?"

"I don't know!" I throw up my hands. "He fae fucked the coordinator's head and made her put me with his company."

Her brows knit, and she slides off her bed, coming over to me. "We'll figure this out, I promise." She purses her lips. "Can you get a new mentor?"

I shake my head, the weight of what I'll have to endure on Monday settling in my chest. Damn that arrogant fae for screwing with me like this.

"I wish there was something I could do," she says, and the worry in her eyes makes me frown.

"You know him better than I do," I say. "What can you

tell me?"

"About Tristan? Or the fae?"

I sigh. "Both."

There's something about Tristan, something that tells me he won't hurt me, or he would have by now. There's a chance my fae lineage will keep me safe when it comes to him. That doesn't mean I trust him—far from it—but if I have to deal with the fae to get my degree, I need every piece of information Allison can give me.

"This conversation should involve alcohol," she says, walking over to her desk and opening the bottom drawer. She pulls out a bottle of tequila and twists the cap open, taking a swig before walking back and passing it to me. "How much do you want to know? We touched on the fae courts but barely scratched the surface."

I blow out a breath, then take a quick drink, cringing as the liquid burns a path down my throat to my stomach. "Tell me everything. Please."

She sits on the end of her bed and pats the spot beside her, taking a deep breath as she folds her hands in her lap. "Let's start with Tristan."

My stomach dips despite myself, and I grit my teeth.

"I can feel that," she says in a low voice, peering over at me.

"What?" I squeak, gripping the bottle tighter.

She gestures around me. "The mixed emotions you have toward him."

I groan, taking another drink.

"Do you want to talk about it?"

"I really don't." Because the more we talk about it, the more I think about Tristan, and I can't... I shouldn't.

Allison nods. "I'm here whenever you're ready to. Perks of being friends with someone who's immortal." She nudges me with her elbow. "Okay, we'll just move right along to the fae courts."

Seelies are from the *friendlier* court—as opposed to unseelie fae—according to the mythology I found during my brief research stint, though I don't know how much of that is true or twisted to fit a narrative.

"Have you met the king?" I ask, tipping the bottle back and forth and watching the amber liquid slosh around.

"No. Both the king and queen stay out of the spotlight. They rule by heavily relying on their knights to be responsible for the fae in their courts, especially as of late with the number of attacks and fae disappearances from both courts that neither will answer for. Tensions have been rising for some time, but it's never been this bad."

My chest tightens, and after another swig, I pass the bottle to Allison. "So the royals are figureheads who don't really do much?"

She takes the bottle and drinks, then presses her lips together, nodding.

The tequila works through me quickly, warming my stomach and bringing heat to my chest and cheeks. It's certainly making this conversation easier. So much so, I ask, "Will you show me what you look like without glamour?"

Her eyes widen. "Why?"

I shrug. "I'm curious. Terrified, but curious nonetheless. I seem to be part of this world now, whether or not I like it. I don't want seeing a fae's true appearance for the first time to catch me off guard—I want to be prepared."

Allison hesitates. "I don't want to scare you."

"Please," I push.

With a heavy sigh, she puts some distance between us on the bed and turns to face me. Closing her eyes, her chest rises as she inhales slowly, then lets it out. The changes are subtle at first, the shimmering bluish tint to her skin, making it appear luminescent, the sharpness of her jaw. But then I notice her ears are no longer rounded at the top but pointed, and when she opens her eyes, I suck in a breath, my heart lurching. *They're glowing.*

"Holy shit," I breathe.

Allison smiles, and my heart nearly halts in my chest. Each of her teeth are pointed—she has a mouth full of fangs. I drop my gaze, and my eyes widen when I see her fingernails have morphed into claws.

My throat goes dry, and I stare at my best friend who still looks like Allison but... not. My heart is in my throat and my pulse is jackhammering beneath my skin. "I... can see why you need the glamour," I finally get out.

She nods, then puts her glamour back up. Her appearance slowly returns to what I'm used to, and I let out a shaky breath. "Okay?" she checks.

I can't stop staring at her, waiting for the razor-sharp teeth and glowing eyes to return. "Yeah. Uh, what's next in the fae tutoring lesson?"

"Let's go back to Tristan. He's..." She starts then stops, as if she's considering the best way to explain the fae knight. "Tristan is a man of his word and he's big into respect."

"Hard to believe," I mutter, leaning over to set the bottle of tequila on the bedside table.

She frowns. "He has a small circle of fae he trusts."

"He doesn't have many friends. Shocking," I remark dryly, fidgeting with my hands in my lap. The more we talk about Tristan, the more I want to hop on a train and get the hell out of Dodge when I think of having to face him on Monday.

"Aurora, this isn't a joke. You may need this internship to graduate, but you need to be careful. Stay quiet. Don't be witty or smart or—"

"Or *me*?" I shake my head. "He's screwing with my life. I won't make this easy for him."

"Aurora." She clasps her hands together in front of her as if she's about to pray. A girl who's never set foot in a church or said grace in the years I've known her. "Please don't put yourself in unnecessary danger."

I sigh, deflating a little. "Relax, Al. I won't be stupid, but I'm also not going to walk on eggshells around him."

"I'm just saying, the guy can be intense. And he's fae—a knight—which makes him incredibly powerful. Like, more powerful than the average fae."

*Of course he is.* "Why's that?"

"All fae have the same abilities, but his are magnified because of his position. Power from the king's ancestors lives inside him, making him stronger than me, for example."

I blow out a breath. "Thanks for the info. I'll keep that in mind the next time he pisses me off." I'd bet good money that'll be sooner rather than later.

She eyes me with concern. "Tristan can be very charming, and he's good at what he does—in both the human and fae communities. As much as the guy freaks me out, I can't deny that. Do what you can to stay on his good side, especially since he's taken an interest in you."

A faint flutter in my stomach makes the tops of my ears burn. "Why do you say that? Because he's stuck? Because I was taken by mistake and now I'm an obligation?"

She presses her lips together. "He rarely pays attention to humans outside of his business."

"I don't want his attention." The slight shift in my

pulse tries to make a liar out of me.

She arches a brow at me. "We both know that isn't entirely true. Regardless, my advice is to keep your head down as much as possible."

I arch a brow. "Does that sound like me?"

"Aurora, I'm serious. This is for your own safety."

"You think he's going to hurt me?" A faint voice in my head says *no*. It holds no merit, and yet, I want to believe it.

"He's not who I'm worried about. Tristan has enemies in the unseelie court."

"That I believe," I grumble.

"You stumbled into this world at potentially the worst possible moment."

I arch a brow. "As if there would've been a good time?"

"That's not... I just mean..." She shakes her head. "The fae courts have been divided for a long time. It's all boring history and politics."

"I want to know," I say without a thought.

"It all started with our ancestors many years ago. I'm talking about the beginning of humankind. Since there were humans, there have been fae. Some were born and some were made—either intentionally or by accident—when the fae were forced to inhabit the human world after ours was destroyed during the last war. That was way before my time. But it's why some fae—from both courts—don't look at humans in the most flattering way. They're jealous. The humans get to live in their own world, while fae—we're stuck here."

I blink a few times, unable to form a coherent response. This is... a lot.

"Do you want me to stop?" she checks. "I can feel your anxiety."

I cringe, leaning away. "What does it feel like?"

"Dark and sticky like molasses."

"Oh." I don't know what else to say. "What else should I know?" As overwhelming as the information is, it'll give me a better understanding of this world I'm trying to wrap my head around.

"The war I mentioned before? It's still going and likely won't stop for as long as we're forced to inhabit the human world."

My lips part. "That's what the war is about? Sharing the human world?"

She nods but doesn't elaborate for a moment, pulling at a loose thread on her shirt. "I'm not actively involved with the politics. All I know is what I've told you."

I let out a breath. "This war, the rules and responsibility, that's a lot to put on one person, fae knight or otherwise."

Allison raises a brow at me, looking at me as if she's attempting to decipher the meaning in my words.

The tops of my ears burn once again, and I fight the urge to take another drink. "I just mean, I couldn't imagine being in that position, that's all."

"The position you *are* in isn't exactly ideal, either." She presses her lips together for a few seconds. "You're sure there's no way around it?"

My chest tightens. "Without this internship, I'll fall behind and won't get my degree in the spring." My voice increases in pitch. Graduating late isn't an option. It'll shred my plan for the future into pieces, and I refuse to entertain that idea.

She reaches over and grabs my hands, holding them firmly in hers. "You can do this." Her expression is serious, her tone certain.

I can't help but smile despite the warring nerves in my

stomach. She's right. I *can* do this—not having a choice in the matter is beside the point. At least, that's what I'm telling myself.

"And who knows," she adds with what looks to be a forced smile, "maybe you'll have…" She trails off, pressing her lips together. "Have…" She sighs, evidently giving up trying to lie. "Okay, if nothing else, maybe you'll learn a thing or two."

---

Friday afternoon, I make a last-minute decision to hop on a train and visit my hometown. I need a break from the city before my internship starts and figure a trip home will be good for me. And if I have an opportunity to do some digging into my supposed fae lineage, I'm going to take it.

Taking an Uber from the train station, I beat my parents and little brother home. A glance at the time tells me they're still teaching at the college across town and Elijah's still in school. I walk up the empty driveway, chuckling at the state of the overgrown front lawn. The rest of the house looks in order. The dull red brick and giant bay window in the front still make me smile, a lightness in my chest that only blooms when I'm home. I unlock the door and let myself in, setting my bag on the bench inside the foyer before slipping my shoes off and padding across the hardwood floor into the kitchen to grab a drink.

Our kitchen has gone through a few renovations over the years—one of my parents' chosen pastimes, as they like to call it—but the one we have now is my favorite, with faux marble countertops and dark wood cabinets, a stark contrast against the stainless-steel appliances. The breakfast bar, where I always liked to sit while I was doing homework in high school, was added at Dad's request. He wanted somewhere to eat that wasn't as formal as the table in the attached dining room.

I plop down at the breakfast bar and sip on the raspberry lemonade I found in the fridge as I check my student email, waiting for everyone to get home.

It's a little after six when the front door opens.

"Roar!" Elijah's voice reaches me, and his nickname for me makes my chest swell with warmth. He's been calling me that since he was old enough to talk. In the beginning, he couldn't say my entire name but learned part of it, and it stuck. I grin when his footsteps pound the floor as he races into the kitchen. I slide off the stool at the breakfast bar seconds before he wraps his arms around me.

"Hey, you," I say, hugging him tightly.

"What are you doing home?" Dad asks when he walks into the room. He's dressed in his normal teaching attire: a suit and tie, and his salt and pepper hair is neatly combed to one side. Our eyes meet, and I'm reminded of how much I wish I had inherited his bright blue ones like Elijah had instead of Mom's hazel ones.

"Nice to see you, too, Dad," I joke.

"You know that's not what your father meant, honey. We weren't expecting you, is all," Mom says with a smile, wrapping her arm around my shoulders. My mom and I share many features. I have her long, wavy blond hair. We're both a little over five feet and curvy in the hip area. If she were a few years younger, we would look more like sisters than mother and daughter.

"Yeah, I just... It's looking like this semester is going to be pretty heavy, and I probably won't be able to come home again for a while, so I thought I'd spend the weekend." I glance between her and Dad. "I was going to make something for dinner, but there's not much besides lemonade and eggs in the fridge."

Mom smiles. "Start of the semester is always busy. And groceries are on tomorrow's to-do list."

"Why don't we order pizza?" Dad suggests.

Elijah and I exchange a grin; pizza is our favorite food group.

An hour later, we're sitting around the dining room table. Elijah tries to steal the slice of pizza I'm going for, and I smack his hand away, snatching it up. He sticks his tongue out at me, grabbing another slice and shoving it into his mouth.

"You had your internship interview this week, right?" Dad asks.

The slice of pizza I have in my hand stops halfway to my mouth. "Uh, yeah."

"How'd it go? Did you get the company you wanted?"

"I didn't get to choose. They matched students with mentors from local businesses," I explain.

"Where did you get placed?" Mom asks.

"A hotel downtown."

"That's wonderful," she praises. "Congratulations, honey."

I grit my teeth for a second, then force a smile. "Thank you."

"When do you start?" Dad asks.

"Monday," I say, "nine o'clock sharp." Using Tristan's words makes it difficult not to cringe.

After dinner, Elijah and I tidy up the kitchen. I should probably use this opportunity to do some digging and find out what Mom and Dad know about our lineage, but I'm still not sure how to bring it up in a way that won't make them worry something's going on. The last thing I need is for them to get suspicious and ask questions I can't answer. That, or worry about my sanity if they know nothing about fae, which is very possible.

We finish the dishes and meet Mom and Dad in the living room to watch a movie. I'm struggling to keep my eyes open for the first half, and by the second half, I'm dozing in and out before I fall asleep.

When I open my eyes again, everything feels foreign.

"I'd tell you not to freak out, but I suppose that's unlikely?"

I gasp at the deep voice and sit up in a flash. My eyes scan the dark bedroom, quickly landing on where Tristan leans in the doorway, wearing casual black slacks and a gray T-shirt. He steps inside, closing the door behind him, and I scramble off the massive bed, nearly slipping off the black silk sheets. "What the hell is going on?" I demand, my heart beating against my rib cage as my eyes flit around the unfamiliar room.

"Nothing," he answers calmly.

I gesture around the room. "What is *this*?"

"My bedroom," he says, moving closer.

I glance back at the bed from where I'm standing at the end, and my cheeks fill with heat. *Oh god.* "Your bedroom... Did you kidnap me *again*? I swear to—"

He chuckles, cutting me off. "You're asleep, Aurora. This is a dream."

My eyes snap to his, and he's suddenly much closer. If it's a dream, why do his blue eyes look so real? So damn captivating? I shake my head, pushing the thought away as I take a healthy step back. "You're in my head? In my dream?"

"That's right. You're dreaming about me."

I cross my arms tightly over my chest. "Why? How?"

"Because I want you to," he explains, sliding his hands into his pockets. "Another perk of being me: dream walking. Evidently not an ability of mine you're immune to."

I shoot him a dark look. I'm not in the mood to learn what other fae tricks he has up his sleeve.

"Do you want me to leave?" His question throws me off, because I'm not entirely sure I do, which is all kinds of messed up.

"I want you to tell me what you're doing in my dream. I'm already stuck with you one day a week. Isn't that enough?"

He offers a charming smile, and it occurs to me that dream Tristan is just as dangerously attractive as the fae knight I've experienced while awake. "You're fiery tonight," he says.

I huff out a sigh. "And you're annoying. Can I have my dream back?"

"You don't like me, do you?" What a loaded question.

I gape at him. "Is that what you want? Because I'm pretty sure medical professionals have a name for that."

Amusement makes his eyes appear brighter. "You left the city," he says suddenly. "I didn't take you for someone who'd run away."

*How the fuck does he know I left?* My eyes narrow. "I came home for the weekend. That's hardly running away." My arms fall back to my sides. "I'll be back in time to start my internship on Monday. I have too much to lose that not even you being there will stop me from showing up."

He steals the distance between us once more, regarding me curiously. "Good to know."

I stare at him for what feels like far too long, still trying to decide if this is real. "Why'd you hijack my dream, Tristan?"

"To see if I *could*," he admits. "You're immune to my power when it comes to manipulation. I wanted to see if dream walking was the same."

"Why does it matter?"

"Perhaps it doesn't," he muses. "But I'm trying to figure you out. Humans are supposed to be simple creatures. They have impulses and fears. Considering what I am and my position in both the human and fae worlds, humans are intimidated by me. And then there's you. The elusive human with fae lineage. You're... everything I can't control."

My breath hitches. "Control is overrated," I say in an uneven voice. "So I've heard."

"An interesting concept. One I'd guess was created by someone unable to grasp control."

I shrug in response, pushing the hair away from my face and tucking it behind my ears, mostly to have something to do with my hands.

"I didn't expect you to run, but I wouldn't have been surprised if you had—especially when you discovered your family's ties to my kind."

"What would've happened if I had? I wouldn't have gotten far and, honestly, I don't have the energy or desire to fight this. So long as it doesn't affect me any further, I can live with it. I think you can agree there are more important things we both have to deal with. You have your world and I have mine. When they overlap, we'll just have to deal with it. Preferably without the two of us having to interact, but I suppose we must make some sacrifices."

His expression is a mix of disbelief and intrigue that makes my pulse kick up as his gaze holds mine hostage. He says nothing as the scene slips away, but the voice in my head is clear: *you're in trouble.*

## CHAPTER
# EIGHT

I wake on the couch with a knitted blanket draped over me and a throw pillow under my head. The TV is off, and the room is dark, save for a crack of light coming from the kitchen.

I stare out into the darkness, replaying what just happened. If it wasn't for Allison telling me about dream walking before, I'm not sure I would've believed this was real and not an actual dream.

Slumping back against the couch, I groan. Not only do I have to deal with Tristan during the day at my internship, but I can't escape him at night, either. Can't escape the way he makes my heart race and my stomach flip. *I'm so screwed.*

Exhausted as I am, this is the perfect opportunity to look through the house for some answers to the whole fae lineage possibility. Sure, I could have asked the fae knight who stole my dream, but the thought of asking him for anything sounds like a bad idea. I need to avoid any perception of owing him, because I have no doubt he'll come to collect.

Forcing myself off the couch, I drop the blanket across the back and slip into the hallway. I have to be quiet; I don't want to wake anyone and have to lie about why I'm searching the house like some kind of supernatural investigator.

I tiptoe into the office, a small room with a couch, a desk, and a chair. One wall is lined with bookshelves filled with old textbooks, some of my parents' books, and our family albums. I cross the room, switching on the desk lamp as I pass, and run my finger along the spines. I crouch and pull out an album.

As I flip through the pages, I find nothing useful. I sigh, glancing at the shelf full of matching binders. These photos are all too recent. If I wasn't half asleep, I'd have realized that before I wasted my time. If I crawled into the attic, I might find something that dates back far enough, but I can't do that when I'm trying to stay quiet. I won't get any answers tonight.

With a yawn, I drag myself to my bedroom and fall onto my bed, hoping Tristan will leave me alone for the rest of the night.

When I find myself in another dreamscape, anger swiftly rises, and I grit my teeth. My eyes focus on the ground beneath my feet. Cracked pavement. I frown as I lift my head and gasp, coughing on the smoke that's heavy in the air, then blink until my vision is as clear as it's going to get in this war-torn environment. There's nothing left for as far as the eye can see. Buildings have been reduced to piles of concrete and metal, and leafless trees have fallen, scattered in the mess. It looks like a scene out of a dystopian movie.

And when my eyes land on the seelie fae knight, realization knocks the air out of me. I don't think I'm in my dream anymore. I think... I'm in *Tristan's*.

He's standing atop a mess of concrete rubble, staring right at me. No, not at me, *through* me, as if he doesn't see me standing here. He doesn't know I'm in his dream. How *am* I here? And where is *here*?

*Is this the fae world?*

My eyes shift back to Tristan. He's a mess. His dark clothing is torn, all but shredded in some places along his midsection, and his hair is darkened with dirt and ash. I walk closer, careful where I step, and watch his face pale. His eyes are bloodshot and wide, with dark circles underneath. They're bouncing all over the place, never stopping in one spot too long, but growing more frantic by the second. His chest rises and drops, and he balls his hands into fists at his sides.

"Tristan," I whisper, my voice cracking, and suddenly I'm fighting this all-consuming urge to comfort him. The pain in his expression is hurting *me*.

I say his name louder, but he still doesn't hear me.

My eyes burn as I watch the seelie fae knight fall to his knees and stare at the ruins with an utterly hopeless expression that makes my blood run cold.

In the next second, my eyes fly open, and daylight streams into my room. I stare at the textured ceiling above my bed, unable to shake the harrowing scene I just witnessed.

I should feel relaxed and rested; there's nothing like sleeping in your own bed at home. Compared to the stiff twin mattress I sleep on at school, this bed usually feels like a cloud of comfort and warmth. Everything about my room makes me want to stay here: the Polaroid photos I have hung on one wall, the desk that's covered with books on business and marketing, the window seat my dad built for me the first summer I got into reading when I was thirteen. The giant bookshelves are the best thing about the room, though. They hold so many books; I'll probably never read them all. I glance longingly at the keyboard set up across the room. If I could somehow make it fit in my room at school, I'd have it there. I've been playing the piano since I was little. Playing always makes me feel in control and at ease. It helps make life less chaotic.

My thoughts go back to the chaos of my dream—rather, Tristan's dream. The image of his face is etched into my memory. The acute pain in his features won't leave me, and I'm shocked by the lump forming in my throat. It doesn't leave me as I go through the motions of getting dressed and ready for the day.

Only am I able to shove it away when I head down to the kitchen and find Mom sitting at the breakfast bar. She's in front of her laptop, with papers scattered all over the counter. "Morning." I keep quiet in case Dad and Elijah are still asleep.

"Morning, honey. How'd you sleep?" She ties the belt on her soft blue robe and yawns.

"Okay," I say automatically. I don't want to think about the vividness of that dream. My stomach is still in knots. I cross the kitchen to the coffeemaker and pull a mug down from the cupboard above it.

She takes a sip of her coffee. "Elijah is happy you're home."

I fill my mug and smile, leaning against the counter. "Me too." For a little brother, Elijah isn't annoying despite being twelve years old. "I'm guessing he and Dad aren't awake yet?"

Mom's soft laugh lightens her eyes. "You know Elijah is a monster to get out of bed before noon, and your dad is running errands."

I glance at the clock on the stove; it's just after eleven. "Gotcha," I say, staring down at my coffee. "We were talking about things running in families in class the other day..." *Nice segue, Aurora.* "Businesses and traditions and whatnot," I add. "Do you know if our family had anything like that, even a long time ago?" What a time to be completely *not* subtle.

She glances at me curiously. "I can't think of any on my side, but your dad's family was always more... eclectic with traditions and such. Maybe you could ask him?"

My lips part as if I'm going to respond, but no words come out. I'm at least able to force a nod. The back of my neck tingles, the hairs standing straight, and my arms break out in goosebumps. *Was Tristan right about my family?* And if he was, does that mean my dad knows about the fae? I doubt it, considering Tristan said the fae in my family were hundreds of years old. My stomach drops. How could I not have thought about it until now? If my ancestors were fae, does that mean they're still alive?

My phone chimes and my throat goes dry when I pull it out of my sweater pocket and read the message.

> I'm in your room waiting for Allison and some guy named Max came here looking for you.

> Did he say why?

> No, he left the second I said you weren't here. Everything okay?

> Yeah. I'll see you guys tomorrow.

I send Allison a message to tell her Max was creeping around. I figure it's best to give her a heads up. As far as I know, she still isn't on great terms with Tristan, so I want to make sure she's safe. I shudder at the thought of Max looking for me, my pulse ticking faster as I try to come up with a reason for his unexpected visit.

"Honey?" Mom asks. "Is something wrong?"

I look up and find her watching me with concern. "Huh? Oh, just school stuff. It's fine."

She frowns. "I know you're stressed about graduating and getting a job right away, but you don't need to be. You can move home and take as much time as you need. I don't want you to rush into anything because you're worried about money."

"Mom." We've had this conversation more than once. "I'm paying you and Dad back. End of story." It'll likely take most my adult life, but so would a high-interest student loan, so I consider myself extremely lucky I could avoid that.

She stands, walking around the kitchen counter and stopping in front of me. "This is your senior year," she says. "You should enjoy it without worrying about all the things you'll have years to worry about as an adult."

I smile, setting my mug on the counter behind me and wrapping my arms around her in a tight hug. "I'm not a kid anymore, Mom. I understand the value of what you did to put me through school." Because not only did they cover my tuition, my parents had to take time away from their teaching jobs when Elijah collapsed at school three years ago, which led to doctors finding a lump under his arm. After surgery and several rounds of treatment, he was cancer-free, but it took a toll on our parents—both emotionally and financially. The important thing is Elijah's here and remains cancer-free, but Mom used to have a rule about not working on the weekend, and the state of our breakfast bar suggests she's putting in overtime.

"And we'd do it again. In a heartbeat." She squeezes me and kisses the side of my head before stepping away. "Now, tell me more about your internship."

---

Dad grabs lunch on his way home—Chinese food from our favorite place across town—and we eat together in the dining room.

I sit there, enjoying a chicken ball drenched in sweet-and-sour sauce, and smile at my family. My thoughts trickle back to Tristan and the mess that I'm going back to at school. I didn't get any answers from coming home as I'd hoped, and not being able to say anything about it makes it harder to bear. I doubt Tristan would take kindly to more humans knowing about the fae, not that I think my parents would believe me, even though my dad likely has fae ancestors. They'd blame it on stress and sign me up for therapy. Elijah would believe me, though. The kid has a killer imagination.

Looking at them now is making me want to stay. I wasn't homesick much in the past, but I feel it now. The urge to stay is strong, but the growing need for answers is slowly overpowering it. I don't want to think about it, but it's looking more and more like there's only one person I can go to for those answers.

"What time do you have to leave tomorrow?" Elijah asks between giant mouthfuls of fried rice.

"Early afternoon. I have some things I need to deal

with before my week starts." Like figuring out why the hell Max was looking for me.

"Your sister is going to be busy over the next couple of months," Mom says with a warm smile, "and we're very proud."

"Thanks, Mom."

Dad cleans up after lunch, and Elijah follows me to my room to hang out while I pack the few things I brought home with me. "I wish you didn't have to leave," he says, lying across the end of my bed on his stomach.

"I don't want to go back, either." I peek over at him and smile. "I'll visit again as soon as I can."

*If I survive this week.*

## CHAPTER NINE

Mondays suck. This morning specifically sucks more than usual. I got little sleep last night, and it isn't because Tristan showed up—because he didn't. Which is a relief, considering there's a good chance I would've slapped his stupid, carved-perfectly-by-the-gods face for invading my dream again. Dealing with him when I'm awake is enough.

Every time I got close to falling asleep, I'd start thinking about this morning. Dread and nerves made it nearly impossible to relax enough to get any proper rest.

When my alarm goes off at six o'clock, I open my eyes and stare at the ceiling. Should I drop out of school? If there were any other way to get this credit to graduate, I would be all over it. Unfortunately, *my mentor is an infuriatingly arrogant fae knight* isn't exactly a believable reason to be exempt.

Swinging my legs over the side of the bed, I get up and move through the motions of showering and blow drying my hair before getting dressed. Then I spend too much time obsessing over an outfit, as if I'm making a first impression on Tristan. I guess I am, which only makes my muscles more twitchy. There's also a pressure building in my temples that isn't doing anything to ease the queasiness in my stomach.

I stand in front of my closet, chewing on my thumbnail. If I'm going based on what I've seen Tristan and Skylar wear, nothing in here is going to cut it. After several chaotic minutes of pulling shirts off hangers only to toss them in a pile on the floor, I settle on a navy blouse tucked into a knee-length black skirt and pair it with my nicest heels.

I'm finishing my makeup when our door opens, and Allison walks in, holding a tray with two cups of coffee and a brown pastry bag. "Morning," she says, setting the tray on my desk. "I brought coffee and muffins. Today is a big deal for you, so I wanted to start it off right."

Despite the nausea in my gut, I smile. "You didn't have to do that."

"Of course I did." She hands me a coffee. "I have class in..." She checks the time on her phone. "Five hours, anyway." She presses her lips together against a smile.

I take a small sip, hoping my stomach won't reject it. "I appreciate it."

"Whatever I can do to make today a little less stressful for you."

I wrap her in a one-armed hug and squeeze her shoulders. "This is why you're my best friend."

She places her hand over mine. "Are you ready?"

"I don't think I'll ever be ready, but I'm as close as I'm going to get."

She offers a sympathetic smile. "Want me to ride with you? I can hype you up the entire way there so you'll walk into that office feeling like you own the place."

I laugh softly. "I'll be okay, but thanks. You're seriously the best," I tell her, because she absolutely would come with me to make me feel better.

She plops onto the chair at her desk, taking a drink of her coffee. "Yeah, well, I have to make up for keeping the whole fae thing from you."

I lift my to-go cup. "Keep bringing me coffee and sweets, and we'll have no issues."

Allison grins at me. "Deal."

When it's time to leave, my stomach twists. *Get a grip.* I clench my hands into fists, take a deep breath, and grab my bag before I head for the door.

"You've got this." Allison shoots me a thumbs-up from her desk.

My lips form a smile as my chest loosens a fraction. "I'll see you later."

The fifteen-minute streetcar ride to the Westbrook Hotel feels like hours. Both the hotel and campus are downtown, but traffic is always heavy in the morning.

I step off with a crowd of people and shoulder my bag as I head for the building. My heels echo against the concrete, and I focus on the repetitive *click, click, click* to keep myself from spiraling.

The hotel lobby is as extravagant as I remember it, and my gaze bounces around the room. A few employees and guests walk around, chatting or watching the morning news on one of the many flat screens attached to the walls.

I straighten, gripping my bag until my knuckles turn white, put on my best pleasant-yet-professional expression, and walk to the concierge desk. I smile at the familiar face. It's the same girl as the day I stormed in, demanding to see Tristan. Marisa, her name tag says. "Hi there. I'm sorry if you remember me."

Her expression is bright, friendly. "Miss Marshall, welcome back to the Westbrook Hotel."

"Thanks. Again, sorry about last time. Tristan—uh, Mr. Westbrook, can be..."

"Don't worry about it. I've worked here for three years." She offers me a grin as if we're sharing some inside joke at Tristan's expense. "Mr. Westbrook instructed me to send you to the office upon your arrival."

I nod, almost smiling. "Right, okay."

"Head over to the elevators across the lobby. Westbrook Inc.'s offices are marked, so you shouldn't have any issues getting there," she says and hands me a lanyard with a keycard.

"Thanks." I glance at the clock behind her and sigh. I guess it would be too childish to whine about how I don't want to go. Pretty unprofessional, at least. "I better get going. Don't want to be late on my first day."

"Good luck." Her tone is light and paired with a kind smile.

"Thanks," I say before walking away, wondering just how much Marisa knows about the man she works for.

I tap my fingers against my thighs the entire elevator ride, glancing at myself in the mirror that covers the back wall. At the thirty-ninth floor—a level below Tristan's penthouse—I approach the office reception desk.

"Hi," I say in the most cheerful voice I can muster.

A black-haired man in an expensive-looking suit, who can't be much older than me, lifts his head. "Good morning. Miss Marshall, I presume."

"That's me." I try to stay pleasant.

"Wonderful," he says, but the edge to his voice suggests he feels the opposite.

*Keep smiling,* I chant over and over in my head.

"Good morning, Miss Marshall."

The smile drops right off my face. My jaw is clenched so tight I couldn't speak if I wanted to.

This was a terrible mistake.

I can't do this.

Fuck it. I have to.

I square my shoulders before turning toward the smooth, commanding sound of Tristan's voice. Seeing him so clean and put together in another three-piece suit, this one a dark navy, only reminds me of how broken he looked in that nightmare.

"Why don't you follow me, and I'll show you to my office?" he suggests in a level tone.

We walk side by side down a long hallway with clear glass doors lining each side.

"Are you not going to speak?"

"You haven't asked me a question."

He arches a brow. "I don't believe for a moment that you're someone who waits to speak until they're spoken to." My stomach dips at his words, and I feel the weight of his gaze on me as we continue down the hall. Tristan is the kind of man who demands attention. I've become hyper-aware when he's watching me, which makes my skin tingle, and I can't decide what to do with that. *Maybe it's a fae thing.*

I almost laugh. "You're perceptive. I'm sure that's useful in your position."

"Indeed."

I jerk my thumb toward the guy sitting behind the desk

in the entrance. "Your receptionist is lovely," I say with a touch of a smile.

He shrugs. "He's not a morning person." *We have that in common.*

"What are we doing today?" I shift the conversation as we come to a set of glass doors.

"*We* won't be doing anything. I'm handing you off to my chief of staff."

"My first day, and you're already rewarding me," I say sweetly.

He smirks. "Good to know you're smart-mouthed at all hours." He opens the door, holding it for me until I enter his office, then follows me inside.

The far wall is made of windows, letting in the natural light and giving the room an incredible view of downtown. Near the windows is a massive oak desk covered with papers and a computer. Off to one side, a couple of couches and an armchair surround a coffee table that matches the desk and the bookshelves lining the opposite wall. A flat screen is mounted above the seating area, and under it is a huge black marble fireplace.

Tristan walks over to the desk and sits before pressing a button on his phone. "Miss Chen, our business student has arrived. Would you be so kind as to collect her from my office?"

There's a brief pause, and then a newly familiar voice asks, "You're really making me do this?"

Tristan says nothing, just sits there with a ghost of a smile on his lips.

"Fine," Skylar snaps. "I'll be right there."

I stand by the door, biting the inside of my cheek, until it flies open and Skylar waltzes through, looking as if she's on her way to the Met Gala. Her long black hair is in a slick ponytail today and her makeup looks professionally done; perfectly contoured cheeks, winged liner, stunning lashes, and a dark red lip bring the look together. Paired with an emerald knee-length dress that hugs her slim waist, I'd say she looks even fancier than Tristan in his suit. And that sure as hell doesn't make me feel confident in the outfit I stressed over choosing.

Tristan stands, buttoning his suit jacket. "Skylar, you remember Aurora. She's a fourth-year business student interning with us, and I would like you to mentor her."

Skylar sighs before glancing at me. "You can't stay away, can you?"

"I need this to graduate."

She looks me over, her dark brown eyes narrowed and filled with judgment. "Lucky me."

"Play nice, ladies."

We both shoot him dark looks.

"Follow me," she grumbles and walks back out the door.

I hurry after her, worried she'll leave me behind, and catch up to her halfway down the hall as her impressively high heels click against the shiny floor. "I know this isn't ideal for you. You don't like me, and that's fine. To be honest, I'm relieved I don't have to work with Tristan."

Skylar stops and whirls around to face me, forcing me back a couple of steps. "You think I'm going to make this easy for you? That you got off easy when Tristan stuck you with me?" She barks out a laugh, shaking her head. "Piss me off, and you will regret it. Is that clear?"

My stomach drops, and I nod as a shiver races through me. "Do you hate all humans?" I ask in a low voice.

She actually smiles. "Yes."

"Okay." I'm not surprised, but her response makes the dread in my chest weigh heavier.

She pushes open a door Tristan and I passed on our way in, and I follow her inside, letting the door close behind us. "I have back-to-back meetings until this afternoon. You can either do photocopying or you can join me."

I try to hide my shock that she's giving me the option. "I'd like to sit in on the meetings." I pull out a notebook and pen from my bag.

"Fine." She gives me a once-over. "Let's go."

---

I spend the morning and most of the afternoon in meetings, scribbling notes as fast as I can with a half hour break for lunch, which I used to step outside and get some air—and an iced coffee from the café down the block.

Skylar leads a lot of the meetings, standing at the head of the long boardroom table. I keep my head down, my hair curtaining most of my face while I try to keep up from my spot at the far end of the table.

I estimate at least half of the staff in this meeting are fae. That, or some of the most ethereal humans I've ever seen. A few look less than pleased I'm sitting with them, which makes me think they're aware of who I am: the human who knows they aren't, who could pose a risk to them living in secrecy. No one says anything to me; I'm not the only human in the room, and I distract myself from their disapproval by taking more notes.

I'm writing a few things about a marketing campaign they're working on as the room empties.

"I'm surprised your hand still works."

My pen stops moving, and I look over at Skylar. "You gave a lot of valuable information," I offer.

She blinks at me, then opens the folder in her hand and drops some papers in front of me. "Don't waste your time writing everything. Listen to what everyone is saying. Next time, I want you to offer an idea. Got it?"

"Okay." I flick a glance at the paper. She gave me her meeting notes.

"See you next week," Skylar says.

"Yeah. Thanks for—"

"Don't," she cuts in on her way out the door.

"Right," I mumble to the empty room.

Leaning back in the chair, I sigh, tossing my notebook and pen onto the table. My eyes close, and I rest my head against the chair back for a minute.

When I open my eyes, I find Tristan leaning in the doorway with a faint grin, and my cheeks flare with heat.

"Long day?" he asks, pushing away from the doorframe to walk into the room.

"I expected nothing less."

He perches on the edge of the table a few feet away from me. "Did you learn anything?"

"Yes."

"Excellent, then my job is done."

I arch a brow. "*Your* job? You did nothing."

"Are you disappointed you didn't get to spend the day with me, Aurora?"

"Was it that obvious?" I shoot back sarcastically.

He chuckles, tilting his head to the side.

"You're being creepy," I say, my brows tugging closer. "Speaking of, what was Max doing at my place?"

His mouth is set in a tight line. "I wasn't aware he had been. When was this?"

"While I was home for the weekend."

"I'll deal with it."

"Good. I don't want him coming around. Ever." I put as much force behind my words as possible. "And speaking of *that*, what the hell was the dream invasion thing you pulled the other night?"

His lips pull up. "It can get boring around here on the weekend."

My jaw locks. For once, I consider my response before I open my mouth. "Don't do it again," I say, forcing my gaze to hold his.

"Did it bother you?"

It didn't bother me as much as it should have, but I'm not about to tell him that. "It's unnecessary. You want to talk to me, pick up the phone."

"Are you asking me to call you?" The twinkle of amusement in his eyes makes mine narrow. "Aurora, you're so forward."

"Seriously?" I want to throw my pen at him. "Stay out of my dreams." I decide not to tell him about what I experienced later that night. I can't see him reacting well to me seeing *his* dream.

He offers a subtle nod and stands. "How was your time away from the city? Enlightening?"

Shooting him a look, I say, "I couldn't come out and ask my parents if they knew of any relatives that had freaky powers and never aged."

Tristan steps closer and licks his lips. "That could've been amusing."

I hold back an eye roll. "The day we met, you said I wasn't fae, so why do you care?"

He shoves his hands in his pockets. "I've never come across a human with ties to my kind. You've certainly piqued my interest."

"I'm not something for you to ogle or study, so unless you're going to give me some answers, don't bring it up again." Fuck. I didn't want to ask for his help. Allison is looking into it for me. That should be enough. Still, there's a tiny voice in the back of my head telling me to.

"I'm not sure what answers you'd like me to give you."

I massage my temples with my fingers, squeezing my eyes shut briefly. "Anything to help me make sense of this."

"The extent of my knowledge is that fae magic touches you."

I sigh. "That's it? You're supposed to be some kind of leader, a fae knight. You should know more."

"My apologies," he says in a dry tone. "I didn't expect I'd have an outspoken human to answer to."

*So much for answers.*

"I can feel your disappointment," he says in a low, measured voice, then sighs. "For what it's worth, I'll look into it and see what information I can find. It might also help my people feel more comfortable with your knowledge of them if they can hear about your connection from one of your fae relatives."

My gaze lifts to meet his. "Really?" The optimism in my voice makes me cringe. I shouldn't be asking him for anything, but there's no one else I *can* ask.

He nods curtly. "You should get going. As I'm sure you can understand, some of my employees aren't keen on the human who knows what they are hanging around."

I collect my things and stand, heading toward the door. I pause in front of Tristan. "Why do you all look down on humans so much? I mean, without us, your kind couldn't survive. I don't care that you're fae, Tristan. That doesn't make you more or less of an ass, which I think it's pretty clear you are. I'm saying, I don't think it's fair you all look upon us as lesser because we aren't like you." Allison told me about the fae being jealous of humans. I guess I thought there was more to it.

His gaze is unwavering as he says, "I don't view humans that way. I wouldn't own a business that interacts so closely with them if I did."

"I'm not talking about you specifically. Not everything is about you. Shocking, I know."

His lips twitch, but his eyes look tired. "You are very brave."

"And you think too highly of yourself." I shoulder my bag and step around him. "Goodnight, Mr. Westbrook. I'll see you next Monday."

## CHAPTER TEN

Over the next few weeks, my life falls into the closest thing to normal I've felt since the existence of fae tilted my world off its axis. Going into the second week of October, the weather has cooled down, making it perfect sweater weather—my absolute favorite time of year.

Heading across campus, I inhale the crisp fall air, smiling as Ruelle's "Exodus" plays in my headphones. My phone buzzes in my pocket, and I chuckle at Grant's message when I pull it out.

> I'm running late and didn't have time to make coffee. I will owe you forever if you grab me one.

> You're lucky I was planning to stop on my way to class.

> *bows down*

Laughing at his message, I slide my phone back into

my pocket as I pass The Iron Lounge and head toward the café.

Once I grab our lattes, I cross one of many outdoor seating areas on campus and walk into the Founders Building, where most of the business management classes are. My ankle boots echo on the linoleum floor, and I open the door to my marketing principles lecture, taking my usual seat near the front of the room. I sip on the caffeinated goodness while I scroll through emails on my phone. There's one from Skylar with homework for me to complete before my internship next week that I flag to read fully and get started on it this afternoon.

"Good morning," Grant says, greeting me with that perfect smile of his. He pulls out his textbook and clicks his pen against our shared table. He's been sitting next to me since we met at the party, and the company is really nice. It's something I look forward to, something *normal*—a break from trying to figure out the fae world.

I smile, sliding the other latte in front of him. "It will be once I finish this." I lift my paper to-go cup, then take another sip.

He chuckles and wraps his fingers around his cup. "I owe you my life," he jokes before he takes a drink, closing his eyes and moaning softly. "Oh, this is *good*."

I laugh, my cheeks warming as he opens his eyes and grins at me.

We spend the class taking notes and delving into a discussion I tune out of, yawning every so often as I fight to stay awake. The latte isn't helping much this afternoon.

After class, I take the long way back to my room so I can grab dinner from the Mexican grill off campus. With the stress of midterms looming, I'm treating myself to tacos and chips with guacamole.

A short distance away, muffled shouting echoes through the air. Figuring it's normal Friday evening pre-partying, I keep walking until I pick up some of what's being said.

"You are pathetic," a delicate female voice seethes. "No wonder Rowan banished you from the seelie court."

I freeze at the end of a brick storefront. *Rowan? Is that the seelie king?*

There's a walkway ahead that separates the two buildings, and by the sound of it, a couple of fae—presumably from opposite courts—decided this was the place for an argument. I doubt they'll take kindly to me interrupting it.

A deep male laugh reverberates against the exterior walls, echoing down the alley. "You're one to talk, considering you betrayed your own court." His unfamiliar voice sounds pissed. "So why don't you tell me where your treacherous court is keeping our people?"

The female growls viciously, and the building shudders. "If I knew anything, there's not a chance in hell I'd tell you."

"Then this is going to be a brief conversation."

The male grunts; she must've hit him before she spits, "You're a fucking hypocrite."

I want to look, but I can't bring myself to peek around the corner for fear I'll get caught. They're too wrapped up in whatever is happening between them to notice my heart pounding in my chest, but I get the feeling they'll react the second they see me.

Her voice sharpens. "The entire seelie court is—"

A firm hand grabs my wrist and pulls me hard, away from the building. I open my mouth to scream, but it's quickly covered. Panic surges through me before my eyes connect with Skylar's. She lets me go once it's clear I won't make a sound.

"What the hell are you doing?" she hisses.

"I was walking home." I look past her. "Why are they fighting?"

Her eyes narrow. "That's what you're concerned about?" She scowls. "Typical human. You realize if they'd seen you, you'd probably be dead right now or being fed on." She cocks her head. "Unless that's what you wanted."

My brows inch closer. "Of course not," I snap. "What are *you* doing here?"

"I was a few blocks away when I heard them and then your annoying little heartbeat."

"And you came to make sure I didn't get hurt?" I almost smile.

She rolls her eyes. "Yes, Aurora. I live to ensure your safety from my kind. Why else would I be here?" The sarcastic tone of her voice makes it impossible not to grin now. There must be some kind of a gray area with fae when it comes to joking and lying.

Whatever I was going to say is cut off by the sight of the male fae flying. He lands with a *thud* on the sidewalk and jumps up, brushing off his black denim jacket. His eyes swing to where Skylar and I stand, and I instinctively take a small step back. Skylar appears more annoyed than concerned, so I have to think the level of danger isn't equal to the amount of anxiety creeping through me.

"What the fuck, Sky? Thanks for the backup." His eyes slide to me. "Hi."

I offer an awkward wave.

Skyler scowls. "I was coming. I got a little caught up." She nods toward me.

"Don't next time. She got away, along with our answers on the latest batch of missing fae."

*Missing fae?* What is he talking about? My eyes flick back and forth between the guy and Skylar, waiting for one of them to explain, but I'm not surprised when neither does. Considering this fae's familiarity with Skylar, I can guess he's seelie, and she doesn't seem worried about him seeing me, so I hope that means I'm not about to become fae food.

She shrugs. "We'll deal with it."

He rolls his eyes and then shifts away without another word, leaving Skylar and I alone on the sidewalk.

I arch a brow at her. "Care to explain what *that* was about?"

She gives me a look.

"Right. Didn't think so."

---

When I get back to the dorm, Allison is sprawled on her bed, already in sweatpants and a hoodie, her hand stuck in a bag of pretzels as she watches something on her laptop. She pauses whatever it is when I tell her about the fae attack, and she frowns.

"The unseelie fae keep launching attacks against our court," she murmurs, concern lowering her voice as she sits up and crosses her legs. "They're getting more careless every day, attacking in the open for any human to see and snatching seelies off the street, from the rumblings I've heard."

I scratch the back of my neck. "You're not making me feel any better."

"Don't worry about it, Ro. Please. Tristan will handle

things, and if it comes down to it, the king will have to step in."

"They're attacking seelie fae. *You* are a seelie fae. Of course I'm worried! I'd lose my fucking mind if anything happened to you."

She smiles, though she doesn't reassure me that nothing will happen to her, and that makes my stomach sink.

"Will you explain the courts to me?" I ask. "I understand they hate each other and fight over the human world, but why? How did it start?"

Allison's lips press into a thin line, and she lowers her gaze to where her hands are folded in her lap. "Fae haven't always been classed into the seelie and unseelie courts." She meets my gaze. "When the king and queen—Rowan and Ophelia—took their thrones, it was because each had different, powerful ideas on how fae should live. For instance, the seelie king believes we should feed only to survive, never take more than we need, and protect the secrecy of our existence at all costs. The unseelie queen... she pretty much believes the exact opposite. Feeding is for pleasure, human life means nothing, and so on."

I blink at her, my mouth dry. "Does that mean fae *choose* which court they're aligned with?"

She nods. "The courts aren't specific locations and they don't have concrete boundaries across the world. I guess you could look at them like political parties. Simply speaking, that's basically what they are."

I sit with that for a moment. It's... humanizing. Come to think of it, knowing what the seelies believe in, how they choose to live, makes me feel better about spending time with Skylar and Tristan at the hotel. It's also a relief, considering my best friend and the person I share a living space with is seelie.

"Are you okay?" she checks, her eyes searching mine, as if she's waiting for me to freak out.

"Yeah," I tell her, "just trying to keep up." With a sigh, I stand and walk over to my desk. I open my laptop and frown at the new email from Skylar.

*Aurora,*

*I'll be away from the office Monday. I'm sure you'll find something to keep you busy. There's always filing to do and coffee to fetch. Enjoy.*

*Skylar Chen, Westbrook Hotel Chief of Staff*

My loud groan fills the room as I close my laptop.

"What's up?" Allison asks, eyeing me from behind her textbook.

"I don't have a mentor on Monday, which means I'm going to be stuck doing coffee runs for people who would rather suck energy out of *me*."

She cringes. "Okay, besides that, how's the internship going?"

I purse my lips. "Not as bad as I was expecting. Skylar can be scary, but she's a surprisingly good teacher. And I think I've only seen Tristan a few times the entire month I've been there." Part of me is relieved we haven't crossed paths often, but then there's this annoying ache, a weird sort of longing to see him. I have no idea where it came from, but I'm sure as hell doing everything I can to ignore it.

# CHAPTER
# ELEVEN

I'm in the elevator on my way to the office Monday morning when it stops and a man and woman in business attire step on. After the door slides shut, the woman looks over at me, tossing her long, dark red hair over her shoulder. She doesn't *look* much older than me. "I cannot believe Tristan let you live," she seethes, her light brown eyes darkening to the point they appear black.

I should ignore her, but my lips move before I can press them together. "I can't believe he puts up with people as ignorant as you. Welcome to the *human* world. Where *humans* live."

Her lips twist into a cruel smile at the same moment the man pulls the emergency stop, halting the elevator.

*Shit.*

My free hand curls into a fist when they corner me, and my pulse skyrockets, fear raging through me as I assess the situation.

The man runs a hand through his black hair and flicks

a glance at the woman. "I'm dying to taste her." He sighs softly, smiling at the other fae. "But ladies first."

My mouth goes dry. This is *not* happening.

The woman laughs. It's a cruel sound that makes the hair on the back of my neck stand straight. "Not so mouthy now." She steps toward me, the tips of her designer heels almost touching my far less fancy ones.

"Don't touch me," I growl. I'm about two seconds away from throwing my coffee in her face. Would that give me enough time to make the elevator move again and get off at the next floor? Maybe if it wasn't two fae against one human...

She rolls her eyes and shoves me hard, narrowing her eyes. "What the hell makes you so special?"

I grit my teeth, my shoulder blades throbbing from being pinned against the mirror-paneled wall. "What's it to you? Don't tell me you're jealous?" If I'm being harassed because this woman has the hots for Tristan, I swear to—

She grabs my face, digging her fingers into my skin, and I can't help the strangled sound that escapes my lips as pain flares across my cheek. "Say another word," she hisses, "and I'll drain you."

I want to make a snide remark about how that sounds rather unseelie of her, but my head spins as dizziness floods through me like a heavy, fatal wave. She's feeding on me, and my arms are bricks of concrete at my sides. I can't move them; my grip loosens on my cup, and I nearly drop it. Lethargy trickles through me, and I struggle to keep my eyes open, my jaw slackening as I slump against the elevator wall and fall endlessly into the fae's glowing gaze.

"Easy," the man says, his voice sounding far away. "Tristan is keeping her around for a reason. I doubt he'll take kindly to you killing her."

"Whatever," she snaps, finally backing off. She slams her fist against the emergency stop again, making the elevator continue its ascent, and I stand there frozen until they exit a couple of floors later without another word. When the door slides shut, I let out a shallow breath and tip my head back. My eyes burn, and I swallow the bile in my throat, gritting my teeth as I stare forward, willing myself not to release the hot, angry tears threatening to spill down my cheeks. I've never felt so fucking helpless.

I spend the rest of the ride trying to shake off the forced calmness in my muscles, squinting at the panel lighting above me. I would like nothing more than to turn around and go back to my dorm, but I can't find the will to even be angry. If anything, I'm numb, feeling as if I'm sleepwalking. I have no idea how much energy that fae took or how it even works, but my eyelids are heavy, each blink burning and my vision slightly blurry as if I haven't slept.

*It's going to be a long day.*

Arriving at the thirty-ninth floor, I step off the elevator and immediately stop when I see Max sitting behind the reception desk. There is no chance—absolutely none—I have the energy for this right now. Literally. Still, I force a neutral expression and keep my face turned slightly away so he can't see the marks left behind from my run-in with the fae a few seconds ago. The last thing I need is a snide remark or goad from him.

He glances up as I approach and smirks. "Morning, blondie. That coffee for me?"

"Did hell freeze over?" I shake my head. "What are you doing out here? Boss man have you answering the phone today?"

His eyes narrow. "Boss man? I'm sure he'd love you calling him that."

I roll my eyes at that, then ask, "What were you doing at my dorm the other day? Oliver said you were looking for me."

Max leans back a little in his chair. "I don't think you'll believe me, despite knowing you're well-versed enough in our world to know I can't lie."

I squint at him. He's saying too many words, and the pressure behind my eyes is already making my temples throb. "Five words or less, please."

He makes a sound that I almost mistake for a snort and lifts a finger for each word. "I came to apologize."

Of all the things Max could've said, I was not expecting *that*.

"Hmm, I can see by the wide-eyed look on your face I've surprised you." He rakes a hand through his hair, pushing the black waves back from his forehead. "The night I brought you here—the way I handled… my mistake—was less than ideal."

I arch a brow. "Is this your first apology?"

His eyes narrow, and he stands, sliding his hands into his pockets. "I treated you like an enemy because I thought you were one. I didn't expect you to hang around, to catch Tristan's interest and join the fold, so to speak." Max sighs. "I'm sorry for how I treated you then."

"I…" I shake my head, wetting my lips. "I appreciate your apology."

Max holds my gaze for a moment before he nods and sits down, going back to work.

I turn away and step toward the office doors. I drop my things at my temporary spot and make my way to Tristan's office, where I find the door ajar, so I knock a couple of times and slip inside, making sure my hair is curtaining my face.

Tristan is sitting behind his desk, having an animated phone conversation. His eyes find me immediately, softening with recognition, and my stomach swirls in response.

Not wanting to disturb his call, I walk over and sit on the couch to drink my coffee, waiting for him to finish. I tap my fingers against the side of my cup, debating whether I should tell him what happened on my way up here. I'm quick to decide against it, noting the conflicted expression he's wearing. I try not to eavesdrop, but the tone of his voice is sharp and agitated. The Tristan I'm used to is the image of control, so hearing him this way is unsettling. His hair looks as if he's run his fingers through it about ten times too many, and his tie is pulled away from his collar.

Even though Tristan is sitting across the room, I feel him everywhere. How could I have forgotten what that was like? That constant presence... It's not all that unpleasant anymore, which makes my head spin; I glance away when he catches me watching him.

He joins me once he's off the phone and sits on the other couch across the coffee table from me. "Good morning," he says in his normal, smooth voice.

"Morning." I take a sip of my coffee before setting it on the table.

"What is that?" he asks, a sharpness latching onto his tone that makes my pulse jump.

My forehead creases in confusion. "What?"

Before I can turn away, he moves across the space separating us and tilts my face to the side, his fingers brushing along my jaw. I wince at the stabbing pain that follows his touch. He drops his hand and pins me with a dark stare. "What happened?" His voice is low, holding me in place.

I bite the inside of my cheek, heat flaring in my cheeks at his proximity. His breath skates across my cheek and his thigh brushes mine. I swallow hard and force out, "Nothing. It's fine."

Those incredibly blue eyes narrow a fraction, barely enough to notice. "You want to play this game, Aurora? Really?"

I scowl. "I'm not playing any game. I just know it's not worth talking about. I can take care of myself."

"Clearly," he remarks, his voice dripping with condescension, his brows tugging closer as if he's disappointed I'm not confiding in him.

I huff out a breath and grab his hand, lifting it to my face until his fingers press against the spot where the fae dug her nails into my skin. She didn't draw blood, but it is bruised—along with my pride. "Can you just heal it so we can move on?"

"Now you're asking—"

"Yes," I cut in, still holding his hand against my face.

He shifts closer, angling his body toward mine and sending my heart racing. "Tell me what happened, and I'll be happy to help."

I drop his hand from my face. "It doesn't matter," I mumble, looking away. *This is ridiculous.* I shouldn't be embarrassed about what happened. But feeling that way, so utterly powerless... I hated every second.

He snags my chin between his thumb and finger, holding my gaze. "I need to know what goes on in my hotel, Aurora. You can tell me and save us both time, or I can find out on my own."

I clench my jaw until my teeth ache. "A couple of fae ambushed me in the elevator on the way up here." I swallow, casting my gaze down as embarrassment floods through me. "One fed on me."

Tristan tilts my head up as the familiar warmth of his healing magic shimmers across my cheek. I lean into him before I realize what I'm doing. His gentle touch is a stark contrast to the hard, violent expression darkening his features.

"Will you please relax?" I don't want to look at him anymore, not when he appears as if he's about to rip something—or some*one*—to shreds.

He pulls his hand away from my face, and I slide across the couch a bit to put some much-needed distance between us. "You'd like me to allow my people to threaten you?" he asks.

"That's not what I'm saying. I just don't want to make a bigger issue."

He chuckles, but it's humorless. "Since when?"

I respond with a mockingly fake laugh. "This is exactly why I wasn't going to bring it up."

The smile fades from his lips. "I'll make sure it doesn't happen again."

"Okay." I tug at the hem of my dress for no reason other than to have something to do with my hands. "Thanks for the healing," I mumble, reaching for my coffee again and taking another drink.

He nods.

"Is everything okay? When I came in, the tension in the air was enough to suffocate a person, human or otherwise."

The corner of his mouth kicks up. "You're worried?"

I blink, ignoring the dip my stomach does when I look at his mouth. "Well, yeah."

"That's interesting," he muses.

I ignore his comment. "What's going on?" I can't help but wonder whether it's related to the fae I saw fighting the other day.

"Nothing you need to be concerned about."

Images of Tristan's nightmare scene flash through my mind. Yeah, I *am* worried.

I set my cup back on the table and cross my arms. "Skylar isn't here to boss me around today, so I've got nothing else to do but sit here until you talk."

He hums, his eyes darkening with something akin to hunger. "I find it amusing you think you have control here." He points at the door. "The moment you stepped into this office, you lost it."

Despite my racing pulse, which he can no doubt hear clearly, I say, "Were you not validated as a child?"

He tilts his head to the side, questioning me.

"I'm curious," I continue. "You couldn't have been born an asshole, so I'm just wondering when you developed this inherent ability to drive people—me, specifically—absolutely fucking crazy."

"Ah, Aurora, charming as ever." He stands and walks back to his desk.

I follow him, leaving my coffee behind. I'm not completely sure what I'm doing, but I can't seem to leave well enough alone. "Should I go ask Max why you have an entire tree up your ass?"

His eyes snap to mine, and he disappears from behind the desk, appearing in front of me a second later. He towers over me, but I don't back down. "Enough," he growls. "We are not talking about this. End of discussion."

"End of...? There wasn't any discussion," I shoot back. I shouldn't care, and I had no right to ask, but something inside of me—maybe my concern for Allison and my curiosity about the fae world—made me ask, anyway.

He exhales a heavy breath, shaking his head. "Why do you care what's going on?"

"Something tells me I'm missing information," I tell him. "I know more about the fae world than I'd ever wish to, but nowhere near everything. Call me crazy, but I don't make a habit of putting down a book halfway through the story."

Tristan leans in close enough the heat of his body radiates against my chest. "What about the ones you don't enjoy?"

I shrug. "Sometimes I need to remind myself to give them a chance."

His eyes dance across my face, reminding me of the night he invaded my dreams and the look he gave me just before it all went away. "You're right," he finally says. "You don't know the whole story."

"I know about the seelie and unseelie courts and how they're divided."

He doesn't look surprised. "We've been at war with the unseelie court for as long as history can remember. They've been killing seelies for centuries."

The idea of Allison being in danger surfaces. Even looking at Tristan, a pang of concern passes through me—something I was *not* expecting. The recognition in Tristan's gaze tells me he either saw the concern in mine or felt it coming from me.

I swallow, but the lump in my throat remains. "Why?"

"The unseelie court has been hungry for power in the twenty years I've been a knight to the seelie king."

I nod, frowning. "What was that phone call about?"

"It's been fairly calm in both courts until recent weeks.

We're losing numbers. Lucky for us, they can't kill too many at once out in the open. It would attract too much human attention." He sighs and rubs his jaw, his posture tense. "The royal court is in search of a solution that results in the least number of tragedies."

"What's your solution?" I ask softly.

"I'd rather not kill anyone, but I will if it comes to that. I refuse to allow the seelie court to continue living in fear. We lost our home once. I will do everything in my power to ensure it doesn't happen again—no matter the cost."

"Have you considered talking about it instead of retaliating physically? Words hold power."

"The time for talking was before the unseelie court declared war on us."

"You want to add to the bloodshed, then?"

A muscle ticks along his sharp jaw. "This isn't your fight."

I huff out a breath. "Forgive me for forgetting my place." I'm not sure why I'm so upset, or why I offered my opinion. There's nothing I can do to protect Allison that she can't do herself, but with this new information, I feel like a caged animal.

"Hmm," he murmurs, and I take a healthy step back as the corner of his mouth lifts. "You're concerned."

I glare at him. "Of course I am. My best friend could be in danger. I don't want her to get hurt. And you—" I bite the inside of my cheek. "It's dangerous," I mutter.

He doesn't miss a beat. "I will protect my court, Aurora."

"Who protects you?" I blurt. If my concern for him wasn't clear by the energy I've been giving off, he knows about it now. It's funny, it doesn't bother me as much as I thought it would.

My heart continues pounding like a drum in my chest as he says, "You never fail to surprise me."

"Why do you say that?"

He pins me with a focused gaze that turns the temperature of my body way up. "You spend your time trying to hate me for what happened when we met, which is fair, but you don't, do you?"

My jaw tightens. "Are you kidding?"

"Your cheeks flush when I'm around, and I make your pulse race." He lowers his voice. "I can hear your heartbeat right now."

"An excellent observation," I remark dryly, despite the dampness on my palms. I press them against my thighs, struggling to ignore the heat blossoming between them.

"I affect you."

My gaze is stuck on his lips as my pulse jumps, and he smirks as if to say *told you*. "That's ridiculous," I say.

"Is that why your heart is trying to beat its way out of your chest right now?"

"No," I insist. "You're wrong."

Tristan cocks his head. "I don't think I am." His eyes shimmer with heat, and my throat goes dry. "Now you look afraid," he muses. "Though I don't think you are based on the fiery emotions coming from you."

My eyes narrow, and I fight the part of me that wants to get up and run away from what he's saying, from his ability to know what I'm feeling simply by looking at me. "Quit reading my emotions."

"Why? Worried I'll see something you don't want me to?"

*Fuck yeah, I am.*

I shake my head, grappling with a response. "Just

because I don't hate you anymore, just because I care if you're in danger, doesn't mean—"

"What?" he cuts in. "That you feel something for me?"

My heart stutters. Maybe I do feel something for Tristan, but I'll be damned if I let myself admit it out loud. I cast my gaze away from him. "I shouldn't have interrupted. You're busy with fae politics. I'll let you get back to it." His words play over in my head on a loop. *You feel something for me.* I need to get out of this room, away from his presence that makes my skin heat and my pulse race.

I stand from the couch, walking toward the door, my heart in my throat and a voice at the back of my head urging me to turn around.

"I never thought of you as someone who'd walk away from a challenge." Tristan's voice carries across the room, stopping me in my tracks.

When I whirl around, he's right there. I instinctively move to step back, but he catches my wrist, holding me in place.

"You are *very* challenging," I mutter, staring at the deep blue of his tie that makes his eyes seem even more vibrant.

A breath of laughter rumbles through his chest. "Touché."

"And you shouldn't... think about me."

"Why?" He steps in closer, brushing his thumb over the pulse in my wrist. "Because you never think of me?"

"Because I'm human," I say, finally meeting his eyes. The desire there nearly knocks the air out of my lungs, but I force myself to continue. "And that would make you a hypocrite."

His brows inch closer. "I don't follow."

"You think you can punish other fae in your court for having relationships with humans while doing *this*?" I pull my wrist out of his grasp. "Perhaps your king should take a better look at who he has working for him."

Tristan's expression smooths into something impossible to decipher. "I think you've been misinformed."

I cross my arms. "What are you talking about?"

He glances down, dragging his tongue over his bottom lip before his gaze returns to mine. "There is no rule against fae dating humans. They need to be careful among them to ensure our abilities remain secret, but—"

"I have to go," I interrupt, my chest tightening under the pressure of Tristan's words. *He thinks about me.* He shouldn't, especially with everything happening in his court, but knowing that he thinks of me, as I think of him, sends a thrill through me. Which is something I can't deal with at this exact moment.

Something in my voice must give him pause, because he doesn't try to stop me from leaving this time.

I make it to the streetcar stop near the hotel just in time to grab a seat before the doors close. Once we start moving, I pull out my phone and send a text to Allison.

> I'm on my way home. We need to talk. Now.

## CHAPTER TWELVE

Allison is sitting on the end of her bed, pulling on her tennis shoes, when I storm into our room and throw my bag down next to my desk. Her eyes widen before I even open my mouth.

"Why did you lie to me?" I ask in a calm tone, trying to allow her a chance to explain before I snap. I don't want to be mad at my best friend, but my voice is low and uneven as I try to keep my cool.

She shakes her head, her brows scrunching together. "What are you talking about, Ro?"

I fold my arms over my chest. "There isn't a rule about fae dating humans."

Her gaze drops away from mine. "I didn't lie—you know I can't—I just... didn't correct you when you assumed Oliver was my indiscretion."

I open my mouth, then snap it shut and take a deep breath. "I'm going to need more than that, Al."

She nods, then sighs. "Oliver doesn't love me." Her

voice is level and calm, as if she isn't upset by what she's telling me, whereas I'm gaping at her, shaking my head.

"Of course he does."

"Not romantically. He loves me the same as he loves you."

"But you guys have been together for years." I seem to be more upset about this than she is.

"I know." She folds her hands in her lap. "We started off as a genuine couple, but since the end of last semester, we haven't been together."

*That was nearly six months ago.* I think about the dates I tagged along for over the years. "I don't understand."

"Oliver and I aren't together anymore. We're keeping up the ruse for his sake. We were going to tell you—we even came up with this whole plan to take you out for brunch so we could get drunk on bottomless mimosas after we told you, but then everything happened with you finding out about the fae, and I didn't think it was the right time. Things were already so overwhelming, and I was really worried about you."

I nod despite the struggle I'm having keeping up. "Why are you still pretending to date?"

"Because Oliver doesn't want to come out in college. He feels strongly that just because he likes guys, it doesn't mean he should have to tell the world."

I stare at her for several moments, processing her words. Oliver is gay. Okay, that doesn't change anything for me—it also doesn't explain why she was in trouble with Tristan.

"We didn't want you in the dark anymore," she adds, "and I promise we weren't trying to keep it from you." She takes a deep breath. "Now I can explain why I didn't tell you what's been going on."

I'm glad she'd been planning to tell me everything, but the fact she kept it from me to begin with still stings.

"What does Oliver being gay have to do with the fae?"

Allison picks at a loose thread on the blanket next to her. "It doesn't, exactly. Oliver wasn't the only one using our relationship as a cover."

My brows tug together. "Are you telling me you're gay? What, fae aren't allowed to be gay?"

She laughs, but it comes out uneven, almost forced. "Being gay isn't an issue for fae."

I glance at the closed door as a rowdy group of guys passes our room. When the noise fades, I ask, "What did you need this fake relationship with Oliver to hide?"

She hesitates. "The guy I *am* seeing."

"Who are you seeing, Allison?"

She stands in a hurry, as if she can't sit still any longer, and walks toward the bathroom before turning back toward me. "His name is Evan. He's a fourth year, like us, and he's fae."

I'm missing something. So far, her explanation has yet to provide a proper reason for her getting in trouble with Tristan.

"I still don't see the problem."

She wraps her arms around herself for a moment before letting them fall back against her thighs. "Evan is part of the unseelie court... and pretty close to one of their knights, Jules."

A weight settles in my stomach. "This sounds more dangerous than you're making it out to be."

She sighs. "I can feel your concern, Ro, but we care about each other. I tried to explain that to Tristan, but..." She trails off, shaking her head. "If I don't end things with Evan, I'll be forced to stand before a tribunal and likely cast out of the seelie court. The unseelie court probably won't accept me either, which means I'll have no protection from either side or any threats outside the courts."

My pulse skyrockets. "What? No. I'm not going to let that happen to you."

She almost smiles. "There's not much you, or even I, can do. I understand the rules. They are in place to keep our court safe." She blinks a few times. "I don't know what to do," she whispers.

I run my fingers through my hair and let out a slow breath, trying to ground myself so I can think about this situation rationally. "Is it worth it?" She looks offended by the question. "I'm just saying, this could cause a lot of trouble for you. Tristan won't accept that you're sleeping with the enemy. From what you've just told me, this is serious." Tristan's unease during the phone call this morning, and his responses during the conversation we had afterward, tell me enough to make that statement.

"I know," she mumbles, her hands balling into fists at her sides. "I don't want to lose him."

"Tristan said the unseelies are killing fae from your court. What if you become a target?" I grab her hands and squeeze them. "I can't stand the thought of you getting hurt."

"I..." She looks away. "I don't know what to say."

"Did you know he was unseelie?"

"I did," she says. "And before you ask, yes, he knew I wasn't, but we decided it didn't matter."

"I think it matters more than you want to admit." Everything I've heard about the unseelie fae urges me to be wary of them. Especially when my best friend is involved.

She scowls, pulling her hands from mine. "How the

hell would you know?" My eyes widen at her sudden sharp tone. That went from zero to one hundred *way* too fast.

I stand there for several beats. Allison never yells at me. I don't think I've ever heard her raise her voice to anyone. It's clear she's not about to apologize for it. "You're right. I don't know everything about the fae, but I will do whatever it takes to make sure you're okay. Even if you're pissed now, you'd do the same for me."

She blinks a few times, her expression softening as she nods. "I'm sorry for snapping. I love you for caring so much, I do, but I need to figure this out myself. I'll be careful, I promise. Please don't be mad at me."

I don't want to be angry, but it takes some effort to push those feelings down. Maybe I'll feel better once I've met the guy. I decide to reserve my judgment until then. I trust Allison. I just hope she knows what she's doing.

"Okay," I finally say. "I need a coffee. Want to join?"

Her shoulders easing, she smiles. "I have class, but I'll catch you later?"

I nod, leaning over to hug her. "Sure."

---

I'm standing at the self-serve station in the cafeteria, putting a lid on my cup, when Oliver walks over with his own. By the looks of his eyes and messy hair, it isn't his first. You can always tell when it's midterms around here. Hell, I'm surprised he's wearing jeans and a T-shirt instead of pajamas. I would be if I hadn't been at the hotel this morning.

Oliver blows out a breath. "It's just after noon, and I'm ready for bed."

"Do you have time for a break?"

His eyes widen. "Break? You'll have to explain that foreign concept to me."

I laugh. "We can sit and talk about something that has nothing to do with study cards or assignments. I've heard it's enjoyable."

"Huh. Let's give it a shot."

We pay for our coffee and find a quiet spot in the corner of the lounge attached to the cafeteria.

"Listen, there's something I've been wanting to tell you for a while now." He fidgets with his hands in his lap. "Did Allison talk to you?"

I smile. "She did. I understand why you guys kept it from me. I'm not mad." I'm a bit upset with the whole situation, but that's my issue to deal with.

He nods. "I'm sorry I didn't tell you. I've felt so terrible about it, especially for Allison, and she's been so amazing about all of it."

"Don't apologize, Oliver. You shouldn't have to say anything. In my mind, you dating guys is no different from you dating girls."

His face relaxes. "Thanks for being cool."

"Of course." I give his shoulder a gentle punch. "Are you seeing anyone?"

He scratches his head. "Not officially. I'm not broadcasting my relationship status, but I'm sort of hanging out with someone."

I press my lips together, hesitating before I ask, "Do your parents know?"

He offers a weak smile, and my chest tightens.

I reach across the table and squeeze his hand. "I'm sorry."

He drags a hand down his face before taking a sip of his coffee. "It's okay. I'm hoping to move into an apartment around here after graduation so I don't have to go home. I figure one day I'll just bring my boyfriend to meet them."

Oliver's parents are picture perfect conservatives, so I can imagine how well that surprise would go over.

"We can get a place together," I say, only half joking. I'll most likely stick around after graduation, and having a roommate would make rent easier to pay.

"Yeah?" The corner of his mouth quirks. "I'll keep that in mind. Unless I'm living with my theoretical super-hot boyfriend by then."

I laugh. "Right, of course."

Oliver gives me a bear hug before he heads upstairs. I grab my textbook and head over to my study session, joining a few of the girls from my program who are in the lounge with their books already open. I plop down, cracking my book open to join in the discussion about the upcoming test.

We're all scribbling away when Danielle, another girl from my program, walks in an hour later with drink trays in her hands.

"Hey, sorry I'm late, but I brought caffeine!" Danielle sets the drinks down on the counter and throws her hair into a messy bun before passing them out. She sits next to me and hands me a cup before taking a sip from her own.

"Thanks," I say with a smile and tip the cup to my lips.

"My pleasure." She returns the smile and opens her book, glancing over at mine to find her place.

I take another sip before returning my attention to my textbook.

"Are we ready for this test?" Danielle asks.

A collective groan sounds around the room.

Two hours later, I'm shuffling down the hallway, headed for bed with an unsettled stomach, an all too familiar sign I've consumed too much caffeine today. My eyes burn—it's a struggle to keep them open. A constant side effect of college life.

Allison is asleep in our room when I close the door and drop my bag at my desk before crawling under the sheets. I can't be bothered to change out of my clothes or even brush my teeth before sleep pulls me under.

I'm not asleep long before my eyes shoot open and an agony-filled scream tears its way up my throat. I clutch my chest as it burns with such fierce pain I think I'm going to faint or throw up.

Allison is at my side in a second, having thrown herself out of bed when I started screaming. She flicks on the lamp between our beds. "Aurora." She tries to grab my wrists and pry them away from my chest, but I hold strong, groaning in pain. "What's happening?" Her tone is frantic, but I can't do anything. I can't speak, not that it would matter—I have no idea what's wrong with me.

I cry out as the sharpness claws deeper, and Allison's eyes widen, her face blurring with the soft lamplight. I thrash against the sheets, and the moment my arms slip away from my chest, Allison pushes my shirt out of the way to look. When she curses, my stomach plummets. Panic clamps down on my chest as I squeeze my eyes shut against the fire raging through my veins.

"Aurora, this is bad." Allison shakes her head, her eyes wide and filled with fear. "I have to call him. I don't know what else to do."

I grit my teeth, willing the pain to recede. "I'm... fine."

"You're not," she snaps. "I think you've been poisoned by a fae." She grabs my hand and squeezes, but I barely feel it. "I'll be right back."

My breaths are quick and short as I try to breathe

through the pain. My vision blurs even worse now, ebbing in and out. *That isn't a good sign.* I should be freaking out, but I can't feel anything but the fiery pain coursing through every inch of me.

I close my eyes for what feels like a second. They snap open when cool, firm hands grip my shoulders, and I find Tristan kneeling at the side of my bed.

"Aurora." His voice is soft, urgent. "You need to keep your eyes open for me, sweetheart."

I think I nod as my eyes drift shut again. *Did he just call me sweetheart?* Maybe it's because it feels as though I might be dying, but I don't hate the sound of it.

"Aurora," he repeats, sharper this time, as he tilts my chin up.

Blinking a few times, I struggle to focus on his face, the sensation of knives slicing through my chest making me dizzy as I groan in pain.

"Are you going to help her?" Allison asks from somewhere behind him.

His jaw tightens, and my heart sinks when he says, "I can't." He glances over his shoulder at her. "Not here."

"Tristan, please," she says in a small voice. "Whatever it takes. Please."

I try to swallow, but my throat is too dry. He drops his hands and scoops me into his arms. His eyes meet mine for a moment before the room around me gives way to nothing but darkness.

---

I'm still shivering when Tristan's bedroom materializes, and I grab his shoulders, struggling to breathe as the weight of the situation tugs at me. He peers at me and frowns, his eyes wild and his mouth set in a thin line. Cradling me in his arms, he walks over to the massive bed I woke up on in my dream. When he lays me on the black silk sheets, I have to fight to keep my eyes open.

*Yeah, this isn't looking good.*

"Do you remember what you told me when we met?" he asks, sitting on the edge of the bed.

His question surprises me, but I try to recall that day. After thinking about it, I lift my gaze to his and nod.

"Tell me."

My jaw is clenched against the pain; I don't think I can speak. If I open my mouth, I'm afraid I'll scream again.

"Aurora," he says. "Tell me."

I close my eyes and force my jaw to unclench. "I told you I wasn't going to die here," I say, the words slow to come out.

"And you're not."

My eyes open at the sound of his voice. "How?" I whisper, and my voice cracks. He sounds so sure, and yet I feel as though I'm breaking apart in front of him.

He lifts his hand and brushes the hair away from my face, tucking it behind my ear. "I'm going to fix this. I'm going to make it better."

I nod again.

His expression focuses as he helps me sit up enough to lift my shirt over my head. I try not to wince, but the pain is excruciating. I suck in a sharp breath when I see my chest. Black veins run under my skin, circling my stomach and disappearing under my bra, which Tristan makes no move to take off.

He presses his palm flat against my skin above my belly button as I lie back, and I hold my breath, my lips pressed together. "I need you to breathe," he murmurs.

Letting out a slow breath, I watch his hand shift upward. The pain fades eventually, and so do the shivers, but the black veins running under my skin remain.

"You can close your eyes now," Tristan says as he stands. "I'll be right back."

I watch him leave the room and wait, eyes open, until he returns, sitting even closer, his expression utterly focused on me.

"Close your eyes."

"What are you going to do?" It comes out as a whisper.

He leans forward and lifts my chin with two fingers. "I'm going to heal you. You don't need to watch."

My eyes narrow. "Tristan..."

He huffs out a breath. "Don't say I didn't warn you." He pulls out a syringe, and my entire body stiffens. "I'll try not to be offended by your level of distrust as I'm saving your life."

I watch his every move as he shrugs off his jacket and uncaps the needle. I look away as he slips the needle into his arm and fills it with his blood.

"Aurora."

I force myself to look at him and notice the needle is out of his arm. He holds it in his hand, waiting.

"This will cure you of the fae poison in your blood, but there could be side effects."

"Like?" I whisper.

"I'm not going to list them for you right now. You need this." His voice is firm; he isn't giving me a choice. Given the alternative involves me dying, I can't find the will to be annoyed by that.

I close my eyes briefly before nodding.

He slips his free hand up my arm and grips it near my elbow. He turns it over so my palm is facing up, and when he lowers the needle, I look away again. As it pierces my skin, I flinch, and I swear I can feel his blood entering my system.

My entire body ignites with searing heat, but before I can react, a calming, icy chill replaces the sensation. Everything is too bright, so I close my eyes and I shift as he withdraws the needle from my arm. Dizziness floods in, and I force my eyes open.

"It's okay." He sets the needle aside and faces me. "You can sleep now. This will take some time to work through your system." He helps me back into my shirt and pulls the blankets around me.

"You keep saving me," I mumble.

He chuckles, but it holds no amusement.

"It's annoying." I take a couple of deep breaths. "I don't want to need saving."

"Get some rest," he murmurs.

Closing my eyes, I curl onto my side to get comfortable. Sleep drags me under before I can feel weird about being in Tristan's bed.

## CHAPTER THIRTEEN

When I open my eyes, it's still dark outside. It takes more effort than usual for me to slide into a sitting position. My entire body aches as if I ran a marathon with no preparation, but the unbearable pain in my chest is gone. Everything else I can handle.

I scan the dark room as I swing my legs over the side of the bed and stand. After flicking on a lamp, I wander the perimeter of the room, never having had the chance outside of my dream to see what it looks like. I shouldn't care, but I'm curious. Squinting, I wobble over to the bookshelves lining one wall. I run my finger along the spines and glance out the windows that cover the far wall, looking out over the city from a magnificent height. Everything is neat and simple. There's nothing that expresses Tristan's personality out in the open. A pang of sadness grows in my stomach. I wonder if he's this closed-off with Max and Skylar. I hope not. Everyone needs people to share things with.

Once I've finished exploring, I grab the blanket off the bed. Wrapping it around myself, I slip out of the room. The black silk trails behind me like a train as I pad down the hallway in search of Tristan. I stop at the only other door in the hallway and poke my head inside to find him sitting behind a desk.

He glances up the moment I open the door and watches me walk into the room. "You should be sleeping," he says in a hushed tone.

"I woke up." I approach his desk. He changed out of his formal attire into a black T-shirt and slacks. I rub at my temples, wanting to close my eyes against the light beside him.

Tristan rises and walks around the desk, making me turn so I continue to face him. "Are you in pain?" The concern is so clear on his face, I'm shocked. It looks as though he cares. *He does*, a voice at the back of my mind sings.

I shrug. "A little. Nothing compared to earlier, though."

He lifts his hand, and I step toward him. He cups the side of my face, and my skin tingles with a familiar warmth as the aching in my body melts away under his touch. My eyes travel over his face—his soft, focused eyes, his strong jaw and the stubble that shadows it, his lips... My gaze gets stuck there too long. I watch the corner of his mouth quirk, and I realize he's no longer touching my cheek.

"How's that?" His voice makes me shift my eyes upward.

Clearing my throat, I say, "Better, thanks."

He nods, and the weirdest part is, I can feel the relief shimmer through him. It's like being wrapped in a warm towel after swimming in cold water. He's glad I'm okay. I don't know how I know that, but—

*...there could be side effects...*

My hand flies to my mouth as my wide eyes meet Tristan's vibrant, shock-filled gaze. He's realized what just happened.

"Holy shit," I breathe, my hand falling to my side.

He licks his lips. "I suppose this evens the playing field a bit," he muses, his brows shifting closer together.

"I can *feel* you."

He nods. "A gift from your fae ancestors, I'd guess. I wasn't sure what my blood would do, but it seems to have stirred a bit of magic in you."

"Magic? Hold the hell up. Am I fae now?" He looks as if he's trying not to laugh, and I smack his arm. "I don't know!"

"You are not fae, Aurora."

I can still feel the light amusement coming from him, like a sunrise peeking through blinds. My eyes flicker across his face as his emotions become more subdued.

His eyes narrow a fraction. "I think that's enough for now."

I arch a brow. "Says the guy that's been able to read my emotions since day one. Sucks to be on the other side, doesn't it?" At least he can block his from my view. I'm not so lucky.

Tristan chuckles. "If you'd like to know what I'm feeling, I have no problem sharing that with you."

I shake my head. "This is too weird."

"Does the connection bother you?"

"I... don't know. Not really." *Not at this very moment.* I purse my lips. "How long is it going to last?"

He shrugs. "This isn't something I've experienced before. A human being able to feel what I'm feeling. It's as new to me as it is to you, I'm afraid."

I release a breath and shoot him a smile. "Lucky us."

He tweaks my chin. "Look at it this way. At least you're not tuned into Max's emotions."

I groan. The thought of being connected to Max makes me shudder.

Tristan's laugh is a deep sound that booms through the room. It's genuine. I know that with a fresh certainty I feel in my chest. This reading emotions thing could get dangerous.

I glance over at his desk. "What are you doing up so late?"

His eyes flicker across my face in the dim light. "I spoke to Allison while you were asleep. She knows you're okay. I don't take what happened tonight lightly. I will find out who is behind this, and there will be consequences." The tang of anger radiating from him makes me frown. I miss the light emotions he was giving off a minute ago.

"What exactly happened to me?" I ask, masking my surprise at his reaction to the situation. I'm not fae—not his to protect.

"You were poisoned with foxglove. It's a rare plant that originated in the fae world, and when our home was destroyed, some foxglove made its way into the human world. In small doses, it can cause severe hallucinations, but the amount you were given... It infected your bloodstream and would've attacked your nervous system without intervention."

The *it would have killed you* goes without saying.

A shiver races through me, making my stomach coil tightly, and I hold the sheet tighter around me. I almost died tonight. I would have if Tristan hadn't come, hadn't saved me. "And you think it was a seelie fae who poisoned me?"

"No, it wasn't."

"Then why do you—"

His anger rises, dark and cold, but his calm and collected expression holds. If I wasn't privy to his emotions, I wouldn't notice the shift. "They won't get away with harming you, Aurora. Whoever ordered this attack knows you're significant."

I swallow, my pulse ticking faster under his gaze. "I don't understand."

"Don't be naïve." His breath tickles my cheek, a reminder of how close he is. "You know I care about you." The worry and attraction swirling inside him becomes muddled, making my head spin. I need to figure out a way to turn this off.

Swallowing, I say, "I'm not naïve, but you also haven't told me anything. Part of me guessed there was something, or you would've figured out another way to approach the situation after you couldn't wipe my memories." I shrug, still pretty drowsy. "And I—" I clamp my mouth shut. I'm not entirely sure what I was going to say, considering my mind is still caught on the whole *I care about you* thing. If I can feel *his* emotions right now, he can feel mine. I don't have to put words to the mix of emotions warring inside my chest. I could tell him I haven't stopped thinking about him since I left the hotel the morning after I was taken. That I caught myself wondering what his lips taste like more than once. That I want to know him so deeply, it terrifies me. But I say, "I understand."

He holds my gaze for a beat of silence before he says, "Good."

I shake my head. "Not good." My throat tingles as if I'm going to hurl. My stomach feels heavy, and my pulse is uneven. "Some fae wants me dead." The words have to fight to make it through the chattering of my teeth.

"Aurora, you're okay."

I clench my jaw, trying to make it stop. My eyes sting as I hold back tears, gripping the blanket until my knuckles are white. It's all too much. My heartbeat is in my throat as black spots dance across my vision and my ears ring. The unseelie fae want to kill me. Tristan is acting differently since I almost died, and Allison is putting herself in danger of being cast out by the seelie fae because of a guy.

"Hey." His smooth, deep voice brings me back from the edge. His hand is on my shoulder. "Breathe."

I stare at him, and he nods.

"Take a deep breath for me, Rory."

*Rory.* I say it over in my head. That's new.

I inhale, and all I can smell is *him*. Fresh, warm... comforting.

"Good girl," he praises. "Again."

I hold his gaze, standing so close I can count his eyelashes. The pressure in my chest eases, and my throat isn't so tight I can't breathe. My grip on the blanket loosens as I exhale again, and my pulse returns to a normal pace.

His eyes flick back and forth across my face. "Okay?"

I swallow the lump in my throat. "Yeah," I say, placing my hand over where his still rests on my shoulder. "Um, thanks."

His lips curl into the most genuine smile I've seen from him when he lets his hand fall back to his side. "How are you feeling now? Are you up for a late dinner?" He glances at his watch. "Or early breakfast, I suppose, considering it's almost five."

"That depends. You said a minute ago I'm not fae, so human energy or emotions or whatever isn't my kind of breakfast."

"Noted. Though you seem to enjoy being able to sense mine." His gaze holds a flicker of humor. "We can have whatever you'd like. I only feed enough to keep me alive—once a week is plenty. That's to say, I eat human food."

I catch my lower lip between my teeth. "You never talk about it."

"About what?"

"Being fae. Sure, you've told me a bit about your world." Allison has told me most things... "But nothing really specific to *you*."

His forehead creases, and I get a faint sense of shock and maybe even a little confusion from him. "I wasn't aware you wanted to hear about it."

There's a subtle shift in my pulse as something flutters in my chest. "I'm saying you *can* talk about it. It won't freak me out." Yep. I definitely need to stop talking.

"No? We're past that?" His eyes lighten as pleasant surprise flares through our new bond in the form of a tingle along the back of my neck. "I'll keep that in mind."

"Okay, then."

He tilts his head, keeping those deep ocean blue eyes on me. "You're quite the human."

There goes my pulse again. "Did you *just* meet me?"

He chuckles. "It feels like I've known you much longer."

That brings an unexpected smile to my lips. "Yeah, I guess you're not so terrible yourself."

"All right, smart mouth. Let's see what we can find in the kitchen."

I drape the blanket over a chair and follow him out of the office.

It's been almost a week since one of the unseelie fae tried to kill me and Tristan saved my life, showing me a different side to the fae knight I've fought every day since to stop thinking about. I have no idea what to do, so I've decided to avoid it—and by *it*, I mean Tristan. As much as possible.

As the days pass, fewer of his emotions come through the bond. The ones that do are a mixture of worry, anger, and uncertainty, as if maybe he's trying to figure something out. It's rare he feels anything light or warm. Considering the constant pressure he's under, it's understandable. Despite that, I find myself wishing things were different for him.

As of yesterday, I can't sense his emotions at all. Part of me is relieved, but hell, it was interesting knowing I had a leg up on at least one of his abilities for a handful of days.

Oh well. I'll take being human over being able to read emotions any day. In the absence of his emotions, I still think about him way too much.

At the hotel, I almost hug Skylar when she tells me Tristan is out of the office all day. I don't because I value my life, but the heavy sense of relief that pours over me is borderline embarrassing.

"Tristan wanted me to talk to you about the charity gala Westbrook Inc. hosts every year," she says. "He'd like you on the event committee."

Excitement bubbles through me. An event like this would look amazing on my resume. "Wow. I mean, this is awesome. I'd love to join."

"Great." She feigns enthusiasm. "You'll be working mostly with me. Max is also on the committee, along with several other employees."

I nod, trying to ignore the unease in my stomach. Since Max apologized for how he treated me when I was taken, I'm not as nervous to be in the same building as him, but it's far easier to forgive than forget. "When do we start?"

"Now. It's also going to take more than one day a week. Can you make that work?"

"Of course. I'm available Friday afternoons and I can do some evenings and weekends if needed."

"Good." She hands me a notepad. "This is everything we have to do."

I scan the paper until the words blur. "Sure, and when's the event?"

"November twenty-fifth," she answers.

I lift my head from the list, my eyes widening. "That's only a month away."

"Good, you can read a calendar. Let's get to work."

After a few hours, Skylar announces she's leaving for the day, and Max takes her place on the other side of the table. He's dressed in more casual attire than I'm used to seeing around here—a navy blue collared shirt with a loosely knotted tie and black jeans.

"You're still alive, I see," he says after sitting across from me.

I force a smile. "Looks like it."

"What's keeping you around, blondie?" he asks, raking a hand through the mop of hair on his head.

"I need this to graduate."

"You don't need the dozens of extra hours this charity event will give you."

"Maybe I enjoy doing something for a good cause. Or maybe I enjoy working here."

"Really?" he inquires dryly.

My eyes narrow. "What's it to you?"

"Absolutely nothing."

"Great, so why are you being so annoying?"

Max laughs. "I don't get to have a lot of fun around here, so I find entertainment in screwing with you. You're such an easy target."

Rolling my eyes, I stand and walk to the door. "I'm taking a break." I make my way through the quiet office and get on the elevator. A couple of minutes later, I step off into the lobby and offer Marisa a quick wave on my way to the door.

"Aurora," she calls after me, so I turn and walk to the reception desk.

"What's up?" I ask.

Marisa frowns. "You look annoyed."

"I'm fine," I tell her. "Just needed a break and figured I'd come down and get some air."

Her eyes light up. "Remember when you told me you play piano?"

I nod. It had been in passing a couple of weeks ago... I'm kind of surprised *she* remembered.

She glances around as if to make sure no one is overhearing our exchange. "I saw some movers bring one into the ballroom." She points to a hallway off of the lobby. "The double doors at the end of the hall. You can't miss it."

"Really?" My fingers are already itching to play. Nothing can consume my attention like playing—it's exactly what I need right now.

She grins and drops a key on the counter. "No one's in there. Go take a break."

"Thank you." I grab the key and head for the ballroom, hurrying down the hallway as if I'm about to be caught doing something I shouldn't.

After unlocking the door and closing it behind me, I

take in the room. It's elegant: gold walls, high ceilings, over-the-top chandeliers. The marble floor is so smooth it makes me want to lie on it and stare at the twinkling lights. And when my eyes land on the piano, I suck in a breath as I walk over to it. It's stunning. I can see my reflection in the glossy black finish as I lift the lid that covers the keys; they look as if they've never been touched. I run my fingers along them without pressing any and then sit on the bench. With a breath, forcing the tension out of my system, I put my fingers to the keys again.

I don't know too many songs by heart, but Felicity's "Poison" is one I fell in love with the moment I heard it for the first time.

As my fingers graze the keys, I sing, keeping in tune with the key of the song that matches the lyrics. By the middle of the song, I'm belting it out with thick emotion laced in every word. I let go completely, losing myself in the music, and it's absolutely incredible.

The song comes to a close. Eyes shut and my hands in my lap, I sit there, taking several deep breaths before I open them again.

Clapping sounds behind me, shooting a wicked shiver up my spine, and I freeze.

"Boundaries mean nothing to you, do they?" Tristan's amused voice carries through the empty room and latches onto my heart, sending it racing.

I scowl and turn to look at him. "You're one to talk."

He approaches at the same time I stand from the bench. "I own this hotel, Aurora. Therefore, nowhere is out of bounds for me."

"Because that's what I meant," I respond dryly.

"I didn't know you could play," he comments, glancing at the piano.

"There's a lot you don't know about me."

"Duly noted." His gaze returns to mine. "You're good."

My cheeks flush, and I want to look away. I rock back on my heels, wishing I could use that fae shifting trick to get the hell out of this room, away from his gaze. "Uh, thanks."

"Max said you took off. What happened?"

"I just needed a minute."

He inhales slowly. "Should I be concerned?"

"If there was a reason to be concerned, you would know. What are you doing here? Skylar said you'd be gone all day."

"All right," he concedes. "I had business to attend to this morning, but my afternoon meetings were canceled, so I came back. Care to join me for lunch?"

I sigh, shaking my head because, hell *yes*, I want to, but I shouldn't. "Tristan."

"Aurora," he levels.

"I'm not sure what you think you're doing with me, but—"

He closes the distance between us in a second, pressing me back into the side of the piano, and cages me in with his arms on either side of me.

My heart lurches, and I lift my eyes to meet his, pressing my lips together. "You keep doing that," I mutter.

His lips twitch. "What's that?"

"Catching me off guard," I admit. "I don't like it."

His gaze dances over my face, and my breathing hitches when his hands drop to my hips. "Hmm, I think you do. You just don't *want* to. Because when we're close, your heartbeat kicks up, your cheeks flush, and best of all, you get this look in your eyes, and I never know if you're going to take a swing at me or let me closer."

"Depends on the day," I say without thinking.

He exhales a short laugh. "How's today looking?"

My eyes narrow. "Not great." I've gotten good at saying the exact opposite of what the voice in my head is saying, and she's getting louder every day.

"Is that so?" he inquires, leaning close enough his breath stirs the hair at my temple.

I tilt my head back so I can look him in the eyes. "You want to get closer to me, then tell me what's going on. Was that meeting this morning about the unseelie fae?"

"You've been avoiding me," he says, ignoring what I asked.

"I have not. Quit evading my questions."

"Quit evading *me*," he counters, his thumbs slipping under my shirt and grazing my skin, making it tingle.

I look away, pressing my lips together as I fight to ignore the pulsing between my thighs and the warmth in my stomach. "I've... been busy."

"You're spiraling," he murmurs, dropping his hands to his sides. "I don't want you to worry. Nothing is going to happen to you."

My mouth goes dry. If I could speak, I have no idea what I'd say. I'd rather know I can protect myself, but his reassurance that my safety means something makes it hard to keep convincing myself I don't want to test whatever is growing between us.

"During the meeting this morning, I was informed that a woman named Danielle was the fae who poisoned you."

I have to swallow more than once before I say, "*What*? No. She... I don't... We're friends."

"She confessed." I can't feel his emotions anymore, but the furrow of his brows and downturn of his lips tell me enough. He's upset that I'm upset.

"But why?" I ask in a small voice.

"I had Max spend some time with her to see whether he could find out. All he gathered is that she felt bitter toward you because of something Jules said. He's always made a game of screwing with people, so I'm not surprised."

"Max?" The idea of him helping me—it's almost unfathomable. "What would this Jules guy have to say about me?"

"We don't know. Danielle stopped talking after she told Max about Jules. She's been dealt with." I knew what that meant. I wouldn't see Danielle in class anymore.

Tears gather in my eyes. "She's dead." It isn't a question.

Tristan nods, his back straight, as if my emotional response is making him uncomfortable. He snags my chin, holding my gaze. "Would you have liked me to spare her?"

My whole body tenses. "I couldn't make that call."

"I wouldn't ask you to." His thumb traces the line of my jaw. "I told you—I will protect my people."

My eyes widen, and heat rises in my cheeks. "If your blood activated some weird magic inside me, why didn't the fae poison she tried to kill me with do anything like that?" I'm annoyed for not thinking of it sooner, but frankly, I've been doing my best to forget that night.

He presses his lips together. "You remember the black veins under your skin? Those appeared as your body tried to fight the poison, but because you're human, it didn't work."

I swallow hard. "Do you think more unseelie fae will come after me?"

"I'm handling it." He lowers his voice. "I won't let you get hurt." His fiery gaze burns into me, making my pulse race as his words terrify me and bring me comfort all at once. Nothing makes sense right now, but I'm pretty sure I enjoyed hearing him say those words a little too much.

## CHAPTER
# FOURTEEN

I've been back on campus for a week since spending that night at Tristan's when I was poisoned, and Allison has been looking out for me. Tristan also assured me there are other seelie fae on campus keeping an eye on me, which in other circumstances would've freaked me out more than comforted me. But that was before the unseelie court made me their target.

Allison hasn't mentioned seeing Evan since Danielle tried to kill me, and I haven't asked. If she thinks seeing him in secret is safe, I have to trust her. I need my best friend.

I use the rest of the day to work on readings and get started on a couple of assignments. I'm stuffing my face with cold pizza when someone knocks on the door. I get up and open it to find a tall guy with sharp green eyes and cropped dark brown hair. He's dressed casually in a T-shirt with a black leather jacket and jeans.

"Can I help you?" I ask, holding onto the door.

The guy scratches the back of his neck as his eyes roam over my face. "Is Allison around?"

"You must be Evan."

He nods, pulling his hand out of his pocket and sticking it out to me. "You're Aurora, right?"

I glance at it, then shake it gingerly, nodding. "Allison isn't here."

"That's too bad." He lets his hand fall back to his side. "Maybe I could come in and wait for her?"

I grip the door tighter. "I don't think so. I'll let her know you stopped by. I'm sure she'll call you." Unease slithers its way up my spine, and considering the last interaction I had with an unseelie fae, it's not unwarranted. My mind goes to the bottom drawer of my desk where my iron stakes are hidden. Maybe I should have one on me all the time now.

He glances at where my knuckles have turned white and frowns. "I'm not here to hurt anyone."

"Forgive me for not trusting you. The last unseelie fae I knew tried to kill me."

He frowns. "Allison told me. I'm sorry."

"She's in class," I say, ignoring his apology. I start to close the door, but he raises his hand.

"Can I come in?" His eyes flick between mine. "Please?"

My heartbeat is in my throat. "No," I say in a firm voice.

"Look, I have no leg to stand on here, but I need your help. Please give me five minutes, and then I'll go."

I arch a brow, though I can't ignore the tiny part of me that wants to know what he's going to say. Finally, I exhale harshly. "Five minutes." I step back, opening the door so he can come in. Once he's inside, I leave the door ajar and move toward my desk, just in case I need to dive for a weapon. "Speak."

"I care about Allison. A lot. Not all of us want to be involved in the war, Aurora. The unseelie court isn't the only side attacking and killing. We may be the more ruthlessly inhuman of the courts in many eyes, but you should know, unseelie fae are going missing and often turning up dead, too."

I cross my arms. *I shouldn't say anything, shouldn't get involved in fae politics, especially during such a volatile time.* Instead of responding to the information Evan offered, I say, "Allison will be in more trouble if whatever the two of you are doing continues. Does that not matter to you?"

His eyes narrow. "Of course it matters." He shakes his head. "What am I supposed to do? Walk away from her?"

"That would help."

"No. It would hurt her."

"Temporarily." I sigh. "The last thing I want is for my best friend to get hurt, but I'd rather she be heartbroken for a little while than be cast out of her court and left unprotected as punishment for sleeping with the enemy."

"I'm not the enemy!" He glances at the door and frowns briefly. "I'm sorry, but I'm no threat to you and certainly not to Allison. I'm not a threat to Tristan either."

The stiffness in my spine doesn't ease. "I don't know what you want me to do."

"You can get Tristan to meet with me."

I scowl. "Do you think I'm his secretary?"

"No, but I know you have influence over him."

I press my lips together to keep from bursting into laughter. "Um, are we talking about the same fae knight?"

"He'll listen to you."

*What has Allison told him about me? About Tristan?*

I lean against the side of my desk. "Say I could get him to agree to meet with you. Why should he want to? So you can plead your case to stay with Allison?"

"Would that be enough for you to agree to try?" he asks.

"If it'll make my best friend happy, I'll do it. But that's me. I doubt it'll be enough for Tristan to listen to you." I don't bother telling him that Tristan doesn't make the rules, that he works for the seelie king. Perhaps Tristan can plead their case, but something tells me it won't matter. The divide between the courts is bigger, more significant than one relationship between a seelie and unseelie.

"But there's a chance," he says, "so I have to try."

"Look, maybe the two of you should just take some time away from each other. At least until things get—"

"Better?" he cuts in with a sharp laugh. "We're at war, Aurora. Things are going to get a hell of a lot worse before there's even a chance of them getting better."

"What happens if Tristan says no? Are you going to stop seeing Allison, or are you going to take the chance of her getting punished?" I can't be sure Evan would get punished by Jules, or whether the unseelie queen even cares if someone from her court is with a seelie fae, but I imagine the rules are the same for both courts. *Don't fuck the enemy.*

"Then we'll figure something else out." He meets my gaze. "Tell me you'll try. Please."

I inhale slowly through my nose, and let the breath out through my mouth. "I'll try."

"Thank you."

I drop my gaze. "You should go."

He steps back, heading for the door. "It was nice to meet you, Aurora. I'll see you around."

I stare at the closed door once Evan's gone, my mind reeling with what he said, and what I agreed to do. Grabbing my phone off my desk, I text Allison.

> Evan was looking for you. He just left.

> Shit, I'm sorry I wasn't there. What did he say to you?

> He wants to meet with Tristan. I'll ask, but I don't know if it'll happen, Al.

> Yeah, I know. I have back-to-back lectures today, then a study group tonight, so I'll be home late. Are you okay?

> I'm fine. Drowning in assignments, so I think I'll head to the library and work there.

> Okay.

> Keep your location on, please.

> Of course. See you later.

---

I make a point never to be late for class. This morning would be no different except I slept through all three of my alarms. I've been in a state of exhaustion since being poisoned. I don't know whether it's remnants of fae poison running through my veins that makes it difficult to keep my eyes open all day, but I'm sleeping more often and for longer than usual.

When I do wake up, I grab my phone to check the time. My loud groan fills the empty room. Allison didn't wake me before she left; that's *if* she slept here last night.

Throwing my comforter off, I force myself out of bed. I

pull a comb through my tangled waves and brush my teeth while trying to throw together a presentable outfit. Out the door with a granola bar and my bag in less than fifteen minutes, I sprint across campus. I'm still half an hour late. Of course, today's class is in the largest lecture hall, and my business finance professor has a guest speaker scheduled.

As I approach, I silence my phone and slip it into my bag, then hold my breath and open the door, tiptoeing inside and scanning the room for a seat. A few heads turn when the door shuts. I cringe as I hurry to an empty seat, three rows from the front of the room, which means everyone watches as I make my way to it.

Once I'm seated and have my laptop on the small fold-out desk in front of me, I let out a slow breath.

"Glad you could join us, Aurora," the professor says.

"I'm—" Words stop forming the moment my eyes shift to the guest speaker. *Fuck.* "Sorry."

Tristan stands at the podium, front and center, grinning like a cat in his usual business attire.

"As I was saying…"

I tune the professor out, sliding down in my seat as if my laptop could hide me and praying to anyone who will listen that this lecture ends early.

An agonizingly slow hour passes, and the professor announces a break before the second half of the presentation. I groan and pull out my phone to occupy myself. Now would be the time to gather my things and get the hell out of here, but if I leave, I'll never hear the end of it from Tristan.

"He's so young and attractive—it's unfair," the girl beside me squeals at the girl next to her.

"Unfair? It's inhuman. Jesus, if he was our professor, I wouldn't miss a single lecture. In fact, I'd apply for extra credit assignments." She pauses. "With lots of after-hours work."

"Mmm, me too," the first girl gushes.

The sudden urge to rip my hair out makes annoyance simmer in me. I sit lower in my seat and press my lips together so I don't respond.

"Oh my gosh, he's looking at me," the one beside me whispers and slaps the other girl's arm.

"Uh, no he's not, babe. He's looking at *her*."

I don't have to look up to know the *her* they're referring to is me. Keeping my head down, I stare hard at my phone. It vibrates in my hand, and I grit my teeth at the message.

> Your annoyance is burning rather brightly today. It's almost as vibrant as your classmates' lust each time they look at me.

My thumbs hover over the keyboard as I try, and ultimately fail, to craft a snide response. I lift my head begrudgingly until my gaze meets his and narrow my eyes, shaking my head. The corner of his mouth kicks up, and he slides his phone inside his suit jacket.

Students who left for the break file back in, and the second half of the lecture gets underway. With Tristan's focus on the lecture and addressing the room, I use the opportunity to look at him. He's dressed how I'm used to seeing him at the office, and today it looks like he skipped shaving. It's a look I could get behind.

He speaks passionately about how he grew his business from the ground up, starting with an idea and a goal. Admiration floods through me as I listen to the story. His eyes pause on me, and recognition flashes in them; my emotions are on display. He smiles at me as if we're sharing a moment, as if we're the only two people in the lecture hall, and then his gaze shifts across the room as he continues to speak.

Another hour later, the room empties, and I attempt to throw my things into my bag to follow everyone out. Only a few others remain in the room. If I'm going to get out without—

"Miss Marshall, a moment, please."

I glance up and lock eyes with Tristan and hesitate before I offer a curt nod.

The professor hangs around until the other students file out and shakes Tristan's hand. "Thank you for joining us today."

"Always happy to, George."

"Can I walk you out?" he asks, his gaze shifting to me for a moment, making the tops of my ears burn.

Tristan offers an easy smile. "No, thank you." He catches the professor's gaze, and I can't stop myself from watching. "You will leave and remember walking me out. We had a pleasant chat about your lovely students."

George's expression is dazed, calm. My stomach swirls with a conflicted mix of unease and attraction as I realize what's happening. Tristan's using his manipulation ability on him, and without another word, George grabs his coffee cup and satchel and walks out of the lecture hall. Maybe I should be bothered by Tristan using his ability on my professor, but I can't stop myself from being attracted to the display of power—especially when he can't use it on me.

Leaving my bag at my seat, I make my way to the front while Tristan packs his things, appearing to be in no rush to leave.

I slide onto the large desk off to the side and let my legs

dangle over the front, swinging them back and forth. "Did you need to mess with his head?"

"Forgive me for not wanting him to get the wrong idea with you staying back after everyone else left."

I arch a brow. "The wrong idea?" His stupid little smirk makes me scowl. "Never mind. You could've just told him you were my mentor."

"Yes, I could have." He zips up his stupidly fancy leather bag. "What was this morning about?"

I look over at him and shrug. "I was late." It doesn't seem like the place to talk about Evan and what he said yesterday.

Tristan leaves his bag at the podium and approaches me. "I know that, Aurora. I'm asking you why. You're never late for work. I imagined school would be the same."

I sigh, rubbing my hands over my face; I didn't have time to put on makeup before sprinting to class. "I'm tired. It's no big deal."

He steps in front of me and grips my wrists, pulling my hands away from my face and setting them in my lap. "It's been over a week since—"

"I know," I cut in. I don't want him to say what went down the night Danielle poisoned me, or the day in the ballroom. It all felt too intimate. "It's fine. I just need to grab a coffee."

"Have you spoken to Skylar?"

"About *this*?" I ask in a sharp tone.

He chuckles. "About the charity event."

"Oh," I mumble. "Yeah. I was going to head to the hotel and meet with her."

"I'm going there, too. Why don't you ride with me?"

I catch my lower lip between my teeth. The idea of riding in a car alone with Tristan sets me on edge, but I also can't ignore the warmth and fluttering in my stomach.

"Aurora," he says in an amused tone.

"Yeah, okay," I say. "Before we go, why didn't you tell me you were coming today?"

"And miss the look on your face when you saw me? No way."

I narrow my eyes. "For an all-powerful fae knight, you sure can act like a twelve-year-old."

He chuckles, arching a brow. "All-powerful, huh?"

I push him back a few steps and slide off the desk. "You really just came here for a guest lecture?"

Tristan sighs softly. "I was also monitoring a situation."

"An unseelie fae situation?"

"I want to make sure you're safe." His eyes meet mine and soften. "I don't want you targeted because of me."

I grind my molars, resenting the fear that zips through me. "Who I spend my time with is no concern of the unseelie fae."

Tristan smiles as if he's trying not to laugh.

"What?" I snap.

"Just you." His tone matches the fondness in his expression, and it makes my heart beat faster.

"Yeah, go ahead, laugh at the human who can't protect herself from the supernatural. I'm hilarious." I roll my eyes. "Mark my words, if I catch wind of more fae targeting me, you can bet your ass I'm going to—"

He rests his hands on my shoulders, their weight anchoring me. "Take a breath, Rory. It won't come to that."

"Danielle tried to kill me. What makes you think someone else won't try?"

"I won't let anyone hurt you," he vows in a deep voice.

I glance away before nodding. "We should go."

Never did I think I'd be walking out of class with Tristan beside me. While I've gotten used to his presence, I'm not used to the eyes that follow us the entire way to the parking lot.

Tristan goes through the Starbucks drive-thru on the way back to the hotel and orders himself a coffee. As I'm about to tell him what I want, he orders my usual iced latte and drives to the window. He's paid attention to the coffee I drink at the office. Something so minimal shouldn't stick out to me so much, but it does.

Max pulls Tristan into a meeting the minute we get back to the office, so I drop my stuff and find Skylar in the conference room, poring over a stack of papers.

"Hey," I say.

"You're late," she snaps.

"By three minutes, and I was with your boss, so take it up with him," I toss back, ignoring her defensive tone, and sit across from her. "What are you working on?"

"I'm going over the donors for the event. We've got more than enough, and I'm still waiting on a few companies to get back to me."

"Great. Is the guest list finalized?"

Skylar pushes a sheet of paper across the table, and I scan it. "This looks good to me," I offer.

She doesn't spare me a glance. "I need you to take it to Tristan and get his approval."

Right. Pushing the rolling chair away from the table to stand, I grab the guest list and head for Tristan's office. I frown when I pass Max in the hallway.

"I wouldn't go in there if I were you, blondie." His voice makes me grit my teeth as I keep walking, knocking briefly on Tristan's office door before slipping inside. I scan in the room, and my gaze immediately lands on Tristan. He's standing at the window, his back to me, and he's not alone. His arm is wrapped around someone's waist. She has one hand pressed against the window and the other resting against her thigh as she leans into him, making soft noises that make my stomach sink. He's not kissing her, not touching her in any way that warrants the moans coming from her, unless... *he's feeding on her.*

Before I can speak, he pulls back, whispering something to the woman, who nods and walks over to the sitting area across the room. His attention shifts to me, his lips set in a tight line, eyes glowing blue orbs that steal the air from my lungs.

"Something I can help you with?" He walks closer, and I instinctively take a step back, my eyes flitting to where the woman appears to be passed out the couch, her eyes shut and a faint blush tinting her cheeks. When I force my eyes back to Tristan, he's much closer. I pull in a shaky breath, my heart toppling over itself.

"What did you do to her?" I whisper, unable to meet the weight of his gaze, and stare at the design on his tie instead. I have no idea why I even asked. Maybe I just want to hear him say it.

"Don't ask questions you know the answers to. It's beneath you."

My eyes snap to his. "Did she know what spending time with you would entail?"

His lips twist into a faint smirk. "You seem very interested in what goes on around here behind closed doors." He moves closer, and before I can side-step him, he snags my chin. "Or are you simply jealous?"

I smack his hand away, scowling. "You're delusional if you think that." Despite the firm tone of my voice, there's a tiny part of me that's curious to experience it when it's *not* against my will. And that's all kinds of messed up.

His eyes dance across my face. "You sure?" He lowers his voice, stepping so close, I reel back and collide with the wall. "You forget I can feel your emotions."

I swallow hard and force out, "That means nothing."

Tristan cocks his head to the side, a bit of his hair falling across his forehead. "Of course not," he murmurs dryly. He leans in until his nose skims mine, and I hold my breath, my heart in my throat as my entire world narrows on him. He braces his hands against the wall on either side of me, just above my shoulders. "Your heart is racing," he muses, flicking his tongue along his bottom lip. "But I don't think you're scared. So what is it?"

"Annoyance," I offer, thankful now more than ever I don't have the same inability to lie as fae.

He chuckles, his breath tickling my cheek. "Hmm... no." His thumb brushes my shoulder, shooting tingles across my skin. "Try again."

I bite the inside of my cheek until I taste blood. "What are you doing?"

Tristan cocks his head slightly. "You recall barging into my office a minute ago, yes? Perhaps I should ask you that."

"Were you going to kill her?" I ask in a voice barely above a whisper.

He arches a brow. "Do you think that low of me?"

"Don't answer a question with another question. It's beneath you."

"No, Aurora, I wasn't going to kill her."

"Just feed from her until she ends up passed out on your couch, then?"

He casts a brief glance toward the couch and exhales a sigh. "Evidently so."

"Such a gentleman," I mutter.

His gaze returns to me, and he steps back, dropping his arms to his sides. "You're free to leave," he says. "Or stay. It's up to you."

My eyes widen. "Stay?" I shake my head. "Why would I want to do that?"

He gives me a knowing look but says nothing.

I swallow past the dryness in my throat, standing straighter. "You told me the day we met you wouldn't feed from me."

"I stand by that," he says. "Unless, of course, you offered."

A flush creeps across my cheeks and chest. "I'm not—I wouldn't."

"What if I was dying?"

I purse my lips; I think he's joking. "I'm sure Max would write you a great eulogy."

Tristan chuckles. His gaze drops to my lips when I press them together before returning to mine. "Perhaps we should pick this conversation up another time."

"It seems finished to me."

"I'm not finished with you," he says in a low voice, "not even close."

My next breath gets caught in my throat. "I need to get back to Skylar," I force out, then quickly remember why I came here. I shove the list toward him. "You need to sign off on this."

He nods slowly, keeping his eyes on me a moment longer before he takes the document from me and scans it, then hands it back. "It's fine."

"Great."

His gaze deepens. "Anything else you need?"

The heat between my legs screams *yes*, but I shake my head no.

The corner of his mouth kicks up, and he steps around me, opening his office door. "You know where I am when that changes."

I leave, ignoring the certainty in his voice. My shoes echo softly on the floor and my pace slows to a stop as voices reach me from behind a meeting room door.

"That's not what I'm saying," Max growls, and I bite the inside of my cheek at the viciousness of his voice.

"What *are* you saying?" a female voice asks.

"Tristan won't allow the attacks to continue without advising the king to take action. What Rowan chooses to do—"

Someone slams their fist on the table, and I suck in a breath, moving away from the closed door, and hurry back to the conference room. I give Skylar the list and say, "All good."

She nods without looking up from her laptop. "I need you to call the bartender and confirm what they're bringing."

"Sure." I glance at my hands, then back at her. "Can I ask you something?"

"If you must."

"When I was on my way back from Tristan's office, I walked past what sounded like a tense discussion Max was having with someone about the issues that have been going on with the unseelie fae."

"That isn't a question."

"Why are you working on this human event and not in there offering your opinion? I'm sure you have one."

She laughs, finally glancing up from her screen. "Talk is boring. I lead the physical training. Teaching fae how to protect themselves and each other. This power struggle between the two sides has been going on for a long time. Too many of ours have died or gone missing. We're going to retaliate soon, and we're going to make sure we have the resources and power behind us to win. That takes time, training, and planning."

"When is this going to happen?" I'm not sure I want an answer.

"Don't worry about it," she grumbles, and with that, she goes back to work as though I'm not here.

All I can do after that is worry about it.

What'll happen when the seelies launch their retaliation? How many innocent humans will get killed in the crossfire?

What will happen when Allison finds out her court is going to attack Evan's?

What the hell is going to happen to *me*?

## CHAPTER FIFTEEN

A few hours later, it's dark outside the massive floor-to-ceiling windows as I collect my things. Skylar left two hours ago, and the boardroom is deafeningly quiet. The charity gala is fast approaching, and being given the chance to spearhead it isn't something I take lightly... which is why I'm still here, checking tasks off our seemingly never-ending to-do list. It'll look fantastic on my resume and it's a great opportunity to gain some contacts for after I graduate, so I'm all for the extra work, even if it means juggling my responsibilities.

I flip the light off on my way out and peek down the dark hallway to find Tristan's office light still on. I hesitate, stuck between talking myself out of and into going to him. I blow out a breath, shaking my head. *This is ridiculous.* I square my shoulders and walk to his office, knocking on the door before I slip inside and let the door close behind me. "Can I talk to you?"

He glances up from the paperwork on his desk, and those deep blue eyes slice right through me. His matching tie is pulled away from the collar of his white dress shirt and the sleeves are rolled up to his forearms.

*Look away, Aurora. They're just arms.*

"Once you've finished eyeing me up, you are more than welcome to ask anything you like." There's a glint of amusement in his gaze.

I ignore that, shoving down the stupid fluttering in my stomach. "I had a conversation with Allison's—uh, Evan the other day."

Any humor in his eyes vanishes. "He approached you?" A muscle ticks along Tristan's jaw. "What did he say?"

"He'd like a meeting with you. Something about wanting to prove he's not a threat."

He arches a brow. "He and Allison are still seeing each other." It's not a question, so I don't offer an answer.

"My loyalty lies with my best friend, Tristan, so I have to ask. I understand there are rules, but will you at least hear him out?"

He regards me thoughtfully as he stands and walks around the desk, stopping a foot away from me. I watch him too closely, my breath hitching the closer he gets. "Unfortunately, it's more complicated than that."

I press my lips together, hesitating a moment. Then I say, "From my minimal experience, there's nothing about your world that isn't complicated." I force myself to hold his weighted gaze and add, "But that's an awfully convenient excuse not to try."

Tristan's eyes flit between mine. "Did you come here to tell me how I should handle fae matters? I've been a knight to the king for twenty years, Aurora. I know what I'm doing."

"But—"

"I'm handling it," he cuts in. "Frankly, you should be

grateful I'm not handing Allison over for a royal tribunal to cast out or decimate as they see fit."

My stomach drops and a single word spills from my lips: "Why?"

"Why am I forsaking my responsibility for a fae I don't know or care about?" A hint of a smile plays on his lips as he cocks his head to the side.

His words, paired with the way he's watching me, fill my cheeks with warmth. "Tristan..."

He closes the distance between us, resting his hands on my hips and sending my pulse racing. "I made it very clear to Allison that she would face the consequences of engaging with a fae from the unseelie court if it continued."

I lick the dryness from my lips. "But you weren't surprised she was still seeing Evan, and you've done nothing about it."

"Do you have a question you want to ask me?"

I open my mouth, eyes narrowing a fraction. Finally, I shake my head.

He lifts a hand and twirls a strand of my hair between his fingers. "You'd rather not talk?" he murmurs.

My heart lurches in my chest. This scenario could go a few different ways. It's clear from the pulsating between my legs and the warmth swirling deep in my belly which way my body wants it to go, but there's an annoying voice at the back of my head telling me to run. "What do you want me to say?"

He exhales a soft laugh, his eyes locked on mine. "What you're thinking."

Panic seizes me, and I'm not even entirely sure why. So what if I'm attracted to him? So what if his hand on my hip is searing my skin, making me tingle and struggle to fight the urge to lean in and—

"Go ahead," he taunts in a low, gravelly voice that shoots heat straight to my core. "Tell me you don't want me, Aurora. Say it, and I won't bring it up again." His eyes dance across my face as he waits for my response. He's giving me an out. All I have to do is say I don't want him.

I can't fucking do it. I can't make the words form on my lips.

"This is ridiculous," I mutter instead, my heart pounding in my throat.

"I'm not asking for much," he says, leaning in.

"You know what you're doing. I'm not going to do this with you. It's late, and I'm exhausted." That's not entirely true. My muscles are aching and tired, but standing this close to Tristan, it's as if someone has shot liquid energy into my veins.

"If only you were in a hotel full of beds," he says with a wry grin.

"You are insufferable."

"Thank you," he replies arrogantly, his gaze dropping to my lips.

I'm leaning in before I can stop myself. His breath tickles my flushed cheeks, and his pupils dilate. The corner of his mouth kicks up, and everything in me tenses. I reel back a step, unable to drag in a breath. My head spins as I turn away from him and walk to the door, yanking it open.

"When you're ready to admit what you want," he calls after me in that deep voice I feel all over, "you know where I am."

I pause for half a second at the door, and then I hurry out of the room, grabbing my things before leaving the building.

I stay in bed for over an hour after I wake up. It's Saturday; I have no assignments due right away—no responsibilities I need to rush out of bed for. I pull my computer onto my lap and answer a few school emails, then scroll aimlessly online. When I've wasted as much time in bed as I can stand, I throw the sheets off and shuffle into the bathroom.

After a shower, I towel dry my hair and wrap another around my body, my fingers and toes pruned and my skin radiating heat. I'm humming as I open the bathroom door to grab some clothes from my dresser, and I stop dead when I find Tristan and Allison standing in our room.

I stand there, staring at them both, and grip the towel tighter around me. Looking between them, I ask, "Do I even want to know?"

Tristan looks as if he's about to pounce on me. The dark, intense focus in his eyes makes my heart pound and the heat between my thighs pulse.

*When you're ready to admit what you want...*

"Hey, Ro. Sorry I wasn't here when Evan stopped by the other day." Her voice is low, almost timid. We've basically been on opposite schedules since it happened, so this is the first I'm seeing her.

I force my eyes to shift over to Allison, noting the unease in her posture and the anxious glint in her eyes, then shrug. "It's fine. He did nothing besides scare the shit out of me, and that wasn't really his fault, anyway. Just the result of some major distrust in the unseelie fae, thanks to our good friend, Danielle." My tone is dry, but saying her name sends an uncomfortable shiver through me.

She sighs and keeps her eyes on me, as if she's too

scared to look at Tristan. "Look, I know no one trusts him, but *I* do."

Tristan chuckles, but his jaw is hard.

"Like you've never wanted something you shouldn't?" Allison snaps. "Something your people don't agree with?" Her cheeks flush and her eyes widen, knowing she said something she shouldn't have.

Tristan glances my way, and I shake my head. He turns back to Allison and says in a low voice, "Perhaps you should take a walk. My patience is running thin, and you do not want to be on the other side of that."

Without another word, Allison grabs her bag off the end of her bed and hurries out of our room, leaving me standing before Tristan in nothing but a towel.

## CHAPTER
# SIXTEEN

Tristan is sitting on the end of my bed when I return from frantically tugging on a pair of joggers and a hoodie in the bathroom. I comb my fingers through my damp hair, and he watches me without a word. I'm not sure why he's still here and I can't seem to form the words to ask, but he isn't leaving.

I walk around the small room in quick, unmeasured strides, tidying things here and there.

"You're pacing," Tristan observes in a calm voice.

I ignore him, busying myself in case that might keep me from having to talk to the fae knight still sitting on my bed, especially after the way we left things last night. I suppose I should be grateful he didn't go after Allison when she snapped at him, clearly defying his rank—and fae law.

Tristan catches my wrist as I pass him and holds it in a gentle grip, stopping me from whizzing around. "Aurora, come sit for a minute. You're going to make yourself nauseous if you continue spinning out."

I peer down at his fingers wrapped around my wrist, where my pulse is humming with the energy of being so close to him. "She's not going to stop seeing him, no matter what you say. She could get hurt, and there's not a damn thing I can do."

Tristan lets go of my wrist and slips his fingers through mine, lighting my skin up; I half expect to see neon veins running the length of my arm when I glance down to where our skin touches. "This isn't your fight, and she is not your responsibility."

I deflate, sinking onto the bed next to him. "She's my best friend. The fae courts are at war, and I have no idea what's going to happen. It seems like she's not concerned about the consequences of her relationship, and we're not talking about a slap on the wrist here." I shake my head. "I don't... Why would she risk being cast out, or *worse,* for one person?"

"You'd be surprised what some people would do for one person."

My pulse ticks faster, and I pull my hand free from his. "Are you going to turn her over to the court?"

Our eyes meet. "Are you asking me to allow her to break fae law?" He regards me thoughtfully. "I can't do that, Aurora. I'm sorry."

A sickening sense of helplessness puts pressure on my chest, and I have the powerful urge to scream. Not at Tristan, but at the situation. At the fact there's absolutely nothing I can do to save my best friend from the danger she's willingly putting herself in. He's looking at the bigger picture. Tristan has the responsibility to take care of the seelies, and until proven otherwise, Evan is a threat.

Thrusting my fingers through my hair, I blow out a breath. "Is Allison the reason you came here?" If he's waiting for her to come back, she likely won't without texting me to make sure he's gone.

He shakes his head and wets his lips. "I've been looking into your family history."

"As most stalkers do," I quip, trying to lighten the mood, hoping to ease the tendrils of anxiety wrapping around me.

His eyes glimmer. "As I recall, you wanted more information, so I did some research."

I bite the inside of my cheek. "You... did this for me?"

"I have a mild interest in the matter as well."

"Okay." I glance at the floor, wiggling my toes. "What did you find?" My heart feels as if it's beating in my throat and sitting still is agony. It seems crazy to think I have fae ancestors, but after the way Tristan's blood affected me, it's impossible to deny my family's past.

"Your fae ancestor had her daughter's magic concealed, which is why it didn't continue down the bloodline."

I frown in confusion. "You said I had dormant fae magic in me."

Tristan nods. "Because the fae whose magic was repressed was female, it only affects females in the Marshall bloodline. You are the first since that fae."

I scratch the back of my neck. "Am I part fae?"

He shakes his head. "You are completely human."

"How?"

"Because a powerful witch made sure of it a long time ago."

My eyes widen. "A witch?"

His brows draw closer. "That's right."

*Witches are real—time to add that to my notes.* "Are any of them...?"

"There is no one left in your bloodline. They were lost during the war when our world was destroyed."

My stomach drops, and I barely force out, "You're sure?"

"Yes. I would know if they were still alive, especially after meeting you and sensing their dormant magic."

"Since *you* can sense their magic in me, can't other fae as well? Were my ancestors not concerned about the potential dangers of that?"

He shakes his head. "That's not something I can say. I wish I had more answers for you." The darkness under his eyes and his tired expression make me think he'd been hoping for more, too. If I have no fae ancestors left, there's little chance of getting the seelie fae to accept me—for my lineage to protect me from those who are against my knowledge of the fae, and the freedom Tristan granted me even though he couldn't wipe my memories.

I inhale an uneven breath, a little surprised at the threat of tears stinging my eyes. "At least I know." I blink them away and meet his gaze. "Thanks for looking into it."

---

The weather cools as the daylight hours become shorter, and midterms pass in a whirlwind of studying and surviving off instant noodles and coffee. And once midterms have passed, I spend just about every free moment at the hotel now that we're only a week from the gala.

Skylar and I have been working all afternoon and have made substantial progress in finalizing things. She leaves the boardroom to have the accounting clerk approve some last-minute expenses, leaving me to finish the menu to send to the caterer.

I glance up from my laptop when Max pops his head into the room.

"Let's go, blondie."

I arch a brow. "Where?"

"It's almost ten o'clock." He takes a step forward and leans in the doorway.

"Okay..."

"We're going out."

"You want me to go out with you?" I arch a brow. "Did Skylar drug your coffee or something?"

He offers a little fake laugh and shoots me a pointed look. "No, but she told me to invite you, so I am. Plus, it'll make Oliver happy."

I immediately frown. "Did Skylar invite him? She better not be screwing with him to get to me."

Max crosses his arms and sighs so softly I almost miss it. "I invited him."

I blink in surprise. "Oh. I didn't know you were—"

"Gay?" he cuts in with a slight smirk.

"Into humans," I clarify.

He shrugs. "Just because I don't like you most of the time doesn't mean I don't like humans. You don't represent them all, blondie."

I flip him off. "How do you even know Oliver?"

"He was fake-dating your fae bestie, and I met him when I was looking for you."

"I know it's not against the rules to be with a human, but I'm still surprised." Oliver and Max? I try to picture it, but I can't.

He laughs, and I'm pretty sure it's the first time I've ever heard something so genuine come out of his mouth.

"There are rules to protect us from being exposed, but none that explicitly say 'don't fuck the humans,' so I think I'm safe."

I press my lips together against a smile. "Does Tristan know about you and him?"

"He does."

I nod as I close my laptop and start gathering my things. "Where are we going?" I ask, then mutter, "I can't believe I'm doing this," under my breath.

Max rolls his eyes. "Relax, blondie. We're just going to a bar." He walks out of the boardroom, and I stare at the empty doorway.

---

Sitting around a bar table with Max and Skylar isn't something I thought I'd ever be doing, yet here I am, sipping a virgin margarita. With Skylar and I working on gala stuff in the morning, I figured I'd better play it safe. She and Max don't follow suit.

The music is loud, but not enough that we can't hear each other speak. Not that any of us say much. The large room is lit with dim track lighting and spotlights from the stage at the front.

Skylar glances at her nails and frowns. "This is boring."

Max takes a swig of his beer and shoots her a quick grin. "You're just cranky. Finish your drink, and you'll feel better."

She glares at him, but doesn't disagree.

Oliver chooses that moment to arrive, which puts Max in a better mood. The way his entire face changes when

Oliver gets here is incredible. I've never seen it before. It's nice. It makes him seem more human.

"Ready?" Max asks, turning to me.

I arch a brow. "For what?"

Skylar chuckles. "You didn't tell her?"

Oliver throws his arm around my shoulders and gives me a half hug, laughing.

Max shrugs, still looking at me. "It's karaoke night." He tilts his chin in the general direction of the stage. "Hope you can hold a tune."

"Aurora can sing," Oliver assures him.

Glancing between Max and Oliver, I say, "Fine, I'll sing, but you're buying my next drink—and coffee for the next week."

Max lifts a brow at me, then shrugs. "Deal."

I have a feeling he's hoping to watch me embarrass myself. I chew on my bottom lip, take another sip of my drink, and then head for the stage. When the music guy looks at me, I lean away from the mic and ask him to play Zoe Wees's "Control" before clearing my throat. Tapping my hand against my thigh to catch the beat, I start singing when the music comes on. My voice echoes through the room, getting louder as I go into the chorus, and the audience claps along. My eyes shut, and the lyrics flow through me. I grip the mic with both hands and sway to the music.

When I open my eyes, I almost stumble going into the last chorus. My eyes lock with Tristan's, where he stands with Max, Skylar, and Oliver.

*When the hell did he get here?*

The song ends, and the room fills with hooting and hollering. I walk toward the stairs to return to our table, and the thick heel of my ankle boot catches on a cable attached to the stage. Everything happens in a blur. I'm heading toward the floor—I'm going to fall right off the damn stage—but then Tristan's arms are there, catching me. He hauls me up against him with an amused glint in his eyes.

"Shut up," I mutter, hyperaware of his arm wrapped securely around me.

He dips his head, his lips close to my ear, and murmurs, "I think the words you're looking for are 'thank you.'"

"Not likely," I shoot back, an annoyingly breathless quality to my voice.

"You're feisty tonight." His arm tightens around my waist, and parts of me like that *way* too much. I should pull away, but the heartbeat between my legs is begging me to press closer. Tristan guides me to the side of the room, sliding his hand to the small of my back, as another person takes the stage. "I'm surprised you left with Sky and Max." His lips brush the shell of my ear, making my skin tingle, and I have to force my eyes not to flutter shut.

"They kidnapped me," I mumble. "That seems to happen a lot around you guys."

His breath tickles my skin when he chuckles. "That's because we like you," he says in a low voice. "Let me get you out of here."

"I can't. Skylar wants me to work in the morning. We still have a lot to do for the gala."

"You're going to spend time with Skylar on a weekend?" The glint in his eyes makes it look as if he almost doesn't believe me, and I'm not entirely sure how to deal with playful Tristan. Seeing him outside of the office, away from the constant fae issues he's forced to deal with, is nice. Normal. I'm attracted to the mystery of him, but I crave moments like these where I can look at him without seeing a knight of the seelie fae court and just see Tristan.

"I am."

"Stay at the hotel. You'll be closer to the office in the morning." He squeezes my hip, making my breath catch.

"If I say yes..." My voice trails off.

"Say yes," he whispers.

Part of me is nervous, but another part feels I owe it to myself—the constant thoughts of Tristan, the way my body responds to him—to explore what this might be. My cheek grazes his chest as I tilt my head up to meet his gaze. "Okay," I say.

He slips his arm from around my waist and grabs my hand, lacing his fingers through mine as we approach the table.

"You done feeling her up?" Skylar quips.

Tristan smirks at me. "Not nearly."

"I'm going to head out," I cut in. "Tonight was... fun." I give Oliver a quick hug.

"You better be in the office by nine," Skylar grumbles.

I mock salute her. "Yes, ma'am."

"Call me that again, and not even Tristan will be able to save you from my wrath." She says it with a smile, which only adds to the menacing tone.

Max barks out a laugh as Tristan leads me away from the table. By the time we step outside, my heart is like a hummingbird trying to escape the cage in my chest.

"Rory." His nickname for me sounds so smooth rolling off his tongue. "Anxiety is pouring off you right now."

Spinning to face him, I cross my arms over my chest so he can't reach for my hands. "This isn't a good idea." I scan the street to make sure we're alone.

He tilts his head, regarding me with a thoughtful expression. His eyes alone make me want to give in—they see right through me. "I won't do anything you don't want me to do." When I don't respond, he takes a step toward me, dipping his face closer. "You have a fire in you, Aurora. It's something I deeply admire. And while you put yourself in unnecessary danger by sticking your nose into fae business, your perspective is refreshing, to say the least."

My mind races. "I don't think... We can't."

"Why?"

The words fall out before I can clamp my mouth shut. "I don't feel like I'm in control when I'm around you." It's not something I wanted to admit. This moment feels different, as if it's setting us on a new path.

He laughs. "You don't think I feel the same? You challenge my every word. You go against everything I know."

"You don't know enough about me," I say, as if that might have the power to deter him from pursuing me. *You don't want it to*, an annoying similar voice to my own says, and it's true. Being scared to want Tristan doesn't mean I don't. If anything, it deepens the allure.

He offers a knowing look. "Come on. You can do better than that." His dark-eyed look sets my body ablaze. "I can hear your heart," he murmurs.

"Good to know I'm still breathing," I mutter, struggling to ignore the palpitations happening in my chest.

When he chuckles, a wicked shiver runs through me, and my mind goes places I wish I could say it hasn't before.

"There's that fire I enjoy."

I uncross my arms and let them fall to my sides. "Can we not talk about this anymore?"

"Why? Because you know I'm right about what's going on between us?"

I shake my head.

"You're afraid because you can control a lot about your life, but you can't control how you feel."

I want to argue his words, but he's right. *Of course he's fucking right.* "I can't see any way for this to work out well. I don't understand why I feel whatever this is for you, because I know I shouldn't. You and I come from different worlds—literally. You'd think that might deter me, that I might be able to walk away from this because of everything that has happened." My chest rises and falls quickly.

"But you can't," he says.

"Shut up," I snap breathlessly, grabbing his face as unbridled need consumes me. "Just... shut up." My lips collide with his at the same moment his hands drop to my hips and draw me flush against him. Eyes closed, I deepen the kiss, sliding my fingers into his hair and tugging at the ends. He growls, gripping my hips tighter as his mouth devours mine. My lips part in a moan that says *finally*, and his tongue slides in, brushing against mine and flicking across the roof of my mouth. I never want this moment to end; I could live here forever happily. My pulse pounds in my ears and my breasts tingle as a delicious warmth spreads through me, and the world fades away.

"I'm taking you home with me," he says against my lips.

I'm nodding before I can think of offering any other response. *I want him.* I want him so badly my body physically aches for him. I've never felt this way about anyone, and it's as terrifying as it is exhilarating.

Tristan takes my hand, and we walk a few blocks until his car comes into view. He opens the passenger side door for me, and once I slide in and buckle up, he closes the door and walks around the front of the car, getting behind the wheel.

Pulling away from the curb, Tristan peers over at me.

"Are you hungry? We can stop somewhere for dinner, if you'd like."

My stomach is filled with too much excitement and nerves to consider food. "I'm okay."

The soft sound of Two Feet's "I Feel Like I'm Drowning" filters through the car speakers, and I stare out the window as we head downtown. My breath catches in my throat when Tristan's hand wraps around my thigh, warming my bare skin, and I'm immediately grateful I wore a dress this morning. His thumb glides back and forth while his other fingers slide to my inner thigh. I press my lips together, stealing a glance at him, only to find his attention locked on the road. My pulse pounds beneath my skin, and I bite the inside of my cheek as I open my legs a little.

"Aurora—"

"Touch me." The words fall from my lips, and my eyes widen.

"Are you sure?" His voice is deeper, smooth like warm caramel.

"If you don't, I will." *Where the hell did that come from?* As if I'm actually going to touch myself in front of him.

"Will you?" he taunts, his eyes flicking toward me for a moment before returning to the road. The darkness in them makes my chest tighten with anticipation.

I bite the inside of my cheek, the throbbing at my core matching the thundering beat in my chest. "I'd rather feel you inside me."

His grip on my thigh tightens as he curses under his breath. He pulls his hand back a little before sliding it under my dress, bunching it up at my hips. I suck in a soft breath as his fingers skim the edge of my panties.

"Is this okay?" he checks.

*Fuck yes, don't you dare stop touching me ever.*
"Yeah," I breathe.
Tristan moves his fingers over the thin fabric, skimming them along my folds. I exhale a soft sigh, closing my eyes and giving myself over to the sensations he's wringing from my body. And when his thumb finds my clit, a strangled whimper escapes my throat before I can clamp my mouth shut. Heat flares in my cheeks, and I turn my face toward the window.
"Hey." Tristan's voice is gentle, low. "Don't look away."
I chew my bottom lip, forcing my eyes to find his as we idle at a red light.
He flashes me a brilliant smile. "That's better." His fingers start moving again as his gaze holds mine, and I nearly buck my hips off the seat when he pushes my panties aside and slips a single finger past my folds. I tense at the sudden intrusion—it's been... a while since anyone has touched me, and even then, it wasn't like this. Intense, all-consuming pleasure floods through me, and I grip the seat on either side of me until my knuckles go white. A muscle feathers along his jaw and his eyes darken as he sinks his finger in to the knuckle, massaging my inner walls. My breathing shallows as he pulls back slowly, then pushes in even deeper, curling his finger and hitting a spot that sends sparks of pure bliss through me.
The windshield glimmers green, and I realize with a start that the light has changed. Tristan hasn't taken his foot off the brake—or his eyes off me, though. His fingers continue their steady thrusts as my heart attempts to break free from my rib cage.
"Tristan," I say in a breathy voice, "the light."
"I'm aware," he replies, the corner of his mouth kicking

up as his eyes shine with determination. "We're not moving until you make that delicious noise again."

My eyes pop wide, and I quickly check the side mirror, exhaling a heavy breath when I realize there's no one behind us. That sense of relief is quickly replaced with arousal when Tristan adds a second finger, scissoring them inside me, and strums my clit like the delicate strings of a violin. Heat pools low in my belly as my core throbs and I clench around Tristan's wicked fingers. Everything in me tightens, and I reach desperately for him, grabbing the front of his shirt and tugging him toward me as our lips crash together. His fingers speed up, and my release slams into me. I moan against his lips, riding the waves of pleasure without holding back.

The sound of a horn blaring from behind rips us apart, and I fall back against my seat, breathing hard, with a grin on my lips.

It's silent between us from the time we get out of the car until we reach the penthouse. I glance around the place; the modern elegance of it catches me off guard every time.

Tristan steps into my line of sight with dark eyes and a wicked curve on his lips. "What are you thinking about?"

I press my lips together, trying to form an answer. "A lot."

"Can I help with that?" he purrs, slipping his arms around me, pulling me toward him.

A smile curls my lips, and I lean into him, sliding my arms around his neck. "This is weird," I admit.

"What's that? Me touching you?"

I laugh. "Me *letting* you touch me."

"And enjoying the hell out of it," he adds with a smirk, his eyes locked on mine. "Do you trust me?"

I swallow, trying to ease the dryness in my throat. "Yes," I answer. Had he asked me that a month ago, I would've laughed in his face, but now? Things are different between us—and I'm not just talking about the amazing orgasm he gave me on the way here.

"Good," he says, and then his lips are on my skin, trailing up my neck. Kissing. Licking. Sucking.

I hold on to him, sighing softly, which encourages him. He kisses my jaw, my temple, and the corner of my mouth before his lips slant over mine. I gasp into his mouth when his lower half presses against me, my mind swimming in a pleasant haze. My eyes close and my hips press into him, making him groan against my lips.

I jump when his phone goes off in his pocket, and we break apart. He pulls it out with a growl and swears. "I have to take this," he says. He swipes at the screen and barks, "What is it?" into the phone.

There are several beats of silence, and then: "I'll be right there." He shoves the phone back in his pocket, and when he turns back to me, his gaze is distant. "I'm needed downstairs."

My stomach drops, and I ask, "What's going on?"

He thrusts a hand through his hair, his jaw working. "A group of unseelie fae attacked Skylar after Max left with Oliver."

My eyes widen. Jules is attacking fae who mean something to Tristan, striking closer to home. "I'm so sorry, Tristan. Is she...?"

"She's alive," he says, his posture stiff. "Stay here. I'll be back as soon as I can."

I stop him before he can turn away. "Be careful," I say in a firm voice and lean up to kiss him.

He returns the kiss chastely and then he's gone.

## CHAPTER SEVENTEEN

A week later, Skylar has almost fully recovered from the attack, which, considering she almost died, is incredible. I don't know all the details, just that she was ambushed and wrapped in iron chains that burned her skin and drained her energy until a group of seelies came across them and stepped in, saving her life.

Despite our rocky start, I'm glad she's okay. That being said, the unseelie fae attacking Skylar only worries me more about Allison. She's adamant about trusting Evan, but I can't help the knot in my stomach every time I think about what happened to Skylar happening to her. But I can't think about that, not today.

Westbrook Inc.'s annual charity gala is here, and I can't remember a time when I've worked this hard on something. Which is probably why I feel as though I'm going to vomit the minute I wake up.

Tristan wanted me to stay over last night, but I declined; I needed to keep a clear head for today.

I haven't slept at the hotel since that night after the

bar. I'm not sure Tristan slept at all with the uproar over the attack on Skylar. He and Max stayed with her while she healed. Meanwhile, I curled up on the couch in Tristan's living room in front of the fireplace.

My dorm room is a far cry from Tristan's penthouse, but a sense of relief fills my chest when I peek over and see Allison asleep. When she's here, that means she isn't sleeping at Evan's. It's not that I don't want my best friend to be happy—that's *all* I want, but I can't stand knowing she could get hurt, or be punished by the king for disobeying seelie law. Tristan hasn't turned her over to the court, and I haven't brought it up. Because if he's doing this for me, going against his king... I can't think about what it means.

I toss back my comforter and stare at the ceiling before getting out of bed and tiptoeing into the bathroom to take a shower. Afterwards, I towel dry my hair and change into a sweater and leggings. I don't plan on putting on my dress until the last moment; I still have work to do at the hotel before the gala, all of which has been on me since Skylar has been out of commission.

My phone is buzzing on my dresser when I walk out of the bathroom. I snatch it up before the sound wakes Allison and swipe blindly at the screen to answer it.

"Hello?" I whisper.

"I wasn't sure you'd be awake yet," Tristan says. "I wanted to check in before you got sucked into the chaos of today."

My pulse kicks up at the deep sound of his voice, and I slip into the hallway, closing the door behind me. "What are you talking about? I'm fine."

"You're deflecting, which is all right. I understand you're nervous. You've put significant work into this event and you're taking it as seriously as I do every year. I am very grateful for that."

I stumble on my words before getting out, "I'm happy to help."

"I know," he says softly. "Would you like to join me for breakfast at the office?"

I catch my lower lip between my teeth and lean against the wall, trying not to smile. "I don't know, Tristan."

"We can order room service. The kitchen makes excellent French toast."

Talking to this Tristan throws me off. It's different from having a conversation with the intense, strong-willed fae knight, always focused on protecting his people. Times like these, I can pretend that he's just a guy asking me to breakfast. Which makes it difficult to say no.

I sigh, a grin touching my lips. "Okay, fine."

Tristan chuckles. "I'll see you soon."

Sneaking back into my room, I throw everything I'll need for tonight into a suitcase and head out.

I arrive at the Westbrook Hotel half an hour later and scan my ID card to get in the back door. Skylar hooked me up with it a couple of weeks ago so I wouldn't have to come in through the lobby.

I fidget with my phone on the ride to the office and step off the elevator to find Max sitting at the desk.

"You're here early, blondie," he says.

"Couldn't sleep."

Max nods. "I think Tristan's in his office."

"Great," I say. "What are *you* doing here this early?"

"I spent the night at Oliver's and didn't feel like going to my place when I knew I'd have to come here later on, anyway."

I arch a brow. "You stayed at the dorm? Things seem to

be getting pretty serious with you guys. I mean, you haven't known each other that long."

His eyes narrow a fraction. "Say what you're thinking, Aurora."

I shrug. "I'm concerned, that's all. Oliver is one of my closest friends. I'm just looking out for him."

He leans back in the chair, keeping his eyes on me. "Do you think I'm going to hurt him?"

I shake my head, recalling how he looked at Oliver the entire time we were at the bar. "I hope you won't, but there are so many things he doesn't know about this world that could hurt him."

"We've barely hung out, so you can chill," he says with an edge to his voice.

"All right, I'm not trying to piss you off, Max, but you can't blame me for showing concern for my friend."

He rolls his eyes. "Whatever." He turns back to his computer, and I don't exist anymore.

I shake off the bad mood talking to Max causes and walk down the hall to Tristan's office. I knock and let myself in. "Tristan?" I call out, glancing around.

"He's still upstairs," Skylar says as she walks in from the connecting conference room. It's the first time I've seen her since the attack, and she looks better than I was expecting, though her typically sharp makeup is missing and her hair is tied back instead of styled. She's also not wearing heels, which is a first in the time I've known her.

"Oh, hey. I'm, uh, glad you're okay."

She nods, her lips almost forming a smile. "Thanks. Tristan is waiting for you."

I nod and walk back to the elevator and ride up to the penthouse.

"I thought we said breakfast at the office, Tristan. I told

you, I don't think—" My voice stops working when my eyes land on Tristan in the kitchen with nothing but a towel tied dangerously low on his hips. My mouth goes dry, and I have to swallow several times before I can speak again. "What... are you doing?"

He grins slowly as I stare at him. "Making breakfast. Turns out I make better French toast than the hotel kitchen staff."

"I don't know what to say." The thought of having a meal with Tristan in his home seems too normal, so why the hell am I so nervous? *Because you want this like you've never wanted anything before,* a voice at the back of my head offers, and it's not wrong.

He chuckles. "I'm going to put some clothes on so you can focus instead of staring at me, and then we'll have a nice breakfast before you get swept into gala prep."

My eyes snap back to his, and I gape at him.

He smirks before walking away, and damn it if I don't stare until he's out of sight.

Once Tristan returns wearing a black T-shirt and dark jeans, I sit at the counter on one of the barstools and watch him slice an apple. The whole scene is way too domestic, and it makes my chest ache with a longing I wasn't expecting. *I want this*—normal mornings with sweet, delicious breakfasts and coffee from Tristan's ridiculously fancy espresso machine.

Tristan pauses, exhaling slowly as he peers over at me. "Your emotions are loud this morning. Anything you want to talk about?"

My eyes pop wide, and I look away, heat crawling up my neck and making my scalp tingle. *Shit.* How much did he feel? *What* did he feel? "Everything is set for tonight," I say, hoping he'll buy the swirl of emotions battling in my chest are associated with the event.

He shakes his head. "No work talk before breakfast."

"What do you want to talk about, then?" My pulse is still ticking too fast.

"Tell me about school." He drops the apple slices onto a plate with strawberries and blueberries before he whisks together eggs and milk for the French toast.

I grab a strawberry and bite into it. "I've been working on my resume and portfolio since the beginning of the semester so I can apply for positions right after graduation. My parents loaned me money interest-free so I could get my degree, and I'd like to pay them back quickly. There are several local companies I have in mind to apply to, and a few out of town as well."

"Have you considered mine?"

I pause. "I didn't know there was a position open."

His lips twitch. "There isn't."

My brows inch closer before I shake my head. "I'm not going to work for you, Tristan."

He dips one slice of bread into the egg before laying it in a frying pan, then does the same with another. "I figured you'd say that."

"Good, then you won't bring it up again."

His deep chuckle is the only response I'm granted.

"Do you have powdered sugar?"

"Top shelf in the cupboard behind you." He nods toward the row of storage behind me, so I hop off the stool and open the cupboard. I reach up on my tiptoes and can almost grab it. I jump a little and still can't manage. A faint laugh sounds behind me before an arm extends past mine and pulls it down, setting it on the counter in front of me.

"There you go," Tristan murmurs, his lips brushing my ear.

"Thanks," I mumble.

"Turn around," he instructs in a deep voice. I don't feel the mental pull I imagine would come with his mind manipulation if it worked on me, but hell if I don't want to do what he says anyway.

"If I turn around, you're going to kiss me." I can't stop my eyes from fluttering shut as his hands come to rest on my hips.

"Am I?" The amusement is clear in his voice.

"Tell me I'm wrong."

"Hmm..." His voice trails off to a light hum as his lips press under my ear. "I can't do that."

"We should eat," I say.

He inhales. "I couldn't agree more." He nips my earlobe, and I gasp.

"That's not what I meant." I press my lips together, trying to ignore the pleasant warmth pooling in my stomach and between my thighs. My pulse thrums throughout my entire body; he must feel his effect on me.

His hands fall away from my hips a moment before he slides an arm around my waist and guides me back against his chest. My cheeks flush when I feel him against me.

I hold my breath. "Tristan."

He spins me around, keeping a small distance between us. "You affect me too, Rory."

I swallow, forcing a nod.

"And you were right," he murmurs, dipping his face closer.

"Huh?" My voice is strained, my senses overwhelmed by him, his arms on either side of me, his cologne tickling my nose, his closeness warming my skin.

He smirks. "I am going to kiss you." He presses his lips against the corner of my mouth, and I turn my face enough that our lips meet full-on when he kisses me again. His hands slide from the counter to my hips, where his fingers dig into my leggings as if he's fighting the urge to rip them off of me. *I wish he would.*

I drape my arms over his shoulders and lean into him, deepening the kiss and sliding my tongue along his lower lip. He lifts me onto the counter with ease, and I wrap my legs around his waist, pulling him as close as the counter will allow. I gasp when he nips my bottom lip, but his mouth swallows the sound.

After several minutes of the two of us battling for control, he leans back and peppers kisses along my jaw before stepping away. He walks to the other side of the counter and plates the food. "Hungry?"

*You have no fucking idea.*

I'm still catching my breath, so I nod, my lips pressed together. Sliding off the counter, I take a seat on one of the bar stools and take a sip of orange juice, which, based on the remnants of oranges on the counter next to the sink, is freshly squeezed.

Tristan sets a plate in front of me, dipping his face to kiss my cheek.

I find my voice and murmur, "Thank you."

"My pleasure." He takes the stool next to me and pours syrup over his French toast before sliding the glass container my way. I drench my toast in syrup, then sprinkle it with powdered sugar. The weight of Tristan's gaze makes my stomach swirl with nerves, and I shove a chunk of French toast in my mouth. I groan at the amazing combination of salty and sweet, closing my eyes to enjoy it as deeply as possible. I take my time chewing, then swallowing, before I open my eyes and find Tristan staring at me, his pupils blown and his jaw set tight. Heat flashes through me, and I bite my lip as I squeeze my thighs together against the ache blossoming between them.

Tristan leans in, snagging my chin and freeing my lip with his thumb, brushing it back and forth across before pulling back. Everything in me tightens when he lifts the digit to his mouth and sucks it clean.

I suck in a shallow breath, snared in his gaze. "This... is the best French toast I've ever tasted."

His gaze darkens, dropping to my mouth, and my heart leaps. That brief look is my only warning before he sweeps in and steals my lips with his, tasting them, devouring me whole. "If I'm honest," he murmurs against my lips with a soft chuckle, "I want to lay you on this counter, spread your thighs, and taste *you*."

My breath hitches as I grab the front of his shirt, holding him as close as I can without pulling him off the stool. "Why don't you?"

He kisses along my jaw, licking and nipping the skin and leaving a trail of tingles in his wake. "Because we have limited time, and once I start with you, Aurora, I won't be interrupted." The dark promise in his words knocks the air out of my lungs, and his shirt wrinkles in my grip. "Have I rendered you speechless? I suppose there is a first time for everything." His tone is mirthful; my responding scowl is half-hearted at best.

# CHAPTER
# EIGHTEEN

I spend that afternoon prepping the ballroom. Skylar and Max help here and there, but mostly, it's up to me and a team of the hotel staff, most of which are human.

Once everything is ready and I've spoken to the bartender, caterer, and musician, I step away to get ready. There isn't much time before guests arrive, so I head up to the penthouse to finish my hair, do my makeup, and put on my dress.

I'm surprised when Skylar comes in and grabs the curling iron while I'm trying to rush through doing my makeup. She goes to work on my hair, pinning part of it up and curling it into loose waves before braiding a portion of it, which gives me time to touch up my face. In true Skylar fashion, she disappears before I can thank her.

I pace around one of the guest rooms in Tristan's penthouse until there's nothing left for me to do but put on my dress. I stare at where it hangs on the closet door. It's a floor-length, sleeveless, rose gold gown that glimmers with every movement. It has a V-shaped neckline, and it is the most gorgeous dress I've ever seen. That I'm wearing it for a work event was my justification for the steep expense, but when Tristan insisted the company reimburse me, I didn't argue. I step into it, pulling the material until it falls into place, and slip on my heels. My breath catches when there's a soft knock at the door. "Come in."

I watch the door open from the mirror in front of me as Tristan steps in and closes it behind him. The world slows. There's nothing but the two of us, and we can't stop looking at each other. I've seen Tristan in formal wear at the office for meetings, but I've never seen him like this. His face is freshly shaved and hair is slicked back, none of the usual unruly pieces sticking out. It looks darker than normal. It suits him. He's wearing a black tux with a bow tie, making me smile at the thought of watching him standing at a mirror tying it.

He walks over to where I'm standing and stops behind me. A look of genuine admiration shines on his face as he stares at me in the mirror.

"You are stunning," he says in a low voice, as if dozens of people fill the room, and his voice is meant for my ears only.

I meet his gaze in the mirror and smile. "Thank you."

He leans in and kisses my cheek. "You've worked hard on this event, so I know you want it to be nothing short of perfect, but try to enjoy yourself."

"It *will* be perfect," I assure him.

He chuckles. "Of course it will."

"I'll have a good time. You don't need to worry about me, Tris."

He tilts his head. "What did you call me?" he asks in a light tone.

"Sorry," I mumble.

"No. I liked it," he admits, making my belly swirl with warmth. His eyes travel the length of me, taking in every curve the material is hugging.

"I just put this on, and you're looking at me as if you're about to tear it off." The idea isn't one I'm completely opposed to, but the dress *was* expensive, and I need it for tonight.

He licks his lips, making heat rush to my cheeks and much lower. "It's a gorgeous dress, but what's underneath interests me much more."

I swallow, my pulse kicking up as he slides his hand into mine and guides me to face him. I grip the lapel of his jacket with my free hand as my heart pounds in my ears.

He dips his face closer until our noses brush before resting his forehead against mine. "You have no idea how badly I want you."

I suck in a breath, but before I can get a word in, his lips seal over mine, and whatever I was going to say is lost in the feel of his mouth. I slide my hand up his chest and grip the back of his neck, tugging him closer as I flick my tongue across his lower lip.

A soft growl rumbles in his throat, and he nips my lip before his tongue darts out to meet mine. His hands grip my waist, rubbing slow circles against the fabric of my dress that I'm suddenly wishing didn't exist.

"How much time do we have?" I ask, kissing the corner of his mouth.

"Not enough," he murmurs against my lips. He leans away and brushes my hair back into place before adjusting his suit jacket. He offers me his arm. "Guests will arrive any minute. We'll have to pick this up later."

I press my lips together so I don't suggest something stupid like missing the beginning of the event. *No,* I silently scold myself. I'm going to be a responsible adult and ignore the delicious throbbing between my thighs.

Placing my hand on his arm, we walk to the elevator. Once we're on, I stand against the wall opposite him. I need a clear head going into tonight, and whenever I'm too close to Tristan, it can prove difficult to think straight—or think about anything other than his hands on me.

Tristan says nothing, but the smirk on his lips is telling enough.

I roll my eyes and keep my gaze trained on the wall for the rest of the descent.

Skylar and Max, along with several other Westbrook Hotel employees, are already downstairs when Tristan and I arrive. We walk into the room, and eyes instantly find us. Squaring my shoulders, I stand straight, refusing to look as nervous as I am. Even with most of the fae working for Tristan treating me somewhat better than when I started at the hotel over two months ago, I can't seem to shake my nerves surrounding the event. But I'll be damned if I let that show.

"That's my girl," Tristan murmurs from beside me.

*My girl.*

My chest swells. I like that statement *way* too much.

Skylar and I stand at the entrance to the ballroom and greet guests as they come in, while Tristan mingles with everyone inside. Tonight is all about getting donations from the high-class attendees. Westbrook Inc. chooses a new charity each year, and this year, the money is going to a queer support group for adolescents that Tristan hand-picked from hundreds of applications. Most of the attendees of this event are successful businesspeople and friends of Tristan's, meaning they are fortunate enough to be able to give.

I shake hands with an endless line of attendees, and by the end, my mouth aches from smiling so much. It's amazing. Potential donors fill the room, and while my job is far from over, this is a decent start.

I spend most of the event chatting with some of the most successful entrepreneurs in the city. It's a dream come true for any business major, and I'm taking full advantage of the networking opportunity. Graduation is always on my mind, especially as it inches closer.

Tristan makes a speech, discussing the organization set to receive this year's charity, and wraps up by thanking guests for coming and donating generously.

I find him after he exits the stage and hand him a glass of champagne. "Nice speech," I say.

He clinks his glass against mine before taking a sip.

I follow suit, giving him a curious look when he takes my champagne flute and sets it beside his on a banquet table.

"Dance with me."

I freeze, my eyes widening. Dance... with Tristan... My heart rate kicks up, heat flushing my cheeks. My fingers are suddenly itching for that glass of champagne.

Tristan steps forward, catching my chin in a gentle grip. "You look more scared right now than the moment we met." There's a hint of amusement in his voice that makes me exhale a sigh and lift my hand to his shoulder as Ruelle's "The Other Side" starts playing. He drops his hand from my chin, resting it on my hip, and I place my other hand on his extended one.

We move in time with the music, and I use this opportunity to glance around the room. Everyone seems to be enjoying themselves; I can't help but beam with pride.

"I can feel that," Tristan says, offering me a faint smile.

I lift my eyes to his. "Good."

We dance until the song ends, and he pulls me against him. "Tonight is amazing. The donations are pouring in. Congratulations on a successful event, Rory." He smiles at me. "I have to speak to some people, but I'll find you later."

I squeeze his hand before letting go. "I'll be around here somewhere."

He tweaks my chin, and his smirk sends my heart racing as he leaves me standing off to the side of the room, surveying my success.

My chest feels light as I watch guests dance around me. I couldn't picture how this event would turn out—nothing would measure up to how wonderful this is.

As I'm grabbing another drink from the bar, I catch Skylar waving me over from behind the donation table. I'm heading toward her when one of the hotel employees taps my shoulder and leans close to my ear. "Your phone keeps going off."

I forgot I'd left it on a table. "I'm a little busy right now," I say, not wanting to keep Skylar waiting.

"It appears to be your mother."

I huff out a breath and take the phone from her, my drink in my other hand. "Thank you," I say, trying to be polite.

I exit the room and walk into the lobby as my phone buzzes again. "Mom, what's going on? Is everything all right?"

"Aurora." Her tone makes my heart stop. "I'm sorry to call you. I know tonight is your big event, but—" Her voice breaks.

"Mom?"

"We need you to come home."

"What happened?" The room feels too warm, too small as it closes in on me, so I retreat outside. The cool night air touches my skin, but little relief follows.

"Your brother is in the hospital," my mom says, and her voice breaks at the end. She sniffles as if she's fighting back tears, and my stomach plummets.

"He what?" I choke. "Why? What happened?"

She takes a deep breath. "We... The doctors aren't sure yet. He, um—" Her voice cuts off, and she sniffles. "He collapsed at his soccer game an hour ago and... hasn't woken up." Mom chokes on a sob, and everything around me slows to a stop.

The glass slips out of my hand and shatters against the marble step. I squeeze my eyes shut. When I open them, my vision is blurry.

"Your father and I are here with him."

I cover my eyes with my free hand. "I'm coming home."

"Your father can come get you," she says in a hoarse voice.

"No." I wipe my cheeks, but it's pointless; more tears spring into my eyes and fall. "I'll take the train or something." A lump forms in my throat, making it hard to speak. "I'll be there as soon as I can." I end the call and stand frozen in place, staring straight ahead as a silent sob wracks my body. Too many things are rushing through my head. My parents must be terrified. I give up trying to fight back tears and cry until my eyes hurt and there's nothing left. My stomach coils up tight, and I think I'm going to throw up all over the steps of the Westbrook Hotel.

This doesn't make any sense. No healthy kid collapses randomly and ends up unconscious in a hospital. Which means... *No. I can't go there.*

I walk back into the hotel where the gala is in full swing. I stop at the coat check to grab my clutch and ask an employee to tell Tristan I had to leave.

Hurrying out of the lobby to the front of the hotel, I pull out my phone to get an Uber, and then I'm spinning around at the hands of Tristan.

"Where are you going?" he asks.

Turning my face away, my hair falls forward. "I have to leave." I try to keep my tone casual, but my voice cracks.

He grasps my chin and turns my face to look at him. "Are you crying?" His forehead creases. "I saw you leave. What happened between then and now?"

I shake my head. "Tristan, please," I beg, and dammit, the tears are back. I blink, and they fall, dripping onto his hand.

He lets go of me. "Tell me what's going on, Rory," he says in a gentle voice.

I swallow the lump in my throat. "Elijah... my brother is in the hospital, and no one knows what's wrong with him."

Tristan's brows tug together. "What do you need?"

"I need to go home."

He doesn't miss a beat. "I'll take you."

I don't have the strength to protest—I wipe my cheeks dry and nod.

Ten minutes later, we're speeding toward the hospital in silence. We arrive after midnight, and Tristan doesn't hesitate to use his manipulation to get us past security, then stays in the lobby while I ride up to the pediatric floor. The hallway is dark, the only light coming from the nurses' stations spread out over the floor. The walls are a dull beige, punctuated by boxes of masks and gloves, sanitizer pumps, and shelves of gowns, while the smell of antiseptic burns my nose.

As I reach Elijah's room, tears roll down my cheeks. I walk closer to where he's asleep on the small bed. He's hooked up to a bunch of different machines. His face is pale even against the soft beige blanket that covers him. His hair is a mess, and even though his eyes are closed, the underneath is dark, making his face appear hollow.

I pull a chair over to his bed and sit. I reach for his hand and hold it in both of mine, listening to the sound of his breathing.

A nurse walks in and pauses when she sees me. "Visiting hours are over. You shouldn't be—"

"He's my brother," I force out, my voice wavering.

"Oh." Her demeanor shifts and her expression softens. "Your parents went home about twenty minutes ago."

I lift my head enough to look at her, my eyes stinging from crying for so long. "Thanks," I whisper as a few more tears slip free.

The nurse checks the machines and glances over Elijah's chart before she leaves the room.

I sweep the hair out of Elijah's face and press my lips to his temple.

"Aurora?" a soft voice calls.

I turn to see Tristan leaning in the doorway. "Sorry to keep you waiting." I dry my cheeks and stand, pushing the chair back against the wall.

"Nothing to apologize for, Rory. I can take you home,"

he offers, and when I nod, he places his hand at the small of my back to guide me out of the room.

Back in the car, I give him directions and stare out my window. I jump when Tristan's hand touches mine. I don't pull away when he slips his fingers through mine.

## CHAPTER NINETEEN

We pull up out front, and Tristan insists on walking me to the door. I texted my mom on our way over, so she's already waiting for us. It's a struggle to get out with my gala dress, but Tristan helps. He keeps his hand at the small of my back as we approach the front of the house.

My mom glances between the two of us before settling on me as her eyes well. "Aurora, I'm so glad you're here." Her complexion is splotchy and pink, which makes the dark circles under her eyes look worse. Her hair is frizzy and tied back in a messy top knot.

I wrap my arms around her in a tight embrace, my eyes burning from hours of crying and the fresh tears forming now. "I wouldn't be anywhere else."

She pulls away and looks at Tristan. "Who's this?"

"Tristan Westbrook," he says. "I'm sorry to have to meet you under these circumstances, Mrs. Marshall."

Mom nods. "Please, come in." She ushers us into our small but cozy living room off of the main entryway.

My dad is throwing more wood into the fireplace when we walk in. I give him a hug, and he shakes Tristan's hand before we sit. Tristan and I are on the couch, and Mom and Dad take the chairs across from us.

"That dress is beautiful, Aurora," Mom says in a hoarse voice.

I try to smile. "Thank you."

"We appreciate you bringing her home, Tristan," Dad says, Mom nodding in agreement.

"Of course." Tristan glances at me. "I should leave you with your family," he says in a hushed tone.

I bite the inside of my cheek. "Please stay." His presence makes me feel stronger, almost as if I have an anchor to keep me grounded, to keep my mind from racing in too many directions. I don't have the strength to hide the emotions that are tied to feeling that way. In this instance, I don't mind Tristan seeing them.

There's hesitation in his eyes before he says, "Okay."

"We'll head back to the hospital in the morning. Elijah's doctor said he was stable and suggested we get some rest tonight. They are going to run more tests tomorrow."

Letting out a slow breath, I nod. "I'm going to change." Tristan follows suit when I rise from the couch.

My parents stand, their hands reaching for each other's, while Dad shoots Tristan a wary look. "Aurora, see if you can find something of mine for Tristan to change into. I'm sure he'll be comfortable staying in the guest room tonight."

"That's appreciated but unnecessary, sir," Tristan says.

Mom and Dad don't push the offer on him. Instead, they walk out of the living room, leaving us alone.

"Thank you for bringing me home," I say, looking at the carpet under my heels.

He cups my cheek and lifts my face so our gazes meet. "I'm glad I can be here for you." His thumb brushes across my skin, and my pulse quickens in response.

"I..." My eyes dart between his, wanting nothing more than to get lost in their calm, deep blue depths. "Will you stay?"

His expression softens. "If that's what you want."

"Unless you need to go back. I know tonight was important."

He smiles. "I'm confident Max and Skylar took care of it."

I nod, leaving Tristan in the living room to say goodnight to my parents, who are drinking tea at the breakfast bar in the kitchen.

"Is there something going on between the two of you?" Dad asks.

"Now's not really the time to talk about that." Not with Elijah in the hospital—or with Tristan in the other room, where his fae hearing can most definitely pick up our conversation.

"It's clear he cares for you," Mom says.

The heat rises in my cheeks, and I shrug, because how the hell am I supposed to respond to that?

"How do *you* feel?" Mom asks.

*What a loaded question.* How desperately I wish I could confide in my mom about the feelings I shouldn't have for Tristan, to give her the distraction from this awful day, but the timing... I can't.

"I feel like I don't want to talk about this right now."

She frowns. "Okay. We'll see you in the morning, honey."

I hug them both before returning to the living room. Tristan looks over at me but mentions nothing about what was said in the kitchen, though I know he heard every word.

Upstairs, we pass Elijah's room, and I pause. My hand is opening the door before I can stop myself.

Tristan steps inside with me and stays silent.

I look around the room, taking in all his old video game posters. Clothes cover most of the floor, and his bed is unmade. All the kid wanted was to sleep until noon on the weekends and play video games. Now he's stuck in a hospital bed, hooked up to machines, with doctors trying to figure out why he won't wake up.

I blow out a breath, my chest heavy and my eyes watering again. "This isn't fair," I whisper.

"I know," Tristan murmurs, sliding his hand into mine and squeezing gently. After another few minutes, he guides me out of the room and down the hall until I stop at my closed bedroom door.

"You can't laugh," I say in a tired voice.

He peers at me. "Why would I laugh?"

"Just promise you won't."

He brushes the back of his hand across my cheek. "I promise."

I nod and open the door before stepping inside. Everything is a different shade of purple. The bedding, the curtains, my desk—everything. "I haven't lived here for, like, three and a half years," I say as though it's an explanation.

He presses his lips together against a smile. "Sure," he says. "It's... nice."

"It's overwhelmingly purple," I mumble. "It's terrible."

Tristan shrugs off his suit jacket, draping it over the

chair at my desk, and slowly unbuttons his white-collared dress shirt. "It's charming."

I sigh, guilt trickling in. I don't really care about my room right now. Not when Elijah is stuck sleeping on a hospital bed instead of his own. "I'll grab you something to wear." I slip out of the room and find a pair of sweatpants and one of Dad's old T-shirts.

When I return to my room and close the door, I find Tristan sitting shirtless on the end of my bed. It takes me a minute to find my voice; my head is in too many places right now. "I'm pretty sure these will fit." I toss the shirt and pants at him and turn away, walking to my dresser, and grab an old hoodie and leggings. Turning back to Tristan, I take a few steps closer and wet my lips. "Can you unzip me?" I whisper.

He closes the distance between us, coming behind me, and rests one hand against my hip while the other glides up my back. He fingers the zipper, dragging it down, the heat of his chest warming my back.

"Thank you," I force out, my heart kicking in my chest.

He leans in and kisses the side of my head before his hand drops from my hip, and I slip into the bathroom across the hall to change. My reflection in the mirror makes me pause. I cringe at the smudged eyeliner and black tear stains running down my cheeks. My hair is still curled and set around my face, which makes it look odd. I grab a makeup wipe and do my best to get rid of it before flicking off the light on my way out.

Tristan is dressed when I come back and turn on my bedside lamp, flicking off the ceiling light and giving the room a soft golden glow.

"Get some sleep," he says, stepping toward the door.

I pick at the hem of my hoodie. "You don't have to sleep in the guest room."

"I don't want to upset your parents."

"They sleep downstairs. So long as you don't snore obnoxiously or something, they won't have a reason to come up here and check where you're sleeping." I press my lips together. "Stay. Please."

He exhales slowly. "Okay." He watches me crawl into bed, then walks around to the other side and sits on top of the bedding.

"This doesn't feel real," I whisper.

"That's understandable." He reaches over and tucks my hair away from my face.

"My head is spinning so fast. I'm trying to figure this whole thing out, but I know there's no explanation."

He frowns. "You're doing what you can. You're here with your family."

"But I can't help him," I whisper as I lie back and stretch out my legs. "I..." I choke on a sob and turn my face to look at him.

His eyes search mine as he gets under the sheets and lies on his side, and then he wraps his arm around my shoulders and pulls me against him. There's plenty of room for two people in my queen-size bed, but Tristan presses right against me, and I don't want him to move. I can't help but think just how substantially things have changed between us since we met. I trust him, care for him deeply, and definitely enjoy how he challenges me.

I never thought the seelie fae knight would be anything more than a threat to everything I've been working toward, and yet, I can't imagine surviving this without him. He showed up for me like I never could have expected, and in doing so ruined any chance I had at ignoring the way I feel about him any longer. I want to be with Tristan, whatever that means, and whatever it takes to make that work. It terrifies me; I've never wanted anything so badly, but there's a beacon of warmth in my chest that tells me I'm moving in the right direction, even though I have no idea where it leads.

I press my face into the crook of his neck and cling to him. He holds me until the sobbing quiets. I knew the silence would come in time, after crying for so long, but the fear of the unknown still weighs on my chest.

He cups my cheek in his hand and draws my face away so that I'm looking at him. An idea hits me so fast I don't have time to register it before I say, "Can you heal him?"

Tristan's face falls, and he shakes his head. "I'm sorry."

"But you healed me—the day we met after Max hurt me—you healed me."

"You had cuts and bruises and a mild concussion. I can heal superficial injuries or even broken limbs, but we aren't sure what's wrong with your brother yet. I can't fix something I don't know."

My bottom lip trembles. "I thought..." My voice breaks, and more tears spring free, rolling down my cheeks.

Tristan wipes away my tears. "You should get some sleep," he says softly.

"I can't sleep." I try to shift away from him so I can get up. "I should go back to the hospital, so I'm there when he wakes up."

"I don't think you should sit at the hospital all night, especially when we don't know when he's going to wake up." Despite the gentle tone of his voice, the underlying *if he wakes up* chips away at the growing crack in my chest.

"What else am I supposed to do?" I snap, sitting up.

He runs his hand up and down my arm and murmurs, "Let me help you."

"How?" I ask, my voice trembling with a fresh onslaught of tears.

"You trust me?" he checks.

I nod without hesitation.

"Lie back and close your eyes. I'm going to take the energy tied to the emotions that are preventing you from sleeping."

"Okay." My voice doesn't waver; he'll take care of me, and every part of me knows that. I follow his instructions and reach for his hand. "You're not going to leave, are you?"

"I'm not going anywhere." He slides his arm around my waist, pulling me against him, and I hug the arm he has wrapped around me. He leans in and whispers in my ear, soft and lulling, until exhaustion floods in; I don't fight the wave of darkness as it pulls me under.

## CHAPTER
# TWENTY

The following morning, I wake in a tangle of limbs. My pulse kicks up as I become aware my legs are wrapped around one of Tristan's. My arms hug his midsection, and my cheek is pressed against his warm, solid chest. His heart beats against my ear as his chest rises and falls in time with the steady rhythm.

Glancing around while trying to keep my head still, I try to think of a way to get off the bed without waking him. I pull back carefully, freeing one arm, but he's lying on the other. I sneak a glance at his face to make sure his eyes are still closed, then shift to the side so I can slip my legs free. Of course, I lean too far back and lose my balance. I'm heading for the hardwood floor, and I'm going to smack my tailbone hard. The fluffy purple IKEA rug won't cushion my fall, either.

At the last second, Tristan grabs my wrist with inhuman speed, pulling me back onto the bed.

I suck in a sharp breath and cringe when he releases me. "How long have you been awake?"

"Long enough," he murmurs with a slight curve of his lips.

I laugh sheepishly, scooting back against the mountain of pillows at the headboard. "Great." As I look around the room, the events from the past twenty-four hours come back in a painful rush. I rake my fingers through the mess of curls on my head and swing my legs over the side of the bed. "I should get ready and head to the hospital with my parents."

Tristan Westbrook is crawling out of my bed—where he slept beside me last night. When I imagined this moment, it didn't include having to go to a hospital... let alone downstairs to face my parents.

He kisses my cheek on his way past and slips out of the room while I get dressed. Once he returns a few minutes later, I tell him, "You should head back to the city. I'm sure you want to check in at the office and see how the rest of the gala went."

"I'm fine right here."

"I don't know how long I'm going to be here, and you can't hang around for me—I won't ask you to. I haven't forgotten everything you have to deal with. You were here for me last night, and you have no idea how grateful I am for that." I pause. "Come to think of it, you probably do, considering the whole fae emotions radar thing you have."

He chuckles softly, nodding.

"You need to be there for your people now."

He sighs, and his brows knit. There's a long moment of hesitation before he says, "You'll let me know if you need anything?" When I nod, he concedes. "All right."

I walk toward him. "Thank you," I whisper, "for everything."

He leans in and kisses my forehead. "Keep me posted."

"I will," I promise.

We walk downstairs, and Tristan says goodbye to my parents. They stay in the kitchen while I walk him to the door, where he pulls me into his arms. "I'll see you soon," he murmurs, his lips brushing my ear. His fingers splay across my cheek, and he rests his forehead against mine. "Hang in there."

The rush of tears that gathers in my eyes doesn't surprise me at this point. "I'm trying," I force out in a hoarse voice.

His lips press against mine in a whisper of a kiss. It's slow and tender and unlike anything I'd expect from Tristan. He smiles before walking outside and heading for his car. My cheeks are warm when I close the door, and I lean against it for several beats before returning to the kitchen, where Mom and Dad are drinking coffee at the table.

"Tristan didn't want to stay for breakfast?" Mom asks.

"He had to get back to the office," I answer, getting myself some coffee.

"He seems like a decent man," Dad says.

I peer at him over my mug. *Where is he going with this?*

"He also appears to care about you a great deal."

I shrug. "He's... It's complicated."

Mom chuckles, but it sounds nowhere near her normal, carefree laugh. "All the best things are."

I'm not sure that's true, but I keep that to myself. "We should go to the hospital."

"Visitors aren't allowed for another hour," Dad says.

"I want to be there the minute they are. If there's a chance he can hear us, he should know we're there."

"All right," Mom says. "Let me get dressed, and we'll head over."

My hands are shaking by the time we pull into the visitor parking lot at the hospital. The three of us ride to the pediatric floor in silence. Mom's hands are clasped in front of her, while Dad has one arm around her and the other shoved in his pocket.

We walk to Elijah's room and find his doctor—Dr. Richelle Collins, according to the blue embroidered name on her white coat—is standing beside his bed. She looks up when the three of us walk in, offering a smile. Mom, Dad, and I stand in the doorway.

"Good morning," she says in a pleasant voice, turning her attention to me. She appears slightly younger than my parents—mid-thirties, if I had to guess. She has deep brown eyes and isn't wearing makeup, save for some concealer to cover a few blemishes on her chin and cheeks. She hasn't bothered trying to brighten the darkness under her eyes, though most of it is shielded by her glasses. "You must be Elijah's sister." She sticks her hand out, and I notice a brace around her wrist as I reach out to shake her hand. "I'm Richelle Collins."

I glance between her and my parents, then nod. "Aurora."

"Nice to meet you." She pulls her hand back. "Would you mind sitting with Elijah for a few minutes so I can talk to your parents?"

I glance over at Mom and Dad, catching their subtle nods. "Sure," I say. After a brief moment of hesitation, I walk over and sit where the doctor was when we came in.

When I look at him, with his eyes closed and the oxygen mask over his nose and mouth, my throat burns. I want to crawl in beside him, but with all the machines he's connected to, I'm worried I'll disrupt one of them. I settle for taking his hand in mine like I did last night, brushing my thumb back and forth across his knuckles.

The clock on the wall counts the seconds passing with an echoing *tick, tick, tick* as I watch Elijah's face, waiting, begging any higher power that will listen, for him to open his eyes. To move a finger. *Something.*

"Hey, buddy," I say in a low voice, willing the lump in my throat to ease. "I'm not sure what's going on, but I'm here." I squeeze his hand. "We're going to figure this out, and *when* you wake up, we'll play video games and eat pizza until we're sick of it. Just... please—" My voice breaks, and I turn my face away from him as a tear leaks free, rolling down my cheek. I quickly wipe it with the back of my other hand, dragging in a shallow breath as I fight to keep it together.

A couple of minutes later, Mom, Dad, and Dr. Collins walk in. There are fresh tears on Mom's face, but she forces a smile.

"What's going on?"

Mom and Dad exchange a glance, then turn to the doctor, who nods and shifts her attention to me.

"Unfortunately, our tests so far have been inconclusive."

I shake my head. "What does that mean?"

She frowns briefly, looking toward Elijah for a moment. "There's nothing physically wrong with him. For a child his age and with his medical history, Elijah is, on paper, perfectly healthy."

I glance between where Elijah lies, attached to machines, and where my parents stand at the end of his bed. "I don't... How is that possible? Clearly, something is wrong with him." My voice takes on an edge that makes

Mom turn to Dad, teary-eyed, her lower lip trembling as she fights back tears.

Dr. Collins steps toward me, offering a sympathetic smile. "I understand your confusion and concern. We'll run more tests—I won't give up on your brother, Aurora." She reaches for me, wrapping her fingers around my forearm, and gives it a firm squeeze. Lowering her voice, she says, "I'm going to find out why this has happened and do everything I can to make him better."

My eyes snap to hers, and something in them makes me freeze. The unease swirling around my stomach grows more intense, and I press my lips together, nodding slowly.

She steps away and smiles at my parents before leaving the room. I sink back into the chair next to Elijah's bed as I fight back the scream of helplessness caught in my throat.

## CHAPTER
# TWENTY-ONE

We stay with Elijah for over an hour before Dad suggests we head out for some fresh air, and Mom quickly agrees. I don't think either of my parents can handle sitting in a room with their unexplainably unconscious son when there's nothing they can do for him. I badly want to stay with him, but it turns out I'm not stronger than they are. If I continue to sit in that hospital room, I'm going to burst into tears, and that won't help anything.

Mom and Dad are understandably pretty out of it when we get home, so I offer to cook. Knowing how much they love it, I make penne pasta in a rose sauce with a kale salad and garlic bread. We sit around the table, but we're all picking at our plates. I stare at the wall of family photos that decorate the dining room and can't help the tears that threaten to spill from my eyes. Memories from summers road tripping up north to Mom's parents' cabin, the Christmas we spent in Florida at a fancy resort where Dad got food poisoning from a shrimp cocktail, and so many other events, big and small, showcasing our family.

Dad breaks the silence, saying, "Your mom and I understand that you'll need to get back to school soon—"

"I'm not going anywhere until he wakes up," I cut in, trying to keep my tone gentle, and nibble on the slice of garlic bread in my hand. My parents are just as concerned about Elijah as I am. I don't want to make it harder on them.

"Aurora, we don't want your education to suffer because of this, and neither would Elijah. You've accomplished so much, honey, and you're almost there."

The food in my mouth suddenly tastes sour; I have to force myself to swallow it, and the bread tastes like cardboard. "Education isn't *always* the most important thing. Especially when Elijah is sick. I've made my decision." Even as the words leave my mouth, the tightness in my chest expands, clamping down hard and stunting my breath. My degree has been my life for the past three years, but my family takes priority over it. I'll figure it out.

Mom sighs. "Okay."

After the three of us give up picking at our food, Dad slips away to clean the dishes, so I retreat upstairs and stand in the shower far longer than necessary. I'm drying myself off when I notice my phone going off on my bed. I rush over and answer it before it goes to voicemail.

"Hey, Allison," I answer, sitting on the edge of the bed. "I was going to call you today."

"Elijah's in the hospital?" Allison asks, and the concern in her voice brings tears to my eyes once again. "I wish I knew you were going home—I would've gone with you."

"Everything happened so fast. I found out last night

while I was at the gala." I explain how I got home as I pull a comb through my hair.

"Yeah, Tristan told me all of that. Do you want me to come? I can be at your place in a few hours."

"It's okay." I sink onto the end of my bed. "I appreciate you wanting to be here for me, but I'm going to stick around for a while."

"I feel like shit just sitting here while you're there."

I sigh. "All I'm really doing here is sitting—that's all we *can* do. According to the doctor, there's nothing wrong with him."

"How's that even possible?"

I have to swallow past the lump in my throat. "I don't know."

"Do you think... I mean—"

"You think the unseelie court has something to do with it?" The words tumble out of my mouth, twisting my stomach in knots. I can't ignore the possibility of fae involvement when medically he's fine. But what if there's magic involved?

"Fuck, I don't know. After Danielle tried to kill you and Skylar was attacked, I don't think we can rule anything out."

I stand and pace my bedroom; sitting still is only feeding the rage brewing in my chest. "I'll kill whoever did this to him," I say through my teeth as my blood pressure rises, making my cheeks flush.

"Take a deep breath, Ro. I know you're upset, but we can't get ahead of ourselves here." She sighs. "Are you sure you don't want me to come? I know your parents are there, but I want to be there for *you*."

Struggling to blink back a fresh onslaught of tears, I shake my head, sitting back down on my bed. "No, no.

Thank you, but you should stay there. I'll keep you posted, though, I promise."

She exhales an uneven sigh, and emotion is heavy in her voice when she finally says, "Okay." She clears her throat. "Do you need me to talk to your professors? I can let them know what's going on."

The idea of missing lectures makes me queasy, but I say, "Would you mind?"

"Consider it done."

"You're the best." I lie down, resting my hand on my stomach. "I haven't checked in with Tristan. How are things?"

"Okay, I think. I've heard a rumor from a few different seelies that Tristan spoke to the king and was granted permission to propose a meeting with Jules, the unseelie knight for this area."

"That's good. Let me know if anything happens?"

"Sure," she murmurs. "Keep me in the loop with things on your end?"

"I will."

"You know I love you. I'm here for whatever you need. Always. And if you change your mind and want me to come, I'm there."

"I know, and I love you right back."

After we end the call, I take a long breath. Not knowing what's going to happen is killing me. My skin itches and my nerves are jumpy. My mind is racing with so many what-if scenarios, and I can't think straight.

Crawling under my sheets, I try to relax. Tristan's absence is tangible; as I gaze at the empty spot beside me, my chest aches. *That's new.* I roll around to face the other way and close my eyes. Drifting off, I'm grateful for the darkness pulling me away from reality. At least when I'm asleep, nothing is wrong and my brother is okay.

When a scene materializes, it takes me a second to realize I'm dreaming. I blink a few times, focusing on the crackling flames in the fireplace in front of me. I'm in Tristan's bedroom.

I turn to glance around the room. Even asleep, it smells like him, warm, inviting—with the hint of sandalwood and citrus I've come to associate with the fae I can't get out of my head or heart. "You can't invade my dream and leave me here alone," I call out.

Tristan walks into the bedroom through a door that materializes from nowhere. "I know you told me not to do this," he says as he approaches, "but I needed to make sure you were okay." He's dressed casually in a dark gray T-shirt and black slacks, his blond hair messily framing his face and his eyes soft as they take me in.

"I wish you were here," I admit.

"I'm right here, Rory," he murmurs, brushing the hair away from my face and tucking it behind my ear.

"You know what I mean. How are things there?"

He shakes his head. "That's not why I brought you here. We don't need to talk about that."

"I don't want to talk about what I'm dealing with."

"Then we won't," he says. "We can talk about whatever you want, or we don't have to talk at all."

"So, you brought me here to...?"

"Offer you some comfort. I spoke to Allison after she talked to you." My eyes widen at that. They've been talking a lot recently, which feels weird considering how nervous she is of him—and for good reason, though he still hasn't made a move to turn her over to the court that I know of.

The thought of *me* being the reason they're talking makes my stomach swirl with nerves that I'm not entirely sure the reason for. "I know what you're dealing with," he continues, "and I want nothing more than to be there with you. This is the closest thing besides physically being there."

I reach out and take his hand. "You continue to surprise me."

"Is that a good thing?"

"Some days, it really is," I say.

We sit on the loveseat in front of the fireplace with my back against his chest and his arms wrapped around my waist. I count the soft freckles spattered along his arm for a minute, enjoying the warmth radiating from the fire.

"Can I tell you something?" I murmur to break the silence.

"Anything."

I press my lips together, hesitating before I say, "I saw your dream. I mean, I was in it, like you're in mine now. Except you didn't know I was there."

He shifts, peering down at me with his brows knit. "You *what?*"

"I don't know how it happened. It was that first night you did it. You left my dream, and then when I fell asleep later on, I somehow entered yours."

Tristan frowns. "That's unusual."

"Random fae magic?" I offer.

He chuckles, but it holds no amusement this time. "Random fae magic sounds about right."

"It only happened that one time." I don't want him to think I've been snooping through his dreams, especially since he's stayed out of mine. "But what I saw... Your world was in shambles, destroyed beyond repair, and you... you looked so defeated. Even then, when I wasn't your biggest fan, my chest ached for you. The pain in your eyes and the hopelessness in your body language, it gutted me."

Tristan sighs quietly, his arms tightening around me. "I'm sorry you had to see that," he murmurs, and covers my hand with his.

I shake my head, running my finger along the collar of his shirt. "I'm sorry *you* had to see that."

We lie together in silence for a while after that. I didn't know it was possible to fall asleep during a dream, but I find my eyes drifting the longer I stare at the flickering flames in the fireplace, basking in the warmth it's radiating.

"Can I tell you something else?" I mumble, sleep tugging at me. I don't wait for him to respond before I say, "I think... I'm falling for you."

# CHAPTER
# TWENTY-TWO

Waking up alone has never sucked so hard. I miss Tristan more than I know what to do with, and I'm still working through that.

Mom and Dad are still in bed after I've showered and gotten dressed. They weren't asleep before dinner yesterday like I was. I don't wake them; they need the rest. Whereas I need to keep busy, because each time I think about the admission I made to Tristan in my dream last night, the tension in my chest expands. I'm equal parts anxious and desperate to know how he would've responded had the dream not ended as I woke up, but even as my finger hovers over his name on my phone, I can't bring myself to call him. There's a good chance that what I told him wasn't news; reading my emotions from the moment we met provides a certain advantage to knowing how I feel.

Heading into the kitchen, I make a fresh pot of coffee for my parents and leave a note to let them know I've gone to the hospital before I swipe Dad's keys off the counter and head out the door.

After finding a parking spot, I text Allison to let her know where I am. Her response comes in less than a minute.

> Give him a hug for me and keep me posted!

I go back and forth, wanting to text Tristan on the elevator ride to the pediatric floor, but the soft *ding* tells me I'm out of time. I'll call him after I see my brother.

I head to Elijah's room and find the door ajar. The nurses' station is empty, and soft conversation filters through the air from several rooms. I step forward to walk inside and freeze at the sound of his doctor's voice.

"I've run all the same tests, and they have provided the same conclusion." There's a pause, as if she's on the phone with someone who's speaking, and then: "I can't be certain without running further tests, but it appears unseelie. The presence of seelie magic is typically lighter in the bloodstream."

My eyes pop wide and my stomach plummets. I shove the door open, then slam it shut, narrowing my eyes at the doctor. "What the fuck did you just say?"

"I'll call you back," Dr. Collins says into the phone, pulling it away from her ear and slipping it onto her white coat. Her cheeks are tinged pink, and her eyes are wide with a mix of surprise and fear. "Before you—"

"No," I cut her off. "You're going to tell me why you're talking to someone about fae magic while standing over my unconscious brother."

She frowns briefly before nodding. "I'm not sure what you think you heard—"

"I know exactly what I heard, so now you'd better start talking."

Dr. Collin's pales. "You... you know about the fae?"

I nod, crossing my arms over my chest. "Clearly, so do you. Are *you* fae?"

"No." Her tone is sharp, and there's a hint of what sounds like disgust. She glances toward Elijah before turning her attention to me and sliding her hands into her pockets. "As I said yesterday, there is nothing physically wrong with your brother."

"You're saying Elijah not waking up has to do with the fae?" My heart is in my throat as I wait for the doctor to confirm my inkling that the fae somehow did this.

Shock crosses her expression before she schools her features. "How much do you know about them?"

Something tells me to keep my cards very close to my chest. "Enough," I answer vaguely.

She purses her lips for a moment before continuing. "I've been researching the fae for nearly six years, and this—what's happening to Elijah—I've seen it before."

My pulse pounds in my throat as my eyes bounce between Dr. Collins and Elijah. "If you've seen it before, that means you can fix it, right?"

"I'm doing everything I can, I assure you." She steps closer to me, pressing her lips together when my back stiffens. "Does your family know about the fae?" she asks in a lower voice, as if she's concerned about being overheard.

I shake my head, finding it harder and harder to pull in a steady breath. "You said fae magic did this to him? What exactly *is* this?"

She hesitates. "In basic terms, Elijah is in a magically induced coma."

My brows knit, and I blink against the burning in my

eyes. "How... *Why* did this happen?" I'm not asking her specifically, mostly asking aloud in horror, but she responds anyway.

"It's hard to say. How many fae do you know? Any that would want to hurt your family?"

Before I can respond, her phone chimes, and she pulls it out, frowning. "I'm sorry. I have to assist another patient. I'll come back as soon as I'm done." She heads for the door, glancing back at me. "Please don't leave."

The moment the door clicks shut, I hurry over to Elijah's bed, kiss him on the forehead, then get the hell out of there.

I have the phone to my ear before I even reach the elevator. I jam my fist against the button, holding my breath as the doors slide open and the call connects.

"Aurora—"

"How quickly can you get here?" The words tumble out of my mouth as I step into the empty elevator and hit the button for the ground level.

"Talk to me," Tristan says in a calm voice. "What's going on?"

I press my fist against my mouth for a moment, willing the tears to recede. "Elijah..." I finally force out. "He's in a coma because some unseelie fae did something to him."

"I'm on my way. Are you at the hospital?"

"I'm going home," I tell him, getting off the elevator and speed-walking toward the doors that lead to the parking lot. "His doctor," I say once I'm outside, "she knows about the fae."

"What's her name?" His voice is deep, and there are muted sounds around him, as if he's walking somewhere and passing people.

"Richelle Collins."

"I'm not familiar with the name. I'll have Skylar look into her."

"Okay," I say, fumbling with the keys before I finally get the car unlocked and slump against the driver's seat. "Can you do your fae thing and just appear here?" I shove the key into the ignition and start the car before reaching to buckle my seatbelt.

"Distance is tricky. I haven't fed recently, and even then, you're too far. I'll have to drive." Right. I forgot about the proximity limitations of shifting.

Staring out the windshield, my vision blurs with tears. I close my eyes, my heart beating hard in my chest after fleeing the hospital. "Tristan, what do I tell my parents?"

"Nothing yet. The truth won't make any sense to them, and until we know how to fix it, it won't do them any good."

Despite knowing full well that he's right, the pit in my stomach grows. "Right. Okay."

"We'll figure this out, Rory," he says in a voice that makes my chest tighten. "I'll see you soon."

---

After updating—read: lying to—my parents about my visit with Elijah, I sit with them at the dining room table, forcing myself to swallow the breakfast of scrambled eggs and pancakes Dad made. I let them know Tristan is coming back, making up some lame excuse about him wanting to check in and see my hometown, which only makes Mom more inquisitive about our relationship. I narrowly escape that conversation by shoving the last bit of pancake into my mouth and washing it down with a glass of orange juice. I quickly excuse myself, grabbing my dishes and carrying them to the kitchen to load into the dishwasher before disappearing upstairs to take a shower. I've got time to kill until Tristan arrives, and the last thing I want to do right now is field questions from either of my parents about him. Because most days, I feel as if I have no idea what's going on between us. I'm drawn to him, I crave him, want to be near him constantly... and I've never felt this way about someone before. I'm entirely out of my element—it's as exciting as it is terrifying, and I'm not sure what to do with that.

Dressed in plain black leggings and Dad's old college crewneck, I sit cross-legged on the porch swing and wait for Tristan, cradling a steaming mug of hazelnut-flavored coffee in my hands. I want to text Allison and let her know what's happening, but with the unseelies' suspected involvement, I'm not sure it's safe. And that feels about as good as a stack of bricks on my chest. She's my best friend, and I want to confide in her, tell her everything. But when it comes to Elijah and making sure we can wake him up, I can't take any chances.

When Tristan's car pulls up to the curb, the urge to jump up and close the distance between us sweeps over me. I set my mug on the windowsill and stand, walking toward the porch steps. Tristan walks around the front of his car, his hair framing his face messily and black sunglasses covering his eyes. The dark jeans and gray T-shirt under his black leather jacket make him look downright—*fuck me, I'm staring at him so hard.*

He climbs the steps, drawing me against his chest without a word. His hand cradles the back of my head, and I allow myself this moment to just close my eyes and be overtaken by his presence, his warmth, his citrus and sandalwood scent. My pulse jackhammers, and I wrap my arms around his waist, burying my face in his shirt. I want to stay here, in this moment, forever. Where, for the space of a heartbeat, my brother isn't locked in endless sleep because of some fae. Where I don't have to worry that my best friend is putting herself in danger by simply being with Evan. Where I don't have to figure out what's going on between me and the fae knight whose arms I'm in.

"I told my parents you came to see my hometown," I mumble against his chest.

A soft laugh rumbles through him, and he pulls back. "Oh? And where are you going to show me first?"

"You've already seen the inside of my bedroom, so everything is pretty dull in comparison."

"No doubt," he murmurs with a faint smirk. His expression smooths, and he brushes his fingers along my cheek. "Whenever you're ready to go back to the hospital—"

"Let's go now." I step away from him and grab my mug off the windowsill. "I'll tell my parents we're leaving."

I slip inside and find them in the living room. There's a sitcom rerun Dad appears to be watching at first, but when I get closer, it looks more as though he's staring into space, while Mom is dusting the decades old crystal in the cabinet beside the front window. My stomach sinks; Mom doesn't clean—*she's distracting herself*. I guess I take after her with keeping busy to avoid things... I certainly can't fault her for it.

"I'll be back soon," I tell them.

Mom looks up, setting a champagne flute we've never used back in the cabinet. "Isn't Tristan going to come inside?"

"Maybe later." I'm already walking to the front door. "I'll bring dinner home," I say before stepping onto the porch and closing the door behind me.

"All set?" Tristan asks from the same spot I left him.

I nod, dropping my gaze to his outstretched hand. Sliding my fingers through his, I shove away the voice in my head asking, *what does this mean?* I don't have the mental bandwidth to consider it at this moment, so I walk next to Tristan, letting him open the passenger door for me and sliding into the car.

The silence between us from the moment we pull away from the curb until we're in the elevator at the hospital is comfortable. There's a good chance neither of us knows what to say, but I finally break the silence as we ride to the pediatric floor.

"What are you going to do?" I ask in a low voice, leaning against the wall opposite him.

Tristan regards me thoughtfully. "When I brought you here a couple of days ago, I didn't really see Elijah. Once I do, I should know more of what we're dealing with."

I nod. "Should we confront his doctor? She was talking about running more tests while on the phone with someone when I walked in earlier—we should find out who, right?"

"One thing at a time," he says softly as the elevator stops and the door slides open. We walk side by side as my heart beats in my throat. Tristan's hand rests at the small of my back, guiding me forward as we walk into Elijah's room, where Dr. Collins is nowhere to be seen.

I let out a shaky breath and approach Elijah, brushing the hair away from his forehead and pressing a soft kiss there, while Tristan walks around the bed, observing my brother. "Anything?" I ask in a quiet voice.

He purses his lips, reaching for Elijah's wrist, and wraps his fingers around it as if he's searching for a pulse. Closing his eyes, several seconds pass before he lowers Elijah's arm back to the bed. His brows tug closer as his lips form a frown, making my stomach sink.

"Tristan?"

He opens his eyes and looks at me. "The doctor was right."

I shake my head. "I don't..." I trail off, looking down at Elijah. "An unseelie fae did this to him?"

"Yes." His tone has a sharpness that makes my eyes prick with tears as I clasp Elijah's hand in both of mine.

"How did this happen?"

Tristan exhales a heavy sigh. "This sort of magic goes hand in hand with the dream walking ability fae possess."

My voice cracks when I say, "Explain, please."

"Aurora, are you—"

"I need to know what's happening to my brother, Tristan."

He nods. "This is the work of a powerful fae—or several. They are keeping your brother locked in a dreamscape."

I bite my bottom lip to stop it from trembling. "Oh god," I breathe. "Does that mean... Are they making him see things?" My grip on his hand tightens.

"It's possible, but based on his stats," Tristan offers, gesturing to the machines with cords attached to various spots on Elijah's body, "he isn't in distress."

That grants me a sliver of relief. "Can you bring him out of it?"

"I wish I could, Rory. Only the fae who started the dream can end it. They're holding your brother captive; if any fae could come in here and pull him out, it wouldn't be very effective to accomplish whatever it is this fae is after."

My stomach roils, and I clench my jaw against the bile rising in my throat. "Are you able to tell who did this?"

"Not with complete certainty."

I frown at him. "What do you mean?"

"I can't tell by looking at your brother, but I have a good idea of who's behind it."

I pull back from Elijah's bed, letting his hand slip from mine, and look at Tristan. "Who?" My voice is low, hard.

"There's only one unseelie fae with the power to do something like this—Jules."

My chin quivers as my vision blurs, and I quickly blink back the tears burning my eyes. "Why would he do this? I've never met the guy. What reason could he possibly have for hurting me like this?"

Tristan drops his gaze, and it feels like a punch to the gut. "He's doing this because of me." He walks around the bed, and I turn to face him. "Jules has targeted you to get at me." A muscle feathers along his jaw. "Because attacking the seelies wasn't enough..." He shakes his head. "Aurora, I am so sorry." His gaze slams into me, filled with darkness and regret, and it knocks the air out of my lungs.

"No," I say in a firm voice, swallowing hard. "This isn't your fault. This is on Jules, and he is going to pay for what he's done."

"I promise you, he will," Tristan vows.

I glance back at Elijah and sigh shakily. "What should we do about the doctor?"

"I'm still considering that," he says. "We don't know what she knows, and it could be helpful to have her looking for a way to bring Elijah out of this."

"Okay," I say hesitantly.

He places his hands on my shoulders, looking into my eyes. "According to the background Skylar was able to access, Collins has a perfect record. Nothing of concern has ever been reported, and she's won several medical awards in the last decade."

"Still," I mumble, though his words make me feel a little better about her.

"We'll continue to monitor things here, and if I need to intervene, you know I will."

"Right." I sigh. "We should leave before she comes back to check on him."

"I'll get someone from my team to come look out for Elijah. Nothing will happen to him here. I give you my word."

"All right," I say, because what other choice do I have?

---

We end up driving around the city with me pointing out the places I frequented growing up. The café my friends and I got coffee almost daily in high school, the pizzeria Mom and Dad ordered from every Friday night, even the park where I had my first kiss—I mean, if you count an eighth-grade dare.

"I enjoy hearing about your life," Tristan says as we head downtown.

My cheeks flush and a faint smile curls my lips. "Yeah, my pre-fae life was definitely not as exciting, but I have some really wonderful memories here."

Tristan chuckles. "Where to next? You wanted to pick up dinner for your parents?"

"Yeah. There's an amazing hole-in-the-wall restaurant a few blocks down."

"You got it." He pulls back out onto the street and holds one hand out to me, keeping the other on the wheel.

I slide my hand into his, resting it on the gearshift. "Thank you," I murmur.

It only takes a few minutes to get to the family-owned Chinese place. My family has been ordering from this restaurant since I was born, and from what I can tell, it's still as amazing as it was over a decade ago.

"Do you want to sit for a little while before I take you home?"

I nod. "That would be nice."

The waitress I've chatted with frequently, Tess, seats us in the far back booth and leaves us with menus. I scan mine as if I don't already know what I'm going to order. I peek over at Tristan, watching him for a moment before his eyes flick up and catch me staring.

He shoots me a grin and sets his menu on the table. "Do you know what you want?"

I nod, dropping mine on top of his. "I always get the same thing."

When Tess returns with water glasses, I hand her the menus and order the kung pao chicken and vegetable chow mein.

"Same for me, please," Tristan says.

Tess scribbles down what we want and smiles before she hurries off to get our order in.

"Crap," I mutter after taking a sip of my water. "I left my phone in the car. I should grab it in case my parents call."

"I'll get it," he offers.

I shake my head, standing. "Toss me your key? I'll be right back."

He fishes the key out of his pocket and drops it into my open hand. "So stubborn," he murmurs.

It's my turn to shoot him a grin as I walk backward to the front door. Outside, I head toward the parking lot at the back, unlocking the car as I approach the passenger side. Swiping my phone out of the cup holder, I slip it into the pocket of my leggings and lock the car after I shut the door.

Before I can turn around, a hand clamps over my mouth as someone slams me against the car. I cry out, pain shooting across my face where it hit the window. I spin around to face my assailant and wince when he grabs me by my throat. His dark brown eyes narrow, his white-blond hair flying all over the place with the wind.

"Aurora," he purrs, cocking his head to the side. He looks over my face as his fingers dig into my jaw.

I try to smack his hand away, cringing at the sharp pain. "Who the hell are you?" I growl as two others step into my line of sight—a guy and a girl who both look around my age.

He presses his knee between my legs and leans in until his face is inches from mine. "Keep quiet," he snaps.

"Ease up," the other guy barks.

"Fuck off, Nikolai," the guy snaps but lets go of me.

"You don't need to hurt her," Nikolai grumbles.

"What if I want to?"

Nikolai thrusts a hand through his messy black hair and shrugs. "Your funeral, asshole."

The girl sighs. "Can we hurry? I'm bored."

I shove the guy away from me. "I'm going to take a shot in the dark and guess that you lot are unseelies."

Nikolai slow claps from where he's leaning against one of the parked cars.

"What gave us away?" the guy still blocking my escape asks with a snicker.

"It certainly wasn't your friendly demeanor," I remark dryly.

The unseelie fae whose name I still don't know growls and rears back to hit me, but his fist never connects. In the time I take to blink, he's flying and smacking against the brick side of the building.

I suck in a sharp breath as Tristan prowls toward the guy crumpled on the ground. "Don't." I grab his arm. No matter how much that fae deserves what he'd have coming to him, I don't think I can watch Tristan kill someone.

"Nice jacket, Westbrook," Nikolai laughs from the same spot against the side of the car.

"You want to live, Sterling?" Tristan snaps.

Nikolai snorts. "Oooh, threatening. Showing off for your girl?"

Tristan steps around me, and faster than my eyes can register, he has Nikolai by the throat. Seeing fae shifting from one place to another so fast makes me queasy. "Since when do you do Jules's dirty work?"

Nikolai cocks a brow. "Who says Jules sent us?"

"Nikolai," the female fae snaps.

"Why *are* you here?" Tristan demands.

"Where's the fun in giving that up?"

"You might get to keep your life. That could be *fun*."

"You're so uptight, Tristan." Nikolai glances over at me. "Anytime you want to get away from Mr. Broody over here, you let me know."

Tristan growls and slams him into the car, shattering the passenger-side window.

I offer a tight-lipped smile. "Not in your lifetime."

He chuckles. "I'm immortal."

"Exactly."

Nikolai rolls his eyes and twists Tristan's arm enough to slip free, stumbling to the side. "Believe it or not, Westbrook, your fight isn't with me."

"My fight is with the unseelie fae," he barks. "Until they—*you*—stop killing my people, my fight *is* with you."

Nikolai fixes his jacket where Tristan wrinkled it. "I haven't killed anyone."

"You're going to act like you weren't going to kill me?" I cut in.

He licks his lips. "I wasn't." He shrugs. "I was going to watch."

Tristan backhands him so hard, he falls to his knees. Tristan hauls him to his feet and strikes again and again, slamming his fist into Nikolai's face until blood is spraying from his nose and mouth.

The female fae's eyes pop wide, and she shifts, disappearing in a matter of seconds.

My focus returns to the battle in front of me. Nikolai isn't getting many hits on Tristan, but it doesn't look as if Tristan is putting much effort in either, and he's practically pummeling Nikolai.

Nikolai disappears, and Tristan whips his head around, growling.

A hand snakes around my waist, and a hand clamps over my mouth before I can scream. *This shit is really getting old.*

"Let. Her. Go," Tristan says in a hard voice.

"Relax, Westbrook. I'm not going to hurt your girl." Nikolai spins me around to face him. "Hi there."

"Fuck you."

His eyes flit toward Tristan as he whistles. "She has a sharp tongue on her, huh?"

I shove him as hard as I can, and between one heartbeat and the next, Tristan catches my wrist and pulls me away from Nikolai.

"Get the fuck out of here," Tristan growls at Nikolai, who rolls his eyes before shooting me a wink and dematerializing. In the time it takes me to blink, he's gone.

The fae on the ground comes to, groaning, and gets to his feet. "Your days are numbered, Tristan," he grumbles. "Jules will make sure of it." With that, he disappears, too.

"Are you okay?" Tristan asks, stepping in front of me.

"I'm fine," I say.

He tilts my head back to look over my face, and his features sharpen. "What happened?"

I reach up to touch my face and wince at the sharp pain above my eye. My fingers come away with blood, and I cringe. "The asshole you slammed into the wall thought it would be fun to slam *me* into a car."

He closes his eyes and exhales through his nose before he traces his fingers along my skin to heal me, erasing the pain along the side of my body that collided with the car.

When he leans down to kiss my cheek, I cup the side of his face and guide his lips to mine, kissing him slowly, letting my lips explore his until I need to catch my breath. Once we break apart, I ask, "What the hell was that about? Jules has fae tracking us now?"

"It's possible."

Pressure clamps down on my chest, and I step away from Tristan. "Are... are my parents in danger?"

"We can't be sure of anything, which is why I've had a protective detail on them for a while."

I let out a breath. The idea of Jules targeting my parents

makes it hard to breathe, but knowing they're protected eases the weight on my chest. "Thank you."

Tristan nods toward the restaurant. "Maybe we should take our food to go?"

I'm not about to argue with that.

## CHAPTER
# TWENTY-THREE

When it becomes heartbreakingly clear Elijah isn't going to wake on his own, I finally concede to my parents' wishes and return to school. Tristan has several fae monitoring the hospital and Dr. Collins to ensure we know the moment anything changes, and I spend weekends at the hospital by Elijah's bedside.

Fall seems to turn to winter in the blink of an eye, and Christmas break is the least restful I've had since I started college. Answering *Merry Christmas* texts from Oliver and Grant with pleasantness and smiling emojis feels like lying, but neither of them know what's really going on, just that my brother is in the hospital and we don't know when he'll be out. Opening presents and baking cookies isn't fun without Elijah. In fact, I hate every minute of it, but it's a solid distraction for my parents, who are at a complete loss. It physically hurts not being able to tell them the truth. I've thought about it every day, but I can't bring myself to drag them into the fae's deceitful and dangerous world.

Back on campus and nearly a month into my last semester of college, tensions continue to rise between the fae. After I was attacked in my hometown nearly two months ago, Tristan explained that, despite a relatively civil meeting with the unseelie knight, he was unsuccessful in putting an end to the killings. Jules also refused to speak to Tristan about Elijah, insisting on meeting with me. Needless to say, both Tristan and Allison won't let that happen, no matter how hard I fight them on it. Which leaves us trying to find a loophole, some way to wake Elijah without the fae who rendered him comatose. It doesn't help that since the day I barged in on Dr. Collins talking about fae being involved, she's completely disappeared. As shady as it is, I refuse to waste time searching for her when we could be figuring out how to bring my brother back.

Besides the weight of Elijah's condition on my shoulders, I'm also plagued with thoughts of being targeted by the unseelie fae because of my relationship with Tristan. They threaten to consume me when I should be thinking about many human things—most importantly, what I'm going to do after graduation in a few months.

While I could dwell on the supernatural shitshow that has taken over my life, what I need to focus on today is the final assignment for my business class.

I sprawl out on the couch in Tristan's office, where I've been hanging out once or twice a week after class despite my internship being over. He invited me to spend time here instead of on campus when I'm not in class, and with everything going on—plus the excuse to see him more—I accepted without hesitation. I'm still figuring out what being with Tristan means, but it makes me happy. Fuck, giddy even. The stolen moments between his meetings, the dark looks filled with the promise of so much more, taunting and teasing me constantly. And while we haven't gone any further than the fiery kisses and lingering touches, this drawn-out challenge between us is exciting.

Pulling out my notebook, I flip to my draft proposal and start reading it over when Tristan storms in and slams the door shut.

"Long day?" I ask, glancing at him over my paper.

He lets out a heavy sigh. "I didn't know you were here."

I frown, sitting up. "I don't have to be. Do you want me to leave?"

He approaches the couch. "That is the last thing I want, Rory." His tone softens when he uses my nickname, and warmth fills my chest as he rakes his fingers through his hair, messing up the already tousled blond strands.

"Okay," I murmur, offering him my hand. "What has you so on edge?"

He slides his hand into mine and sits on the coffee table in front of the couch. "Four seelies were found dead this morning. I sent Max out with a team to get some answers."

My stomach sinks, and I lean forward. "What happened at that meeting with Jules, Tristan?"

He bows his head, looking at our hands as he brushes his thumb across the top of my knuckles. "Jules is hell-bent on seeing me fall." He says it so calmly, so matter-of-factly, but his words make my chest tighten as I squeeze his hand.

"Why?"

Tristan shrugs. "Power over the seelie court, perhaps. Some fae are open to the idea of coexistence, and Jules wants to capitalize off that, gain support from fae outside his court."

"Again, why?"

"To garner favor with the queen, I'd imagine," he answers distantly.

"Have you met her? The unseelie queen?"

Tristan nods.

My voice is lower when I ask, "Did you ever consider joining her court?"

"No. I don't share Ophelia's ideals or beliefs in many things, namely the exploitation of humans for sport. Hunting and feeding for pleasure as opposed to necessity." I shudder at that before he continues. "The queen is, of course, one of the most powerful fae from both courts, rivaled only by her brother."

I arch a brow. "Her brother?"

"Rowan, the seelie king."

My eyes pop wide and my lips part in a silent gasp. "They're siblings?" I don't know why I thought they were strangers or maybe ex-lovers, but royal siblings sure as hell weren't on my fae world bingo card.

Tristan's lips twitch at my shocked expression. "Just when you thought you were getting the hang of my world, huh?"

I exhale a heavy breath. "No kidding. I have so many questions, I don't even know where to start. At the same time, I'm not sure I really want to know any more." *Yeah, I definitely need a minute to wrap my head around this.*

"Take your time, Rory. I'll answer any questions you have whenever you're ready."

My brows furrow. "Do you think the queen knows what Jules is up to?"

He frowns. "Her knowing and giving it any attention

are, unfortunately, very different things. If she knows, which I'd guess she does, she won't intervene. Jules isn't breaking any fae laws, and she certainly won't care that he's targeting a seelie knight."

My jaw clenches. "Then we have to do something."

"Are you worried about me?" A hint of a smile touches his lips.

I raise my eyebrows, pulling my hand free from his. "Are you kidding? Of course I'm worried—your enemy is planning to kill you!"

"It's been that way since we both became knights twenty years ago. To be honest, this wouldn't be a priority for me if not for the unseelies killing seelies."

I press my lips together, hesitating before I ask, "What can I do to help?" I shoot him a look when he chuckles. "I'm serious. I want to help."

He leans forward, brushing the hair away from my face. "I know you do. After everything you've been through in my world, you still want to help. You can't imagine how that makes me feel."

"Tristan Westbrook, knight of the seelie fae court, *feels*?" I gasp mockingly. "Alert the press."

He tweaks my chin. "Smart mouth," he says.

"Hmm... touché," I murmur.

His eyes move to the paper I was working on. "What's that?"

I pick up my notebook and hand it to him. "My final assignment proposal for business class. It's not perfect, but I think I can make it work."

It's something I've been thinking about for almost a decade. I want to open my own independent bookstore and café.

Tristan scans the pages, his expression unreadable, and

I become more nervous by the second. "I think you should do it," he finally says, setting the paper on the table beside him.

I release the breath I was holding. "You think it's good enough for my assignment?"

"I do, but that's not what I meant. I think you should open the bookstore."

I shake my head. "I... can't. It would require a commercial building, employees, marketing, and, oh yeah, money. I've spent tens of thousands of dollars getting my degree. I'm dead broke."

"Let me pay for it," he says in a casual tone.

My brows tug together, and I gape at him. "No. No way. Absolutely not."

"Then partner with me. You can't start this business without an investor, so partner with me. I have the funds, and you have the ideas. It's simple."

"I think the word you're looking for is *crazy*, Tristan. This is a college assignment. I haven't even graduated. I can't open my own business. I have approximately zero experience, and—"

"You have plenty of experience. You've worked here for months. Do you think I would've given you the responsibility I did if I didn't think you could handle it?" He sighs. "Aurora, I arranged the placement for your protection. There was no way to know what would happen after you found out about the fae, and with your lineage being a dead end, I couldn't count on that to protect you—from my people as well as the unseelie fae. That aside, the choices I made regarding your work at my company were smart business decisions. You've impressed everyone who has worked with you here. You *can* do this."

I thrust my fingers through my hair and try my best to

wrap my head around the idea of Tristan protecting me from his world even back then. "I don't know," I mumble, biting my bottom lip.

He smiles. "I'm not expecting an answer right away. Think about it. Talk to your professor about using it for your assignment, but consider how amazing it would be to truly create it."

"You're serious," I breathe.

"I'm serious."

I wrap my arms around his neck and pull him forward until our lips meet. I close my eyes and kiss him hard, my fingers gripping the ends of his hair as a lump forms in my throat. He grabs my waist and lifts me onto his lap, taking control of the kiss as his tongue teases its way into my mouth. I gasp against his lips when he presses against me, my heart racing when his fingers trail up my shirt until they reach the edge of my bra. I pull away enough to look at him, my chest rising and falling fast. "Maybe we should slow down," I suggest, despite every nerve in my body tingling with need.

His eyes are dark with lust, the pupils blown as he gently shifts me back onto the couch. "Are you okay?"

"That was... I have a lot to think about."

He studies my face. "You do."

I glance at the floor, pressing my lips together. "I haven't exactly made this thing between us easy, and I'm sorry. I thought the first day I met you would also be the last day." I lift my gaze until our eyes meet. "It's no secret that when I saw you after that day, it wasn't a good thing. I dreaded those moments when you popped up out of nowhere with your hidden agendas and ridiculous fae charm." When he chuckles, I shoot him a look. "We challenge each other every single day. It's our thing."

He tilts his head to the side, a hint of a grin playing at the corner of his mouth as if he agrees.

"It was easier to hate you than to admit I had feelings for someone who kidnapped me, someone *fae*, who I didn't know existed until said kidnapping." Glancing away, I blow out a breath, but it still feels as though something is keeping my lungs from working properly.

"Aurora," he says gently.

"I'm still struggling with... this. I have no idea what I'm doing when it comes to you." Some of the tension in my chest releases at the admission. It feels fucking *good* to tell him, to put words to the chaos going on inside me. "Every other aspect of my life is under my control, for the most part. Everything has a plan. That's how I've chosen to live —it's what keeps me sane. So, when you came along, and I fell for you, I panicked. You being in my life forced me to consider a different future for myself than the one I've had planned forever. You didn't just nudge me out of my comfort zone, Tris, you launched me so far away from it, I'm not sure what it feels like anymore."

"Aurora—"

"No, please, just listen for a minute." This is something I need to get out. "I'm not saying this is going to be easy, but..." I flick my eyes up until they reach his. "I want to try."

Tristan leans in and cups my cheeks, his thumbs skimming across my face. "You're too good for me," he whispers, resting his forehead against mine.

"That's not true," I say. "Please, tell me you'll try."

He kisses my forehead and flashes me a soft smirk. "Oh, I'm all in."

My heart races at his words, knowing just how deeply I am, too. In the time I take to blink, Tristan moves forward, grabbing my hips and laying me across the couch. He gives me no warning before his lips crash against mine, moving gently. His tongue darts out, flicking along my bottom lip, teasing and soft, until my lips part to grant him entrance. Our tongues dance, while my head spins as my pulse ticks faster, and I slide my fingers into his hair, gripping the ends. I get lost in him, letting his touch consume me, take me away from the stress of everything, if just for a moment.

Boldness grips me, and I push against his chest until he moves back, keeping his lips on mine as I sit up. We move to the end of the couch, where I take control, straddling him and grinding against the hardness between his legs. The heat pulsing between mine makes my cheeks flush, and I break the kiss to catch my breath, my heart as loud as a drumbeat. I drop my head to his shoulder, my chest rising and falling fast.

"Tell me what you want," he says gruffly.

A single word spills from my lips: "You."

Tristan guides my head up so our eyes meet. "I'm going to need you to be a bit more specific, Rory."

I lick the dryness from my lips and grab his hand, guiding it between my legs where I'm aching for him. He catches on fast, and the curve of his lips shoots heat straight to my core. Tristan grips my hips and flips me around so I'm sitting between his legs with my back against his chest. I yelp at the blurring movement, turning my head to shoot him a look, which he only smirks at as he snakes an arm around my waist, locking me against him. His other hand glides along my thigh, back and forth, making my skin tingle under my leggings. My breathing hitches as his fingers delve between my legs, and I press my lips together against a soft moan when his thumb brushes my clit. A heady mix of anticipation and desire floods through me as Tristan kisses the beating pulse at my neck. I tip my head back against him, spreading my legs wider, an invitation for him to slide his hand into my pants, which is exactly what he does. His fingers trace along the line of my panties before slipping inside, and I suck in a sharp breath when he skims my slit with a single digit.

"Like this?" he checks, his lips tracing the shell of my ear.

"Yes," I breathe. My hips lift, but he holds them down, circling my clit with his thumb until my thighs are shaking. Just when I think I can't take any more teasing, he eases one finger into me, stealing my breath. I squeeze him, breathing heavily, and turn my cheek so I can press my lips to his jaw. He pulses his finger inside me while continuing to work my clit, and his mouth finds mine, swallowing my moan as I fight his grip, desperate to grind against his hand.

Tristan's chest rumbles with a deep growl that makes me clench around him, and I whimper against his lips when he adds a second finger, curling them deep inside me and hitting the spot that's going to launch me over the edge. His lips leave mine and trail along my jaw.

"Are you going to come for me, Rory?"

*Fucking hell.* That does me in. He picks up speed, and I make an embarrassingly strangled sound at the back of my throat, hanging onto him as a wickedly powerful orgasm tears through me. Everything in me tightens, and I come apart on his fingers.

He kisses the side of my head as he pulls his fingers out, plucking the pocket square from his jacket and wiping his fingers clean before returning it to his pocket with a devilish smirk.

When he shifts me away and stands, I frown at him. "What, um... what about you?"

He cups my chin, tipping my face up to look at him. "Don't think I got nothing out of that." His thumb traces along my bottom lip, making it tingle. "And believe me when I say I'd much rather take you to my bed for the afternoon than go to a budget meeting."

My stomach dips, and I pull my lip between my teeth, imagining all the things we could do with an afternoon, none of which involving clothing. "And I'd rather stay here with you than go to my accounting lecture."

He grins, then bends and steals my lips in a soft, slow kiss that leaves me lightheaded when he pulls away. "I'll see you later?"

"If you're lucky," I offer with a faint smirk as I gather my things, taking his outstretched hand and standing.

Tristan walks me to the elevator, and his goodbye kiss promises so much more than the tease on his office couch before the doors close and he's gone.

## CHAPTER
# TWENTY-FOUR

To focus on school—read: distracting myself from worrying about the fae—I text Grant the following afternoon to meet up and work on our e-commerce presentation. It's been nice having him in another class, though I no longer look at and get a fluttery stomach, and he hasn't tried to push for anything more than friendship. It wouldn't matter, anyway; for better or worse, I've completely fallen for a knight of the seelie fae court.

Grant texts me the address for his apartment a few blocks from campus, and I head over mid-afternoon.

"It's open," he hollers from inside after I knock, so I turn the knob and let myself in. The space is open concept and modern, with worn hardwood floors and light furniture. The kitchen, dining, and living rooms are all combined, so I see Grant the moment I walk in. He looks effortlessly put together today in dark jeans and a light gray V-neck shirt. His hair had grown longer since we met four months ago at the beginning of the school year, and the shaggy surfer look definitely suits him. I still recognize how attractive he is. It just does nothing for me now.

"Hey," I say as I move toward the kitchen, where I find him chopping vegetables at the island counter. "You're cooking." Clean white cabinets and cupboards line two of the walls, forming an L, with gorgeous gray marble countertops. He has stainless-steel appliances, including a fridge with an ice dispenser, like the one I've always wanted; this space looks as if it should be featured in a home and style magazine. So much so, I almost ask if his parents own it, because a college student living here makes little sense.

He tosses me a lopsided grin when I look at him. "I thought we could eat and then work. Food is always better than homework."

I lean against the counter and watch him chop a few more pieces off a carrot. "You don't have to convince me. Can I help with anything?" I ask, glancing at the garlic bread on the counter.

He grabs a dish towel and wipes his hands. "You can slice the tomatoes." He walks around the counter and hands me a knife, setting me up with a few Roma tomatoes and a marble cutting board.

I slice into one of them, and Grant watches from beside me, his shoulder brushing mine, as if he's worried I'll screw it up. The thought brings a smile to my lips... until my head starts spinning. Squeezing my eyes shut at the familiar sensation, I drop the knife onto the cutting board with a clatter and grab the counter.

"Easy," he murmurs, his hand against the small of my back.

"W-what...?"

"You're okay." His eyes meet mine. "Sit down." His

hand drops from my back, and he returns to his place on the other side of the counter.

I stare at him without moving.

He peers over at me and frowns. "Interesting."

*Wait a fucking minute.*

My eyes go wide. "You just..." My mouth goes dry, and my ears ring. "Oh my god." My fingers grip the edge of the counter until my knuckles go white.

"Would you look at that? You finally figured it out." He pops a piece of carrot into his mouth. "All those months of feeding from you, waiting for you to notice. But you never did." He claps his hands together, and I flinch at the loud sound that echoes around the room. "Phew, I'm glad I don't have to hide it anymore."

*He's been feeding on me?* My stomach churns, and my throat burns with bile.

"You... you're fae." The words spill out of my mouth, stating the obvious as I reel back. "What court are you from?" I ask, though the pit in my stomach tells me I already know, which means I am royally fucked.

"Are you sure you'd like me to answer that? Things are going to get far more unpleasant once I do."

My eyes flick around the room, and I swallow hard. "Why am I here?" My thoughts immediately go to the last undesirable interaction I had with the unseelie court. I can't help but think this is going to end a lot worse than being slammed against the side of a car.

"You're what I need to win this war."

I shake my head, my brows pinching together. "Why would you—" My voice breaks and my jaw clenches until my teeth ache in protest. *Oh no. No, no, no.* "Jules." The name falls from my lips as fear digs its claws into my chest, because I'm standing in the same room as Tristan's enemy—a knight of the unseelie court.

The same fae who put my brother in a magic-induced coma, and the only one who can bring him out of it.

Rage lashes across my chest, white-hot and all-consuming as Jules walks around the kitchen island, blocking my escape path. "Well done. One point for you."

Desperate to put distance between us, I move backward. "This isn't a game, Grant. Or Jules. Or whoever the hell you are." When he steps toward me, I immediately lean away, but he grabs my arm and forces me to stand before him. Without hesitation, I swing my fist at his face, but he catches it all-too easily before it connects. "Why are you doing this?" I demand sharply, pulling my hand back and wincing at the tingling sensation left behind. "Why did you go after my brother?"

Quick as a snake, Jules wraps his arm around my shoulders and holds me against him, his grip too tight to break no matter how hard I struggle. He smoothes a hand over my hair, and a sickening drowsiness floods in as he feeds on my energy. I should fight him off, but standing seems like too difficult a task. My eyelids flutter, and my body falls against his. "That's it," he croons. "Close your eyes."

---

Once awake, I blink several times before my vision clears. I turn my head to look around the room. It's simple, fair in size, and set up with a dresser, desk, and bed. The bed that I'm lying on. I bolt upright. *Where am I?*

Before I can panic, the door opens and Jules walks in,

carrying a tray of breakfast food with a glass of orange juice and a steaming mug of what smells like coffee.

"You're awake," he says in a pleasant voice, and sets the tray down on the table beside me.

I scramble off the bed, trying to put as much distance between us as possible as my heart pounds in my chest. This is bad. So fucking bad.

"How are you feeling?" he asks.

Something akin to anger flares to life in my chest, mingling with the fear living there. "You don't give a shit about me."

He frowns and walks toward me.

I jump onto the bed to get across to the other side, away from him, but he catches my leg and pulls me back, maneuvering himself on top of me, and pins my arms to the mattress above my head.

"Get off of me," I scream, tears pricking my eyes as I buck my hips to get him off. I grunt, digging my nails into his hands, and he bares his teeth at me, and I shudder. Each one is razor sharp, gleaming, and ready to rip me to shreds.

"Scream away. No one can hear you." He grins, and I think I'm going to be sick.

My scream rips through the air, and I lift my knee to catch him in the stomach as hard as I can. He grunts but doesn't move, so I do it again. He lets go of one of my hands to cage my leg, so I use that opportunity to lash out, dragging my nails across his cheek.

He hisses and rolls off of me, standing beside the bed. "You should eat something," he says in a tight voice, his teeth appearing normal again. "I took a lot of energy. You should replenish it."

There's no way I can stomach anything right now.

With a snarl, I kick the tray off the table, sending it to the floor in a pile of food, juice, and shattered glass. My temples throb with an impending headache. "Why are you doing this?" I ask again, sitting up and pressing my back into the headboard.

He exhales through his nose. "Because, sweet Aurora, you're the way to Tristan's heart—and I'm going to use that to destroy him."

My eyes widen, and I stare at him for several beats. "I thought you were my friend." The words come out quieter than I wanted, and I clench my jaw at the feeling of weakness.

"Hmm... I could be," he offers.

"What's your plan? You think you can just keep me here?" I clench my hands into fists so I'm not tempted to scratch my nails down his face again, though I'd like nothing more. Right now, I need information. *I need him to bring Elijah back.*

"Help me destroy Tristan Westbrook, and you can go back to your mundane life and do whatever you want—as can your brother. All you have to do is say yes."

My pulse ticks faster at the weight of his words, and I hate myself for even pretending that working with Jules is an option. "What does eliminating Tristan mean for you?"

He studies me for a moment, as if he's considering whether it's safe to share that information. "Tristan is one of the most powerful fae in existence. Of course, that's why the seelie king knighted him."

"I imagine the unseelie queen knighted *you* for a reason," I point out.

He laughs, but there's not an ounce of humor in it. "I was merely her plaything for many decades before she decided to use me for something more significant."

"So what? Getting Tristan out of the way will reflect well on you in the eyes of your queen?"

"For someone new to this world, you catch on fast."

*It's not that complicated.* My snarky remark gets stuck on my tongue.

Tristan was right. Jules wants power over the seelie fae. He's crazy if he thinks I'll help him. But maybe if I play along, I can figure a way out of this with betraying Tristan or losing my brother.

"Consider what this could mean for *you*, Aurora. You could get your brother back and return to your old life, just like that."

Silence stretches between us, and I drop my gaze to my lap, squeezing my eyes shut and biting my bottom lip to stop it from trembling. I'll figure out a way to save them both, but for now, I have no other option.

"Fine," I finally say, and that one word feels like I've already lost.

When I force myself to look at him again, he narrows his eyes as if he might not believe me, but then he says, "You're making the right choice."

He leaves the room, the door clicking shut behind him, and I press my face into the pillow to quiet the sound of my sobs.

---

It's dark outside the window when I open my eyes. I use the bathroom connected to the bedroom, and while I'm washing my hands, I catch my reflection in the mirror. *What am I doing?* I need to find a way out of here before Jules has the chance to force me into doing something that will hurt Tristan.

When I leave the bathroom, I stop dead when my eyes land on Allison's unseelie boyfriend standing in the other room. He left the bedroom door wide open...

My eyes narrow. "You're involved with this?"

Evan hesitates. "In a way."

His words make my stomach roil. What are the odds of me getting past him and out of Jules's apartment? Probably really fucking slim. Still, I flick a glance past him to the hallway beyond the open door, but I can't see anything helpful.

"What are you doing here?"

"Jules asked me to see if you'd like dinner now."

"How long did you know he was going to do this to me?" I snarl, tasting the venom in my words. "Do you know what he did to my little brother?"

"Listen, Aurora—"

"No," I snap, squeezing my hands into fists at my sides as I inch toward him. "Does Allison know what's going on?"

Evan shakes his head. "You won't believe me, but I care about her. While things may not have started that way, I—"

"You knew I knew Jules, but that I didn't know who he *really* was."

He nods.

That's when I snap. I launch forward and slam my fist into his face. He stumbles back, and I follow, swinging at his face again and again, almost surprised that I'm getting some decent hits in. Either he's letting me, or he isn't as coordinated and fast as most fae. Blood sprays from his nose and drips from a cut on his lip, but watching them heal as fae magic works through him makes my rage burn hotter. I hit him harder, faster, over and over until someone grabs me around the waist and pulls me away.

"Aurora." Jules's voice doesn't help the part of me that wants to murder Evan with my bare hands.

"I'll kill you," I hiss at Evan, trying to break free of Jules's hold. "I swear, I will end you."

Jules pulls me back and turns me to face him, grasping my chin with his free hand.

I try to break his grip. "Get the fuck away from me."

"Stop fighting me," he orders.

I swallow hard and stop struggling. It's not doing any good, anyway. "You sick son of a bitch," I growl. "He deserved that." My heart pounds from the adrenaline rush, making my hands shake as they grip the front of Jules's shirt. My knuckles are bloody and already bruising.

Jules holds his hand over them until the cuts seal and the bruises fade. He sighs heavily. "Let's have dinner. I did cook, after all."

I blink at him, my lips turning down as I struggle to grasp his motive for healing me. I open my mouth to question him, then snap it shut when Evan grumbles, getting up from the floor, and walks out of the room without a word.

---

Jules and I sit across from each other in his small, modern dining room. He brings out two plates with chicken breast, broccoli, and roasted potatoes. He pours me a glass of white wine and one for himself before he looks at me. "Eat," he instructs.

I narrow my eyes at him but pick up my fork and knife.

I slice into the chicken, watching the serrated metal cut into the meat. How fast could I—?

"I wouldn't," Jules says in a casual tone, lifting a piece of chicken to his mouth. My eyes snap to his, and he smirks. "Your rigid posture and permanent scowl are fairly telling, Aurora."

Glaring at him, I drop the utensils and cross my arms. "You can't blame me for thinking about it."

He tilts his head, chewing and swallowing, before he says, "I don't. However, I know how it would end if you attempted it, and I'd rather not see that come to fruition."

"How kind of you."

"There's no reason for you to get hurt. It wasn't your fault you became a part of this world. Once we deal with Tristan, you can go back to your life, and you'll be happy. I'm giving you an out that benefits me as well."

"You're forcing me to take it," I correct in a sharp tone.

He sets his fork down and takes a sip of his wine. "It's for your own good. You'll see that eventually."

"You don't need me for what you're planning. You overestimate Tristan's feelings for me." I know how Tristan feels, though, enough to know Jules's plan to use me against him could work. The thought makes my chest ache. For all those weeks I dreaded seeing Tristan, he's the only person I want right now.

Jules laughs. "I've seen the way he is with you. That's never happened before in the nearly thirty years I've known him. Humans don't do it for him, but you do."

I push away from the table and stand. "I'm done talking about this. When you let your people kill his, you started the war. You want to destroy Tristan and make your queen happy so she'll see you as more than a pathetic toy she can play with? You're on your own. Good fucking luck." I storm toward the door to get away from him.

Halfway across the room, Jules grabs my wrist and spins me around. "Stop."

"Go to hell," I snap.

His lips curl into a twisted grin. "Your fear and anger are intoxicating," he murmurs. "Such strong, genuine emotions."

My heart races at the intention behind his words. "It's called being *human*. You've tried it, remember?"

Amusement glitters in his eyes. "It's a shame that didn't work out, but college can be so dull."

"Then you know what it's like to spend time with you," I remark dryly.

He sucks in a breath that almost sounds like a laugh. "Maybe you need more time to think about my offer." I barely catch sight of his fist before the sickening sight of him goes black.

I blink a few times, my head already pounding, and my ears ringing. I spit out a mouthful of blood before I gag on it and groan.

"You hit her?" Evan says, and his voice sounds far away.

Jules grumbles. "Put her back in the other room. I have shit to deal with."

I watch his shoes as he walks out, and I barely see Evan approach before my eyes shut on their own.

---

When I pry open my eyes this time, I recognize the space around me. I'm in Tristan's bedroom. I struggle to keep my eyes open long enough to see him sitting on the end of the bed, watching me with a dark expression. His hair is a mess, as if he hasn't brushed it in days.

"What..." I stop. My head is spinning so fast I have to squeeze my eyes shut, or I'm going to throw up.

Tristan shifts closer and lays his hand across my forehead. The dizziness recedes enough for me to open my eyes again and look at him. He brushes the hair away from my face and assesses my appearance.

"Am I dreaming? How did I get here?" I ask, trying to figure it out in my head. There's a chunk of time missing, but I can't fill in the blanks.

His jaw clenches, and I wish I hadn't asked. "You don't remember?" he murmurs, his eyes on me. "This isn't a dream. Evan brought you back to us a few hours ago."

I shake my head, confused and unsure whether I'm able to speak anymore. *Evan brought me back?*

"I'm so sorry," he murmurs, putting his arm around my shoulders.

I lean against him, taking a deep breath. "How do I know *this* is real?"

His fingers slide along my cheek, making my skin warm and tingle. "The day we met—the moment you slammed into me when I stepped off the elevator—the determination in your eyes to overcome, to *survive*, it stirred something in me I haven't felt in a very long time. Part of me knew, even then, you would be important to me. I needed to know you. I wanted *you* to know *me*."

His words send my heart racing, memories from our time together since the moment we met filling my head. My internship interview, the gala, being there for me with Elijah in the hospital.

When the images morph to my time with the unseelie knight, I squeeze my eyes shut; attacking Evan, Jules feeding off me—the scenes play over in my head like a twisted movie, and a whimper escapes my lips.

"Shh," he soothes. "Listen to me, Rory. Listen to my voice. You're okay. Just keep breathing." He runs his hand up and down my arm, trying to help me through the montage from hell.

The pictures stop, and all I want to do is kill Jules for what he did to me. Some things are still blurry, like how I got here. I remember being in the back of a car and someone carrying me into the service entrance of the hotel. I don't understand why Evan brought me back...

"It's all right." Tristan grazes my cheek with the back of his hand. "You're safe. We'll figure this out, and then I'll deal with that bastard." He lifts my chin until our eyes meet. "For now, you need to rest and eat."

My stomach churns, and bile rises in my throat at the idea of trying to put food in my body, but after a moment, I nod.

Tristan kisses the side of my head and stands. "I'll be right back."

I watch him walk out of the bedroom and replay his words.

*Part of me knew... you would be important to me. I needed to know you. I wanted you to know me.*

I press my lips together, closing my eyes at the sudden sting of tears as realization settles over me. No matter what happens, I can't go back to my old life. I can't give Tristan up. I won't.

## CHAPTER
# TWENTY-FIVE

It's been two days since Evan brought me back from Jules's. No epic battle has broken out; no more seelie fae have been killed; Elijah is the same. Nothing has happened. I think we're all going crazy waiting for *something*. My thoughts are toppling over each other and the weight on my shoulders about what Jules wanted me to help him do... As badly as I want my brother back, I won't sacrifice someone else I care about. I'll find another way—*I have to.*

In the office boardroom, I glance up from the stack of papers on the table in front of me when the door flies open, and Allison charges in with determination in her eyes.

"We have a problem," she says, setting her hands on her hips. Allison has been spending time at the hotel since yesterday when she ended things with Evan over his involvement with Jules. It was a brief phone call she made with me in the room, holding my hand with tears in her eyes while she broke it off. I think him helping me escape was his way of trying to make things right, but Allison didn't care. I don't blame her, but I'm also sorry she got hurt.

"Is it an emergency?" I ask. "Skylar needs this done ASAP, but we can get drinks when I'm finished here." I want to tell her what Jules wants from me and get her thoughts on what I should do.

"I, uh, don't really know."

I frown, flipping through some papers, and pull out the one I'm looking for. "This problem—is it human or fae?"

She curls her fingers around the belt loops on her washed-out jeans. "Fae."

Before Allison can answer, Tristan walks through the other door from his office and flicks a glance at us. "Ladies."

"Perfect," I say, jerking my thumb toward where he stands. "Allison, I'm sure Tristan would be happy to help with this problem, as he is a beloved knight of your court." I drop my eyes back to the marketing report I was reading and uncap my pen. "We can talk about this later, I promise, but until then"—I point at Tristan again without looking up—"fae knight," I say, then point back at Allison, "fae problem."

"Okay, but I'm holding you to that drink. I think we could both use it." She's expressed several times how guilty she feels over Evan being there when Jules kept me captive, regardless of my assurance that I don't blame her. There's nothing else I can do—we just need to move past it together.

The two of them walk through the door into Tristan's office, closing it behind them.

I'm still buried in paperwork when they come out almost an hour later. Allison says a quick goodbye before she leaves, and I offer her a wave.

Tristan approaches and perches on the table next to me. He watches while I work, and I can only ignore his presence for so long.

"What's with the lurking?"

"Am I distracting?" he inquires in an amused tone.

The crispness of his cologne tickles my nose. I want to wrap myself in that fresh scent like a soft, comforting blanket of Tristan. I knock the thought out of my head and say, "You're blocking my light."

"My apologies," he purrs, leaning down so his lips are at my ear. "You've been sitting here for hours." He shifts so he can place his hands on my shoulders and massages them slowly. "How about a break?" His breath is warm against my lips as his eyes search mine.

I swallow, my chest rising and falling fast. "Tris..."

His mouth curls into a wicked smirk, my only warning before he drops his hands, gripping my hips and lifting me onto the table. I suck in a sharp breath, and my eyes land on his. He dips his face close to mine and presses his lips against my jaw, trailing his mouth toward my ear. He sucks the lobe into his mouth, and I gasp, pressing my lips together to muffle a moan as my eyes drift shut.

I grab his waist to steady myself and lean into him as he ravishes me with his mouth against my skin. Goosebumps rise on my arms as he takes his time exploring each inch of bare skin, bringing heat to my cheeks.

Someone could walk in at any moment.

We should stop.

*I don't want to stop.*

He pauses briefly before his lips collide with mine, and my belly gives a happy flip as I move with him. He groans, and we fight for control, pressing closer to each other.

I wrap my legs around him, and he responds with a

growl and teases my lips with his tongue. They part, and his tongue grazes against mine, sending a pleasant warmth deep into my belly. I grip his suit jacket as our tongues dance, and he gives my hips a gentle squeeze before dragging his hands up my sides. One hand dives into my hair, holding the back of my neck while he kisses me slow and soft, and my body jerks forward when his other hand skims my breast over my shirt. His lips curl against mine as his thumb deliberately brushes over it again. I gasp, but the sound is muffled by his insistent mouth.

Breaking away before I'm even close to wanting it to end, I succumb to the need for air. I rest my forehead against his chest, and he slides his hand out of my hair to cup my cheek, his thumb brushing across my skin. I lean back and meet his deep blue gaze, unable to help the grin that touches my slightly swollen lips as I push my fingers through the mess of soft blond hair hanging across his forehead.

"I'm never going to get this paperwork done," I mutter as I catch my breath.

"Keep talking about work, and I'm going to take you to my room and give you something else to do with that mouth," he warns, making the warmth in my belly spread to the pulsing between my thighs.

I arch a brow. "I might believe you if I didn't know you have a meeting tonight," I say with a sweet smile.

His eyes narrow. "You think I won't cancel that to be inside you?"

"Do it," I say in a defiant tone despite the race of my pulse.

He smirks. "You're sexy when you're feisty."

I scowl, but it's half-hearted. "You think I'm not serious?"

"Oh, I know you are." The hand holding my hip slides down and grazes my thigh. I watch his fingers move lower before he tips my head back up. "You never miss the chance at a challenge."

I sigh. "For someone who was complaining about me talking, you're sure slow to shut up."

He raises a brow. "Clever."

I nudge him back far enough so I can slide off the table and straighten my shirt. "If you're not going to follow through with your threats, you shouldn't make them," I say cheekily as I reach for my notes to get back to work.

Tristan grabs my wrist and pulls me back against him. His lips are quick to find my neck, and his teeth graze my skin, sending shivers down my spine. "Upstairs?" he breathes.

I nod before he shifts, transporting us from the boardroom to the main bedroom of his penthouse. I lean up on my tiptoes and brush my lips over his bottom one. His arms come around me, sweeping me off my feet as his mouth seals over mine. As he presses me back against the closed door, he nips my lower lip, making me suck in a breath. He chuckles as I wrap my legs around his waist. I bury my fingers in his hair, tugging at the ends as my lips move against his. Our mouths are frantic, losing coordination in our desperation for more.

His lips leave mine for a second, and I drag air into my lungs while he trails his mouth along my jaw, kissing and nipping gently. His hands grip my hips, his thumbs moving in slow, sensual circles.

"Aurora," he breathes.

"Kiss me," I demand.

"This isn't the slow pace you mentioned before."

I lean back enough to look at him. "I don't want slow," I admit. "I want *you*."

The hue of his eyes darkens into a look so filled with desire, heat floods through me. My entire body is tingling with a wicked sensation, a need to be touched.

"You're saying—?"

"I'm saying, *kiss me*, Tristan."

I don't have to ask again. His lips are on mine in an instant, pulling soft whimpers and moans from me with ease. He spins us around and walks across the room, setting me on my feet when we reach the side of his bed. My heart surges forward, and my eyes snap to his.

"Are you sure?"

I nod, reaching for him.

He catches my hand and presses it flat against his chest, over his heart. It pounds against my palm. "I need to hear you say it, Rory."

A smile touches my lips. I lift my other hand to his face and cup his cheek. "I want you, Tristan Westbrook, so much it terrifies me. I want you so badly it hurts."

His eyes widen slightly, and he slides his hand up my neck, cradling my head as his lips capture mine. He lays me on his bed and leans over me, planting short, soft kisses along my jaw, down the side of my neck, across my collarbone. My skin heats at his touch, pulsing between my legs each time his lips brush across an additional part of me.

Tristan lifts his shirt over his head, dropping it on the floor before reaching for the buttons on my blouse. Undoing each button with care until he can push it off my shoulders, he then tosses it on the floor with his shirt. He dips his head and licks along the top swell of my breasts, making me gasp. I grip the waistband of his pants, tugging on his belt until I can get it to unbuckle. He steals my hands and pins them above my head with one hand, using the other to unclasp my strapless bra. It falls away, leaving my upper half bare and bringing heat to my cheeks.

His eyes catch mine as he releases my wrists, and he smiles. "You are so beautiful," he murmurs and brings his lips back to mine in a sweet, slow kiss. He drops his mouth to my chest and kisses around my breast, flicking his tongue across it, hardening the nipple before he sucks it into his mouth. I groan as he circles his tongue around it while tweaking the other with his fingers. I arch my back, and he answers by switching sides and delivering the ministrations all over again. The heat between my thighs pulses with need, and almost as though he senses it, he presses his knee higher, and my hips jerk in response.

He trails his lips down the length of my stomach until they reach the edge of my pants, then pulls them past my knees. I kick them the rest of the way off, and Tristan helps me slide back farther so my head rests against the pillows. He hovers over me, kissing each of my cheeks, my forehead, my nose, before his lips return to mine. His hand presses against my stomach and slides lower. My hips buck when his fingers brush over my panties, making me gasp against his lips.

"You like that?" he murmurs.

"Yes," I breathe.

My head spins when he slips his hand into my panties, and I grip the black silk sheets on either side of me as he slides a finger inside me. His thumb circles my clit while his finger thrusts in and out, making me writhe against the sheets. He takes his time stroking me, stealing my moans as his lips move against mine in a feverish kiss.

Shifting his body, he trails his lips down my neck and

across my collarbone. My pulse kicks up when I realize where his mouth is heading. His free hand slides down my side as he moves his lips lower to my stomach while his fingers still move slowly inside of me, eliciting small, soft moans from me. He kisses just below my navel, then lifts his eyes to mine, and I immediately get lost in the depths of lapis lazuli. The sight of him before me almost does me in, and when a smirk touches his lips, my heart races.

In one quick, smooth motion, Tristan pulls my panties off and tosses them aside, lowering himself to comfortably lift my leg over his shoulder. Pausing, he raises a brow at me. An invitation.

I take the cue and lift my other leg. Tristan lowers his gaze to my core, his dark lashes fanning his cheeks. His fingers slow and slide out, making me sigh, but before I can protest, his tongue replaces them. I press my lips together, and my eyes shut on their own accord as he flicks his tongue against my clit.

My next breath sounds more like a moan, and I bite back a string of expletives when he pushes his tongue inside. *Holy shit.* Doing this has never felt *this* amazing before. *You've also never had Tristan Westbrook's tongue between your thighs.* If I'd known it would feel like this, I don't think I'd have been able to hold off this long before admitting what I feel for him.

"Tristan..." My hips jerk off the bed, and he chuckles, shooting vibrations straight to my core as he holds me against the mattress. I grip his hair, holding him there while he pulls more moans from me, making my head spin and setting my body on fire.

My breath comes in short, quick gasps, my heart pounding in my chest as my hips grind against him. He flicks his tongue over me once more, thrusting in deep, and I explode, crying out my release.

He presses a kiss to my stomach and gets off the bed, giving me a minute to catch my breath while he steps out of his pants and boxers. My mouth drops open in awe of him.

Sliding his hands up my thighs, he crawls over me and reaches into the nightstand, pulling out a condom. He tears it open and rolls it on with ease, kissing the corner of my mouth. He tilts my chin until our eyes meet. "You're still sure?"

"Yes," I say, running my fingers through his hair.

His leg nudges mine apart as he settles between my thighs. His lips find mine as he leans forward, and I feel him against me. He dips inside of me, and I wince at the discomfort, a reminder that it's been a while since anything besides my fingers and vibrator have been down there.

"You need to relax, Rory," he murmurs, his lips brushing my cheek. "Let me in."

I take a deep breath and let it out, allowing my muscles to unclench. He slides in a bit more, groaning as he rests his forehead against mine.

"You're so tight." He pushes in farther before sliding almost all the way out. When he thrusts back in, it steals my breath, and he doesn't move for several beats. "Are you okay?"

"Don't stop," I breathe.

He slides out, then fills me again, making me clench around him. "Fuck, Rory," he groans.

A few more thrusts and the discomfort dissolves into a pleasant fullness. He quickens his pace, making me moan, and kisses the pulse at my throat.

"That's it," he encourages, reaching between us to tease my clit with his thumb. He thrusts a few more times, and the pressure builds again. My head spins with pleasure as he thrusts into me again and again until everything tightens, and I come hard, moaning his name.

"You still with me?"

"Always," I murmur, still basking in the aftershocks.

Tristan grips my hips and drives into me hard and fast, changing his pace every few thrusts. Some are deep and slow, others quicker. His eyes shut as he groans, the sound rumbling in his chest, and seals his mouth over mine, kissing me sweetly.

I lift my hips to meet his thrusts, and we pull each other closer, our lips battling for control with each stroke, each thrust, until Tristan reaches his own climax, growling deep in his throat.

Our heavy breathing mingles as we break away slightly. He takes his time sliding out of me and gets off the bed. "I'll be right back," Tristan says, still a little breathless, and less than a minute later, he's lying next to me again, his head propped on his hand. His grin is wicked. "We should've done that the night we met. I could've won you over a long time ago."

I roll my eyes and push him clear off the side of the bed, smiling at the *thud* he makes hitting the floor.

He gets up, unfazed, and kisses my shoulder. "I'm sorry. I didn't mean to ruin the moment."

I flick a glance in his direction, unable to stop the smile from touching my lips. "Nothing could ruin what we just did."

We lie together in silence. The only sound is our quiet, steady breathing. Tristan traces slow circles on my shoulder with his finger, lulling me into a sleepy, content state. He pulls the sheet across my naked body and wraps his arm around my waist. Despite the number of times I've slept beside Tristan in this bed, anticipating this day, it is so much more satisfying than I imagined.

At this moment, there are no seelie or unseelie fae. There's only us, and that's all I want.

## CHAPTER
# TWENTY-SIX

I wake with the most delicious ache between my legs, and a smile curls my lips before I even open my eyes. Last night was incredible. It felt like something I've been waiting my entire life to experience, and it surpassed my expectations of what being with Tristan would be like.

I blink a few times, squinting at the sunlight shining in through the window. Tristan is still asleep beside me. I lie on my side, watching the rise and fall of his chest. I could watch this forever, basking in the normalcy of it, but the longer I lie there thinking about how great last night was, the more panic trickles in. The light, pleasant feeling from only minutes ago is gone, replaced with a pit of unease in my stomach. Even while looking at Tristan's relaxed face, all I can think about is Jules plotting his next attack to kill Tristan. My chest tightens, and I fight the urge to reach over and touch his face. I don't want to wake him.

My phone buzzes from the nightstand, and I roll over and grab it. I read the message three times before the words register.

> Morning, honey. We didn't want to wake you with a phone call. Your dad and I spoke to Elijah's doctor this morning. She thought he was showing signs of waking up through the night, but his condition hadn't changed as of this morning. They are running more tests today, and we will keep you posted. Love you.

Oh my god. Elijah started to wake up?

My chest tightens with such anger, it steals the breath from my lungs, and I stumble out of Tristan's bed.

Jules is taunting me. Instead of attacking Tristan directly, he's coming after me—my family.

*You're the way to Tristan's heart—and I'm going to use that to destroy him.*

Jules's words play on repeat until I'm clenching my hands so tightly my fingernails slice into my palms. *Shit.* I hurry into the bathroom, close the door, and turn on the sink. I hold my hands under the water, wincing at the bit of blood that washes away.

There's a soft knock at the bathroom door. "Aurora?"

I close my eyes, swallowing past the lump in my throat. "I'll be out in a minute."

"Are you all right?"

"Yeah," I choke out.

The door opens slowly, and Tristan steps inside, meeting my gaze in the mirror above the sink. Worry fills his deep blue eyes, and he presses his lips together for a moment. "Talk to me," he murmurs.

I exhale a shaky breath and turn to face him. "They thought my brother was waking up."

Tristan's brows knit. "What happened?"

I let him read the text, and when he goes to hand my phone back, he notices the marks on my palms. Without a word, he sets my phone on the vanity behind me and takes my hands, brushing his thumbs over the red crescent-shaped cuts. My skin warms under his touch, tingling as his healing magic erases the marks.

"Thanks," I mumble, blinking back tears.

"Aurora—"

"I'll kill Jules for this." I pocket my phone and look at him. "At least I would if I didn't need him to wake Elijah up."

A dark look passes over Tristan's face. "Killing him would sever his magic. It would no longer exist."

My eyes widen, a sudden sense of urgency making my skin itch. "Does that mean... If we kill Jules, will Elijah wake up?"

He nods, lifting his hands and resting them on my shoulders. "We should take a beat. Figure this out with Skylar and—"

"No," I cut him off as my pulse kicks up, pushing away from the vanity and walking back into his bedroom. "I'm not waiting any longer. I'm going after that son of a bitch." Once I go home and shower, change, and arm myself with the iron fence stakes I picked up weeks ago.

*Will I be able to bring myself to kill him? Will I be strong enough?*

The questions echo through my head, the answer to both coming almost immediately.

*I'll do whatever is necessary to bring Elijah back.*

Tristan follows me. "I'll take you back to campus. You should at least talk to Allison, and I can brief Skylar so we have backup. We aren't doing anything without a solid plan in place." His voice is firm, his expression sharp and focused. Seeing him like this reminds me just how much power he holds in the fae world—something I'm still figuring out; I have to trust his judgment here, because mine is clearly impaired by my desperation to wake my brother up.

I don't want to tell Tristan about Jules's plan to use me against him, and so long as we deal with Jules permanently, Tristan doesn't have to know.

I nod. "Let's go."

---

After I take the fastest shower of my life, I change into black leggings, a sweater, and boots. I pull a comb through my hair and tie it back so it's out of the way. Standing in front of my desk, I hesitate before I open the bottom drawer and grab the iron stakes.

I slide one into each of my boots and another one at the back of my leggings. I hold the last one in my hand for a moment and slide it up my shirt, securing it between my breasts.

Tristan sits at the end of my bed, closing his eyes and letting out a breath. It's such a human thing to do. When he opens his eyes, he reaches for me, but I flinch away. If he touches me, I'll come undone. "You shouldn't have to do this, Rory. We can find another way."

I immediately shake my head. The only other way is Jules waking Elijah himself, which he won't do unless I agree to help him kill Tristan, so this is our only option. Facing Tristan again, I school my emotions. I can't let myself feel right now—I need to focus. "I think I should go in first. Let him think I snuck away from you and came to him alone to get my brother back. If he thinks he has the upper hand right off the bat, we'll have the element of surprise."

A muscle feathers along his sharp, stubble-shadowed jaw. "You have no idea how badly I want to stop you from being involved in this at all."

My mouth goes dry, my brows knitting. "Stop me? This is my brother, Tristan."

"I understand, but I'm not sure *you* understand how dangerous this is. If he catches on to your ploy, what then?" His voice is calm, but I see the fire raging in his eyes.

"He won't," I say in a tight voice.

"Aurora."

"I don't know! Okay? But I need to do this, so I guess we better hope I can make him believe I did this on my own long enough for you to swoop in and deliver the final blow."

His dark expression doesn't change. Fuck, what I wouldn't give to feel his emotions right now.

I swallow hard, struggling past the lump of fear creeping up my throat. "If you try to stop me from saving Elijah, I won't forgive you."

Tristan holds my gaze, frowning. Several beats of silence pass between us before he nods. "Once we kill Jules, there's no going back. Many of the unseelie fae will want a life for a life. My court is prepared for this, to fight, but I want to make sure you know what you're getting into."

This whole thing—the fae war—isn't about me, but the moment Jules messed with my life, my family, it became about me on some level. He made it personal when he manipulated me and put my family at risk, and now he's going to answer for what he did. I don't like the thought of taking a life—even a psychotic one like Jules's—but I will do whatever it takes to get my brother back. So whether or not I'm prepared—

"I'm sure." My voice cracks, but my resolve holds. I pull

out my phone, taking a deep breath as I open my messages, grimacing at the chain with Grant's name. I tip the phone forward so Tristan doesn't see what I type.

> I'll do it.

Jules's response comes less than a minute later.

> I knew you were smart. Meet me in an hour. Alone.

The next message that comes through is a location pin to The Iron Lounge pub on campus.

"We're set," I say in a low voice, pocketing my phone.

---

Campus is quiet as I walk across it toward The Iron Lounge. My boots crunch in the newly fallen snow and my breath fogs the air in front of me. I'm not surprised to find the pub door unlocked, even though it isn't open yet. My heart hammers in my chest as I step inside. The place is empty, televisions off, and chairs on tables. The silence is deafening, and the faint scent of alcohol lingers in the air. My boots feel as if they weigh a thousand pounds each and my mind races with all the ways this could end. I push the possibilities away, knowing it's too late to consider them now.

"I expected an entourage." Jules's voice makes me stiffen, and my eyes dart toward the sound to find him walking out of a room marked STAFF ONLY. "I didn't think you'd heed my direction to come alone." He looks at ease, no creases in his forehead, no sharp, calculating expression. He's as casual as the day we met, in jeans, a navy button-down, and combat boots—somehow that only pisses me off more.

My jaw clenches at his cliché line, but I say nothing.

He tilts his head to the side, his eyes wandering over my face. "I'm surprised you came at all, especially after Evan took you back to Tristan. It's a shame I had to kill him for helping you. He didn't know what loyalty was."

My eyes widen at the same moment my stomach sinks. Evan is dead. I wasn't crazy about him or the danger his relationship with Allison posed, but he got me away from Jules, and I'm grateful for that. He didn't deserve to die. "What do *you* know about loyalty?"

He smirks, ignoring my remark as he prowls closer, stopping a foot away and making my heart pound harder in my chest. "Have you finally come to your senses?"

I swallow, shaking my head. "You used me."

"It was never about you, Aurora. Not really."

"Then let my brother go. Wake him up."

Jules's lips curl into a slow grin that makes my stomach roil. "I'll be happy to pay Elijah a visit and help him," he pauses, "once Tristan Westbrook is dead."

My heart beats in my throat. "You're insane if you think any of the seelie fae will follow your queen if you kill Tristan. Not to mention what the king will do if you take out his knight. You really want to add fuel to an already raging fire of war? The seelie court will destroy you."

It's silent for several moments, and then he sighs. The soft sound makes my blood run cold. "Shame." He moves faster than my eyes can track, slamming me into the wall, and I cry out as stars dance across my vision. "Hmm," he hums, his brows lifting for a moment before he shoves his hand up my sweater and rips the iron stake from between my breasts. Growling as it burns his skin, Jules tosses it across the room. It clatters against the hardwood, and I wince, trying to break free of his grasp. Jules tightens his grip on me. "This could've gone a different way, Aurora."

"I doubt that," I say through my teeth, shoving him hard.

He backs up, a dark smirk plastered on his lips. "You came here to kill me?" He lifts his arms out, palms up. "Have at it," he taunts, letting his arms fall back to his sides.

I bend and pull the iron stake out of my left boot, holding it in a tight grip.

Jules laughs, shifting his gaze to the weapon in my hand. "Did you stop at the hardware store on your way here?"

I step forward, swiping the air so he'll move. I circle him and kick out with my right leg, but he catches it, and the other iron stake slides out of my boot and hits the floor. *Fuck.*

He pushes me back, and I stumble over my own feet and almost lose my balance, catching my footing at the last second.

"Do you truly believe you can win this fight?" Jules doesn't give me a chance to answer before he charges forward, grabbing me by the throat and throwing me to the ground, holding me effortlessly. His fingers trail along my jaw, and I shiver in horror when I feel his *claws* against my skin. "I'm almost sorry I have to kill you."

I choke on the fear clogging my throat and try to push him off, panting as I struggle beneath him. The pity in his glowing green eyes has my stomach roiling, and then he slams me against the floor again, making me suck in a shallow breath.

*Where the fuck is Tristan?*

I lift my leg and kick him in the groin as hard as I can, screaming at the top of my lungs. He rolls off me with a throaty growl. I throw myself on top of him and barely manage to wrap my fingers around his throat with one hand, using the other to grab my last iron stake out of the back of my leggings.

"You have quite the collection," he sneers at me, baring his razor-sharp teeth. "I guess that's smart, considering the crowd you spend time with."

"Shut up," I shout, tightening my grip around his neck, digging my nails into his skin. Claws would be more convenient. I could slash his throat, his chest—the soft, charming face that made me befriend him.

In a second, he has us flipped over, and now he's on top again, holding my arms at my sides. "You're making this too easy." When his lips brush my ear, dread squeezes my lungs, making it hard to breathe. "Do you think Tristan regrets what he's put you through?"

I buck my hips, trying to get him off, but all it does is exhaust me. Tears blur my vision. "He'll destroy you," I say through my teeth, my muscles shaking from exertion and marrow-chilling fear.

Jules laughs, and then the snap of bone echoes in my ear. My left arm explodes with excruciating pain, causing black spots to dot my vision, and a scream rips from my throat. The sick glimmer of amusement in the unseelie knight's eyes makes my stomach clench.

The room blurs, and I fight to keep my eyes open. I refuse to pass out, and by the frustrated, borderline angry expression on the face above me, I'd say that's exactly what Jules wants me to do.

"You shouldn't have come alone," he says with a snarl.

*I didn't*, I want to say. Tristan should be here, kicking

the door off its hinges and making Jules suffer for all he's done. But he's not.

*Something is wrong.*

Despite the fear filling my chest with an almost unbearable pressure, I bark out a laugh. "You really wanted to see Tristan, didn't you?" I wince as the throbbing in my arm intensifies. "Do you have a thing for him or something?" Sarcasm laces my tone. Good. At least I'm holding on to my wit. "I don't blame you. He's hot."

Jules growls and wraps his fingers around my injured arm, squeezing hard, and I scream again. "Where's your fire now?" he taunts.

I close my eyes as tears spill down my cheeks and clamp my jaw shut so I'll stop screaming. If I'm going to die, I refuse to give him the satisfaction of seeing my devastation. There's a moment where Jules's grip on my arms loosens. When it happens, my body moves on autopilot, responding instinctively. I rip my arm free and raise it, ready to slam it into his chest.

"Aurora, don't!"

Tristan's words register too late as I drive the iron stake home, right into Jules's rib cage. I know the moment the iron pierces his heart. He cries out in pain, a sound so excruciating, I want to cover my ears. He falls, rolling off of me, but still holds my broken wrist in a weak grip. Jules's mouth forms a perfect 'O' as his breath stutters, and his eyes widen in shock for a moment that seems to last forever before they close for the last time.

Tristan stalks across the room, his footsteps thundering in my ears as he approaches. My eyes snap to where Jules's fingers remain wrapped around my wrist when the contact burns. It quickly becomes unbearable, and I struggle and claw at his skin. Tristan drops to the floor next to me and tries to pry Jules's fingers open, desperation overtaking his hardened features. Tingles shoot up my arm, traveling to the rest of my body, and my heart pounds in a panicked frenzy. *Something's happening to me—this isn't normal.* Fire races through my veins, burning everything in its path. I throw my head back, screaming in agony that seems to last forever.

Tristan pulls me against him, talking into my ear, but his words are static; I can't make them out over my agony-filled sobs. He pulls my wrist free from Jules's lifeless grasp, and I fall against his chest as everything goes dark.

# CHAPTER
# TWENTY-SEVEN

The wood floor is hard against my back, and I take a minute to pry my eyes open. The room feels brighter, warmer, and the sharp scent of alcohol is stronger. I glance sideways to where Jules's body lies with the iron stake sticking out of his chest. Sitting up slowly, I peek at my arm and frown when I find it's uninjured. I move it carefully in confusion. *Did Tristan heal me?*

"Aurora."

My head snaps up at the sound of Tristan's pain-filled voice, and everything comes rushing back. Not that it helps me make sense of anything. "Where were you?" I gasp at his disheveled appearance. His hair is a mess, his clothes are ripped, and dried blood is caked above his brow, under his nose, and along his jaw. "What happened?"

Tristan doesn't answer. His eyes are dark and glowing with fury, his jaw clenched sharply. He shakes his head, kneeling before me and helping me to my feet.

I immediately lift my hand to his face, brushing my fingers over his skin. "Tristan, what happened?"

"We need to get out of here," he says lowly, his face pale and his jaw clenched. "I'll explain—"

Footsteps pound the pavement outside before two men come barreling through the front door. One appears to be in his late twenties, and has sandy brown hair, and the other is younger-looking, with dark red hair. They look as if they could take me out in a matter of seconds. Against muscles like that, I wouldn't stand a chance. I'm not sure even Tristan could take them both.

Glancing between me and Jules's body, the redhead growls deep in his throat. He makes a move forward, and Tristan steps in front of me.

The older fae grabs the younger one, pulling him back. "We can't touch her now."

"The hell we can," he snaps. "She killed—"

"Look at her," he cuts the other one off firmly. "We can't."

I step out from behind Tristan. "What the fuck does that mean?"

"You took the life of a fae knight," he says in a cool tone. "You answer to the unseelie court now."

Tristan's stance goes rigid, and I shake my head. "I'm human."

The men exchange looks, and my stomach twists.

"Not anymore."

Those two words shatter my world.

My mouth goes dry. "I..." I look at Tristan, the image of him blurry.

"You're fae," the older one says to me.

The redhead shakes his head, his glowing eyes filled with disgust. "We need to advise the queen." His gaze slides to Jules's body for a moment before he shifts, dematerializing before my eyes. The other fae spares me one last glance before he disappears too, his words echoing in my head.

*You're fae.*

My legs give out, and Tristan catches me around the waist before I hit the floor.

"You son of a bitch," I growl at Jules as tears spill down my cheeks. I pull away from Tristan and drop to my knees beside Jules's body, ripping the iron stake from his chest, crying out when it burns my skin. I drop it immediately, and it clatters against the floor.

Between one moment and the next, the front door flies open, slamming into the wall, and Allison storms into the pub with Max. They're both as disheveled as Tristan, with ripped, bloodstained clothing and strained expressions.

Stopping dead in their tracks, they stare at me with wide eyes. Max glances at Jules's lifeless body, and the recognition that flashes in his eyes is mirrored in Allison's expression. I'm immediately overwhelmed by her mix of shock and terror. It's dark and spiky, like thorns grazing along my chest. She looks as if she wants to say something, her brows tugging together and her lips parting, but nothing comes out of her mouth.

"Allison, let's move," Max says in a low voice.

Her eyes hold mine a moment longer, glassy with unshed tears, before I cast my gaze down as she and Max move around me to grab Jules.

Tristan clears his throat, and Max looks to him, seemingly for direction. "Go back to the hotel." He nods at Jules's body in Max's arms. "Take his car. It's around the back of the building." His throat bobs when he swallows. "We'll meet you there."

Allison reaches into Jules's pocket and retrieves his

keys, while Max nods, tossing his own set of keys to Tristan, who catches and pockets them.

"She's in no condition to shift," Max comments, not unkindly. In fact, the softness of his tone is rather surprising. I watch the entire exchange, feeling as if I'm living outside my body.

*This doesn't feel real.*

I don't experience any of Max's emotions when they pass me again and carry Jules out the door, and Allison's fade as a car starts, and they move away from the pub.

The room is silent, and then it isn't. I can hear Tristan breathing, his heart pounding. I hear the faint sound of his shoes against the floor as he closes the distance between us, the soft hum of the lighting above us and the cooling system behind the bar. Things I couldn't hear before, I suddenly do.

"Aurora," he murmurs, and his voice cracks, his hands balling into fists at his sides.

I can't bring myself to look at his face. My chest tightens, and my hands shake at my sides at the devastation in his tone. I don't feel his emotions as I did Allison's, and something tells me he's making sure of that.

"Look at me." His voice is tight, as if he's struggling to hang on.

I shake my head, clenching my jaw.

His presence fills my chest with a dull ache before the tops of his shoes move into my line of sight. He reaches out and cups my face, allowing me to keep my head down. His thumbs brush across my cheeks, and my heart cracks at the way they're shaking.

"Look at me, please," he begs, his posture unnaturally stiff.

I lift my face enough to meet his dark gaze, and more

tears roll down my cheeks, wetting his fingers. His eyes are wide and panic filled. His face is pale, and his expression is strained; he's terrified.

"What have I done?" I breathe. And then I shatter.

Tristan catches me before I hit the floor and cradles me in his arms, brushing my hair out of my face as his eyes search mine. He guides us the rest of the way to the floor and pulls me against him. I bury myself there as he holds me to him, and it takes me a minute to realize the unfamiliar movement in the rise and fall of his chest.

He's crying.

*What have I done?*

# PART TWO

Who am I then? Tell me that first, and then, if I like being that person, I'll come up; if not, I'll stay down here till I'm someone else.

— LEWIS CARROLL, *THROUGH THE LOOKING GLASS*

# CHAPTER
# TWENTY-EIGHT

Tristan's heart pounds in his chest, his pulse uneven beneath his skin as he holds me against him. I can *hear* it, the increased and desperate rhythm. Everything around us finally breaks through the noise. A shudder ripples through me, my stomach filling with nausea, and I grit my teeth against the bile rising in my throat.

"Aurora." Tristan's voice sounds far away. He draws me back, cupping my face in his hands again. I immediately want to look away. The pain and fear in his deep blue gaze, the glassiness of his eyes as he fights tears... It's breaking my heart.

I swallow hard. "What happened?" *Where were you?*

Tristan's brows pinch closer. "A group of unseelie fae ambushed me. I could hear you fighting, but I... I couldn't get to you—until it was too late. You weren't supposed to be the one to kill him, Rory."

My bottom lip trembles as the burning in my eyes threatens tears. "I don't understand."

"I knew you killing a fae as powerful as Jules *could* trigger the fae magic in you, but I truly didn't believe it would be an issue because we agreed I would be the one to end his miserable existence." His back is ramrod straight and his gaze is filled with desperation, as if he's terrified I'm going to blame him for this. "I can't tell you how sorry I am."

I force a stiff nod and swallow the lump in my throat. I'm not entirely sure I'm registering what he's saying. "Tristan, am I really fae?"

His gaze falls from mine, and the knots in my stomach twist tighter. A strangled sound of surprise bursts from my lips when my phone rings. I slip it out of the thigh pocket in my leggings, and suck in a breath when I register my mom's number on the screen.

"Mom?"

"He's awake," she cries. "Elijah is awake. All his tests came back normal, but the doctors want to keep him for a few more days just to be safe."

The air leaves my lungs, and I choke on a sob, squeezing my eyes shut. So many emotions are at war in my chest, it's impossible to breathe.

"Aurora, are you okay?" Mom asks.

"Elijah's awake," I gasp out, my heartbeat tripping over itself.

"Mom, please stop crying," Elijah says in the background.

"Do you want to talk to him?"

My gaze meets Tristan's, and despite the encouraging albeit faint smile he offers me, the weight of everything that's happened slams into me at full force. I'm teetering close to the edge of falling apart again, and that's the last thing I want Elijah to hear. "I really do, but I can't right now."

"I understand, honey. We'll talk to you soon."

"Bye, Roar!" Elijah shouts.

I end the call before my mom can hear the agony spilling from my lips. Tristan moves toward me again, but I reel back, shaking my head.

"You saved your brother, Aurora," he says in a gentle voice.

I nod.

"We should get out of here. There's a lot we need to talk about now that... You need to know what this change means for you, but that conversation can wait until you've had some time to collect yourself."

Another nod.

We walk out of The Iron Lounge and get into Max's car. I stare blankly out the windshield the entire drive to the hotel, moving robotically from the private parking to the staff elevator. Really, the trip from the pub to Tristan's penthouse is a blur. My senses are utterly overwhelmed to the point everything is too loud, too bright, too sensitive against my skin. I've never had an out-of-body experience, but I'd wager it feels something like this.

Once we're inside, Tristan guides me through his bedroom to the en suite bathroom, and I watch him pull a towel from the cupboard beside the vanity. He hangs a white fluffy robe on the hook next to the shower and turns it on before coming back to me. I don't feel any emotions coming from him like I did when he healed me of the foxglove with his blood, which tells me he doesn't *want* me to know what he's feeling right now.

"Take your time," he murmurs, leaning in and pressing his lips to my cheek. "I'll be right outside."

When I say nothing, he exhales a soft breath and leaves me alone, closing the door behind him.

After getting undressed, I stand under the hot spray of water, staring at the marble tile for a while before I wash myself off. Maybe if I stay in here long enough, everything will sort itself out, and I won't be fae anymore. I almost laugh at the thought; I'm not naïve enough to believe it. The pit in my stomach is evidence enough of that. Not to mention the guilt ravaging me, because I am so fucking relieved Elijah is awake, but the thought of being fae absolutely terrifies me.

*I don't want this. I don't want this. I DON'T WANT THIS.*

I got my brother back, but I can't help feeling as if I lost so much more.

Stepping out of the shower after I've rinsed the soap off, I wrap myself in the robe, towel drying my hair as I pad over to the sink. Standing in front of the large vanity mirror, I gasp at my reflection. My eyes are glowing and my skin holds the same blue and silver hue I've seen on other fae. Holding my breath, I tuck my hair back, and dread fills me like heavy, wet sand at the sight of my newly pointed ears. I blink at my reflection, slightly confused but mostly relieved that my teeth at least appear normal, not the razor-sharp mouth of fangs like I feared. But why? Do I have to earn them or something?

I let loose an unsteady breath and run my fingers through my damp hair. There are other, less noticeable changes, like the sharper angles of my face, the smoothness of my complexion. Of course, then there's the heightened senses, which already have my head pounding with pressure.

I don't want to leave this room. I don't want to go out

there and face Tristan—face what I did by killing Jules. Most of the questions I have are terrifying to ask.

After I get dressed in the clothes Tristan left for me, I pace the bathroom a few times. When I can't reasonably stall any longer, I open the door and step into the bedroom to find Tristan sitting at the end of his bed. He looks up and stands, waiting for me to approach.

"Hey, you," he murmurs.

My lips form a smile, but it isn't real. "Where are Allison and Max?"

"Max said he was going to see Oliver and Allison is downstairs with Skylar. She didn't want to overwhelm you."

I nod and cross my arms over my chest, hugging myself as fear digs its claws into me.

"It'll be an adjustment," he says. "For everyone."

"Right," I say, unable to look at him.

"It's not going to be easy, but we will figure this out. You're not alone, Rory."

"I think... I, um, need some time."

"Of course—"

"Alone."

Tristan drags his hand through his already messy hair and down his unshaven face. He looks as wrecked as I feel. "You want to leave?" The confusion on his face makes the ache in my chest blossom, especially when a bit slips through the shield he's keeping around his emotions.

"No." I shake my head. "But I have to."

"Let me help you through this." He reaches for my hand, but I step away before he can touch me. I'll lose the strength I need to leave if I let him touch me.

"Don't," I breathe, my lower lip trembling. "Please let

me go." My chest is so tight it feels as if it's about to explode.

"Why?" he challenges, desperation creeping into his usually confident tone.

"Because," I say, fresh tears filling my eyes. "This—*us*—is considered treason in your world, remember?" Until I know what *you answer to the unseelie court now* means, I assume I have no place in the seelie court.

His hands clench into fists, as if he's fighting the urge to reach for me. "We'll figure that out. Remember what you told me? About not putting down a book before you finish the story? Our story isn't over yet." His words knock the air out of my lungs in a swift, painful *whoosh*. "Aurora." My name is a prayer on his lips. He's begging me not to leave. I can see it in his eyes. In fact, it's the last thing I see before I back out of the room and walk out of his suite.

## CHAPTER TWENTY-NINE

It's been a week since I killed Jules.

I haven't left my dorm since I collapsed into bed after getting back from the hotel—*after walking away from Tristan*.

Allison has barely left my side since she came home later that day and found me crying on our bathroom floor. No words passed between us as she helped me up and back into bed, where she sat with me until I fell asleep.

During the following days, I don't leave my bed much. My joints ache and my head pounds. Medication doesn't touch the pain, and I can barely eat anything or drink water without it coming back up.

With each day that passes, the... *symptoms* of becoming fae are getting more severe, likely because I haven't fed yet. Along with the physical pain, the weight of guilt on my chest for walking away from Tristan is all but unbearable. And yet, each time he asks to see me—whether it be through Allison or the missed calls and texts—I ignore him.

I've texted my parents a few times, telling them I caught some wicked flu on campus and don't want to bring the germs around Elijah. That buys me a couple more weeks without having to stress over visiting them for the first time since I changed. I'm desperate to see my brother, to see for myself that he's okay after Jules kept him in a coma all that time, but I can't get past the fear of being around them when I'm like this. It clings to me like Saran Wrap.

Allison keeps telling me that feeding will make things easier—at least physically—and she even offers to teach me on several occasions, but the thought makes my stomach churn.

"I spoke to your professors today," she says, walking into our room and closing the door. "They've agreed to let you transfer to online courses without academic penalty."

I sit up, leaning back against the headboard. "Really?" It's a damn shame; I enjoy class and learning among my peers, but being stuck in a room with thirty or more people for hours sounds like the worst idea right now. It's currently the winter study week, meaning there aren't any classes, but the thought of going back next week makes me nauseous.

She nods. "I told them about your brother being in the hospital, and they understood you'd want to be with him and your parents as much as possible. A couple of them suggested deferring your semester since it's only February, but I made sure they were supportive of you graduating on time. I know how important that is to you."

My chest swells, and I manage a small smile. "Thanks, Al." I wince at the sudden build-up of sound from the hallway. A group of students are having a normal conversation, but their voices are like nails on a chalkboard. I want to cover my ears, to turn the sound off.

"You'll be able to control your senses better once you've fed," she says gently. "I'm shocked you've lasted this long, though that probably has something to do with the energy you took from Jules."

"Right..."

She sits on the side of her bed, facing mine and pressing her lips together as her brows scrunch closer. "We need to talk. I know you don't want to see Tristan, but there are some things you just can't avoid any longer—like feeding. You should know, once you feed for the first time, your teeth will change and you'll grow, um, claws, like you saw on me."

My stomach drops. I was sincerely hoping by some miracle I had dodged the mouth full of fangs thing, and the thought of having *claws* makes me want to cry.

"Okay," I force out, the back of my neck tingling as my anxiety climbs.

"After human energy has nourished your body, you'll rely on it more. You won't be able to go for a week without feeding like this. But you'll be able to use glamour to hide your inhuman features—the ears, eyes, skin, claws, and teeth. It's one of the easier fae abilities, so long as you stay fed. It'll become as natural as breathing, and you'll need it to survive in the human world."

I nod slowly, fighting the urge to cry that is growing stronger by the second. *I don't want this.*

"Do you have questions?"

"Probably a thousand," I say in a thick voice, my gaze focused on the blanket in my lap as I pull on a loose thread. As much as part of me wants to accept her help, I'm finding it difficult to do so. Allison has been my best friend for three and a half years, but the thought of her seeing me this way, struggling to adapt to this new life, it's a hard pill to swallow and one I continue fighting. Not as adamantly as I am with Tristan; it's a little difficult to avoid her completely when we live together.

Allison laughs softly. "I'll do my best to answer any questions you have along the way as you figure things out. That said, we don't have a lot of time."

I glance over at her. "What do you mean?"

"The seelie king isn't as concerned with what happened, aside from what the unseelie court is planning in retaliation. Tristan is concerned about how the unseelie queen is going to respond. She lost a knight."

"So what? She wants my head on a spike?"

Allison frowns. "We don't know. There have been fewer attacks since Jules's death, which makes us think he was orchestrating a lot of them behind the queen's back. Maybe even plotting against her. Who knows?"

My eyes widen. "How does that happen?"

"I have no idea. She'll be looking for a replacement, though."

"Please don't tell me I'm expected to take Jules's place because I killed him?"

Her brows lift. "Oh. I don't think so. I'm pretty sure the queen chooses her knights. It isn't like a you kill the alpha, you become the alpha sort of thing."

A tiny amount of tension leaves my chest, and I press my fingers to my temples, closing my eyes against the pressure behind them.

"He's worried about you, you know," she almost whispers.

I sigh in response.

"What should I tell him? Because he asks about you all the time."

I open my eyes and tip my head back to stare at the ceiling. "Tell him I'm... figuring things out." I don't want him to worry about me, but the thought of seeing him makes the panic fill my veins like ice. I'm not ready.

That said, I fucking miss him.

"Why don't we get out of here for a bit?" Allison suggests.

"I can think of a million reasons why that's a terrible idea."

"Come on. I think it would be good for you. You've been cooped up in here for a week, Aurora."

I exhale a heavy breath. "I can't go out looking like this."

Allison purses her lips, staring at me for a moment. "Here's the deal. I want you to feed so you'll feel better, but I understand why you're struggling with it. Until you're ready, I'll use my glamour to conceal your fae-ness so we can go get a drink and try to remember what normal feels like."

*Normal.* Right.

"Okay," I say hesitantly.

She shoots me a reassuring smile. "If we get there and it's too much, we can turn around and come right back here. Deal?"

"Deal."

"Great!" She gives me a once-over. "You shower, and I'll find you something to wear."

I groan softly, throwing the blankets off and getting out of bed. I shuffle across our room, hoping to hell this isn't a disaster.

An hour later, we're standing out front of The Iron Lounge. I wasn't sure coming back here would be a good idea, but I quickly decided that Jules wasn't going to ruin the places on campus I enjoy.

Even though this place is filled with the memory of my last moments as a human.

Allison grabs my hand before I can reach for the door handle. "You just say the word if we need to leave, okay?"

I nod, looking through the old stained-glass door to see people walking around, sitting and talking at the bar. "Are the fae in there going to know who I am?" I ask with a slight tremor in my voice, trying to squash the fear that's rolling through me like dark, violent waves. Maybe coming to a bar with fae wasn't the best move.

"Some might, but no one is going to give you any trouble. Much to Tristan's dismay, I have friends from both courts, some of which are inside." She takes my hand and squeezes it. "I've got your back."

"I... Okay."

Heads turn the moment we walk inside, making it clear which of the patrons are fae. I suppose the good news is that the place is also filled with humans, making it easier for me to walk across the room without being ambushed by angry fae. Looking at some of their faces makes me want to hightail it out of here and never come back. To be fair, they don't *all* look like they'd enjoy seeing my head on a stick.

Allison walks ahead, stopping at the bar, and the lone bartender turns to face us. He's rocking some epic stubble, and his dark brown hair falls across his forehead as if he's tired of pushing it out of his face.

"Can we get a couple of beers, please?" she asks, sliding onto a stool. "Whatever you have on tap is fine."

"Sure thing." His eyes slide to mine and the grin fades as I take the stool next to Allison. "Aurora Marshall," he says in a deep voice.

My heart lurches in my chest. *This guy knows who I am.*

"Um, hi. I don't think we've met?" I say, because how else do I phrase, *how the hell do you know who I am?*

"Nope. But you've quickly become the topic of a lot of conversations. Girlfriend of the seelie king's favorite knight and the human who killed one of our knights." *So he's unseelie then.* "You're the talk of many around here."

My stomach sinks. "How... how'd you know that was me?"

He shrugs. "Fae are nosy. Someone must've looked you up, because your picture has been circulating in a few unseelie circles."

*That's fucking great.*

"Oh."

"Gotta say, you don't look like someone I'd expect to take down Jules, though I suppose if you're with Westbrook, there must be something special about you."

"Deacon," Allison cuts in, glaring at him. "Be nice."

He pours us each a beer and sets them on the bar, looking mostly at Allison. "On the house."

"Thanks." I take a small sip, hoping my stomach won't reject it.

Deacon nods at us before walking away to serve a customer on the other side of the bar.

"I want to ask how you're doing," Allison says in a quiet voice, as if she's hoping I won't hear it, then takes a sip of her beer.

I turn to her. We're sitting close enough together and

far enough away from the others at the bar that, if they're human, they won't overhear something they shouldn't. "So ask."

"You don't want to talk about it. I can tell by the look on your face, but it's been a week since it happened, and I need to know you're okay."

"I'm not," I say. "I'm not sleeping. I can barely stomach food. I'm tired and dizzy all the time, and I have no idea how to deal with everything."

She takes a deep breath. "Most of that will go away once you feed. The last time I went that long without feeding..." She shudders, shaking her head. "Please, just let me take you to a feeder unit."

I blink at her. "A *what?*"

"A place where humans go to be fed on and fae go to, well, feed."

My eyes widen. I'm not sure why this is the first I'm hearing of it. Granted, every other time Allison has brought up feeding in the last week, I've quickly shut her down. "Is that legal?" Somehow, I doubt it. A lot.

"Human laws aren't written with consideration to the existence of fae." She takes a drink of her beer. "Either way, the humans aren't in danger and are well paid."

"They're paid?" That sounds... dirty. Wrong.

Her eyes scan me. "Your emotions are all over the place."

I glance at her but see nothing. "I can't see yours, so I'm assuming there's a way to hide them? Can you show me how?" This doesn't feel like a great place to work on my fae abilities, but we're here and I need to figure this out—now, preferably. The sooner I can hide my emotions, the better I'll feel in front of the other fae. "I don't need the fae knowing my insecurities, and if I run into Tristan, I don't want—I mean, it would be easier if—Please just show me."

She nods, her eyes filled with understanding. "Don't think we're done with the feeding conversation, though. Are you ready to do this now?"

I chew my lip. "I think so?"

"You need to visualize your emotions. What makes it easier for me is to associate a specific color for each different emotion you're feeling. Love is red, blue is sadness, green is concern or worry—you get the idea."

"Seems simple enough." I run through what she said and close my eyes, trying to picture each emotion I'm feeling as a burst of color radiating from my chest. Right now, it's uncertainty, which I see as a muddied brown color, and fear, which is orange. "Can you see it?" I ask her.

"Yes."

"I get the color thing. How do I make it disappear?"

"This is where it gets tricky."

"What do I need to do?"

"We all do it differently. I visualize myself wrapping those colors up in a blanket."

"Okay." I try it her way. She can still see it.

We go back and forth for almost an hour. She tries suggesting different ways of shielding what I'm experiencing, but nothing sticks. She lets her emotions show for a minute, and I watch her process of hiding them. Even when she verbalizes what she's doing as she's doing it, I can't pick up her technique.

I ball my hands into fists so I don't lash out and hit something in frustration.

Allison gives me a sympathetic look. "Keep trying. No giving up."

I arch a brow at her. "Nice pep talk, coach."

"Thank you. I've been thinking of becoming a motivational speaker."

I crack a smile. "Don't count on it."

She whistles. "Ouch. Come on. Try again."

With a deep breath, I try something else. Instead of trying to cover up what I'm feeling, I try to pull it into myself. I picture myself grabbing the orbs of color in my fists and pulling on them, yanking them into my chest. It's painful in the weirdest way. Almost like an anxiety attack, where I'm feeling everything too strong, all at once, but there's something different about it. I'm controlling it. It's not something I don't understand, and knowing I can make it stop when I want makes it bearable.

"I don't know what you're doing, but I can't see anything."

I exhale. "I did it?"

She smiles, nodding. "I wish I could say the rest of what you'll encounter as a fae will be this easy to overcome, but this is about the easiest thing to get a handle on. So, what's next? Shifting? Mental manipulation?"

"That's enough for now." As for the shifting—it was something I found creepy as hell as a human. It's not something I *want* to learn how to do, at least not now. "Thank you for showing me the shielding thing. Now I don't have to worry about the fae being able to see my emotional meltdowns."

"Of course. I'm glad you're letting me help you." She presses her lips together as if there's something more she wants to say.

"What?"

"Why are you willing to let me help you with this, yet you're avoiding Tristan?"

My brows inch closer, and I chew my bottom lip. "It's...

I can't look at him, Al. I know he blames himself for what happened, because he wasn't there to kill Jules like we'd planned. I see that guilt in his eyes and I can't stand it. Maybe it'll go away in time, but for now..." I trail off, shrugging as I drag my finger through the condensation on my glass.

"I understand that, and I'm so sorry." She sighs. "In the interest of transparency, you should know he offered me a job. I start officially after graduation."

My stomach dips at the shocking news. "For what?"

"My official title is media coordinator. I'll handle all the hotel's online presence stuff. It's pretty awesome. I've been hanging out there a lot in between classes, training and whatnot." Considering she's spent thousands of dollars getting a media degree, this is a great opportunity.

I manage a smile. "Allison, that is amazing. Congratulations."

"Thanks," she says after finishing her beer.

Having completed our impromptu fae lesson with success, Allison waves Deacon back over, ordering us a couple more beers. I even snack on a few peanuts from the dish in front of us.

The crowd near the stage on the other side of the room goes wild, and I wince at the sudden influx of noise. Allison frowns at me as if she's asking if I'm okay. I force a nod and a smile.

"They fucking fawn over him," Deacon comments, grinning at the crowd who's still going nuts all around the room. "Cocky bastard is pretty damn talented, though, and considering he owns this place now that Jules is gone, he can do whatever the hell he wants."

My eyes pop wide; surprise shines in Allison's as well. "Jules owned this place?" I ask in a shallow voice.

Deacon nods before turning when someone across the bar calls his name.

"Are you okay?" Allison asks.

I manage a nod, then take a sip of my beer as the guy starts singing. Immediately, I understand why the audience is going nuts. His voice is pure silk, which is probably why most of the crowd surrounding the bar—men and women alike—look as though they want to wrap themselves in the sound of his voice. Hell, I wouldn't blame them. This guy can sing. I keep my back to the stage, wanting to face Allison while she's talking to me about her new job, but I fight the urge to turn my head.

The moment he goes into the chorus, the crowd cheers. Some women even scream. I swing around the bar stool to look at what has these women all riled up, and the moment my eyes land on the singer, the breath gets caught in my lungs.

Suddenly, I'm back in that parking lot of the Chinese restaurant where the gang of unseelie fae ambushed me.

Front and center on the stage in front of what appear to be adoring fans, Nikolai Sterling, the unseelie who took on Tristan that day, meets my gaze and grins.

## CHAPTER
# THIRTY

I can't look away. We continue to stare at each other as if we're the only ones in the room. Finally, he blinks, turning his attention back to the row of people below him. He goes into the chorus again and extends his hand to the audience. Several women latch on immediately, hollering louder, as his voice envelops the room in the song's tune. The lust they feel is suffocating; I'm seeing everything through a hazy, pink film. It makes me scowl until I watch it dim slightly. My eyes narrow on where Nikolai's hand is brushing over several of theirs, and then my gaze flicks at his closed eyes.

*Son of a bitch.*

He's feeding on them.

I whirl around to find Allison isn't paying attention to the stage, but having a conversation with the bartender. "What the hell is he doing?" I demand. It's more of a rhetorical question. I'm looking for an explanation *why* he's feeding on the crowd. Aren't there rules against this sort of thing? I should find out; it doesn't seem moral.

Though something about Nikolai tells me not much about him is.

Deacon's gaze shifts to mine, and he shrugs, stepping away to fill some drinks before he returns to where we're sitting. "He does it all the time." He puts his hand up to stop me before I can say anything. "Nikolai has never hurt anyone here. Those women he's feeding on likely won't even feel a difference, and if they do, they'll chalk it up to the drinks they've had."

A muscle ticks along my jaw as I look at Allison.

"Deacon's right," she assures me. "He's not hurting them."

I bite the inside of my cheek before blowing out a breath. "Okay, then. Wait, if they're drunk, does that affect the fae feeding on them?"

Allison shakes her head. "Alcohol affects the bloodstream, and since fae don't drink blood, that isn't a concern."

"Gotcha." I lean back enough to look across the room to where the bathrooms are, and frown at the line. "I'll be right back," I tell Allison.

"I'll save your seat."

The pounding of the bass quiets as I'm in the bathroom. When I'm done, I pace the hallway for a few minutes, my mind spinning. I can't stop thinking about the day Nikolai and Tristan fought, the way they bickered like brothers. Nikolai said he wasn't our enemy, and Allison doesn't seem concerned about him, so maybe I need to give him a chance. Some time to prove what he said to us that day. And if I'm stuck in the unseelie court, it's probably a good idea to have some allies. Unless Nikolai was friends with Jules, in which case, I'm screwed there.

I head back toward the bar as exhaustion clings to my

muscles. A rush of dizziness hits me halfway down the hall. I press a hand to my forehead, forcing deep breaths until it passes, and blink until my vision rights itself before I keep walking. A dark figure steps out of a room and blocks my path.

"I was wondering when I'd run into you." Nikolai's voice is smooth, warm. Friendly, yet arrogant.

I look him over, noting the slight curl of his pale pink lips, the dark stubble along his sharp jaw, the glimmer in his emerald-green eyes. His black hair is damp with sweat from the stage lights, and messily swept across his forehead. Paired with a plain white V-neck shirt, dark blue jeans, and combat boots, he fits the rock star persona to a T.

"You shouldn't feed off unsuspecting humans."

His deep laugh echoes off the surrounding walls in the hallway. "Don't get upset with me feeding just because you don't want to, Aurora."

My eyes narrow as my heartbeat kicks up. *How does he know I haven't fed?* I try to reach out and feel his emotions, but I hit a cold, dark, solid wall. I recoil, shivering. It's the first time I've actively tried to seek another fae's emotions, and Nikolai is clearly blocking his. I scoff before I can stop myself.

"I like to keep that private," he murmurs lazily, his eyes dancing over my face.

"What do you want, Nikolai?"

His grin is a flash of perfect teeth. "You remember me."

Bitterness laces my tone when I say, "You rarely forget the faces of those who attack you."

"Are you always this dramatic, or is it because you're hungry? I heard you talking to your seelie friend about feeder units, and no offense, but you definitely look like you need to visit one."

I cross my arms. "What's it to you?" The pettiness in my voice makes me cringe, but this guy is annoying.

The quirk of his lips sets me on edge. "We've both been... *promoted* recently. And it's pretty obvious how you're handling it."

"How is that any business of yours?"

"Hmm... perhaps because you're to thank for my promotion."

I arch a brow at him before the realization hits me. "You're the new knight?"

Nikolai's grin is answer enough. He leans against the wall, holding my gaze. "Believe it or not, I'd like to help you, Aurora. Not all unseelie fae would agree," he says, lowering his voice, "but I'm relieved Jules is gone. I've grown rather bored with the fighting between courts, so I wouldn't mind it ending. There's more of a chance of that happening now. Especially considering you and Westbrook—"

"Don't," I cut him off, shaking my head.

He arches a brow. "What? You two aren't...?"

I shoot him a look. "We are *not* talking about this."

"Fair enough. But you can't keep hiding and you need to feed." His eyes flicker between mine. "You'll fade quickly if you continue to avoid it. It's not a choice. You feed or you die."

I look away, swallowing the lump in my throat. This is the last thing I want to talk about right now. I just want him to leave me alone.

"I can help you." The softness in his voice takes me by surprise. "If you let me, I can show you how to live with this."

My pulse dips as I stare at him. Despite knowing he's telling the truth, I can't help it when my eyes narrow. Nikolai is not Jules, but my thoughts still go back to the time when I trusted who I thought was my friend, Grant, only to be betrayed and used when I discovered he was actually Jules.

"Thanks," is all I say. Not, *Hey, dude, remember that time you stood by while that other guy was tossing me around like a rag doll? Not cool.*

Nikolai nods. "When you're ready, let me know." He steps aside, giving me space, and I hurry past, walking back into the bar, not entirely sure what to do with his offer, but I can't ignore the sensation in my gut that tells me he's being genuine. Safe to say, I'm completely torn when it comes to Nikolai.

"Hey!" hollers a familiar voice.

I lean back to look past Allison and find Oliver and Max sitting at the bar, beers in hand. Forcing a smile, I say, "Hey." My eyes shift from Oliver to Max, then back to Allison. A weight settles on my chest as I note seelie and unseelie fae mingling in one room. She gives me a reassuring smile and pats my leg. I shouldn't be so wary of the idea, considering this—both sides living together peacefully—is the goal. I'm worried a fight is going to break out at any moment and someone is going to get hurt.

Forcing myself to relax, I try to enjoy the conversation our group is having. I smile and nod along, but after a while, I struggle to keep my eyes open.

During a break in the conversation, I say, "I'm going to head back to the dorm."

Allison turns to me, her back to the guys. "You okay?" she asks, trying to keep her voice down. It's still clear over the loud music, thanks to my newly heightened senses.

"Just tired," I answer, then say goodnight to the rest of the group before I force my legs to carry me out the door.

Once I get to our room, I don't bother changing before I crawl under the sheets and try to get comfortable. I toss and turn, wrapping the sheets around myself to warm up, but it doesn't work. I'm bundled up tight and still shivering. I clench my jaw to keep my teeth from chattering and rub my hands together. This is ridiculous.

I get up and look through the closet until I find my heated blanket, then take it back to bed with me and plug it in, turning it to the highest setting as I wrap it around myself. Slowly, I stop shivering and get comfortable.

When my eyes open, the room is dark and Allison isn't home yet. I lean over to check the time, but the clock is flashing twelve o'clock. The power must've flickered out after I fell asleep.

I turn on the lamp next to my bed and get up to grab a glass of water from the tap in the bathroom. Walking back into the bedroom, I freeze as a scream tears its way up my throat, and I drop the glass, spilling water all over the floor at my feet.

Sitting at the end of my bed with the lamplight behind him is Jules.

I blink hard, but he's still there. "N-no..."

He shoots me an easy grin, as if the fact he's sitting in my room a week after I killed him is amusing.

"You're dead," I force out, my voice raspy.

He nods.

My head shakes. "Why—*how*—are you here?"

He blinks once. Twice. Doesn't say a word.

I narrow my eyes, closing my hands into fists at my sides. "What, you're not going to talk?" A bitter burst of laughter escapes my lips. "You ruined my life and now you've got nothing to say?" The anger in my voice echoes through the room as if it's empty, and when I glance around, I find it is. Every piece of furniture save for my bed is gone. My eyes snap back to Jules, but he's no longer there. I blink, and we're at The Iron Lounge where I...

Jules slams into me, knocking us both to the hard floor. I gasp, forcing air back into my lungs as he hangs over me, baring his razor-sharp teeth. He reaches back and pulls out an iron stake. My eyes widen at the sight. *Why isn't it burning him?* Before I can fight back or roll away, he drives the stake into my chest, stealing the breath from my lungs. Searing pain explodes in my whole body, but when I scream, no sound comes out. I try to push him away as he pulls the stake out, but I can't move. He lifts his arm and then brings the stake down again. The stone cold, unforgiving iron pierces my heart—

My eyes fly open, and a high-pitched, ear-curdling scream fills the room. I shoot upright and reach around until I find the lamp on the table beside me, flicking it on, still gasping for air. My hair is damp and sticking to my forehead. The rest of my body is in a cold sweat.

I jump at the sudden pounding at my door. Scrambling out of bed, I start toward it before hesitating a few feet away.

"Aurora." Nikolai's voice startles me, but I step forward and unlock the door, opening it a few inches. He's dressed in the same clothes I saw him in at the pub, along with a black leather jacket.

"What are you doing here?" My quiet voice breaks, and I cringe inwardly.

The green in his eyes is too bright, wild. "I was coming over to see you." His brows tug closer. "You screamed as I was about to knock."

My bottom lip trembles; I'm not fully awake yet. "I..." Fucking hell, I should *not* be showing this guy weakness, but even if I wanted to put on a brave face of indifference, I can't right now.

His eyes flicker across my face, and he pushes the door open a bit more. "Why are you shaking?" When I step back, he takes it as an invitation and enters the room, closing the door behind him. "What happened?"

I press my lips together until my teeth bite into them and it becomes uncomfortable. "He was here," I mumble.

"Who?" he asks in a calm voice, peering carefully around the room, his gaze focused, then returns his attention to me.

"J-Jules." Saying his name brings hot tears to my eyes, and I try to wipe them away before Nikolai can see. "Not *here*," I explain. "In my dream."

He frowns, raking his finger through the mess of black hair on the top of his head. "You had a nightmare about Jules." It isn't a question, but I nod anyway.

"It was like the day I killed him, except it went the other way around, and he..." My voice trails off, and I swallow the lump in my throat.

"Killed you?" he offers.

I sniffle. "Yeah."

He nods, then steps forward and tweaks my chin. "Head up, gorgeous. You survived him. Don't forget that."

The smile that touches my lips surprises me, and I meet his gaze. "Thanks, Nikolai."

He nods. "I'll let you get back to bed."

I exhale a heavy sigh, the thought of falling asleep again making my stomach clench with unease. "What time is it?"

"Just after one," he answers.

I arch a brow at him. "And you were coming to see me?"

He laughs. "Yeah, but it can wait. It's late, and you're upset."

I wrap my arms around myself as I stand there. "I don't know why you're being nice to me, but, um, thanks."

"I believe you're going to shake up our world," he says, "and frankly, I'm very much looking forward to that and would enjoy being part of what feels long overdue. That said, I'm happy to be your unseelie confidant and teach you whatever it is you need to adjust. Hell, if you want me to hang out here, I'm down." He smirks. "I'm very good at warming beds."

My brows shoot up my forehead as my cheeks fill with heat. "Are you... coming on to me right now?"

He tilts his head to the side, those green eyes sparkling with mischief. "Confidant can mean many things."

I make a sound akin to a weak snort. "Pass."

"Huh," he muses. "That's a first."

"Sorry to hurt your ego."

He smirks. "It's all good. Keeps things interesting." His playful arrogance makes me laugh, which is a welcome distraction after the night I've had. "Seriously, though." His expression evens out, the playfulness gone from his eyes. "We don't know each other well, but I have this weird inkling, a voice telling me to help you. You don't want to feed, and I get that. Fearing something you've never done before is understandable, so I'm going to offer you this on a very limited basis."

My brows lift. "What are you talking about?"

"Give me your hand," he says.

"Uh, why?"

"I'm going to give you the energy you desperately need."

"You're..." I trail off, my eyes widening. "Fae can feed on each other?"

He chuckles. "No, they can't. I'd be transferring energy to you I took from a human. It won't be as strong as if you'd fed from them yourself, but it'll do it in a pinch. It's also shorter-lasting, meaning you'll still need to actually feed soon."

I nod, offering him my hand. If this can delay sucking energy out of a human, I'm willing to try it.

Nikolai clasps my hand in both of his, drawing me closer, and my breath catches as he inhales deeply, closing his eyes and exhaling slowly. His breath skates across my cheek, and my posture stiffens as energy zips through my veins like a shot of caffeine.

"Holy shit," I breathe, my pulse racing.

"Pretty good, huh?"

"That feels... *amazing*." Euphoric even, which could get dangerously addicting very fast.

"It's better directly from the source," he says with a wink, letting go of my hand.

I nod slowly, my head still swimming in a haze of warmth and pleasure. "Thanks, Nikolai."

"You're welcome. Goodnight, Aurora," he says, backing toward the door. "And forget Jules. Dream of me next time, will you?" He flashes me one more grin before he walks out of my room.

# CHAPTER
# THIRTY-ONE

The rich aroma of coffee lures me to the land of consciousness. I pry my eyes open to find sunlight streaming into our room and Allison standing at the foot of my bed with to-go cups in each hand. She's wearing an oversized hoodie with leggings, and her hair is thrown into a messy bun at the top of her head.

"I knew the coffee would rouse you," she says with a smile.

Sitting up, I lean against the headboard and take the cup she offers, cradling it in both hands. "Thanks." The heat radiates against my palms, warming my skin. A quick glance at the clock that Allison must've reset tells me it's shortly after nine. "You're up early for a Saturday."

She crosses our small room and sets the other cup on her desk. "I thought we could give the feeder unit idea another shot."

The coffee cup stops halfway to my mouth as I freeze,

panic clamping down on my chest in an instant. "Allison—"

"I won't drop it, Ro," she says firmly, leaning against her desk and folding her arms over her chest. "Even though you look a little better than yesterday, you still need to feed."

I take a sip of my coffee, enjoying the moment of peace its warmth gives me. "About that..." I bite the inside of my cheek, debating how to say what comes next. "Nikolai gave me some."

She shakes her head. "There isn't a part of the sentence I understood."

I frown. "He transferred energy into me."

"Uh, okay." She drags out the word, her forehead creasing. "How'd that even happen?"

"It's kind of a long story, but the short of it is that I met Nikolai a while back when I was human. Last night, we chatted a bit, and he offered to help me. He said something about wanting to change the way the courts coexist. Plus, I'm the reason he's now a knight to the unseelie queen. He took Jules's place."

Her eyes are wide by the time I finish speaking. She opens her mouth to respond, but before she gets a word in, there's a rapt knock at the door. Huffing out a breath, she crosses the room and opens it. "What are you doing here?" The door is blocking my view of the hallway, so I can't see who's standing there.

"Nice to see you too, Allison." Nikolai's voice is smooth like melted caramel and filled with humor.

I set my coffee on the bedside table and stand, walking to the door. "Hey." I give Nikolai a once-over; he appears slightly less casual today in a black peacoat, his hair combed neatly. "What's up?"

His attention shifts from Allison to me, and he says, "Your presence has been requested."

"By who?" Allison asks.

He doesn't have to answer. The tension unfurling in my stomach tells me exactly who.

*You answer to the unseelie court now.*

"Why?" I ask, my pulse ticking faster.

"Ophelia wants to meet you."

"Absolutely the fuck not," Allison chimes in with a sharp tone, evidently having caught on. "You're not taking an audience with the unseelie queen. No way."

I glance between her and Nikolai, jerking a thumb in his direction. "I'm guessing by his presence, I don't have much of a choice."

"Yeah," Nikolai confirms. "'Requested' wasn't the best word choice."

I swallow hard, picking at the hem of my sweater. "When do I have to see her?"

"I've been instructed to bring you now."

Allison curses sharply, her posture going rigid as if she's going to fight Nikolai to keep me from having to go.

I exhale a shallow breath, glancing down at the loungewear I slept in. I can't very well meet the unseelie queen like this.

"You can have a few minutes to change," Nikolai offers.

"Fuck this." Allison slams the door in Nikolai's face. "I'm calling Tristan."

My pulse skyrockets at the thought of bringing him into this. As much as being saved from having to face Ophelia would be a blessing, involving a seelie knight seems like a bad idea. Not to mention what that could mean for Tristan, because he'd do whatever was necessary to protect me, and that could put him in danger.

"I wouldn't." Nikolai's deep voice is muffled through the door that he doesn't bother trying to reopen.

I face Allison. "We knew this was coming, right?" We could've guessed it, at least. "If she wanted to kill me for what I did to Jules, something tells me I wouldn't be standing here now."

Allison's skin shimmers blue and her eyes glow faintly; her glamour is slipping in her upset state. "I don't like this."

"I'm not exactly thrilled about it, either." In fact, I'm chilled to the bone with fear.

She chews her bottom lip, glancing between me and the closed door. "Are you sure you don't want me to call him?" she whispers.

I nod firmly. "And please don't tell him. He doesn't need to worry when there's nothing he can do about it."

Allison sighs. "Fine." She opens the door again and grabs Nikolai by the collar of his coat, pulling him into our room and kicking the door shut. "If anything happens to her, and I mean *anything*, I will release terror upon you like you can't imagine. Got it?"

There's a flash of amusement in his eyes, but he nods. "Understood."

I grab a pair of fleece lined leggings and a cream-colored sweater along with fresh underthings and slip into the bathroom to change. After quickly washing my face, I apply some light makeup before twisting my hair into a fishtail braid over one shoulder. I haven't colored it recently, so the blond has yellowed some, but at least it's freshly washed instead of filled with dry shampoo.

Allison stares at me with concern when I come out of the bathroom and pull on socks and boots before grabbing my coat off the back of the door.

"Where exactly are we going?" I ask Nikolai.

"I can't tell you that. The safety of the ruler is a knight's top priory, followed closely by that of those in their court."

I arch a brow at him, shoving my hands into my coat pockets as my fingernails dig into my palms. "Won't I see how we get there?"

He offers me a wry smile. "Nope. We're shifting."

I tense, stealing a glance at Allison, who is watching Nikolai like a hawk. "Do we have to?" My voice sounds small, and I hate it.

"You won't be doing the actual shifting, I will." He offers me his hand.

I press my lips together, the muscles in my stomach coiling tight with unease. At least we can't be going *too* far, considering the distance limitation of shifting. "Can you at least assure me I'm not walking—or shifting—to my execution?"

Nikolai sighs. "I, like you, believe if Ophelia wanted to punish you with death for killing Jules, it would have already been done."

That appears to be the closest thing to reassurance I'm going to get. I take a deep breath and step toward him, but Allison blocks my path, her eyes searching mine.

"I'm freaking out, Ro. I feel like I shouldn't let you leave." The panic in her voice makes it crack, and my chest tightens.

I grab her shoulders, squeezing them. "None of this is on you, Al. Stay here, or better yet, go hang with Oliver. I'll let you know when I'm... back."

She looks as if she desperately wants to argue, but finally, she nods.

I release her, and she steps aside to let me pass. I meet Nikolai's vivid green eyes and close the distance between us, sliding my hand into his. When the room slips away, I squeeze my eyes shut and pray to every deity in existence I'll survive this.

---

It's not until there's solid ground under my boots that I finally exhale. My heart tries to break free from my rib cage and my throat is clogged with fear. I pull everything I'm feeling close to my chest, blocking it from view just how Allison showed me.

"Aurora."

Nikolai's gentle voice coaxes my eyes open, and I blink a few times as what appears to be a farmhouse with modern characteristics comes into focus before me.

"This is where the queen lives?" I ask, my breath fogging the cold air, and take in the three-level house—its pristine, white exterior with black-framed windows and a wide front porch with stained wood pillars. The front door is twice the size of what would be normal and made of frosted glass.

"From what I've gathered, Ophelia lives many places, moving wherever necessary." He glances toward the house. "We should get inside—she doesn't like to be kept waiting."

We climb the steps onto the porch, and Nikolai knocks on the door. Seconds later, a man with soft hazel eyes and a face of wrinkles opens it. He has to be at least seventy and smiles warmly at us.

"Please, come in, come in. It's a chilly one today."

Inside the house, the man takes our coats and hurries away down the long hallway before us. At the end is a staircase that winds up to the second level, and a chandelier hangs from the ceiling there.

"Is he—"

"Human. Yes." Nikolai walks forward, keeping his boots on, so I follow suit. We step through a wide, rounded archway into a formal living room with leather furniture and a roaring fireplace that fills the space with warmth. Bookshelves line the wall on either side and stretch from floor to ceiling, while the adjacent wall has a few windows draped by heavy, deep red curtains.

I glance at Nikolai, unsure of what to do. Sit? Stand? Am I supposed to bow to—

"Well done, Nikolai," a smooth, feminine voice purrs, and I turn as what must be the unseelie queen glides into the room barefoot, wearing a flowy lavender dress that trails along the floor behind her. I stand straighter on instinct, pressing my lips together as I take in the inhuman features she's not glamouring. Her light blue eyes glow so bright they appear almost silver, and her long auburn curls are tucked behind pointed ears. She's the most stunning person I've ever seen—and she carries herself as if she knows it. There's an air of sophistication about her, and despite her appearing to be in her late twenties, knowing she's over a century old makes me shudder.

Her gaze lands on me, the weight of it dizzying. "You must be Aurora. What a lovely name."

"Th-thank you," I force out. I'm not sure how to address her. In hindsight, I should have asked Nikolai before we came inside. That said, I'm not sure she deserves the reverence associated with something like *your majesty*. Because even as she stands in front of me with a seemingly pleasant demeanor, I can't forget that she leads the court of fae who believe they're entitled to humans for whatever they wish—feeding, hunting, *playing with*...

She flicks a glance toward Nikolai, her lips curving into a faint smile, before returning her attention to me. "You can relax, love. No harm will come to you here."

I nod slowly, but the tension in my muscles doesn't go anywhere. "With all due respect," I say carefully, "why *am* I here?"

The queen inhales slowly. "For several reasons." She gestures to the seating area near the fireplace. "Shall we sit?" She poses it as a question, but her tone and posture tell me it's an order.

Nikolai crosses the room and stands near the fireplace as if he's guarding it, or perhaps the queen.

Ophelia sits gracefully on the couch and pats the spot next to her for me.

Grinding my molars, I force my legs to carry me to the couch and sit. My pulse is still racing, and my lips are dry, no matter how many times I lick them.

"I'm glad we could meet, Aurora," she begins, pushing her hair over her shoulder. "When I was informed of Jules's death, I was prepared to kill Tristan Westbrook myself."

My back stiffens, and I nearly choke on the dryness in my throat as a dagger-sharp anger flares to life in my chest. I bite back a possessive snarl, the abrupt sensation dizzying. I don't mistake my killing Jules to mean I'd stand a chance against the unseelie queen, but her mention of killing Tristan shoves me dangerously close to not giving a shit about logic. A stark reminder of just how out of my element I am.

The queen's lips twitch. "I see Rowan's favorite knight means something to you." When I say nothing to that, she continues, "I was surprised to learn the person responsible for killing one of my knights was human."

"He deserved it." The words leave my lips before I can clamp my mouth shut.

Her brows lift as she purses her lips. "I'm not interested in hearing your defense, Aurora. What's done is done."

I grit my teeth, sliding away from her. "You don't want to know that your knight deceived me for months, put my brother in some magic coma, then tried to use me to kill a seelie knight?"

"No, I don't. Nor do I care." She smooths her hands along the purple material pooled in her lap. "I'd like to discuss your future in my court. I believe we can help each other."

"I don't want to be in your court." My tone is bordering on snippy, and Nikolai's brows tug closer as he watches us silently, his eyes sharp.

Ophelia seems to consider that. "So you'd like to embrace the myriad of restrictions in the seelie court?"

I shake my head. "I don't want to be part of any fae court."

"Interesting," she muses.

"If you were planning to use me to get at the seelie court like Jules was, that's not going to happen." I stand and move away from the couch. "I didn't choose to become fae, and I sure as hell don't choose the unseelie court." I look at Nikolai for a moment before my gaze returns to Ophelia, who's now standing. "If that's everything, I'd like to leave. My human life may not matter to you, but it matters to me, and I have midterms to study for." I walk out of the formal living room, my boots echoing on the hardwood, and hope Nikolai follows, because I have no idea how to shift out of here.

## CHAPTER
# THIRTY-TWO

After Nikolai shifted me back to the dorm yesterday afternoon and told me we'd catch up later—he must have recognized I wasn't in the headspace to talk after meeting the unseelie queen—Allison grilled me on what happened.

I gave her the lowdown, which only made the panic in her eyes deepen. She respected my wishes and didn't tell Tristan where I'd gone, but urged me to tell him myself. Except, that would require talking to him, which I still can't bring myself to do. It's hard enough thinking about the career fair Allison, Oliver, and I are going to tomorrow at the Westbrook Hotel. The possibility of running into Tristan makes me want to back out completely, but my determination to get a job as soon as I graduate hasn't changed. Especially with the time my parents took away from work while Elijah was in the hospital... They won't say it, but they need me to pay them back for the tuition money they lent me, now more than ever.

I munch on a granola bar as I sit at my desk and scroll

through job postings. My eyes flit to the framed photo of my parents, me, and Elijah from our cabin trip last summer, and my chest aches. I haven't spoken to them or gone home since Elijah miraculously woke up and have only kept in contact with brief texts every few days, using the excuse I'm drowning in schoolwork. Good thing fae can lie via text.

I sigh, closing my laptop and picking up my phone to call home. It rings twice before my mom answers.

"Aurora, how are you?"

"Hey, Mom." I avoid answering her question and instead say, "Sorry I haven't come home yet."

"That's okay, honey. Elijah knows you're busy with school. Are you feeling better?"

"Don't worry, my friends are taking care of me," I tell her, because that's the only truth I can come up with. "How's Elijah doing?"

"He's perfect. After all that, he's absolutely fine. The doctors wanted to send him to a different hospital across the country for more testing, but your dad and I refused. Eli's been through enough."

"Definitely," I agree firmly. Besides the fact it's true, it would be pointless. What happened to Elijah wasn't scientific—it doesn't have a medical explanation. Fae magic kept him locked away in a state of unconsciousness until I killed the fae who trapped him there. I shove the memory of that day away. "Did you see Dr. Collins the last few times you were there?"

"No," Mom says, "though another doctor mentioned she'd transferred hospitals."

The knots in my stomach give a painful squeeze. I still don't know the extent of Dr. Collins's involvement in the fae world, and it looks like now I never will. I remind myself it doesn't matter. Jules is dead and my brother is okay.

"What have you been up to?" Mom asks.

I press my lips together. *If only she knew.* "I was just looking through some job postings online. Allison, Oliver, and I are going to a job fair tomorrow, so I'll probably edit my resume this afternoon and make sure it's perfect in case I want to give it to any of the companies."

"Good plan." I can hear the smile in her voice. "You must be getting excited for graduation, or are you too buried under schoolwork and studying right now?"

I laugh. "Yes, but also yes."

"You've worked so hard, Aurora. I just... I hope you know how proud of you we are."

A lump forms in my throat, and I blink back tears. "I know, Mom. Thank you."

She sniffles. "I'll let you get back to it. Elijah and I are heading to the mall in a few minutes to get a new game he's had his eye on."

"Have fun," I say. "I'll talk to you soon."

"Love you."

"Love you," I echo before ending the call and setting my phone down on my desk with a shaky sigh. I miss my family and I want to see them, but that doesn't feel like something I'm ready for yet. What if it's so overwhelming I can't glamour my fae features? I can't imagine, especially after everything they've been through lately, they'll be able to handle their daughter with pointy ears, glowing eyes, and all the rest. Until I know I can control it all, I have to keep my distance.

I wake with a gut full of nerves and a wicked headache, not to mention feeling as if I'd run a marathon and didn't sleep all night. It's safe to say the energy Nikolai transferred to me has worn out. I don't have time to think about that now. Sucking energy from a human is going to have to wait until after the job fair today.

Once Allison is done in the bathroom, she returns to the bedroom and glamours me to conceal my inhuman features. I'm thankful she's still willing to do it, but I know there will come a day soon where I'll have to do it myself.

With a quick, "thank you," I slip inside and put on the same formal black jumpsuit and blazer I wore to my internship interview. I curl my hair into loose waves after doing my makeup, dabbing a little extra concealer under my eyes to hide the evidence of my restless night.

Oliver meets us outside our building, and the three of us take an Uber to the Westbrook Hotel. My knee bounces anxiously the entire drive there, and my pulse is all over the place as I get out of the car.

My heels echo on the marble stairs, and it takes everything in me not to think back to the time I stormed up these stairs, demanding to see Tristan after Allison was taken. Being back here—it doesn't take much for my head to go there, to those first encounters I had with Tristan. When he was just Tristan Westbrook, the infuriatingly arrogant and equally attractive seelie fae knight. Before he was the man I called mine.

Allison, Oliver, and I walk inside together, and I can hear my heart beating over both of theirs. I need to relax. Deep breaths. I *can* do this.

Marisa rushes over from the concierge desk as we make our way across the lobby. "Hey!" Her voice is cheerful and warm; the smile on her face is genuine and pleasant.

I smile, my eyes doing a quick scan of the room before they land on her. "Hey, Marisa. How are you?"

I tune out the second she starts talking. People are walking around, checking in and out of their suites, sitting around the lounge area, watching one of the flat screens attached to pillars that separate the room into smaller, cozy sections. Listening closer, I pick up on bits of conversations happening in the hotel restaurant; the orders being given in the kitchen, and the buzz of activity coming from the ballroom we're headed for.

Allison taps my elbow, and I snap back to the moment, offering an apologetic smile as Marisa leads us to the ballroom as if I don't know where it is, chatting with Allison until we reach the open double doors.

Allison reaches over and squeezes my hand before we walk in, getting enveloped by the buzz of dozens of separate conversations.

I grip the manila folder filled with copies of my resume and take a deep breath as I look around the room at the different presentations. Oliver goes one way, while Allison and I go the other and start walking down the aisle of tables and scanning the different company names.

We inch closer to Westbrook Inc.'s table, and I pause when my eyes meet Skylar's. She offers me a nod, but I don't approach. I'm not sure what keeps me away, but I blink in surprise when Allison walks over and starts chatting with her.

I turn in the opposite direction and walk to another row of tables, reading over the different company names until I come across one for a publishing company. I smile at the middle-aged woman behind the table and take an informational pamphlet from the stack, skimming it as I keep walking.

"Aurora, hey!"

I turn to find Lucas, a guy from my program, coming toward me. We've shared several classes over the years and completed a few group projects together. He has soft brown hair and a kind smile, and he's wearing a flattering black button-down and slacks, looking much fancier than I've ever seen him.

"Hey," I reply, slipping the pamphlet into my folder.

"How's it going?"

"Pretty good." He glances around. "Find anywhere worth looking at?"

"I haven't been here long," I tell him. *And I don't plan to stay much longer.* The crowd is only getting bigger, and it's making me more on edge than I was expecting. I stupidly thought a room as big as this one would give me room to breathe.

Lucas nods and starts talking again, but I don't hear a word. My throat tingles as if I'm going to throw up, and the pressure in my chest feels as if my lungs are growing thorn-filled vines that are restricting my air.

"Are you okay?" Lucas's voice sounds far away, drowned out by the ringing in my ears. My heartbeat is ticking faster, making breathing a harder task than it should be. And then it's not just mine. It's every single heartbeat in the room, pounding loud in my ears. I swallow hard, suffocated by raging emotions. Excitement bubbles in my chest, stress makes my shoulders heavy and triggers a twitch in my eye... Hell, my body—namely between my thighs—tingles with the warmth of arousal. It's too much. I can't make it stop, can't push it away. Everything is bombarding me at once, cranking the temperature of my body way up. Sweat dots my brow as I try to get it under control. My muscles shake, and I feel lightheaded, as if I'm going to pass out any second as I fail to control the landslide of emotions.

I step away, muttering a quick apology as I flee the room. It doesn't take long for Allison to spot me leaving and catch up with me. I make it to the lobby, relieved to find it almost empty, and lean against the wall near a sitting area. I suck in a breath, trying to force air into my lungs as Allison appears in front of me.

"What's going on?" she demands, her voice thick with concern.

My jaw clenches so hard my teeth ache. Putting distance between the room full of people helped some, but I'm still hyperventilating. "Sorry," I force out.

She shakes her head, rubbing her hands up and down my arms. "It's okay, just keep breathing."

Keeping my eyes closed, I shake my head. "I don't think I can do this." My voice cracks. "I feel like I'm drowning. Everyone's emotions were pulling me under back there, and I couldn't break free." My bottom lip trembles, and Allison squeezes my shoulders.

"Aurora," she says softly, "you need to feed."

Once my head stops spinning, I open my eyes, and then my entire body goes rigid.

"What is it?" Allison asks.

Our eyes lock, and even from across the lobby, I feel him everywhere. He looks the same, but different. His hair is shorter, his stubble thicker, his eyes the same blue that pierces right through me. The two weeks it's been since I saw him last feels like an eternity, and as I stand here staring at him now, it's as if I'm seeing him for the first time with the feeling of having known him forever. Nothing makes sense.

"I can't..." I'm speaking to Allison, but my gaze hasn't left Tristan's. "I have to get out of here."

I push past her and hurry toward the door, terrified he'll follow. The echo of my heels against the marble is loud in my ears, and it's not until I reach the sidewalk and get into the back of what is definitely someone else's Uber I can breathe again.

"Laura?" the driver checks.

"Drive," I order, then tell him where. My tone is dark; I picture it as inky purple tendrils I'm sending toward him, bending him to my will as the swirls of color wrap around him like a spool of ribbon. I focus one thought: I need this car to move. Projecting that onto the driver, I force my need to become his. I've never tried to use my mental manipulation ability until now. I don't know if I'm doing it right, but when he stares out the windshield and nods, I figure it worked. It doesn't matter how. All that matters is that we're driving away from *him*, from everything. For now.

## CHAPTER THIRTY-THREE

Aside from snapping at the Uber driver when I threw myself into the backseat, I've kept it together the rest of the ride. I apologize before I get out, tossing a twenty into the front seat.

After he drives away, I walk toward The Iron Lounge. At first, I wasn't sure why I told the driver to bring me here, but standing in front of it now, the reason seems clear. This was the last place I was human. In some twisted way, it feels... comforting coming back, even though it's also the place I took a life. Like I said, *twisted*.

Frowning when I spot the CLOSED FOR INVENTORY sign stuck to the door, I decide to knock anyway, hearing the faint sound of at least two heartbeats.

The bartender, Deacon, opens the door a minute later, looking me over before letting me inside and locking the door again.

"A little overdressed for a drink," he comments, returning to the bar where he appears to be restocking bottles.

I nod at his faded Metallica shirt. "A little underdressed for work."

He grins, his hair falling into his face, and he doesn't bother pushing it back. "Hey, we're not technically open. You shouldn't even be in here."

I slide onto a barstool. "Why'd you let me in then?"

"Because you looked all sad out there."

"Gee, thanks."

Deacon chuckles softly, pulling the box off the counter and stowing it under the bar. "I have some inventory stuff to do downstairs. You good here for a few? Nikolai's around somewhere if you need anything."

*Just what I need—Nikolai witnessing me drowning my sorrows in booze.* "I'm fine."

With a nod, Deacon hops over the bar and disappears down the hallway. A door closes a few seconds later, and I let out a sigh before walking around the bar and snatching a full bottle from the shelf without looking to see what it is. It doesn't matter.

I kick a few of the stools away and sit on the floor, my back against the wood of the bar. I hug the bottle, glancing down to see that it's tequila before I crack it open and take a long drink, cringing as it ignites a path of warmth from my tongue to my belly. It isn't until I've polished off a quarter of the bottle that I realize I'm buzzed—and crying. The tears roll down my cheeks as my shoulders shake.

*I can't fucking do this. I don't want to.*

I clench my jaw, hauling myself off the floor before I scream, choking on a sob and throwing the bottle against the faux brick wall. It shatters, glass and liquor covering the old wood floor. A floor that's likely seen many spills, but probably few intentional ones. I should clean it up before it ruins the wood. *Fuck. Why do I give a shit about the damn floor?*

My head whips around at the sound of another heartbeat close by. Nikolai leans in the doorway across the room with his arms folded over his chest.

"Feel better?" he asks.

I narrow my eyes, ready to snap, but all that comes out is, "No." My voice is broken, and I'm still angry. Angry that I can't control my body, angry that what was supposed to be a great opportunity for post-grad job leads has been shadowed by it.

Now that I'm not surrounded by humans, I'm left to tread in my own emotions. It should make me feel better, but the dark, heavy combination of everything whipping through me is less than pleasant. I'd much rather feel nothing.

Nikolai uncrosses his arms and approaches. His vibrant green gaze is steady, and his heartbeat is calm. I wish I could say the same for mine; it's attempting to break through my rib cage.

"Aurora." His voice is soft like velvet. It should be soothing, but it flips a switch in me and I snap. My arm swings out, but he grabs my hand before it can connect with anything. I growl and swing with the other. He catches that one as well and holds them both in his, all the while continuing to murmur words of understanding until I stop trying to attack him. My chest is heaving, and my mouth is dry as I catch my breath and finally settle down. I'm still crying; I can't make it stop.

"You're okay," Nikolai says.

I shake my head and try to disagree, but no words come out. I don't even have the energy to fight him, plus my head is still swimming. Pretty sure I can thank the tequila for that.

Once he's sure I won't attack again, he releases my hands, and I let them fall to my sides.

"We'll clean up the mess later," Nikolai says. "I think you and I should have a chat."

---

Turns out, Nikolai lives in the loft above the pub. He unlocks the door, gesturing for me to walk ahead of him. I hesitate in the hallway, waiting for alarm bells to blare in my head about the potential danger of being up here with Nikolai alone. But then I consider everything he's done for me since I became fae; he hasn't given me a reason not to trust him. Besides, as bad as it sounds, I'm finding it really difficult to care whether this is safe, so I step inside and look around.

There's a small, simple kitchen right off the entryway with stainless-steel appliances, faux marble countertop, and white cupboards. I can't picture Nikolai preparing meals for himself, but the dishes in the sink displace my assumption that he doesn't cook.

The kitchen island and seating area open into the living room, an open concept design that makes the place feel modern and large. There's a flat-screen television and an L-shaped couch with a dark wood coffee and matching side table. It's very simple and impersonal. It's the complete opposite of what I'd picture for Nikolai.

He stands in the kitchen and brews a pot of coffee, pouring us each a mug before joining me in the living room and settling onto the couch.

"What do you want to talk about?" I ask.

He takes a sip before setting his mug on the coffee table, then turns to look at me. "Let's start at the beginning."

I arch a brow, sipping on my own coffee. "As in the night I was taken by the fae?"

"Why don't we start with the night you killed Jules?" The suggestion is gentle, but that doesn't make the thought of talking about it easier. I haven't spoken to anyone about it, and the idea of opening up to Nikolai, someone who knew Jules—hell, the fae who took over his position in the unseelie court—feels wrong.

I wet my lips. "How do I know I can trust you?" Not sure why I'm bothering to ask now, but the words leave my lips nonetheless.

His smile is faint. "Are you sure you'd like me to answer that?"

I shrug. "Sure."

"There have been ninety-seven optimal opportunities for me to take you out since you killed Jules."

My eyes widen. "What the hell?"

"There's a reason the queen chose me to take over Jules's position."

I frown from behind my mug as I take another sip. "You could kill me right now," I mutter rather pointlessly. I think it's fairly obvious.

Nikolai chuckles. "Relax, Aurora. I have no desire to kill you or to see you dead by any other means."

My responding laugh is breathy. "Good to know." I set my mug down. "I'm kind of surprised you're still being nice to me after how meeting your queen went."

"You were quite bold," he says. "Ophelia would never say it, but I think your resolve impressed her."

"Really?" I ask with an arched brow.

Nikolai shrugs. "It impressed me." He takes a sip of his coffee. "But you should know that being unaligned could pose further challenges for you. It leaves you unprotected from both courts."

I frown at the similarity to the situation Allison faced being with Evan. I suppose it's pretty hypocritical of me not to choose a court when I harped on her about the potential of not having one.

I can't argue with what Nikolai said, so I pose another question. "What were you doing the day we met in my hometown?"

His brows lift. "Hmm. I figured that would've been your first question when I ran into you last week."

"To be fair, you caught me off guard. I wasn't expecting to see you on stage—or anywhere, really."

He nods. "What did you think?"

"About what?"

"My performance."

"I told you. You shouldn't feed off humans like you did."

He rolls his eyes. "Not what I meant. We'll come back to that, though."

I shake my head. "Okay?" I run my fingers across the soft cotton throw on the back of his couch. "You meant your singing? Are you seriously fishing for compliments right now?"

He grins. "Nah. I know I'm awesome."

I refuse to stroke his ego, even though his voice *is* amazing. He doesn't need me to tell him that.

"All right, all right. So, the day we met. Before I knew much about you, like before Jules targeted you, there was a small group of us who were tiring of the guy."

A shiver runs through me, and I frown. "So you *were*

going to let them kill me?"

He waves me off. "Chill out, gorgeous. They weren't going to kill you. They were going to use you to get the shit they wanted from Jules. He wanted to use you to get to Tristan, and they wanted to use you to get to *him*."

Nikolai's explanation doesn't make me feel any better. *How were they going to use me?* I suppose it doesn't matter now that Jules is gone.

"Anyway, that plan was ruined when your annoying Prince Charming got involved."

I scrunch my nose. "He'd kill you for calling him that."

Nikolai smirks. "He'd try."

I shoot him a look. "I still don't understand why you're trying to help me since I've made it clear I want nothing to do with the fae world you seem to think I'm going to change."

"You're right," he muses. "I should just let you go to your fae friends for help." He leans in a little and lowers his voice. "Oh, wait. You won't."

I press my lips together and stay silent as my eyes narrow. I can't disagree with him, though.

"Hey, I don't blame you. I get it. That's what's so great about me—well, one of the great things about me. There are many."

"Nikolai," I mutter, rubbing my temples. This conversation was supposed to make me feel better; it's just giving me a headache.

"You'll let me help," he says, "because I mean nothing to you, so you don't care what I think of you."

Huh. That actually makes sense. That, or spending time with Nikolai has clouded my judgment.

He meets my gaze. "I'm not asking you to trust me

blindly. I understand that's something I have to earn, and that's fine."

I catch my lower lip between my teeth as silence stretches between us. Finally, I say, "What happened with Jules went down far from what we'd planned. Tristan knew that me killing Jules would trigger the dormant fae magic in me, which is why *he* was supposed to be the one to kill Jules. It didn't happen that way, and now we both have to live with shit—me being fae, and Tristan the guilt of not getting there in time to execute the plan or warning me what would happen if I delivered the killing blow."

Nikolai frowns. "You had fae magic in you as a human?"

"Long story short, that's what brought Tristan and I together."

"Okay, then. I'm definitely curious about how you bagged one of the most powerful fae in history, but perhaps now isn't the best time to delve into that."

"Yeah." I'm not in the headspace to recount meeting Tristan.

"Let me get this straight. You left Westbrook because you don't want him to see you struggling?"

The room is silent, save for the sound of our heartbeats. "I left," I say, "because I need to figure this out on my own. Tristan blames himself for what happened, and I'm scared that guilt is all he'll feel if he sees me like this."

His brows pull closer. "Something tells me he'd disagree with your decision."

I almost laugh. "That's his favorite thing to do."

Nikolai's lips quirk.

Letting loose a heavy sigh, I say, "I can do this without him." I flick my gaze across his face. "I have you, remember?"

He beams. "That you do. Now, listen to me carefully." He pins me with a deep stare. "You can't survive on food alone, Aurora. By now, you have to know you need to feed."

I stay silent.

"You can feel it, can't you? Your body shutting down?"

Squeezing my eyes shut, I nod reluctantly. "I'm exhausted all the time. My head won't stop spinning, and the idea of eating makes my stomach sick." It's a damn shame, too, because I love food.

"That sounds about right," he muses, and I open my eyes to look at him. "What's your big idea? How are you planning on making it through this transition?"

I don't have a response because I don't have a plan.

His eyes narrow a bit. "Unless you weren't planning on making it through at all."

I scowl as that familiar ache blossoms in my chest. "I wasn't going to off myself, jackass."

"Then what? Did you think you could magically survive without feeding? That maybe you were so damn special that you could continue to live as a human regardless of the fact you're not?"

My pulse spikes, and I snap, "Fuck you. How is this supposed to help me?"

"Consider it a reality check. I can't help you if you don't want to be helped."

Crossing my arms over my chest, I let his words sink in. I don't want to die. This new life isn't something I would've chosen for myself, but it's because of me I'm forced to live with it. In this case, I'm my own worst enemy. "I want help," I say in a quiet voice.

He reaches over and pats my leg. "Glad to hear I'm not wasting my extremely valuable time, then." There's that easy arrogance back.

I nod. "Please teach me. Not today, though. It's been disastrous enough, and I don't have the strength for any more. But when I'm ready, you'll teach me how to feed and how to deal with crowds of people and their emotions suffocating me? Because I don't think I can handle that happening again."

"Please. Once I'm done with you, you'll be the poster child for the perfect fae."

I roll my eyes. "You're not creating 'the perfect fae' with me, Nikolai. You're teaching me how to survive."

He gasps mockingly. "What's the point of surviving if you're not living?"

"Like you're some expert?"

Darkness clouds the bright green of his eyes, and I suddenly wish I hadn't spoken. His lips turn down and a soft sigh escapes his lips. "Aurora, I've done a lot of living in my life, but like you, I've also done a lot of surviving. I'm sure it will surprise you to know that I wasn't always this awesome." He exhales a laugh, shaking his head. "I think that's a story for another time."

## CHAPTER
# THIRTY-FOUR

After chatting with Nikolai yesterday, I have a new sense of optimism. I'm going to figure out how to be fae. It won't be easy, but I've always thrived when presented with a challenge, and I refuse to let this be any different.

With this newfound resolve to figure things out, I can't help but think about what this could mean for me and Tristan. Maybe once I feel better, more like myself again, we can reconnect. My stomach drops when one invasive thought takes hold. I may have forsaken the courts, but Tristan is very much aligned with the seelies. I couldn't see the seelie king accepting us when I *answered to the unseelie court*, but I have absolutely no idea how he'd view one of his knights—his favorite—being with a fae who refused both courts. Will it matter?

I'm spinning out at my desk in the dorm when a knock sounds at the door. Allison's in class, so I get up and open it to find Nikolai standing on the other side, looking like a model ready for a photo shoot. His hair is tousled—no doubt styled that way—and the dark, form-fitting leather jacket brings the whole James Dean look he's got going on to another level of attractive.

"Hi..."

Nikolai struts inside as if he owns the place.

"Uh, sure," I grumble, "come on in." I close the door and turn as Nikolai drops onto the end of my bed.

He grins, flashing his stupid, perfect teeth. "Ready to learn how to feed?"

"Can't wait," I remark dryly. There's a part of me that longs to get this shitty learning stage over with. To feel better—not as if I'm nearing my deathbed at twenty-one years old—which is why I've agreed to let Nikolai teach me today.

"You're in excellent hands," he praises himself. "I'm awesome at this." Recalling him feeding off the crowd at the pub gives me a bit more faith in his words, but his excessive enthusiasm makes me want to call the whole thing off right now. "Let's get out of here. I'm starving, and there's this café nearby I've recently become obsessed with. We can talk strategy before trying anything."

I'm not sure what *strategy* entails, but I nod. "I'll go get changed."

His eyes flick to my less than modest sleepwear. "I mean, *I* have no issue with your attire, but the rest of the public might stare."

I flip him off and walk into the bathroom. After changing into thick leggings and a comfortable sweater, I return to the bedroom.

"All set?" he asks.

I blow out a breath. "I guess so." My optimism from earlier is fading, replaced by skepticism and nerves.

He shifts, appearing right in front of me, and grabs my

arms before I can step back. "If you believe you're going to fail, you will." His dark lashes lower. "You want to get better, right?"

My eyes fly to his. "Of course, I do."

His hands slide down my arms and drop away. "Good."

When he starts toward the front door, I sigh. "Nikolai, I need you to glamour my appearance. Allison's been doing it because—"

"Because you can't if you don't feed," he interjects, turning back to me. In a matter of seconds, he conceals my pointed ears, glowing eyes, and blue tinted skin before stepping back. "Let's do this."

---

Sitting across from Nikolai in a café isn't as weird as I thought it would be. That's not to say I ever thought it would happen, because until the night at The Iron Lounge, I didn't think I'd see him again.

Over the years I've gone to school in the city, I've never been to this coffee shop. I take in the sleek, modern decor. The worn oak table we're sitting at has wrought-iron chairs with plush cushions. I make a point not to touch the chair with anything but my ass on the padded seat for fear of iron burn. The floor is clean, shiny white tile and the walls are a light gray. The front is made of windows, letting in the natural light; the whole place has a pleasing aesthetic. I understand why Nikolai enjoys coming here. Breakfast food has always been my favorite. There's never a wrong time to eat it—except when you feel as if you'll hurl if you eat anything.

Nikolai orders us some coffee, while I slip into the bathroom near the back of the café to splash cold water on my face, willing the nausea rolling around my stomach to recede. When I return to our table, he's fully engrossed in the menu. My eyes flick over it, but most of the selection makes me want to gag right now.

"You look like you're about to vomit," Nikolai comments, peering at me over his menu.

I don't even have the energy to fake a smile. "I feel that way, too."

His brows tug closer. "It could be—Wait. You and Westbrook. Did you...?"

My eyes narrow. "I'm not pregnant," I whisper-yell. "God, Nikolai." I huff out a scowl. "Can fae even get humans pregnant?"

Nikolai's expression transforms, going from light and at ease to something dark, hard. Haunted. "Yes," he says in a low voice. In the space of a heartbeat, his face returns to his normal, but my head is spinning. I want to ask him what happened, but I can't bring myself to do it. Not with the way he looked moments ago.

"You need to order something." His eyes return to the menu as mine flick toward the sound of coffee beans grinding in a machine behind the counter at the front of the café. "Their French toast is a-fucking-mazing."

My chest tightens. "No French toast." I struggle not to think about the morning before the gala in Tristan's kitchen.

"All right," he says. "I'm going to eat my weight in blueberry pancakes. Feel free to join me."

I take one more look at the menu as the waiter stops at our table, then order a fruit bowl before Nikolai asks for the largest plate of blueberry pancakes available.

Once the waiter is gone, Nikolai leans in and lowers his voice. "Here's the plan: after we eat, I'm going to take you to the feeder unit. I would've taken you there first, but this place was on the way, and as we established, I'm fucking starving."

I prod the inside of my cheek with my tongue. "I'm not sure about the whole feeding unit thing." The whole thing still seems freaky.

He takes a sip of coffee. "I'm going to be with you the whole time, so you don't need to worry. Your first feed can be overwhelming, but I'm confident it'll go well."

"Because you're going to be there?" I ask sarcastically.

He smirks, leaning back. "Now you're getting it."

I stop myself from rolling my eyes. Nikolai can be a bit much, but while he's helping me, I'm going to have to deal with it. Until I can feed without fear of hurting someone, I need him.

Allison and Tristan would both hate me not going to them for help, but I can't. They're too important. Nikolai doesn't know me. He's someone I can learn from, and he seems to enjoy showing me the ropes.

"How often will I have to feed?"

"The norm for most fae is once every couple of days. Older fae can go up to a week between feeds, though most don't because that also means their abilities aren't as strong. That said, it'll be a learn-as-we-go sort of process to see what feels best to you. You've gotten away without feeding for so long because you took the energy Jules had when he died and what I gave you. Once you've fed for real the first time, we'll have a baseline to go off."

I'm not sure what I was hoping to hear—probably that I didn't have to feed at all, which is absurd—but the weight on my chest feels heavier.

Nikolai wolfs down his food, cleaning his plate, while I

pick at the fruit in front of me. I'm hoping that once I feed, I can go back to eating like normal.

After breakfast, we head down the sidewalk. I don't know where we're going, so I follow Nikolai.

"Is feeding immediately after eating human food a good idea?" I ask.

"Eating human food fills our stomachs, while feeding boosts our energy and abilities." He glances over at me. "The feeder unit is a few blocks ahead."

"Do these humans know about the fae? Or do they have their memories wiped?"

He shrugs. "It depends on the human. They're extensively evaluated after their first feeding session to see if they're likely to commit to more, and if not, someone from the security team will erase any memories that human has of the fae."

"Are there some who keep their memories?" That sounds like it has the potential to be dangerous. Aren't they worried about exposure?

"Yes," he answers. "Feeding can be addictive for both parties, but usually more so for the human. They enjoy it, and most want to continue being fed from. They are monitored and most live normal, mundane lives outside of the feeding units."

"How many units are there?" I suppose I should be relieved that there are places fae can feed safely.

"In the city? Last I heard there were ten, but more will open in the future. It's a safer alternative to feeding in public."

"You don't seem concerned about doing that," I mutter.

He chuckles. "That's because I've been feeding for a long time, Aurora. I'm good at it and I won't hurt anyone.

Feeding from crowds is typically safer than taking from an individual."

I nod, then hesitate before asking, "How old are you?"

He flicks his tongue over his bottom lip and smirks a bit. "Old."

"First fae war old?"

"Not quite. Older than Tristan, though."

"Hmm." I scratch the back of my head. He doesn't seem open to giving me his actual age, so I move on. "Do a lot of the fae use these feeding units?"

"Some. From both courts, though we stick to different units. Others don't like feeding in such a controlled environment." Those fae probably aren't concerned about hurting humans like I am. Part of my reluctance to feed stems from this deep-rooted fear I'll end up losing control and won't be able to stop. Especially after the taste of energy Nikolai gave me—how intoxicating that felt—it seems like a valid concern.

Several blocks later, we come to a stop outside a plain-looking storefront. The small window in the front is tinted, and the door is a solid sheet of dark gray metal. It's not welcoming, but that's probably the point. Unless you know what it's there for, the fae don't want you to pay it any attention.

Nikolai steps in front of me, leading us around the side of the building through a narrow, damp alley, and stops at another metal door. I stand frozen beside him; my heart is ticking faster, and my palms are clammy. My body is reacting as if *I'm* the one being fed on. I shouldn't be this nervous, not with Nikolai here, but I can't shake the unease.

"Aurora," he says. "You're going to do fine. Once you

get through one feed, it'll be a breeze, and you'll start to feel like yourself again."

Inhaling through my nose, I hold my breath for a moment before letting it out through my mouth, then nod. "Let's go."

He opens the door and holds it for me. I step inside ahead of him and take in my surroundings. It's what appears to be a waiting room; the walls are a calming lavender color, and the floor is a dark hardwood. Chairs line one wall and there's a reception desk on the other side of the small room.

Nikolai nudges me forward and walks beside me to the desk where an attractive brown-haired woman sits, smiling brightly.

"Hello," she says with a warm smile. "Good to see you again, Nikolai."

He winks at her, and I fight the urge to roll my eyes. "Always a pleasure, Destiny."

She giggles before turning her attention back to me. "You must be Aurora. It's so great to finally meet you. You're quite the talk of the fae world right now. Tristan must be pouting somewhere. He loves when people talk about him."

Oh boy, do I feel uncomfortable. I force a smile. "Thanks. Nice to meet you, Destiny."

"I'll get a couple of rooms set up for you."

My stomach drops before Nikolai says, "Just one for today, please."

She doesn't question him, just nods and says, "Of course." She disappears into another room, leaving Nikolai and I alone.

"She's human," he comments, "in case you couldn't tell."

I hadn't taken a close enough look to even attempt to decipher any potentially inhuman features. "Hmm. You just come on to everyone then, don't you?"

A grin plays on his lips. "You jealous?"

I scowl. "Please."

"You don't need to beg, gorgeous. Once we're done here, I'd be more than happy to—"

"All set. Last room on your right," Destiny says in a chipper voice, walking back into view just in time to stop me from having to reject Nikolai a second time. I can't deny his attractiveness, but it just doesn't do anything for me. I don't think it ever could, even if I wanted it to. And the playfulness in Nikolai's eyes makes me think he isn't serious about it either.

I nod to tell Nikolai to go ahead so I can follow him, and he obliges. At the end of a hall, Nikolai opens the door to another room and steps inside. After a moment of hesitation, I enter, closing the door. The room is a perfect square with plain white walls and a plush carpet beneath my feet. The only thing inside is a black leather recliner and two smaller chairs on either side of it. A speaker in the ceiling plays soft instrumental music. The atmosphere is calm, subdued, and yet my pulse is racing. I don't know if I can go through with this. When my eyes fall back to the curvy, dark-haired woman sitting in the chair, I suck in a breath. She's smiling as if she's happy to see me, *as if we're friends*. Not as if I'm here to feed off of her energy. She looks to be around forty, but the brightness in her eyes makes her appear younger.

"Hi," I say after clearing my throat.

"Come sit, dear." She pats the chair on her right as Nikolai sits on the one to her left.

Once I'm sure my feet aren't cemented to the floor, I

approach and lower myself onto the chair, turning to face her and Nikolai. "I've never done this before," I admit.

"Don't worry. I've done this plenty of times."

Nikolai smiles politely at her.

"How long have... I mean—"

"How long have I been a feeder?"

Cringing at my awkward inability to get out the question, I nod.

"About five years."

I want to ask how she got into it, but that doesn't seem appropriate. I'm also taken aback by the attitude of this woman. She *wants* to be here. Nikolai said they're compensated and that it can be pleasant for them, but it still feels kind of icky to me. Having been on that side before I became fae, I don't think I'll ever understand the desire to be fed on. The invasion of privacy and autonomy makes my skin crawl.

"I don't know how this works," I say, wiping my hands on my thighs.

"That's what I'm here for," Nikolai chimes in. "The feeding process is quite simple. Being fae, you need human energy to survive. It sustains us. Don't ask me why. I'm not into science or magic or whatever the hell you want to call this. Anyway, we siphon energy, which stems from human emotions. Some fae have a preference of which they enjoy most, but at this point you might not be able to tell different emotions apart in terms of how the energy makes you feel. We'll have to see. Now, for the good part." He winks at the woman, reaching for her wrist, and holds it where it sits on the armrest, wrapping his fingers around it. She closes her eyes, sighing as if she's enjoying herself. After a couple of moments, Nikolai pulls his hand away and shoots me a grin, his eyes glowing faintly. "Easy as that," he says simply, not as if he just sucked energy out of a human being.

"Easy?" I echo. "I don't know what you did."

Nikolai offers me his hand. I blink at it a couple of times before placing mine on top. He turns our hands over and guides mine against the woman's arm. "Close your eyes," he instructs. "It'll help you concentrate."

"Do I have to touch her?"

"Yes."

I nod and follow his direction, letting my eyelids flutter shut, feeling the warmth of his hand on mine and mine on the human's.

"Visualize yourself pulling the energy out of her. See her emotions as a physical thing. A ribbon of color. Pull it out of her and feel it flow into you."

I picture her energy as a bright pink rope that's wrapped around her. Once I grab it, I gasp at the influx of energy that surges through me. It seeps into me as I continue pulling on the rope.

Nikolai lifts his hand off of mine, letting me feed on my own, praising me in a soft voice as energy keeps flowing into me, easing the aches in my muscles and the nausea in my stomach until it's gone completely. Waves of emotion trickle through that ribbon. My lips curl into a blissful smile, my shoulders feel light; I feel *good*. Oh my god, this is amazing. Euphoric, even. I feel more awake, more alive than I ever have. I don't want this feeling to stop. Even when my gums throb with pressure, and I suck in a breath as my teeth transform into a mouthful of razor-sharp fangs.

"Aurora," Nikolai cuts into my warm, fuzzy thoughts. "That's enough."

My grip tightens on the woman's arm as if I'm worried

he'll take her away from me. She whimpers under my touch, but I keep my eyes closed, still pulling energy from her. A flicker of panic cracks through my veins, almost like a pins and needles sensation shimmering across my body, but I can't let go. This sensation is all-consuming—I can't give it up.

"*Aurora*," Nikolai snaps, ripping my hand away from her arm. She slumps in the chair, her eyes fluttering before she passes out. The sight of her still form and pale face is like a bucket of ice water being dumped on me.

I suck in a sharp breath and cough on the dryness in my throat. "I..." My legs move on their own, lifting me from the chair and hurrying down the hallway and out of the building. I ignore Destiny when she calls after me, her voice drowned out by the pounding of my heart.

Someone grabs my elbow and spins me around. My eyes lift to Nikolai's soft gaze. Understanding fills the bright green irises, which makes me feel worse, as if he was expecting this—for me to mess up and hurt that woman.

"Aurora, it was your first time." He lifts a hand and glamours me so my teeth return to normal.

"Don't," I plead. "I don't want you to tell me what I just did was okay, because it wasn't. I could have killed her." This is exactly what I was afraid of. If I can't feed without losing control, how am I supposed to survive being fae?

"But you *didn't*."

I shake my head. Even as my entire body sings with energy and power, all I can feel is shame wrapping its dark, heavy tendrils around me.

## CHAPTER
# THIRTY-FIVE

When Nikolai asks me to come to The Iron Lounge with him instead of going back to the dorm, part of me thinks he just doesn't want to leave me after what happened at the feeding unit. I don't question him, though, mostly because I really don't want to be alone right now.

When we walk inside and I see Skylar standing at the bar, my stomach sinks. *What is she doing here?*

Deacon throws his hands up and comes around the bar, putting a cigarette between his lips. "I'm going for my break," he mutters to Nikolai on his way past. The door slams shut behind him. A few sets of eyes turn to look, but quickly lose interest.

Skylar huffs out a breath, shaking her head before tossing her pin-straight, inky hair over her shoulder. Her eyes flick past me to a booth.

I turn and find a fae glaring at Skylar. I don't expect him to do or say anything, not with human patrons close by, but hell, if looks could kill.

Skylar rolls her eyes and turns her attention back to me, crossing her arms. She's dressed formally, as I'm used to seeing her, in an emerald, knee-length dress over sheer, dark stockings. Her long black wool coat likely cost ten times what my winter jacket cost when I bought it three years ago. "I went to your dorm. Allison was on her way out and said you weren't there."

"She was with me," Nikolai cuts in, grinning like a cat.

Her eyes flick toward him, giving him a quick once-over. She doesn't look impressed. "Wonderful." The sarcasm is clear in her tone.

"What's up, Sky?" I ask, earning her attention again.

"We need to talk."

I frown, nerves unfurling in my stomach. "That sounds unpleasant."

"Good to know you're just as perceptive now." She presses her lips together as if she's making sure the bright red lipstick is still in place. "Perhaps we could have some privacy?" Her eyes slide to Nikolai, who's still standing at my side.

"You can use the office," Nikolai offers.

I step forward to walk across the room, but Nikolai catches my arm. I arch a brow at him. "What?"

"I'm coming with you."

"You don't have to. I'm not in danger."

Skylar snorts, and Nikolai narrows his eyes at her. "Watch it," he growls.

"Down, boy," she remarks in a bored tone.

"Okay," I cut in before they can get into it in front of all these people. "Let's go."

Skylar sneers at Nikolai—whose only response is a wicked smirk—before he leads the way toward the hallway. I exhale an uneven breath before following him, with Skylar walking next to me.

The three of us step into the office, and Nikolai closes the door, leaning against it as if he's guarding the thing. "Speak up, kitten. We don't have all day."

Skylar whirls on him. "What the fuck did you just call me?" Her jaw is sharp enough to cut glass.

He whistles, thrusting his hand through his already messy hair. "Easy. Put the claws away." Her claws are glamoured; Nikolai is baiting her.

"Nikolai," I groan. This will go downhill fast if he keeps opening his mouth. Turning my attention back to where Skylar has perched on the edge of the desk, I ask, "What's going on?"

She crosses her arms, looking at me. "The king has summoned Tristan."

My pulse skyrockets at the mention of him, and anxiety bubbles in my chest, threatening to boil over. "What does that mean?"

"It could mean many things. Regardless, he'd like to see you tomorrow morning at the hotel before he meets with Rowan."

"No," Nikolai cuts in. "There's no way we're walking into a building full of seelie fae right now. I don't care that the attacks have decreased since Jules kicked off. It still isn't safe."

Skylar doesn't even spare him a glance. "Nine o'clock," she tells me.

"Absolutely fucking not." Nikolai pushes away from the door and prowls closer. "I don't trust anyone there, especially not Westbrook."

"And I don't care, Sterling." She looks at me with a

passive expression. "See you tomorrow." She slides off the desk and steps past me, but Nikolai blocks her exit.

"We're not done here," he barks at her.

She huffs out a laugh. "Oh, yeah?"

I frown at the two of them in the middle of a glaring match. The sight is comical; Nikolai towers over her by at least a foot, even with Skylar in heels. He's leaning toward her as if he's ready to pounce. While she looks tiny opposite him, I'm confident she could hold her own if it came to a fight, which I really hope it doesn't because I'm not sure I'd be skilled—or brave (stupid?)—enough to step between them.

"You think it's a good idea for her to walk into a building full of your people?" Nikolai shoots at Skylar.

"I walked in here without a problem."

His eyes don't leave hers. "She's not going alone."

I don't bother interjecting, though part of me wants to tell Nikolai that Tristan wouldn't let the seelie fae hurt me.

Skylar arches a brow. "Please, by all means, join her."

Nikolai's eyes narrow. "I wasn't looking for an invitation."

She scowls and moves to step around him, but he blocks her again. "Get out of my way," she snaps, but the usual venom isn't laced in her tone. It's almost as if she's... enjoying this—and I'm not really sure what to do with that besides watch awkwardly from the sidelines.

"Why?" He smirks tauntingly, while I decide to sit this one out and let the two of them deal with each other.

"You think you can handle me, Sterling?" The challenge in her voice sounds more like an invitation. One an arrogant man like Nikolai would never decline.

His eyes flash as he leans closer to her face. "I'm quite certain of it, kitten."

She bares her teeth, flashing her mouth full of fangs. "Move," she growls. I'm waiting for her to punch him. I shouldn't want to see it, but I kind of do. He could handle getting knocked down a peg or two, and Skylar could take care of that.

Finally, he steps to the side, letting her past, and she throws the door open, storming out of the office.

I let out a breath. "Was that necessary?"

He's grinning when he says, "Most definitely."

---

The following morning, I wake with a stomach full of knots and what seems like never-ending hot flashes. I haven't been this nervous since the day I had my internship interview.

I want to cancel. To stay in my bed wrapped in blankets like a burrito and pretend the fae courts don't exist. Pretend I don't have to face the seelie fae knight I fell for over the last five months after being dragged into his world and becoming fae. Seeing Tristan... It's not something I'm ready for.

Reminding myself of what Skylar said yesterday about the seelie king calling for a meeting with Tristan forces me out of bed. I need to know he's okay.

I shower and get dressed in a navy sweater and black high-waisted jeans, drying and straightening my hair before putting on makeup. I don't have to cover up the physical proof of my fae struggles with concealer today. In fact, my reflection looks more refreshed than ever. Even so, the unease in my chest grows, along with a conflicting fluttering in my stomach.

My phone chimes with a text from Nikolai, letting me

know he's outside. Part of me isn't sure about him coming—the last thing I need is to deal with a fae fight between him and Tristan—but if I run into any seelies who aren't too happy to see me, I want backup.

In the car, Nikolai glances over at me and stares as if he's trying to see what I'm thinking.

"Quit it," I mutter, squirming under his gaze. He's checking up on me, and while I appreciate it, now is not a great time to gauge how I'm feeling. Not with the ribbons of nerves winding around me.

Nikolai shoots me a grin before he pulls away from the curb, and we spend the drive to the hotel in silence. We pull into the guest parking lot, and Nikolai finds a spot near the front of the building. I peek down at my hands in my lap and clench them into fists so they'll stop shaking.

Nikolai turns to face me. "You've got this, Aurora. No sweat."

I choke on a laugh, meeting his steady gaze. "We're about to walk into a building where many people hated me as a human. I can't see them approving of me more as an unaligned fae." I'm not sure if it'd be better or worse if I chose the unseelie court, but either way, I'm glad Nikolai is with me.

"If it makes you feel better, I promise they hate me more than they hate you."

I catch my bottom lip between my teeth. He's probably right, but that doesn't make this meeting any easier to walk into. Taking a deep breath, I let it out slowly. "Okay," I say, putting as much force and confidence into that one word as I can.

The lobby is buzzing with people as Nikolai and I approach the concierge desk, where Marisa greets us with a wide smile.

"Aurora, welcome back." Her voice is soft, friendly. Her eyes flick to Nikolai, who is standing behind me. "Who's your friend?"

"Nikolai Sterling," he says, eyeing her name tag. "Lovely to meet you, Marisa."

"I have a meeting with Tristan," I chime in before Nikolai can start flirting with her. We don't have time for that, and I'm not in the mood to watch him charm Marisa.

"Of course." She clicks away at the computer for a few seconds. "I see there's a meeting on the calendar, so he should be in his office, if you want to head up." She hands me a guest badge.

I force a smile, taking it from her. "Thanks."

Nikolai and I head for the elevator. Once we're riding to the thirty-ninth floor, my pulse kicks up. I stand frozen against the back wall until Nikolai nudges my shoulder.

"You need to relax."

*Yeah, there's no fucking chance of that.*

"I haven't spoken to him since the day I killed Jules."

The elevator stops on the tenth floor and slides open before Nikolai has a chance to respond. A woman steps on and glances at me. My mouth goes dry when I recognize her as the fae who attacked and fed on me in this very elevator months ago. I clench my jaw as my heart pounds in my chest, anger bubbling violently. This was *not* an obstacle I needed to face today. It must be the universe's idea of a twisted joke.

She shoots me a dirty look, and that's all it takes for me to lose control. I'm moving before I can stop myself, slamming her against the side of the elevator, just as she did to me. My fingers wrap around her throat without a second of hesitation, cutting off her air.

"Aurora," Nikolai warns in a low, calm voice, but makes

no move to stop me, as if he's not concerned I'll genuinely hurt this woman.

A smile touches my lips as her face turns red, and her eyes bulge. She tries to fight back by clawing at my arms, but it doesn't faze me. I revel in the fear radiating from her. While I'm not feeding off it, just the sight—the stark ribbons of color shooting out of her chest—is euphoric. I've never *seen* emotion like this before, and it's... beautiful. I recognize how messed up that is, but the resentment I have toward this fae drowns out reason.

I'm too caught up in my anger to realize the elevator stopped. I look over my shoulder to see the door open to the office lobby and Max standing there, looking shocked for the first time since I've known him.

Nikolai snakes his arm around my waist and pulls me away from the woman.

She gasps for air, dragging in quick, shallow breaths as she glares at me. "You're a real bitch," she snarls, blinking back tears.

"You—"

"That's enough," Nikolai cuts in.

Reminding myself that he's looking out for me, I close my mouth and turn my back on the fae woman as I step off the elevator into the familiar reception area of Westbrook Inc.'s offices.

"Long time no see, blondie." Max shoots Nikolai a dark look before shifting his gaze back to me. "Tristan's waiting in his office."

"Thanks, Max." I lead the way, knowing where to go, and Nikolai follows. He knocks on the door I stop in front of.

"Come in." Tristan's voice is muffled through the door, but still, my heart races.

My gaze meets Nikolai's as I inhale, focusing enough to build a wall around my emotions. I picture it as if I'm stacking bricks around the colors of emotion, blocking them from radiating from me. Nikolai nods, having noticed what I was doing; his gaze is full of unwavering support, which pushes me to square my shoulders and open the door, stepping over the threshold into Tristan's office.

My eyes land on him, and I swallow hard. He's standing behind his desk with his back to us, looking out the window. I jump when the door closes and Tristan turns.

The sight of him threatens to knock the air out of my lungs, but I force what I hope is a calm, neutral expression. I take him in, unable to stop myself from staring. Glimpsing him at the job fair wasn't enough. I want to take my time and ingrain every detail of him to memory.

He looks polished and pristine, as usual, in a black suit and dress shirt, though he's without a tie today. His hair is neatly styled and curling a bit at the ends, making my finger itch to run through it.

Tristan's eyes freeze on me, making my heart pound against my rib cage until he flicks a glance to where Nikolai is standing behind me. His eyes, the color of brilliant lapis lazuli, narrow as a growl rumbles in his throat.

Nikolai's posture stiffens as he bares his teeth at Tristan.

I let loose a sigh. "Really, guys? Can you not?"

Nikolai chuckles, but Tristan's stubble-shadowed jaw clenches.

I focus on Tristan. "You asked us here," I remind him, mustering a strong, even voice.

"I asked you here," he says. "*Not* him."

"We're a package deal right now," Nikolai purrs in an

arrogant tone, and my jaw clenches at the sound of Tristan's low growl.

I ram my elbow into Nikolai's ribs and meet Tristan's narrowed gaze. "Ignore him. I'm sure there are more important things we should talk about."

A muscle feathers along Tristan's jaw before his expression smoothes, and he gestures for Nikolai and I to sit on the other side of his desk as he undoes the button of his suit jacket and lowers himself into his chair.

We walk over and sit. Nikolai crosses his arms while I set mine in my lap and press my lips together.

"Skylar told me you were summoned," I say, the pit in my stomach keeping me from telling him what I desperately want to. *I fucking miss you.* "Do you know what the seelie king wants?" I have to assume it has something to do with me; otherwise, why would he ask me here?

His eyes roam my face, drinking me in, and the breath gets caught in my throat. Finally, he says, "I have a good idea." His eyes slide to Nikolai as he seems to get sidetracked. "I understand your queen has made you a knight."

Nikolai nods. "I'll assume your congratulations were lost in the mail."

A muscle ticks along Tristan's jaw. "Yeah, do that. And then you can tell me why I've received reports that unseelie fae are plotting to ambush the king during the spring equinox ceremony next month."

Nikolai leans back in his chair, crossing one knee over the other. "I've only had an audience with the queen twice since I took over for Jules. This didn't come up."

Tristan's eyes narrow. "You don't know anything about it?"

"Am I being interrogated right now?" Nikolai asks in a hardened voice.

"Right now, you're avoiding my question."

Nikolai's back straightens. "You have some nerve, Westbrook. I brought your girl here—after taking care of her since she became fae—to make sure you weren't in danger, because she was worried about you. I'm not going to sit here and—"

"Nikolai," I cut in, heat filling my cheeks.

Nikolai shakes his head, his eyes blazing with thinly veiled anger. "I don't know about any unseelie fae targeting your precious king," he sneers at Tristan. "Though I *have* heard a rampant increase in attacks on the unseelie fae. Perhaps we should talk about that?"

*What? There have been more attacks on the unseelie court?* This is the first I'm hearing of it, and based on the grim expression painting Tristan's sharp features, I have to think he's learning it just now, too.

"Do you have specific information you'd like to share?"

Nikolai pauses before shaking his head. "That's not my area of expertise."

Tristan makes a sound between a snort and a scowl. "Hmm. What exactly *is* your 'area of expertise'?"

"How about keeping Aurora alive?" he shoots back, and my pulse jackhammers as the air leeches from the room, making it hard to breathe.

Tristan grips the arms of his chair, and I'm half-expecting his claws to protrude from his fingers, but he keeps his human appearance. "I will look into these attacks you've mentioned," he finally says in a low voice.

"Good," Nikolai grumbles.

Tristan's eyes shift to me again as he scratches the stubble lining his jaw; he hasn't shaved in a while.

*I miss the feeling of that against my cheek.*

"I understand you had an audience with the queen."

Tristan's words make my chest tighten. His expression is strained, his jaw sharp.

I hesitate before asking, "How did you know? Did Allison—"

"No," he cuts in gently. "There are several other seelies in your dorm who I've had keeping an eye—and an ear—on things. I apologize if that's intrusive, but I had to know you were okay."

My heart beats in my throat as I stare at the fae I'm still completely enraptured by. "O-okay. Is that why you wanted to meet me?"

"I wanted to see you," he admits. "If it wasn't to ask about the queen, I would've found another excuse." That sends my heart racing, and I tuck my ankles behind the chair legs so I don't do something crazy like launch myself across Tristan's desk and straddle him despite Nikolai sitting next to me. "Will you tell me what happened?" Tristan asks.

I blow out a breath. "It was a short meeting where I basically told her where she could shove it, because I don't want to join the unseelie court."

Those deep blue eyes shine with admiration, and he drags his tongue over his bottom lip as if he's attempting to hide a smile. "I'm sure she took that well." I expect him to look at Nikolai, but his eyes stay locked on me. "I'm happy to hear it. The seelie court is lucky to have you."

My brows knit, and I drop my gaze to the desk that separates us. "Oh. Um, I'm not..." I trail off, the knots in my stomach growing rapidly. "I'm not choosing a court," I force out.

There's a long stretch of silence before Tristan sighs. "Aurora—"

"It's my choice." I drag my gaze back to his. "It's also

my hope that the courts will one day coexist so me not picking one won't be such a big deal."

The tension in his expression is reflected in his posture, and it puts me on edge. "I understand," he finally says. "I don't like it, but I... respect your decision."

My eyes widen, and I shift in my seat, clearing my throat. "Thank you." Needing the conversation to move away from me, I bring it back to the previous topic and ask, "What's the spring equinox ceremony?"

Some of the tension leaves Tristan's shoulders. "A celebration among the seelie fae. It used to be a period when passage between the fae and human worlds was easiest; however, that became obsolete after the war that destroyed our world and we moved here permanently."

"But you still celebrate it?"

Tristan nods. "Hoping to return to our world one day, I suppose."

I take a moment to try to read him. When I hit a mental brick wall, it's clear he's blocking his emotions just as I am. My pulse jumps when Tristan's eyes flit toward me. Heat flares in my cheeks, and I drop my gaze, feeling as if I've been caught doing something wrong.

I try to cover up my embarrassment by saying, "Maybe this planned attack you heard about is a rogue group of fae, not something orchestrated by the queen?"

"It's possible," Tristan offers, flicking a glance toward Nikolai, "but *he* should know what's going on in the unseelie court."

"Because you always know everything happening in yours," Nikolai remarks dryly.

"I've been at this for decades longer than you, Sterling," Tristan says in a short tone, sitting straighter.

"Then protect your king and have your little party." Nikolai turns to me and stands. "I think we should go."

Tristan growls, but I focus on Nikolai as I nod stiffly and get up. This meeting feels unfinished, but it also doesn't seem like it's going anywhere good.

"Aurora." Tristan's voice makes me freeze halfway across the room. "Could I have a moment?"

Nikolai whirls around, but I grab his arm and shake my head. "It's okay." He stares at me with a hard expression before he gives me a curt nod and leaves. The door closing echoes in the silence.

Tristan walks around the desk, closing the distance between us. The butterflies in my stomach flutter crazily, attuned to his presence, which sets me on edge.

Tristan's eyes flick across my face, taking me in as if he's doing it for the first time. His face is different. His fae knight mask is gone; this is the Tristan only I get to see. He tilts his head slightly. "How are you doing?" His voice is soft. It makes my chest tighten.

Tossing the question around in my head, I try to decide the best way to answer it. "I'm—" The word *fine* won't come out. I try again. "I'm—" *Okay* doesn't want to work either. I can't say the words I want to. My brows tug together and my jaw clenches.

"First time you've tried lying since you became fae?" he asks.

I close my eyes, exhaling through my nose. When I open them again, he's still watching me, waiting for an answer. "Things are different." I stumble to the side when my head spins out of nowhere. *Why do I feel like this already?*

Tristan reaches for me immediately, but I pull back fast enough so he doesn't touch me. "You aren't well," he observes with a frown. The concern and confusion are etched on his face; I don't need to read his emotions. "When was the last time you fed?"

"Yesterday."

He frowns, rubbing his jaw idly. "You may need to feed daily for a while until your body gets used to this new sustenance."

Panic is like ice in my veins; I don't *want* to feed every day. "Don't worry about it."

"Aurora—"

"I'm figuring it out, okay? I'm... managing." When my voice cracks, I cringe. I need to leave. I can't keep looking at him.

"It didn't look that way at the job fair."

"I'm better." It's not a lie. I *am* doing better since then, though I know I'll slip back to that place if I don't feed again soon.

He wets his lips. "Are we going to act as though we mean nothing to each other? You don't want me to care about you anymore?"

*Fucking hell.* My eyes burn, but I force the tears back. "Please—"

"Tell me you don't care about me."

I glare at him. "You know I can't do that. Of course, I care about you."

"Then try. It won't ever be easy. We knew that going into this. But isn't it worth fighting for?"

Every fiber of my being wants to surrender, wants to lay myself bare to him and fight for everything we are. Everything we *could* be. But I can't, because as much as I don't want to admit it, there's a part of me unsure it'll work, and that terrifies me.

Not to mention, I won't put him in danger of reprimand from the king should he choose to take issue with me not aligning myself with his court.

Tristan has earned significant status and respect over the years, but that doesn't mean the king will approve of him being with a fae not from the seelie court. Even if Tristan will risk it, which I have to think he is considering he hasn't brought it up, I'm not. Maybe in time, once I get the hang of the whole fae thing, we can talk about it—working together to realign the courts—but that just isn't something I have the strength to take on yet.

"I can't do this right now," I whisper. "I'm sorry. I'll talk to Nikolai and get him to find out anything he can regarding the attack you heard about."

Tristan's brows tug closer. "What does Sterling have to do with this, exactly? With you?"

"He's to me what Max is to you. A confidant—a friend," I say, then frown at the look he gives me. "He can be an asshole and he's annoying as hell at times, but he's been helping me."

"I see," he says in a clipped tone, shaking his head. "It should be *me* helping you, Rory. You wouldn't be in this mess if it wasn't for me."

"I never blamed you, so please, try to let go of that guilt, because it kills me to see it in your eyes when you look at me." I lower my gaze and tug at the hem of my sweater, not sure what else there is to say.

The near desperation in his gaze makes his eyes brighter somehow—it also makes me want to close the distance between us and kiss him until it goes away.

"I understand you need time to adjust to your new life," he says in a smooth voice. "That being said, it doesn't need to keep us apart. At least, I don't want it to, and I have to believe you don't either. And you not choosing to join the unseelie court means I don't have to commit treason," he adds with a brief laugh.

"Me not choosing the seelie court either doesn't pose the same issue?"

He shakes his head. "And if it did, I wouldn't care. Call me a hypocrite."

My head spins and my palms feel damp. I wasn't prepared for *this* conversation today. I inch back a step, not sure how to form the words to tell him I'm too overwhelmed at this moment to talk about what's between us. "I... should go."

He looks as if he wants to argue, to call me out for shutting this down, but he only nods, making the sinking feeling in my stomach grow more pronounced.

"Aurora," Tristan calls after me just as I reach the door.

I pause, turning back to look at him; I'm not sure how much more I can handle.

"Please take care of yourself." His eyes hold mine for a moment that feels like an eternity, and then I walk out the door without a word.

# CHAPTER
# THIRTY-SIX

Once we're back in the car, Nikolai doesn't ask what happened after he left, which I'm grateful for. It was hard enough in the moment. The last thing I want to do is sit and rehash it.

We pull up outside the same feeding unit Nikolai brought me to for my first feed, and he cuts the engine. Pulling the key out, he messes with them before unlatching a building key from his ring. He holds it out to me, and I hesitate before taking it.

"What's this for?"

"I'm giving you a job," he says, pocketing the rest of his keys. "That's to the front door of The Iron Lounge."

I turn a confused expression on him. "Huh?"

"I need help running the place, and you'll have a business degree in a couple of months."

My forehead creases. "I don't know the first thing about running a pub."

He drums his fingers against the steering wheel. "Something tells me you're a quick study."

I consider it. I haven't let go of the dream of owning a bookstore—postponed it, but not forgotten it. That being said, I will need a job, and working with someone who understands what I'm going through is probably the best-case scenario. "Okay," I finally say. "Thanks, I guess."

He grins. "If you could sound less enthused, that'd be great."

I sigh, glancing back out to the window toward the feeding unit. The nerves in my stomach tangle tighter and form a heavy pit. "Why are we here, Nikolai?"

He drums his fingers against the steering wheel. "To adopt a puppy," he remarks dryly.

"Hmm. Fine line between lying and joking, huh?"

Nikolai chuckles. "Yep. Now, let's do this. Practice will make you better."

I arch a brow at him, unbuckling my belt and dragging in one breath after another, trying to calm my jitters over feeding again. "Not perfect?"

"One step at a time, hotshot."

We walk into the feeding unit, and despite my nerves, I try to keep an open mind. I have to be careful here—I need to get better at this. Inhaling through my nose, I'm reminded of the last time we were here. The pleasant, fresh smell is reminiscent of a spa. Exhaling brings the release of some tension from my chest and shoulders as we step up to the reception desk. Relief shimmers through me when I see a different human behind it today, someone who didn't see me rush out of here after nearly killing the first human I fed on.

"Hello there," the guy says, offering a kind smile. "Can I get you both set up with feeders?"

"Just her, please," Nikolai answers.

We're led to a private room like the first time, and

Nikolai stands near the door, while I sit next to the human in the recliner—she can't be much older than me.

I take her hand, recalling Nikolai's past direction. I take a deep breath and close my eyes, brushing my thumb over the girl's palm. A quick gasp escapes my lips as her vibrant, warm energy zips through me. I pull it in, consuming each tendril of colorful emotion as she sighs softly.

I let go, my pulse pounding and my chest rising and falling faster than normal. When I open my eyes, Nikolai is observing me.

"You can take more," he says.

I press my lips together for a moment. "I don't want to hurt her."

He nods. "You won't, I'm here. Keep going if you want to."

With a steadying breath, I rest my hand on her knee this time, keeping my eyes on her face while I latch onto her energy again. Her eyes flutter shut as a smile curls her lips, and she makes a soft sound at the back of her throat. She's enjoying this, which is good for her—so long as I'm careful not to take too much. Pleasure floods through her and into me, warm and sweet like pink taffy, and a blush creeps across my cheeks. My thoughts veer, returning to the meeting with Tristan this morning. As hard as it was to see him, it was also... really nice, because I fucking miss him and want him and *crave* him. The heat from my cheeks dips much lower, and I squeeze my thighs together, pulling my hand off the girl's knee. I've taken enough from her; I feel freshly revitalized, as if I've just woken from the best nap of my life. Between the crackle of energy and the heat of arousal flooding my body, I take a moment to stand.

Nikolai opens the door for me, and we walk out of the

private room, stopping at the reception desk to pay—which feels incredibly weird—before returning to the car.

"I'm proud of you, young grasshopper," Nikolai says, shooting me a grin. "You crushed it this time."

"Thanks, mentor," I offer with a small smile.

"Now that you've fed properly, you should have no problem glamouring yourself. Think you can give it a shot?"

"I feel like I can do just about anything right now."

"Good. You'll have to let down the existing glamour and build your own. It's all about visualization. Find a place in your mind where you can focus and picture those human features being stripped away."

I close my eyes and listen to the deep sound of his voice, following his instructions. "No one's walking by the car, right?"

"You're good," he assures me.

I blow out a breath, clenching and unclenching my hands and feet to get to a place of deeper calm, deeper concentration. I focus on each feature—my ears, my eyes, my teeth, my skin—and pull back the glamour as if I'm removing one of those face masks that looks as if you're peeling off your actual face. It works effectively based on Nikolai's words of encouragement.

"Time to glamour yourself now," he says. "It's kind of the same idea as shielding your emotions, except you're hiding physical attributes instead of internal ones."

"Right, okay." I think back to the night at the pub when Allison taught me to hide my emotions and put that into play as I picture the point of my ears becoming rounded and human. Next, I work to hide the blue hue of my skin, visualizing it like a light fading before turning out completely. Once each of my physical fae characteristics are, to the naked eye, gone, I exhale a heavy breath and open my eyes.

"Damn," Nikolai whistles. "You did that in record time. See what happens when you stop fighting what you are and allow yourself to embrace it? The small things aren't such a struggle."

I can't help the smile on my lips as a mix of pride and relief blossoms in my chest, because he's right. That went exceptionally better than the last time, and it gives me hope that each time after will get easier.

---

A few days later, I finally visit home—after I ask Nikolai to take me to the feeder unit so I'm sufficiently fed and fully glamoured before seeing my family. I haven't seen them since Elijah woke up and I became fae. We've been in touch over the phone and text, but I'm finally in a place where I feel somewhat confident about seeing them.

The four of us sit around the dining room table, stuffing our faces with the best pizza in town for dinner Saturday night after spending the day outside in the snow, shoveling the driveway and sidewalk, and having an epic snowball fight—parents versus kids.

It feels like old times, like before I stumbled into the fae world and everything I knew was flipped upside down. Elijah grins at me before stealing the last slice of pepperoni, and for a short, blissful moment, I forget I became fae to save his life.

After dinner, I help my mom clean up the kitchen.

"How are things with you and Tristan?" she asks while the sink fills with water.

With a sigh, I say, "I don't really know."

She rinses the dishes and hands them to me to put in the dishwasher. "I can see you're in pain." Her voice is soft as she hands me a plate. "Did he hurt you?"

"No," I say in an instant, sticking the plate on the bottom rack with the others. Tristan has done nothing to hurt me. He wouldn't.

She presses her lips together, pinning me with a stare. "What's going through your head?"

*This could take a while*, I mutter in my head. "You and Dad," I say in a low voice. "How did you know you were right for each other? That it was going to last forever?"

Mom laughs and sets down the dishcloth, wiping her hands on her thighs. "Oh, honey, I didn't know it would last for our whole lives."

"And you married him anyway?"

She nods. "Anything as important as love is worth the risk. At least in my mind. You might find this amusing, but when I met your dad, I really didn't like him." She flashes a faint smile, rinsing a few more dishes.

"Are you serious?" Evidently, Mom and I are more alike than I knew.

"Yes. But damn him, he made me fall for him. Hard, too. I couldn't stop thinking about him. It was infuriating."

A smile curls my lips. I've never heard this story before. "What made you decide he was worth it? The risk of getting hurt?"

Her eyes flick across my face. "I knew because of the way I felt around him. I felt better, stronger, *happier*."

My stomach flutters a bit, and I bite the inside of my cheek as I put the last cup on the upper rack of the dishwasher. "Thanks, Mom."

She leans over to close the dishwasher and kisses my cheek. "Anytime." She walks over to the stove and turns on the burner after filling the kettle with water. Pulling a few mugs out of the upper cupboard, she drops tea bags into them.

Dad walks through the kitchen, talking on his cell phone. When he frowns while mentioning Nan's name, my pulse jumps. My dad's mother is no spring chicken, and her health hasn't been the best over the last handful of years.

"What's going on at Nan's?"

Dad grabs his cup of tea off the counter and kisses Mom's cheek before walking back into the living room, still talking on the phone.

"She's okay," Mom says, leaning against the counter. "She and your dad decided it was best for her to move into a care home where she'll be able to live mostly independently, but there's help when she needs it."

I let out a breath, relieving the pressure in my chest. "That's good."

Nan has lived in the same old Victorian home since I was a baby. It was the house she grew up in; the property has been in my dad's family for decades.

Holy shit. Why didn't I think about that months ago when I was looking into my family history? Dad had nothing that dated back far enough to the fae in our family, but Nan might.

"Do you need help with the move?" I ask.

"Are you sure? We weren't going to ask. Your dad and I didn't want to make you feel guilty if you didn't have time."

"I have time," I tell her. "I can help."

"That's great." She sighs. "I love her, but that woman is a serious packrat. The attic is full of stuff that has to be over a hundred years old."

I arch a brow. "Really? What does she even have that is that old?"

Mom shrugs. "Heirlooms, according to your father. She kept everything that was passed down from your granddad's family after he died. She did nothing with it, of course, it just sat there, collecting dust all these years."

I laugh a little. "Awesome. Glad I'm sticking around to help, then."

She presses her palms together as if she's about to pray. "Thank you."

I wave her off, grinning at her display. "Oh, come on. It can't be that bad."

---

Okay, yeah. It *is* that bad.

We've been here three hours and haven't come close to making a dent.

Nan, Mom, and Dad are downstairs packing up the breakables in the kitchen and dining room, while I quickly offered to climb into the attic to go through the piles of dust-covered boxes. I could use a minute to myself and there's still a part of me that hopes I'll find something tied to my fae lineage.

There are enough heirlooms up here for a Marshall family museum. I've sneezed so many times my head feels heavy and fuzzy and my throat is scratchy, as if I'm getting sick. I duck my head from the low, exposed wood ceilings and crack the lone window open enough to inhale some fresh air.

Keeping the window open, I walk away from it and gulp down some water, tossing the empty bottle toward the garbage bag I started, and move onto another box. This one is just labeled *family stuff*. Nice. Very specific. The words are faint, probably written long before even Nan was born.

Holding my breath as I rip the deteriorating tape off the flimsy cardboard, I squint at the darkness inside. I toss the ball of tape in the garbage and drag the lamp I've been using for light closer so I can see what's inside.

Paper. It's filled with yellowed, worn paper.

I push the flaps of the box back and reach inside, pulling a bunch out. Thumbing through the delicate sheets, I note the dates go back at least a century.

"Holy shit," I mumble.

Some of it looks like old receipts, most of which have such faded ink I can't make out what's on them. I empty the entire box, glancing over a few things. A folded piece of paper falls to the floor as I flip through a leather-bound notebook. I pick it up and press my lips together as I open it, surprised to find the writing well preserved.

There are names scrawled across the top with small black and white headshots and lines connecting them to others all the way down the page. Written in neat cursive across the top is *Marshall Family Tree*.

I've never seen this before. I'll bet my dad hasn't either. Nan probably didn't even know it was in one of these boxes, considering by the looks of them, they haven't been opened in the last century.

I run my finger across the crinkled paper, taking in all the names and dates. Some names are familiar, while others are complete strangers. The last name on the page —the last relative that was added to the tree—is my great-great-grandfather.

Pulling my phone out of the back pocket of my shorts, I open the camera and snap a picture. I go into my gallery and select the photo to make sure it came out clear, and frown. There's a glare from the flash halfway up the page, drawing my eyes to a familiar name. Mine.

Of course it's not *me*, but my eyes widen. I didn't know I was named after a distant relative. This Aurora wasn't born a Marshall. My gaze slides over to her spouse—the Marshall of the pairing—and the air leaves my lungs in a painful *whoosh*.

"What the hell?" I breathe, blinking a few times. There must be dust in my eyes. I'm not seeing straight. This isn't—this *can't* be real.

Across from my namesake is the face that still gives me nightmares.

*Jules.*

My body jumps into action, moving on autopilot down the ladder from the attic and into the bathroom. I slam the door shut and get the lid of the toilet seat up a second before I empty my stomach into the bowl.

My eyes burn as my vision blurs in and out, and my ears are ringing so loudly I almost don't hear someone knocking on the door.

I flush the toilet and rinse my mouth out before taking a deep breath and opening it to find Nan and Mom standing there.

"Are you all right, honey?" Mom asks.

I swallow hard. "I just—"

"She probably found a dead animal up there," Dad says, walking past the hallway. "That attic hasn't been clean since the damn house was built."

Nan frowns. "Was there a dead animal?"

*You could say that.* I get away with nodding, unable to vocalize the lie.

Instead of getting answers, I'm left with a million more questions, and I killed the only person I could ask.

"I think that's enough for one day," Mom announces.

"Are you sure?" I ask hoarsely.

Nan nods, guiding me away from my mom. "You head home. You've been a great help. Thank you, Aurora."

I force a smile for her. "Hey, Nan? I found an old Marshall family tree in a box in the attic. I think it was in a box of Granddad's things. Neither of you are on it, but I was wondering if you'd seen it?"

Her face crinkles as she thinks about it. "I can't say that I have. I'm an old girl, but I still have an excellent memory, and I don't remember any family trees."

I offer her a smile, even though I feel as if I'm going to cry. "Do you mind if I take it?"

"Take whatever you like. Everything is going to a thrift store or the trash."

"Thanks, Nan."

She reaches for my hand and kisses it. "You're very welcome."

Nan goes back into the living room, and I force my legs to climb back into the attic, where I stand, staring at that piece of paper—that one name—until my head is spinning.

Jules is—*was*—my great-great-great-great-grandfather. He was part of the Marshall bloodline—*my* bloodline.

I slide to the floor, gripping the paper in my hands, and lean against a stack of boxes. I don't care how dirty the old hardwood is. My knees are shaking so hard, if I didn't sit down, I was going to fall on my ass.

Jules being a distant fae relative doesn't make me feel anything new when it comes to ending his life. It got my brother back, and I don't regret it for a second.

I pull the box across the floor toward me and tear through the rest of it. There's nothing else with any mention of Jules inside. Instead of going home, I spend the rest of the afternoon searching through the remaining boxes, but the family tree I have folded in my pocket is the only thing I can find. It might be all I have to go on, but it makes one thing clear: when I didn't think any of my fae ancestors were left, Jules was there the whole time. I can't help wondering if he knew...

---

I'm on a train back to the city Sunday night after dinner with my family. I stare out the window, watching the farmland and greenery transition into suburbs, then high-rises. Pulling my phone out, I hover over Tristan's name for a second before opening a new message.

> I'll be back in the city twenty minutes from now and I'm coming to see you. Alone.

We need to talk so I can tell him what I found out about Jules, and I want to give him a heads up Nikolai won't be tagging along for this meeting.

Marisa is standing behind the reception desk at the Westbrook Hotel when I arrive a half hour later after taking an Uber from the train station. I wave hello on my way to the elevators.

The ride up to the penthouse is uneventful. I've had enough ambushes on this damn elevator to last a lifetime... er, eternity. Whatever. I have given little thought to the idea that I'll live forever. It's too overwhelming. Living day by day is hard enough right now.

Stepping off the elevator into the small, simple

entryway outside Tristan's suite, I freeze before I get the chance to knock. This is ridiculous. I've been here countless times. I've even seen Tristan since I changed, and yet, my insides are still a mess of nerves. Despite the nerves, though, there's also a flicker of excitement about having an excuse to see him, especially when Nikolai isn't here to get into a pissing match.

I take a deep breath, trying to build up the will to reach up and knock. Before I get the chance, the door opens and Tristan stands there with a curious expression. He must've sensed my presence or heard me out here trying not to lose my shit. His eyes dance with amusement, making my stomach flip. *I miss that.* The way he affects me.

"Hi," I say in a low voice.

"Aurora," he greets smoothly. "You've never been the type to strike me as a booty call."

My eyes widen, and I shake my head. "That's *not* why I'm here."

He wets his lips. "You texted me, 'I'm coming to see you. Alone.'"

Okay, maybe that sounded a bit like I was coming over for, well, *not* the reason I came over.

I cringe. "Fuck. I meant Nikolai wasn't coming."

His forehead creases as his brows lift. "There would never be a time or a place where I'd be down for that."

I can't help the grin spreading across my lips. For a moment, I forget why I'm here. "You're such a smartass."

"Coming from you, that's a high compliment." He leans against the doorway. "Are you coming in?"

My eyes narrow a fraction. "Not a booty call," I remind him, stepping past him into the suite. I try to ignore the tingle that shoots up my arm when it brushes his. I pause in the entryway, stepping out of my shoes and leaving them by the door like I'd gotten so used to doing.

"Can I get you a drink?" he murmurs, closing the door before walking toward me.

"Please."

We end up in the living room, sitting opposite to one another on the couches with glasses of white wine in our hands. My eyes flick around the room as the tightness in my chest refuses to let up. I miss this place. For as much shit that went down here, the Westbrook Hotel—Tristan's penthouse—became a home to me. *Tristan became home to me.*

I shove the thought away, but it leaves a bitter film of memory behind. I'm not sure how to jump into the whole, *Jules was my fae ancestor thing.*

"How are things?" Tristan asks.

"Better," I tell him. "Nikolai has been helpful."

A muscle ticks in his jaw. "I'm having a hard time with you being around him so much."

"I can see that," I say mildly and take a sip of my drink. "I know the two of you don't like each other, but you're both going to suck it up because in the grand scheme of things, your past minor issues don't matter."

His lips twitch. "I miss that wit of yours."

"It didn't go anywhere."

"No, but you did."

The invisible grip on my heart pulses painfully. "Tristan..." I shake my head, as if I'm begging him not to bring that up tonight. Because with the way I'm feeling after finding out I'm related to Jules, to the fae I *killed*, I might just be tempted to throw everything aside and let myself get lost in him. And that wouldn't be fair to either of us when I'm still struggling to figure everything out.

He frowns. "You came to me. We could've just as easily had this conversation on the phone."

Heat rises to my cheeks. He's right, and we both know it. I didn't need to come, and yet, here I am, because even if I'm struggling with what we are, an inherent part of me craves him—needs to be around him still. "Right. I know that."

"I'm worried about you, Aurora."

I force what I hope is a believable smile. "You don't need to be. You have more important—"

"No," he cuts in firmly, shaking his head. "Don't dismiss this."

"I'm not trying to."

His gaze meets mine. "Promise me something?" The softness in his voice wraps around me like the black silk sheets that dress his bed.

"Okay," I whisper after several beats of silence.

"Take care of yourself. You are important to me."

The rush of emotions slams into me like a brick wall, as if he's let down the shield on his emotions, and my lips part. "I..."

"Please." His unwavering gaze makes my heart pound harder.

"I promise."

He lets out a breath and thrusts a hand through his hair. "I fucking miss you, Rory."

*I miss you.* The words scream loud in my head, but I can't force them past my lips. Not because it's a lie—it's the hardest truth I know—but because I'm still so scared. I've never been so out of my element, and with the added layer of complication courtesy of the fae courts, I feel like I'm drowning. My thoughts jump back to the conversation I had with my mom over the weekend.

*Anything as important as love is worth the risk.*

I set my glass beside Tristan's and stand, mainly so I won't throw myself over the table and into his lap. At this moment, I want nothing more than to give in to the pounding of my heart against my rib cage. Even with the time that's passed, *I know* what wrapping myself in Tristan's arms would feel like. *Home.*

"I came over because I found out something about my lineage." What I'm about to tell him—not knowing how he'll react—has made my entire body tense.

He wets his lips, his eyes focused on my face. "I'm listening."

I blow out a breath. "My head has been spinning since I found out." I pull the paper out of my back pocket, unfolding it before I hold it out to him.

He glances at my face before looking at the paper, taking it from me.

I hold my breath, watching his eyes scan across the page. His posture stiffens; he's seen it. "Aurora..." His voice is low, rough. The shield he keeps on his emotions snaps, and I'm whipped in the face with his red-hot anger. My cheeks burn, and I cringe, wanting to move away from him. His rage is like a vise around my throat. It's not cutting off my oxygen, but the sensation is dizzying.

"Tristan," I say in a firm voice.

His eyes lift to mine and he swallows hard, pulling his emotions back, getting them under control as he stands. "I'm sorry I didn't find any record of this when I looked before. Most of my sources were seelie, but I made several inquiries in the unseelie court and came up with nothing."

I shrug, because in the grand scheme of things, it doesn't really matter at this point. "It's not your fault my great-great-great-etc. grandfather turned out to be the psychotic unseelie knight determined to take you down." There's a twinge of sarcasm in my words, but they still feel heavy.

"He was your blood and he still was determined to use you against me," he whispers, disbelief making his voice low and breathy.

"That's assuming he knew we were... *family*." The last word tastes bitter on my tongue. "It's kind of irrelevant now, anyway."

Tristan nods tightly, then growls, "That son of a bitch."

"Yeah, well, he got his."

Tristan frowns. "I'm sorry," he murmurs. "I don't—What do you need, Rory?"

*You.* That one tiny word is on the tip of my tongue—so I press my lips together and stay silent.

He exhales a heavy sigh. "I'm glad you're here. I was going to contact you before I got your text."

I can't help it. The butterflies that have been rather dormant in my stomach lately give a subtle flutter. "Oh?"

"I met with Rowan earlier today."

My stomach drops, obliterating the butterflies. "What did he want?"

He rubs at the stubble along his jaw, and I suddenly wish we were still sitting. "As expected, he wanted to know about you. How things went down with Jules and how you triggered the fae magic in you."

"Did you tell him I won't choose a court?"

Tristan nods. "To my surprise, he was impressed."

My eyes pop wide. "Really? Why? I would've thought he'd be angry that I don't want to align myself with him."

"Don't take this personally, but Rowan has plenty of other things to worry about aside from recruiting my..." He trails off, his cheeks turning pink, and I nearly rock back on my heels. Tristan Westbrook is *blushing*. He clears his throat. "He understands you're important to me. His focus is on the war with the unseelie court and the growing number of fae who are disappearing from both courts as we continue to fight one another."

"Right," I say, my heart beating faster as my eyes remain locked on his. I get lost in their stunning depths and feel a pull toward him. The urge, the near-carnal desire to close the distance between us nearly takes over. My throat goes dry as my palms dampen, and I can't ignore the way my breasts tingle or the heat gathering between my legs. But when Tristan steps closer, I shake my head. "I should go. I just came to tell you what I found. I'm, uh, glad the audience with the king went okay."

Without another word, I head for the door, praying Tristan doesn't ask me to stay. *Would I?* I can feel him standing behind me as I wait for the elevator.

Once it arrives and I get on, I turn to face Tristan where he's standing in the hallway watching me. Our eyes meet, and I have to grab the railing to keep myself from getting off and wrapping my arms around him.

Reaching over, I press the button for the lobby without looking away from him. "I'll see you around," I say in a low voice.

His response is a curt nod before the door closes and I'm left alone as the elevator descends to the lobby. I'm such a coward. I'm tired—*exhausted*—of fighting my thoughts and feelings. They're at war with each other, much like the fae.

I leave the hotel and head for The Iron Lounge, figuring I should share my discovery with Nikolai as well. Plus, I could use a drink.

The pub is closed by the time I get back to campus. I

unlock the door and slip inside before locking it again, then head for the hallway that leads to his apartment. Because if he can show up unannounced at my dorm, I can return the favor.

I freeze when I hear muffled voices coming from the office. Frowning, I lean closer, but I can't make anything out. Nikolai wouldn't be down here this late. My hand reaches for the handle as the sound gets louder. I open the door and step forward, only to let loose a startled, ear-shattering scream.

## CHAPTER THIRTY-SEVEN

"Oh my god!" I slam the door shut as I jump back into the hall and will the vivid picture of what I just witnessed out of my brain.

Moments later, Max and Oliver join me in the hallway. Oliver is tugging on his shirt, while Max is taking his time zipping up his pants—still without a shirt.

"Guess you missed the sock on the—" Max stops talking as his eyes flick to the door. "Whoops."

I'm grinding my teeth to keep from yelling at him, and my cheeks are flaring with heat.

"We should go," Oliver pipes up.

I force a tight-lipped smile. "I think it's best you do."

Oliver nods. "Sorry, Aurora."

Max pulls on his navy dress shirt, leaving it unbuttoned. "Sorry, blondie." His voice is more amused than apologetic, and considering it's paired with a smirk, it doesn't quite sound genuine.

After they leave, I climb the stairs I've only been up once before and knock on Nikolai's door. When he opens it wearing nothing but black sweatpants hung low on his hips, I fight an eye roll. I walk past him into the apartment and say, "You need to bleach the office."

"What happened?" He asks, sounding like an adult speaking to a child. "Did you kill someone?"

I scowl. "Of course not. I walked in on Max and Oliver fucking on your desk."

Nikolai bursts out laughing. "Did you see anything good?"

"Can you be an adult for two seconds?"

The laughter quiets. "Relax, *Mom*." His tone is light, paired with that charming grin of his. His expression softens as he looks into my eyes. "How are you doing?"

"Better every day." The truth of those words makes my chest feel a little lighter.

"I have an idea that might help you. Remember the night you saw me singing at the pub?"

"Unfortunately," I remark dryly.

"Be nice," he comments. "You called me out for feeding on the crowd. That's always been my preferred method. Taking from groups of humans is faster and less messy. I don't have to worry about anything. There are always enough people; I'd overdose on energy before I ever took too much from one person."

I arch a brow. "Is it actually possible to take in too much energy?"

He laughs, shrugging. "I've never done it. That's not the point. I'm saying this is a foolproof way to feed without the fear of hurting anyone. Feeding the individual way is easier to teach. Now that you've done it a couple of times, it's worth trying another method."

My pulse ticks a little faster. If he's right—if this works, it would make my life a hell of a lot easier. "Okay," I agree. "Let's try it when the pub is open."

Nikolai nods. "What should we do now, then?" His suggestive tone makes me smile reluctantly.

"I don't know, we could watch a movie like normal people... or I could tell you about the family tree I found at my nan's house that revealed Jules was my ancestor."

Nikolai blinks at me. "Sorry, what?"

I pull out the paper for the second time today and offer it to him, waiting as he looks it over as Tristan did.

"I'll be damned," he comments.

I fold my arms over my chest. "Creepy, right?" I try not to think about the times I was definitely flirting with him before I knew who he really was... *Gross*.

Nikolai shakes his head, his forehead creased with confusion as he folds the paper and hands it back to me. "You were named after your great-great-great grandmother, who was married to him?

"I always thought Aurora was taken from my nan's middle name. I didn't know the name went back that far."

"Are you going to look into it more?"

"I don't see the point," I tell him. "It won't change anything that happened. That, and there's no one alive to get information from. Tristan looked into my lineage when we met—we *thought* they'd all perished in the fae war."

Nikolai nods thoughtfully. "Let me know if you change your mind about looking into it. I may have some contacts Westbrook doesn't."

Nikolai wanting to help brings a genuine smile to my lips, which is rare these days. "Thanks, Nik."

"Oooh, I got a nickname." He grins, bumping his shoulder against mine.

I roll my eyes in response.

"What should I call you? We could stick with gorgeous, because it's true, but I kind of want something a little more... original."

"How about my name?" I offer dryly.

Nikolai sighs dramatically. "You are so boring sometimes."

---

When I get back to the dorm, I change into the comfiest sweats I own before grabbing one of the many unread books from my shelf and curl up on my bed. Glancing over at Allison's, I frown as I realize how infrequently I've seen her these days. She's as busy as I am with school, and we always just seem to miss each other at the dorm. Once the semester ends, I'm going to insist we take a trip to celebrate graduation, mostly so I just spend some time with my best friend.

I'm only a chapter into my book when a knock sounds at the door. My eyes flick toward the sound, and I hold my breath. Not wanting to deal with anyone else tonight, I ignore it, focusing on the book in my lap.

My gaze darts up from the page as Max appears. He stops near the end of my bed and crosses his arms.

"What the hell?" I breathe, clutching my chest. "Way to waltz in without an invitation."

He barks out a laugh. "You're one to talk."

I narrow my eyes. "What's with the shifting? You never used to do that."

He shrugs. "Tristan didn't want us doing it around you. He thought it'd freak you out as a human, but I figured now that you can do it yourself, that request no longer applies."

"Whatever," is all I say, because I *haven't* done it myself yet. "Why were you in the office earlier? You couldn't have done that elsewhere?"

"Ollie and I were having drinks at the bar and we stumbled in there to find some quiet." He smirks. "We lost track of time." It's clear by the lines in his forehead and the twist of his lips he's got something more to say.

"What can I do for you, Max?"

His eyes meet mine, then drop to the book I'm holding. "You can read?"

"Funny."

He tilts his head as if he's trying to look at the cover. "Huh. Anyway, I need your help."

My brow lifts. "*You* need *my* help?"

He scowls. "Try not to sound so thrilled about it, would you?"

"Sorry," I say, but my tone is unapologetic. This moment is everything.

"I want to do something for Oliver's birthday next weekend. I tried to talk to Allison, but she wasn't much help in the idea department."

My eyes widen at the same moment my stomach drops. *Shit.* Oliver's birthday is next week, and I forgot. "You want me to help you plan his party?"

"Yes."

"What did you have in mind?"

Max walks over to my desk and perches on top, resting his feet on the chair. "Something at the pub. Drinks, food, music—the lot. I want to rent the place Friday night."

"I can ask Nikolai. You should get Allison to send invites. She'll know who to contact. I can handle the food and drinks, so all you'll have to do is get Oliver there."

For a split second, Max looks shocked, as if he didn't

think I'd agree to help him. It's cute. "Sure," he says, "I can do that."

"Good. Is that everything?" Just as I finish speaking, my phone rings from the bedside table. I glance over and see Oliver's number, making me smile slightly. "Speaking of the birthday boy." I pick up the phone, swiping across the screen to answer the call. "Hey, what's up, Oliver?"

"I wanted to apologize again for what happened earlier, and I was thinking, Max and I are going out tomorrow night, and I thought you and Tristan could join us for dinner. Sound good? I don't want things to be awkward after tonight." After I walked in on him ass-naked, bent over the desk, with Max—*Nope*. I refuse to relive it.

I look away from Max's arched brow. "I don't think I can." I don't want to tell Oliver that Tristan and I aren't together. That would invite a lot of questions I can't answer while maintaining his unawareness of the fae world.

"Is something wrong?" His concern is evident. *Fuck*. I don't want him to worry about me.

"I just started a new job and I'm still getting the hang of things. Life's been pretty exhausting." It has nothing to do with the reason I don't want to go out, but it's not a lie.

"No worries. We'll go out and celebrate once you're feeling up to it."

"Absolutely. I'll talk to you later." After I hang up and set my phone down, I look over at Max to find his eyes narrowed. "What?"

"What's the deal with you and Tristan, anyway? He won't talk about it."

"What makes you think *I'm* going to?"

He shakes his head. "I don't get it, blondie. You're fae

now. You'd think that would simplify whatever is going on between the two of you."

I slide my legs over the side of the bed and stand, needing to stretch and move. "I'm sure the seelie king would be thrilled about his knight being with a fae who refuses to choose a court."

A flicker of surprise passes over Max's face as his gaze tracks my movement. "You seriously won't pick one?"

"I feel that doing so wouldn't bode well for bringing the courts together."

His brows lift. "Since when is that your job?"

I open my mouth to respond, then pause, considering it. "If it's going to work, I think it's the job of all fae."

He nods slowly, rubbing his jaw. "Okay, then. Fuck the courts. Don't let them keep you apart."

My eyes widen, and I stop pacing near where he's sitting on my desk. "I just... I need time to figure things out."

He crosses his arms over his chest, wrinkling his dark blue dress shirt. "Figure out what? If you love him?"

*Love.* That tiny, four-letter word punches the air out of my chest.

"It's more than that," I mumble. It's a lame response, and by the irritated expression on Max's face, it's clear he agrees.

"I don't know what it's like for you, but I do know Tristan. He's never looked at anyone the way he does you." He sighs, as if this conversation is as awkward for him as it is for me. "I understand you're scared, and that's fine. Love is terrifying. But you shouldn't let your fear keep you from being with the person you don't want to live without. Fight for it, Aurora. Otherwise, what's the fucking point of this?"

Tears prick my eyes, and I struggle to hold his gaze. "He blames himself for what happened to me, Max," I say in a low voice. "I can see it when he looks at me, and it *hurts*."

"That won't go away if you keep avoiding him." His arms fall back to his sides. "Take time and figure your shit out, but if you allow what happened to keep you from Tristan, you're letting Jules win."

I stare at him, wide-eyed, for the longest minute of my life. He's right—so fucking right, it makes my chest fill with pressure, as if it's about to explode. "How did we end up talking about this? We were planning a birthday party. *You* came to get *my* help."

"I guess you needed me more than I needed you." He shrugs. "You repeat this conversation to anyone, and I'll kill you. I don't give a shit that you're fae now."

I almost laugh. "Believe me, this conversation didn't happen." Even as I say that, I'm sure Max can see the swirls of gratitude surrounding me like a warm fleece blanket on a chilly day, and I make no effort to hide it.

He turns his face away so I don't see the touch of a smile on his lips. "I'll see you at the party." With that, he shifts out of the dorm, leaving me standing there still struggling with that deep ache in my chest.

---

I meet Nikolai at the pub the next morning. It isn't open yet, so it's safe to talk without worrying about eavesdropping humans. He wraps me in a one-armed hug; it's not weird, which is kind of weird.

"Hey," he says, sliding onto the bar stool beside me.

I smile. "Hey."

"How's it going?" he asks, his eyes flicking across my face as if he's assessing my appearance.

"Fine, I guess. We're throwing a party here on Friday, by the way. It's Oliver's birthday, and Max asked for my help."

Nikolai purses his lips. "Sure, you can take over my pub to host your human friend's party. Thanks so much for asking."

I roll my eyes. "Since when are you one to pass up a party?"

"So, this is my formal invitation?"

"That depends. Are you going to be able to handle yourself without pissing off Skylar?"

He smirks. "It's just so easy."

I shoot him a pointed look. "I'm serious. Oliver doesn't know about the fae, and this is important. He deserves a normal party that doesn't deteriorate into a battle between the fae courts."

Nikolai lets loose a heavy sigh. "Relax, gorgeous. I'll be on my best behavior. There will be other humans attending, I assume?"

"Of course."

"Good. I'll show you how to feed on them."

My eyes widen, my chest swirling with a mix of excitement and anxiety—the two are often hard to tell apart these days. The idea of feeding on Oliver's friends makes me uneasy. "You promise it won't affect them?"

"You'll only be taking small amounts from each person—they'll be completely fine."

I chew my lip as I contemplate it. "Okay."

He flashes his usual charming grin. "Should I book a stripper? I'm sure I could find a dancing police officer or something."

"Yeah, consider yourself *un*invited."

He pouts. "Oh, please. It isn't a party without yours truly."

"You know, I think we'd manage."

"I'm going," he insists.

I slide off the barstool, zip up my jacket, and meet his gaze. "I'm serious, Nik. No funny shit. Okay?"

His expression smoothes as he raises his hand. "Scout's honor."

Nikolai behaving in a room full of people—specifically with women—would be a miracle. I'm not counting on it, not with his zest for romancing anything with boobs. *Was he always like this?* I can't help but be curious, especially after his comment about fae being able to get humans pregnant.

Despite my better judgment, I say, "The other day, when you were talking about humans and fae... were you speaking from experience?"

His brows furrow as a muscle ticks along his jaw. It makes me want to reach for him and apologize for bringing it up, but before I can move, he clears his throat.

"I had a son," he whispers.

My heart lurches. "What?"

"It was a long time ago." He scratches the back of his neck, glancing away for several beats before he continues. "His mother's name was Layla. She was captivating and so fucking genuine. She was human and knew I wasn't. I fell in love with her the moment we met. I wanted to be with her forever, however long that would be for us. Forever came too fast."

"What happened?"

"She died," he says, "giving birth to our son."

Tears burn my eyes. "Nik..." I can't form adequate

words to express how horrible I feel. I shouldn't have brought it up.

"He survived one week in the hospital, but he just couldn't live without his mother. Sometimes, I wonder how *I* lived after she died." He swallows hard.

"He only lived a week?"

He scratches the back of his neck again, looking down. "Yeah. The social workers and doctors wanted us to stay in the hospital to make sure we were stable after losing Layla. One morning, I left the room to get a coffee, and his heart stopped. There was no warning. Nothing that gave me time to prepare for losing him days after I'd lost the woman I loved."

I reach for him, taking his hands in mine and squeezing them. "I'm so sorry. I don't know what to say."

"Like I said, it was a long time ago." Nikolai rubs his hands down his face and clears his throat again. "I'm sorry, Aurora, I—"

"No," I cut him off, gripping his hands tighter. "You don't need to apologize." I tug on his hands until he looks at me. "Okay?"

He nods, forcing a smile, and my stomach plummets. I've never seen Nikolai like this—sad and vulnerable. He stiffens when I wrap my arms around his waist. A moment later, he hugs me back, resting his chin on the top of my head. The breath he exhales is weighted, and I hug him tighter.

Whatever this is between us—a deep understanding or maybe even the start of a friendship—I definitely didn't see it coming.

# CHAPTER
# THIRTY-EIGHT

I've never been so grateful for the weekend. The past week has been crazy as I caught up on assignments and online lectures. Nikolai took me to the feeder unit a few times, and the idea of feeding doesn't absolutely terrify me anymore, which is a tremendous relief. It's still not something I *want* to do to survive, but I've slowly come to accept it.

Now that Friday has rolled around, I get to focus on throwing a kickass birthday party for Oliver. We put a sign on the door this morning, letting everyone know the pub is closed for a private event tonight, and we've been working all afternoon to get the place ready.

Between class, spending more time at The Iron Longue with Nikolai and Deacon to learn how things work, and still adapting to my new life, I am effectively run off my feet. That said, keeping busy has always been my preferred distraction, so it's working well.

There's still a few hours until people arrive for Oliver's

party, so I'm behind the bar making sure we have enough booze to last the night.

Allison is hanging the last of the streamers from the ceiling, and Max dropped off black and gold balloons earlier this afternoon. I sent Nikolai to pick up the cake we ordered from a local bakery, and once he returns, I'll slip upstairs to shower and get changed. I normally wouldn't—that's not a level of intimacy I'd like to add to our friendship—but I didn't want to waste time going back and forth from the dorm, so when Nikolai offered his place, I accepted.

I continue buzzing around the pub, making sure things are perfect, and Allison waves on her way out, letting me know she'll be back in time for the party.

Max is texting me constantly, making sure everything is set. Under normal circumstances, it would annoy the hell out of me, but today it makes me smile.

My phone rings as I'm walking upstairs to Nikolai's half an hour later.

"What's up, Al?"

"I forgot to ask before I left. Is Tristan coming tonight? I didn't know if I should invite him, so I left it up to you."

"I'm sure Max invited him."

"Do you want me to ask him?"

"No," I answer too fast. "I mean, he's probably busy. Don't bother him."

"Right." She draws out the word, making me roll my eyes. "I'm sure he has plans on a Friday night when most of his friends are attending the same party. You're right. His schedule is probably jam-packed."

"Yeah," I mumble. "I have to hop in the shower. I'll see you soon."

"Bye," she sings before hanging up.

I get in the shower, tossing around the idea of Tristan showing up tonight. I want him here, but I'm also nervous about what I'll do if he shows up. *Get it together.* I can control myself. Just because I want him so badly it hurts doesn't mean I can't be in the same room and keep my hands off him.

Turning the water off, I step out of the shower and wrap myself in a towel. After I've finished drying and curling my hair into loose waves, I put on a bit of makeup and walk into the other room to grab my dress.

My eyes find his immediately, and my mouth goes dry.

His eyes are sharp, ablaze with hunger, making heat pool low in my belly. One look—one fucking look, and I'm ready to drop my towel, the only thing between my body and his gaze.

"Surprise," Tristan murmurs, rising from where he was sitting on the end of the bed.

I swallow hard as he stops close enough for me to reach out and touch. "It's not my party," I say, taking a moment to build a shield to cover my emotions from his view. That too has become easier the more I practice and, begrudgingly, the more I feed.

His mouth curls into a smirk. "I'm practicing." He pushes a hand through his hair, messing it up a bit. "The guy behind the bar said he thought you came up here. I knocked, and the door was open," he explains.

"I didn't think you were coming." I use that opportunity to take in his casual attire. I'll never tire of seeing him in a suit, but this laid-back, dark jeans and T-shirt look makes me melt all the same.

"You thought I'd miss seeing you like this?"

I arch a brow, heat rising in my cheeks. "In a towel?"

He chuckles. "Relaxed and having fun with your friends instead of worrying about being fae or the future."

A smile touches my lips. "So long as Nikolai doesn't say something that makes Skylar kill him, I'll actually be able to relax and have fun."

"You make a good point. I have yet to understand how Sterling gets under her skin. He's the only one I've seen who can."

"That's because there's no one stupid enough to try. She'd claw their eyes out."

"Then why is he still alive?"

I shoot him a look, and he smiles. "I need to get dressed," I say instead of responding.

"Of course," he says, but makes no move to leave the room.

I bite the inside of my cheek. "I can manage on my own."

Amusement flashes across his face. "You sure?"

I press my lips together before I do something stupid, like invite him to stay and forget about the party. "Tristan," I say softly. "I'll be down in a few."

His expression smoothes, and he holds my gaze a few moments longer before leaving.

I press my hand against my chest to feel the way my heart is hammering, and my lips curl at the giddiness swirling around my stomach from seeing Tristan. I replay the moment on a loop as I change into the casual long-sleeved maroon dress and heels I packed, then head back downstairs.

People fill the pub, chatting and drinking while we wait for Max and Oliver to arrive. Allison bounces over and hands me a beer, which I take a long drink of.

"This is a great turnout, Al. Thanks for taking care of the invites."

She beams. "Not a problem. I just hope Oliver is surprised."

I nod in agreement.

"I see Tristan came." She lowers her voice and gives me a look. "I also noticed him coming down from the loft not that long ago." She wiggles her eyebrows.

I chuckle. "Nothing happened."

She purses her lips. "But you wanted it to." It's not a question.

Of course, I choose that moment to scan the room and lock eyes with Tristan, who looks as if he's waiting for me to answer Allison.

"We should get ready." I take another drink. "They'll be here any minute."

She arches a brow. "Nice."

I roll my eyes, walking away from her to where our friends are gathered at the bar. I set my beer down and say hello to everyone just as my phone chimes—it's Max letting me know they just pulled up outside.

"They're here," I shout, and the room quiets as someone flips the lights off.

We all stand in dark silence for a couple of minutes until the door to the pub opens, and Oliver mumbles, "I think they're closed, babe."

The lights turn on, and we all yell, "SURPRISE!"

Oliver's eyes widen, and Max stands beside him looking the happiest I've ever seen him. His expression while he looks at Oliver makes my chest tighten. *He loves him.* I recognize that look. *It's the way Tristan looks at me.*

Oliver leans over and kisses Max on the cheek before grabbing his hand and walking toward the bar, greeting people as they pass. When they make it to where our group is standing around the bar, I pull Oliver into a tight hug. "Happy birthday," I say with a grin. "I hope you were surprised."

He's still beaming. "Are you kidding? This is amazing, Aurora."

I peek over at Max and almost freeze when I find him smiling. At me. "It was a team effort."

Oliver gets pulled away by a group of friends, taking Max with him.

I watch them go, smiling at the utter happiness they're sharing. This is everything I could've hoped for. It's the perfect distraction from the stress of all things fae. I grab a bottle of water and lean against the bar, surveying the room. People sing and dance to the music, and there's a small group surrounding the food table.

I refill the chip bowls, then slip down the hall to the storage room to grab more plastic cups and take a minute to breathe. I'm having a good time, but being around this many people is still somewhat challenging.

When I turn and find Tristan leaning in the doorway with his bare arms crossed over his chest, I almost drop the cups I'm holding. "Uh, hey," I say, adjusting them in my arms and instinctively checking to make sure my emotions are still unreadable. When I feel the mental wall give a resisting tug, I'm assured the shield I put up is still in place.

"Need some help?"

"Unless you'd prefer to stand there staring at me," I remark in a dry tone.

Tristan chuckles, pushing away from the doorframe and approaching me. He takes a couple of sleeves and helps me shift the others in my arms.

"Thanks," I mumble, feeling the heat of his body

against my skin. I stare hard at his chest, at where his shirt stretches over his muscles.

"Looks like you planned a successful surprise party."

I smile. "I'm glad you're here."

"I wouldn't miss it. Especially when it's all Max talked about today."

"That... seems so unlike him. It's cute."

He arches a brow. "I wouldn't make a point of telling *him* that."

I push the hair out of my face with my free hand and step around him. "We should get back."

"Of course. We wouldn't want to keep these cups from their drinks."

"Let's go, smartass." After we walk into the hallway, I close the door and head down the hall in front of him. The urge to drop what I'm holding, turn around, and kiss the crap out of him is overwhelming. I press my lips together until the pressure is uncomfortable as I keep walking, forcing myself to keep my gaze forward.

Tristan and I set the cups behind the bar before Max and Oliver drag him into a game of darts. The sight of Tristan laughing and having fun makes warmth blossom in my chest. I can't help the grin spreading across my lips as I go in search of Nikolai. It's time he shows me how to crowd feed. Anxiety crackles through me at the thought of losing control again, but like Nikolai said, this way is safer. I'm not focusing on one person, and there are plenty of humans here to pull energy from.

With a quick scan of the room, I locate Nikolai near the food table, chatting with a group of girls. *Color me surprised.* I walk over, plastering a fake-ass smile on my face and poke him in the side.

He glances over at me. "Hey, gorgeous. Delightful party."

"Yeah, thanks. Do you have some time?"

His eyes flick between mine and his brows raise as if he's questioning me, so I nod. "Of course." He turns his attention back to the girls. "Excuse me, ladies." He throws his arm around my shoulders and guides me away.

I scowl and try to push his arm off, but it's too heavy. "Seriously, Nik?"

"Jealousy is a powerful tool, Aurora."

Rolling my eyes, I elbow him in the ribs. "You are so annoying."

He grunts, finally dropping his arm once we're off to the side of the room. "Let's go over a quick game plan before we start." The typical amusement is out of his eyes, replaced with pure concentration that I try my best to mirror. "This is how I do it, and if it doesn't work for you, we'll find another way. Close your eyes and visualize each human in the room as their own color. Let me rephrase that. You can use the same color for more than one person, but try to see them as a different shade. Make sense?"

I arch a brow at him. "Sort of?" Pushing the hair away from my face, I ask, "Where should I start?"

"It doesn't really matter." He shrugs and points to a group of humans near the stage across the room, laughing and dancing to the music. "Try them."

I nod, flicking my eyes between the people, assigning them each a different shade of orange in my head—one bright like a traffic cone and the other burnt like roasted carrots.

Nikolai steps closer to my side. "Once you see their colors, you'll need to focus on them. The next part is physical touch, when you'll pull their energy into you. It's brief

—a few seconds at most—which is why you need to focus and capture their emotion before you make contact."

Following his direction, I continue to identify each human's color. "Okay, got it. What now?"

"Walk through the crowd, open yourself up to receiving the energy you've focused on, and touch each person. A quick shoulder touch works. Brushing arms in passing should also do the trick."

"Got it," I tell him, wiping my palms on my thighs and taking in a deep breath to center myself. I'm not as nervous about this as I was feeding on an individual, which is a pleasant surprise. In fact, there's a subtle flutter of excitement in my belly at the prospect of this feeding method being easier and helping me get better at living as a fae. Even having Tristan across the room, no doubt aware of what Nikolai and I are up to, isn't sending me into a tailspin of anxiety as I expected it would. I'd like to think that means I'm growing into my new life.

Stepping away from Nikolai, I move through the crowd, touching the shoulders of the humans I assigned colors to, smiling and feigning a quick greeting in passing. My posture straightens as I take in wisps of energy from each person, and my muscles feel steadier. I find I'm not worried about being dizzy or sick. With each touch, energy flows through me stronger, until the sheer amount of it becomes just shy of overwhelming. Stopping is easier this way, I realize immediately, which I very much like. I catch Nikolai's gaze from where he's standing in the same place I left him, then make my way back to his side.

"That was amazing," I say, my heart beating faster, this time with elation. I feel lighter overall, as if I could float away.

"Atta girl," he praises.

A grin spreads across my lips, and I throw my arms around him. "Thank you."

He rubs my back, laughing. "You did the work. I just told you how."

I step back. "I don't just mean for this. For everything you've done for me since I became fae. I really appreciate you, Nik."

He grins and shoots me a wink. "I appreciate you, too. Now, let's get back to the par-tay. I think we could both use a drink, though I feel I should warn you in case Allison hasn't yet. Drinking too much can affect your ability to block your emotions, so just keep that in mind."

I tuck that piece of information away. "Good to know."

A while later, I catch sight of Allison with a girl I'm not familiar with. They have their arms draped over each other's shoulders, giggling while watching a game of darts on the other side of the room.

"Do you think she'll ever follow the rules?" Tristan comments mildly, leaning against the bar next to me. The girl Allison's chatting with must be unseelie. "I suppose I can't say much, considering it could be seen that I'm breaking them now, too."

"No, you're not. You and I are... keeping things professional," I say, but it sounds half-hearted, as if I wouldn't protest if he leaned in to kiss me right now.

"I can be very professional with you, Aurora." He lowers his voice as he leans in, closing the space between us. "Why don't you let me show you?"

I try not to laugh. "What is this? *Fifty Shades of Fae?* Forget it."

"Fifty what?"

My cheeks flush. "Never mind."

He reaches up and brushes his fingers across my cheek,

making my skin tingle. "Show me what you're feeling," he murmurs.

Those words make my heart race. I can't do that. If I do, he'll know. He'll see how much I want him. How much I—

"Aurora!"

I turn away from Tristan and toward the sound of Allison squealing my name. By the sloppy grin and semi-bloodshot eyes, it's safe to say she's drunk.

She stumbles over and throws her arm around my shoulders, tugging me away from Tristan. "I'm heading out," she says.

I arch a brow at her. "Are you sure that's a good idea?"

The unseelie, whose name I don't know, chooses that moment to walk over, holding Allison's clutch in her hand. "Would you like me to take her home?" She glances between Tristan and me. "I haven't been drinking. I'll make sure she gets there safely."

I weigh the odds and go with my gut, nodding at her. "Thank you." I don't know this girl, but she seems genuine, and she can't lie. Still, I reach out to get a read on her emotions and I'm met with soft wisps of yellow and orange, echoes of happiness and compassion. The warmth of her emotions makes me feel better about Allison being around her, especially when she's allowing me to feel them.

She takes Allison from me, sliding her arm around her waist to keep her steady as they walk to the door and out of the building.

I glance back at Tristan, who's watching the two of them with sharp eyes. "Are you worried about her?" I ask, trying not to sound as surprised as I am.

"She's one of mine. Of course I am. The attacks have

decreased significantly after Jules, but that doesn't mean I'm anywhere near trusting the unseelie court."

Before I can respond, Max and Oliver come over, smiling and laughing.

"We're going to take off," Oliver says, pulling me into a hug. "Thanks for such an amazing night."

I lean back and smile. "It was my pleasure. Happy birthday."

After Oliver and Max are gone, everyone else trickles out. Some stick around to finish their drinks and order Ubers, but it isn't long before it's just Tristan and me. No, my bad, Nikolai and Skylar are still here chatting with the last of Oliver's friends. Before long, Skylar and Nikolai start bickering before the two of them go their separate ways, Nikolai catching the attention of one girl. She blushes a deep pink and loops her arm through his before they head for the hallway that leads upstairs to Nikolai's apartment.

I'm behind the bar, stacking plastic cups, when Tristan comes over and sits at the counter, watching me. I stop what I'm doing to arch a brow at him. "What are you looking at?"

"You," he murmurs. "Need some help back there?"

Shaking my head, I drop the cups into the trash under the counter. "It's all good. Deacon can tidy the rest up tomorrow." Nikolai gave him the night off, figuring the party wasn't big enough to require a bartender.

He nods and taps his fingers against the bar top. "Will you come home with me?" He flicks his tongue over his bottom lip at the same moment my heart rate kicks up. His eyes meet mine, and the lust there tells me he can hear my thrumming pulse beneath my skin.

I want to go home with him. It's simple, really. So why am I over complicating it?

"Breathe, Rory," he murmurs. He knows me so well he can sense the panic that unfurled in my chest as control slipped away and anxiety poured in. "Come here," he requests in a gentle tone.

I hesitate before rounding the bar, watching him turn in his seat, then stop in front of him.

"Give me your hand." Once I oblige, he lifts it and places it against his chest. His heart beats fast against my palm, and my breath catches. "Okay?" he murmurs.

I manage a nod.

"Let me in." His eyes flick back and forth between mine. "Please."

I keep coming back to the words my mom said. *Anything as important as love is worth the risk.* The conversation I had with Max the other day still lingers on the surface of my thoughts as well.

Swallowing hard, I squeeze my eyes shut and let the reins loose on my emotions until they're visible, radiating from me like a beacon of multi-colored lights. The dark blue fear, the muddied brown uncertainty, the vibrant pink, all-consuming love. It's all out in the open for him to see. To *feel*.

"Open your eyes," he whispers.

"I'm scared," I breathe, my hand still pressed against his chest.

"I know." He lifts his free hand to my cheek, brushing his fingers along my jaw. "Open your eyes," he repeats, and this time I do.

His eyes are gentle, and his expression is soft, understanding, *loving*. He loves me.

"Tristan—"

"It's okay, Rory. You don't have to say anything."

I nod, biting my bottom lip to keep it from trembling as

I let my arm fall back to my side. "I showed you mine. Now show me yours." I smack his shoulder when his lips twitch. "Funny," I mutter.

"I'm sorry," he murmurs, pushing the hair away from my face. He closes his eyes and relaxes his posture. Moments later, color flows from him, surrounding us in a bubble of his emotions. They are like the warmth of the sun on my face and bring me comfort, clarity, reassurance. There are sparks of nervousness and uncertainty, but knowing he feels it too makes me feel better.

Tristan opens his eyes and meets my gaze. "Okay?" he checks.

"No." The word spills from my lips, the weight of what I've needed to say since Nikolai and I were in his office pushing against my rib cage. "I shut you out after I killed Jules and became fae for more than one reason. Of course, I feared what the future held. How I was going to survive the transition and learn everything to stay alive in this world. The thought of having to take from another person to live haunted me. I'm still trying to get to a place of complete acceptance, though I'm not sure I ever will."

Tristan's gaze bores into mine. "I would've been there for you, Rory, every step of the way. I wanted to be."

I swallow hard. "I know. But I... I didn't want you to see me struggling. I was so scared that if I let you in then, all I'd see when you looked at me was pity or guilt over what happened that day."

His gaze drops, the sound of his pulse beating louder, but he doesn't blanket his emotions when they darken with tendrils of sadness and guilt like seaweed at the bottom of a lake. "I never should have let you go after him." His words come out low. "If I'd thought there was even a possibility you'd be put in the position of having to kill him, I wouldn't have..." He trails off, glancing upward, and his throat bobs as he swallows.

"It was my choice," I say firmly, tears pricking my eyes. "I went after Jules. The consequences of that choice are mine too, Tristan. Not yours. I know you wanted to protect me, and you would've done anything to stop what happened if you could have. But there isn't a world where I blame you for what happened, so I need you to let go of the guilt you're clinging to. Please."

His eyes are glassy as he nods. "Will you stop hiding from me?" When I blink, a tear slips free and rolls down my cheek. Tristan steps in and thumbs it away, sliding his fingers along my jaw and into my hair to tilt my head back. "Because I can't stay away from you anymore."

I lick the dryness from my lips, blinking back more tears. "I don't think I can stay away from you anymore, either."

He pulls me into his arms and, finally, after the weeks of being utterly lost, I feel like I'm home.

## CHAPTER
# THIRTY-NINE

We're barely in the elevator at the Westbrook Hotel five seconds before our lips are locked, fighting for control as we grasp at each other desperately. I've never felt a need so strong. The only way to describe this feeling, this exchange between two people who have lived without each other, is a lust-filled frenzy. My head is swimming in a haze of warmth and Tristan's clean, crisp scent. Neither of us are blocking our emotions from the other's view, which only amplifies the passion and desperation flooding through our veins.

I'm sandwiched between Tristan and the mirror-paneled wall, my core clenching with desire as his erection presses against my lower stomach. The heat and powerful emotional energy crackling between us steals my breath and has me vibrating in anticipation of what this is leading to.

He nips my bottom lip, earning a soft moan from me. "It's taking every ounce of self-control I have not to pull the emergency stop and take you right here." His words shoot liquid heat to the growing need between my thighs.

I wrinkle the front of his shirt in my grip, kissing the corner of his mouth. "If you're looking for me to dissuade you from doing that, I'm not going to."

His chuckle is a whisper of air against my lips. "I want to do this right, Rory. Rushed in an elevator isn't that. I want to ravish every inch of your body until you're trembling and the only word you can think straight enough to form is my name."

My stomach dips, and I suck in a short breath before his mouth is on mine again, stealing the strangled sound of pleasure I make. His fingers dig into my hips, and he slides his hand into my hair, cradling the side of my head as he deepens the kiss until my head spins.

We break apart at the chime of the elevator reaching the penthouse, and we stay that way for the time it takes to get inside his suite. He kicks the door shut and pins me against it, kissing me hard. I taste the sweetness of his relief, but there's a tang of worry lingering.

We reach for each other's clothes, unable to get them off fast enough. He growls, and I growl right back, until we're both laughing and fumbling with zippers and buttons. I get his shirt off before he distracts me with his lips, taking the lead.

Tristan spins me around and unzips my dress as his lips drop to my neck. I gasp, my eyes rolling back as I lean into him and feel his hardened cock against me again, kicking up the temperature of my body until the tops of my ears burn. This time isn't going to be slow and sweet, and I don't want it to be. I turn to face him, kissing him hard before pulling back enough to see his face.

My dress slips off my hips, pooling on the floor, and his

gaze darkens when it lands on my bare chest. "You bring me to my knees."

A grin tugs at my swollen lips. "Can you take your pants off first?"

He chuckles, shaking his head. "What am I going to do with that smart mouth of yours?"

I lick my lips. "I have a few ideas."

His eyes widen, and he closes the last bit of distance between us, sealing his lips over mine as he grips my hips, holding me against him.

My eyes close as I lean in, losing myself in the feel of his mouth and his body pressed flush against me. *This is home.* My heart pounds in my chest, and I break away suddenly, choking on a sob. I've missed him so much I can't breathe.

"Aurora?" His voice is soft but urgent, filled with concern.

I turn my face away, swallowing hard as I try to stop my pulse from jackhammering. "I'm sorry," I force out.

He trails his fingers along my neck and slides his thumb under my chin, turning my face to meet his gaze. "Talk to me. Please, Rory."

I blink back tears. "I've missed you so fucking much. And I'm sorry... that I didn't let you help me."

"I understand why you did what you did. I hated every minute, but I understand."

A tear leaks free, rolling down my cheek. "How are you so accepting?"

He tilts his head to the side. "Because the alternative isn't something I can live with."

I suck in a shaky breath. "But I hurt you. I—"

"Rory, you are everything to me." He tips my face up, gazing into my eyes. "*Everything*. Hurt me as much as you like. I am yours."

Warmth floods through me at his words, and I reach up, sliding my finger along his jaw. "Mine," I nearly growl, overcome with the need to make it very clear where we stand.

His gaze darkens. "And you're mine," he purrs. "From the moment I laid eyes on you, something in me cracked wide open, and I knew. You were it for me."

My eyes widen at his admission, and I lace my fingers together at the back of his neck, leaning up on my tiptoes. "Kiss me again," I whisper.

His chest rumbles with a soft growl that heats my cheeks. "I plan to do much more than that." He tilts my head up with a finger under my chin. "It's going to be a long night."

Without warning, he lifts me, and I wrap my legs around him as he carries me into the bedroom, kicking the door shut behind us.

I giggle against his lips. Not because this is funny—it's far from it, but because it almost doesn't feel real.

Tristan's mouth freezes against mine, and he sets me down. "Is something *funny*, Aurora?"

I press my forehead against his and murmur, "No. Keep kissing me."

He leans back enough to look at me. "You laughed. I'm about to ravish your body, and you're laughing."

Biting my bottom lip to keep from doing it again, I shake my head. "I wasn't sure we'd be together after... everything. I was having a moment."

His stoic expression remains. "You were laughing."

Stubble tickles my skin as I run my fingers along his jaw. "Kiss me, please."

The corner of his mouth curls and the look in his eyes makes me wonder what he's thinking.

I swallow hard, my heart hammering inside my chest. "Tristan…"

He tips his face, resting his forehead against mine as his eyes close. "I should take my time with you—I very much want to—but I don't think I can tonight."

Boldness grips me, and I reach between us, palming the front of his pants. "I want you in every way possible."

His lashes flutter, but his eyes stay shut. "Fuck," he growls, "I've missed you." He plants his mouth on mine as his hands roam over my thighs and grip my hips, making me moan.

I push against his chest, hoping he'll get the hint to move toward the bed. When he complies instantly, I grin. Tristan and I have always been in a constant struggle for power, but in situations like this, the fight makes my heart pound louder for him.

He stops walking once he hits the side of the bed, and we lean away, keeping our arms locked around each other. My eyes roam over his face slowly, willing my mind to commit it to memory. I want to keep this picture in my head forever: Tristan standing here, offering me all of him. The notion steals my breath as I push him onto the bed, falling on top of him in nothing but my black lace panties before sealing my lips over his. His hands slide up my body while his expression darkens, the hunger clear in his eyes. My skin tingles as his gaze devours me.

"Jesus, Rory," he murmurs, propped up on his elbows.

I grin a little. "You like?"

He wets his lips. "You have no idea." He reaches for me, pulling me back on top of him.

I squeal, landing against the firm muscles of his upper body. "I think you're about to show me."

"Oh, I most certainly am." His lips press against the

base of my throat, where I'm sure he can feel the insane speed of my pulse. He swipes a condom from his bedside table and rolls it on.

I push my fingers into his hair, gripping the ends and tugging as his mouth lowers to my chest. I gasp when he arches his hips, pressing himself against the throbbing between my legs.

"You're ready for me, aren't you?" he murmurs against my skin, heating it with the sultry tone of his voice.

I let out an unsteady breath. "I've been ready all night."

He nips at my skin, making me yelp. "Glad we're on the same page." He rolls me over so he's hovering over me and makes quick work of removing the remaining clothing between us. He's between my legs before I have a second to blink. "I'm not going to last long," he advises in a deep voice.

"It's okay." I cup his cheek so he'll look at me. "I just want you."

His lashes lower as he leans in and presses his lips against mine in the same moment he thrusts into me. He starts off slow, moving in and out, but after a few thrusts, his pace quickens, eliciting moans from me and filling the room with his own. His lips move from mine and trail along my jaw until he reaches the side of my neck and nips my earlobe.

I grip him tighter. "Tristan," I breathe, my voice thick with lust.

"I know." He increases the pace of his thrusts again as he slides his hand between us, finding the spot he knows will drive me crazy. He strokes me with his fingers and fills me with all of him, shortening my breaths.

His climax rides in quick and hard, making him groan

as I clench around him, and his lips land on mine once more, muffling our sounds of pleasure.

Tristan presses his face into my shoulder, still breathing hard as he pulls out of me before feathering kisses across my skin, dipping lower and making my breath catch. He takes his time spreading my thighs, causing my heart to race. My chest rises and falls fast from the anticipation of his touch, my skin tingling in its wake. His tongue darts out and licks a fiery path toward my core, stopping just before he reaches it. His eyes flick up to mine, the mischief in them making the blue brighter; if breathing was difficult before, it's almost impossible now.

He lowers his gaze, and I swallow hard. The moment his lips touch me, I let loose a shaky breath, my eyes fluttering shut. He flicks his tongue in lazy strokes as his hands slide along my legs and holds my hips against the mattress, keeping me open to him. And if that isn't the hottest fucking thing...

My hands fist the sheets on either side of me when his lips close around my clit, and when he moans against me, I almost come undone at the intense vibrations.

"Tristan," I hiss, fighting to push myself closer to him. "Please."

"Mmm," he moans against me again, making my hips buck, and I reach down and grip his hair, pushing him deeper.

With a subtle flick of his tongue along my folds, he dives into me, and I cry out. His thrusts are quick and hard, and he adds a finger, teasing me with lazy strokes until I come, moaning his name. He laps up every drop of my release, and my muscles jump at the oversensitivity.

"That's my girl," he murmurs and kisses my inner thigh, my stomach, my neck before his mouth lands on mine. My head is swimming with desire as I taste myself on his lips.

We break apart, and he rolls to his side, landing on the pillow next to me. Once I'm confident my voice won't crack, I turn to look at him with a blissful smile. "We're going to do that at least twice more tonight."

A deep laugh rumbles through him as his gaze holds mine. "You'll get no argument from me." He leans over and kisses my brow, tucking my hair behind my ear and brushing his fingers across my cheek. "I missed that—missed *you*."

I'm not surprised by the sting of tears in my eyes as I echo, "I missed you."

Before we pass out in each other's arms, I lose track of the number of times he makes me come. I haven't been this happy since... before I became fae. I sleep soundly for the first time in weeks, lulled by the steady sound of Tristan's heart beating beneath my cheek.

---

I need to stop leaving Tristan naked in his bed after we've had sex. It's not quite morning yet—at least, not time to get out of bed, but I need to move.

I tiptoe out of the bedroom and into the kitchen. Pouring myself a glass of water, I gulp down half of it before I set it on the counter and walk down the hallway on the other side of the penthouse. I open the door to what I remember being his home office and gasp. His desk is gone and in its place in the piano from the ballroom.

I approach, running my finger along the smooth lid before lifting it off the keys. I haven't played since the day Tristan overheard me, and if I wasn't worried about waking him with the noise, I'd sit on the bench and play a bit. Instead, I settle for closing my eyes, taking a centering breath, and gliding my fingers along the keys, pressing none of them. Their smoothness brings me back to the many evenings and weekends I shut myself in my bedroom and taught myself to play; I was so excited the day I could play my first song from start to finish without fumbling. I'll never forget that feeling of being on top of the world. Of course, I can't stand in front of this piano and not think about the day Tristan caught me in the ballroom, caging me against the side of it. It's almost laughable to think of that time when I tried desperately to deny what I felt for him. I pull my bottom lip between my teeth, reaching up to press my palm against my racing heart. My breasts tingle as I picture what could've happened had I not taken off that day. Flashes of Tristan taking me against—or on top of—the piano fill my thoughts, and heat pulses at my core, tempting me to slide my hand into my panties and—

My eyes open at the sound of the door closing. I blink a few times until the sight of a shirtless Tristan leaning against the closed door with a faint smirk clears.

"Morning," I say softly.

He pushes away from the door and approaches. "Barely," he sighs, as if he's about to scold me. "When I woke up and you weren't there..." He trails off, and the shadows in his expression make my chest tighten.

"Sorry," I murmur, lifting my hands to his face, and brush my fingers along his cheeks. "I'm right here. I'm not going anywhere."

His eyes flick between mine, and there's something painfully raw about the worry in their deep blue depths, in the way I feel it in my chest. "Promise me."

My eyes widen. I'm not used to seeing Tristan like this.

So... vulnerable. "I promise I'm not going anywhere." I laugh softly. "Except the shower."

He chuckles. "I could use a shower." He leans into me, pressing his lips just below my ear. "You know," he whispers, "saving water is important for the environment. We should probably shower together."

I close my eyes, smiling like an idiot. "Oh, yeah?"

His teeth scrape against my neck, making my skin tingle before his lips cover it. "Definitely."

## CHAPTER
# FORTY

I reach for Tristan's hand, pulling him toward the bathroom, and squeal when he swats my ass before curling his arm around my waist and lifting me off my feet. He carries me inside, where he sets me on the plush bathmat and kisses my nose.

I run my hand through his well-fucked hair, pushing it away from his face as I lean in to press my lips against his cheek.

He turns his face at the last moment, sealing his lips over mine, and grips my hips, tugging me toward him. "I'm not sure we're going to make it into the shower," he murmurs, nipping my lower lip as he trails his hands up my sides.

"Says the one who can't keep his hands to himself."

He chuckles. "Those certainly aren't *my* hands on my ass."

I giggle, pulling away and reaching over to turn on the shower. I slip out of my clothes, my heart pounding, knowing Tristan is standing behind me with that dark, hungry look in his eyes, as if he's about to devour me. Heat pools low in my belly as I step out of my panties before turning to face him. My chest is flushed and my eyes dart to his. There's that look. Hooded lashes, lust-filled gaze, and soft, kissable lips.

He shakes his head, bowing it as he closes the distance between us in a couple of steps. "I have to be the luckiest man on earth," he says in a low voice, and by the time he finishes speaking, he's so close his breath grazes my cheek.

My lips twist into a grin. "Yeah?" I slide my hand up the solid muscles of his chest and curl my arm so it drapes around his neck.

He leans in to kiss me again. "Mmm." His lips brush mine, and he backs me up until I step under the warm spray of water. He runs his fingers along my shoulders, dropping them to my waist as his mouth possesses mine.

After several long, delicious moments, we break apart to fill our lungs. Tristan grabs my hand when I reach for the bottle of body wash, taking it from me. My pulse gives a healthy kick as he pours some into his palm and guides me back against him.

My eyes close when his hands touch my skin. He starts at my shoulders, massaging me with the soap and easing the tightness out of my muscles. I bite my lip to keep from moaning, though it'll only encourage him to keep going.

"Does that feel good?" he murmurs, his lips brushing my ear and sending a shiver down my spine.

"Yes," I breathe.

"Good." He slides his hands down my arms, lathering soap there before moving to my back, where he works out the knots and leaves my skin radiating heat and tingling under his touch. His hand slides to my front, trailing a line of suds from my waist to my breasts. He caresses my chest, dipping down and flicking the nipple.

This time, I don't hold back my moan. It fills the room as my head falls against his chest, his cock hardening against my back. He presses his lips against the side of my neck as his fingers tweak and massage my breasts until my breathing quickens.

Just as I catch my breath, his hand dips lower, brushing my stomach on its path toward the heat at my core. My heart slams against my rib cage when he rinses the soap off his hand and slips it between my thighs, caressing my folds with a single digit.

I suck in a breath. "Tristan…"

His lips curl into a grin against my skin, and he drags his finger along my slit at an agonizingly slow pace before pushing in to the first knuckle.

"I need you," I moan when he hits a sensitive spot.

He inhales, easing his finger out of me. "You have me, Rory. All of me."

My chest swells with bright yellow elation. I turn to face him and see nothing but love and adoration in the depths of his blue eyes. When I open my mouth to speak, the words get lost on my tongue.

Tristan guides me back against the opposite wall of the shower. When he steps back, I frown, immediately reaching for him. He chuckles. "I'm grabbing a condom from the vanity."

I snag his wrist and pull him back to me. "I'm on the pill." *And I don't want to wait for you to put a condom on.* Call me an irresponsible, horny twenty-something. I don't give a fuck at this very moment. "So long as it still works now that I'm fae?"

"There's no evidence to the contrary," he offers in a voice thick with arousal.

"Good. Then fuck me."

The hunger in his eyes flares. Between one second and the next, Tristan lifts my feet off the shower floor, and before I can make a sound, he sinks into me, morphing my gasp into a choked sound of pleasure.

"My god," I mutter, wrapping my legs around him as he thrusts, slow and deep.

He pulses inside me, and I clench around him, my mouth muffling the deep groan that tears from his throat as he picks up his pace. My head falls back against the wall, and my lungs need a minute to fill with air before my lips seek his once more. My chest is heaving, my cheeks are flushed; I'm not going to last much longer. The urgency in Tristan's thrusts and the way his mouth is dominating mine tell me he won't either.

"Aurora," he murmurs against my mouth, his voice thick with lust.

"Yes," I breathe. "Keep going."

He grunts and thrusts hard, hitting the spot that ignites the frenzy of pleasure inside me.

I cry out my release, the sound quieted by his lips on mine. He follows not long after, holding me close and burying his face in the crook of my neck. Tristan guides me down, keeping his arms around me even as my feet touch the shower tile. He grabs the bottle of shampoo and pours some into his palm before running his fingers through my hair, washing it gently but thoroughly.

I close my eyes at the delicious drowsiness filling me from his touch. It feels fucking amazing. And despite my recent orgasm, my clit is pulsing greedily again as Tristan rinses out the shampoo and switches to conditioner. I lose myself in his touch again, my head spinning with the heat of the shower and the sensations flooding through me.

Once my hair is rinsed out, Tristan pins me against the wall, the length of his body pressed against mine in all the right places. Evidently, his need is yet to be sated.

I meet his gaze, and a grin touches my lips. Putting my hands on his shoulders, I push him back until he's against the wall. Then I surprise us both when I sink to my knees before him, trailing my fingers along his torso.

"Aurora." His voice is gruff.

I flick my eyes to his face, licking my lips and smirking at the responding rapid beat of his heart. "Mmm?"

His eyes narrow. "What do you think you're doing?"

I offer a flippant shrug. "I'm finding something to do with my *smart mouth*." Dropping my hand to where his cock is standing proud in front of my face, I wrap my fingers around him before sliding my hand up, keeping my eyes locked on his.

"Fuck," he grounds out, leaning back against the wall.

My chest swells with an odd mix of pride and possessiveness, watching him under *my* touch. It's empowering. Heady, even. I apply a bit more pressure, pumping my hand up and down, increasing the pace as his breathing picks up. He curses again when I lean in and flick my tongue along the tip. I slide my fingers up to the hilt, and this time, my lips follow. Inch by inch, I slowly take all of him into my mouth, my eyes watering when he reaches the back of my throat.

He pushes his fingers into my hair, guiding me up and down his cock as it throbs between my lips. "You'll be my undoing," he growls.

My pulse surges, my eyes closing as I moan against him.

The muscles in his thighs tighten, and he groans deeply as his cock hits the back of my throat. "Rory," he murmurs, touching my cheek and making me pause. "I want to come inside you again."

The heat between my thighs pulses. Parts of me are *definitely* into that. I'm aching from getting fucked against the shower wall, but that won't stop me from doing it another time. Not when Tristan makes it feel so damn good.

He wraps his fingers around my wrists and pulls me up until we're face to face. Face to chest, anyway, and he kisses my forehead. He reaches over and shuts off the water, grabbing a towel from the pile just outside the shower and wrapping it around my shoulders. Tristan picks me up without warning and shifts to the bedroom, depositing me onto his bed, the towel lost somewhere along the way.

In the space of a heartbeat, he has me beneath him with my wrists pinned to the bed above me. He lines up the head of his cock with my aching entrance, dipping inside teasingly as I try to free my wrists from his grasp. My efforts are half-hearted; part of me enjoys giving him control like this. That thought shoots heat straight to my core, and I attempt to buck my hips to push him inside, but he traps me with his, bearing down hard, which likely would've hurt as a human. Now, it's just fucking hot.

I'm writhing against him, moaning as he thrusts into me with abandon, rolling his hips to hit the deepest, most sensitive spot. "Oh my... *yes, right there.*"

"Are you close?" he growls.

All I can do is bob my head up and down as I grip the silk sheets on either side of me and give myself over to the flood of sensations consuming my body.

He doubles his efforts, and I see fucking stars. His thrusts hit hard and fast, and when he reaches between us to strum my clit with expert fingers, my vision blurs, my thighs tightening as I clench around him.

"Come for me," Tristan says in a gruff voice, dipping his face to capture my lips in a demanding kiss.

Pleasure crashes over me like a warm, weighted blanket, and I whimper against his lips, grinding my hips as I come around his cock. His lips leave mine, and I suck in a breath to fill my lungs, moaning when his mouth finds the racing pulse at my neck.

And then Tristan bites me.

He doesn't break the skin, but the strength behind it is definitely going to leave a mark. The thought of him claiming me has heat pulsing through me as his thrusts pick up, and I cling to him as he bites down harder and growls against my skin, announcing his own climax.

The drumbeat of our pounding hearts is music to my ears, and I shiver as Tristan pulls out of me, swirling his tongue over the marks his teeth left in my neck.

After we recover from the aftershocks of our shared climax, we lie facing one another. Tristan pulls the sheets over us, then strokes my arm. My eyes flick to his the moment he transfers energy to me. "You don't have to do that," I whisper, though I don't want him to stop. Aside from nourishing me, it also makes my skin tingle with warmth, a pleasant euphoria settling over me.

"Let me take care of you," he murmurs.

I lean up and press my lips against the corner of his mouth. My stomach grumbles, permeating the silence between us. "I think I need some human food."

Tristan chuckles. "I think we can manage that." He smoothes my hair and kisses my head before getting off the bed. He steps into a pair of dark gray sweatpants and winks at me. "French toast sound okay?"

The immediate grin on my face is answer enough.

He nods before turning and walking out of the room.

After watching his backside until he's out of sight, I grab a pillow to prop my head up and sigh, staring at the ceiling. I'm not sure if we've made it back to the place we were before everything happened with Jules, but when we're together, it feels as if we're getting there. I missed it —*him*—more than I could imagine missing a person.

I find my clothes and get dressed before joining Tristan in the kitchen. He has breakfast cooking, so I walk over to the fancy-ass espresso machine and make us some coffee. Leaning against the counter while it brews, I watch him with a smile on my face. I will never tire of seeing this side of him. With all the crazy we've experienced, being able to fall asleep next to each other and cook breakfast like normal people makes the rest bearable.

I leave the coffee and walk around the island in the middle of the kitchen, stopping behind Tristan and wrapping my arms around his bare torso.

"Hey there," he murmurs, turning so he can see me out of the corner of his eye.

"Hey," I say, my cheek pressed against his back.

"You doing okay?"

"Yeah." I sigh. "I wish we could stay here forever—wish the conflict between the fae courts would resolve itself."

"Me too." He shifts enough to wrap his arm around me and pulls me against his side.

I stick my finger in the bowl of icing sugar on the counter, then lick it off. "Yum," I say, grinning a little.

Tristan bends and steals a kiss. "Yum indeed."

We spend the rest of the morning eating breakfast in

between kisses and teases. We're forcing ourselves to keep our clothes on, knowing we'll end up in bed all day if we're not careful. I wouldn't complain, but I have to get to the pub to work with Nikolai, and Tristan needs to get to the office.

"You'll come back tonight?" he asks, leaning against the doorframe as I walk into the hallway to get on the elevator.

I slip on my heels. "Maybe."

He arches a brow, the wicked smirk on his lips waking the butterflies in my stomach. "Maybe?"

My lips twist. "Hmm."

His eyes narrow as he steps toward me. "You're teasing me." He places a finger under my chin, tilting my face until our eyes are level. "I just got you back." His voice is lower, softer. "Let me see you tonight."

"I guess I can cancel my date. Too bad, though. Nikolai and I were going to this really nice sushi place." I press my lips together to keep from grinning.

"Cute," he deadpans in a grim voice. Tristan's hands drop to my hips, and he pulls me flush against him as he lowers his voice. "And you are sorely mistaken if you think I'll let that happen. You are mine, now and forever, just as I am yours. I'm not letting you get away again." He brushes his lips across mine in a whisper of a kiss that sets my soul on fire before he steps away.

My mouth opens, and I'm about to say the most important words I'll ever speak, but my throat closes, and I'm unable to get it out. It's different from when I try to lie; my brain knows I can say it, but it's my *heart* that won't allow the words to pass my lips. It doesn't make sense. I *want* to say them. Now is the perfect time. Instead, I step on the elevator, wait for the door to slide shut, and glare at myself in the mirror-paneled wall until I reach the lobby.

Groaning on an exhale, I fight the urge to punch something. I'm glad no one else is witnessing my meltdown because it's embarrassing as hell. Hot tears prick my eyes, and I shake my head as I step off the elevator.

I walk through the lobby, glancing around at the beauty of it, remembering my first time taking it all in. The smile drops off my face when I catch Marisa heading toward the kitchen, her eyes puffy and red. I turn and change direction, closing the distance between us as I call her name.

Halfway down the quiet hallway, she stops, slowly turning to face me.

"What's going on?" I frown at the dark waves of dread pouring off her.

She shakes her head and forces a watery smile. "Nothing. It's fine. I just need some air."

"Talk to me," I say. "Maybe I can help?"

She chews her bottom lip before nodding. "Can we go outside?"

"Lead the way." During my time here, I never used this hallway or spent time in the kitchen, so I'm not sure where to go.

She keeps walking, and I follow her outside to what appears to be a delivery entrance. There's a black escalade with tinted windows parked near the dumpster, but other than that, the lot is empty.

Marisa sighs, sniffling, and leans against the exterior of the building.

"What's going on?"

There's a moment of hesitation before Marisa lifts her head to look at me. "I hope you believe me when I say I wish I didn't have to do this." She wipes the tears from her face.

My brows tug closer as panic and confusion flood in. "What are you talking about?"

She says nothing. She doesn't have to.

When I'm grabbed from behind and the stick of a needle pinches my neck, my blood runs cold.

"If you had just stayed human..." She trails off and shakes her head again.

My eyelids droop and my legs no longer want to hold me upright. I fall against the guy holding me as black splotches dance across my vision and my head spins so fast everything blurs.

*Fuck.*

I open my mouth to scream, but no sound comes out.

Marisa frowns, her mouth forming, *I'm sorry*, and then the world slips away.

## CHAPTER FORTY-ONE

My ears register the constant *beep... beep... beep* of a machine before I open my eyes. A sharp antiseptic smell burns my nose. I recoil from it with nowhere to go. My eyes sting as I blink them open. Light overwhelms my vision, and I squeeze my eyes shut against the harsh lights above me. I go to move my arm to cover my face but meet resistance. I try my other arm—same thing. They're secured to the bed I'm lying on. *What the hell?*

I lift my head, blinking until my vision clears, and the room slowly materializes around me. My pulse skyrockets as I take it in—everything is white. The bed, the sheets, the walls, the shirt and pants I'm wearing.

*Marisa. She... let someone take me. Who? Why? Where did they take me?* Too many thoughts and questions are running on a loop in my head, too fast for me to focus on one.

I never thought I'd experience a moment where I regretted not letting Nikolai teach me how to shift. I'd been terrified of it so deeply and didn't get to a point where I was comfortable enough with all the other fae abilities I was learning to give it a shot. If I'd known I would need to escape capture, I would've sucked it up and taken a few lessons.

Hindsight is a real bitch.

I close my eyes and picture Tristan's penthouse, as if that's all I need to do to transport myself there, to be in his arms and have him assure me everything's okay. His suite is clear as day in my mind, from the neutral furniture to the warmth of the fireplace. Hell, even the faint lemon scent in the air. When my skin tingles, my pulse races. *Holy shit, is it working?*

The seconds tick by, and when I open my eyes, my stomach sinks. My chest rises and falls fast as my throat goes dry. I'm still trapped in the all-white, sterile room that's smaller than a hospital room—but that's what it looks like. Moving my hand as much as I can, I wince when the IV attached to it moves, searing pain through my fingers. I follow the clear tubes up to the bags they're hanging from and swallow the bile rising in my throat. I don't have a clue what's being pumped into my body—I probably don't *want* to know—and I have no way of stopping it.

Panic rolls through me like a wicked, unforgiving storm, and I snap. Screaming at the top of my lungs, I fight the restraints, kicking hard and pulling at the binds around my wrists. Pain slices at my skin, burning hot as I realize the padded cuffs holding me to the bed are constructed with iron.

*Son of a bitch.*

I lie back, my breathing heavy and my forehead damp with sweat. Before I can make another attempt to break free, the metal door to the room opens, and Dr. Richelle Collins walks in, smiling as if she's happy to see me.

My eyes widen and my head spins so fast I wince, squinting once again at the brightness of the room. Dr. Collins looks as I remember her from Elijah's time in the hospital, all the way up to her stiff white coat. It turns my stomach, and I clench my jaw.

"Aurora," she says with a sad smile, closing the door behind her. The sound of a heavy lock sliding into place makes my stomach sink. "I'm disappointed we have to meet again under such circumstances."

I narrow my gaze at her. "And what circumstance is this exactly?" She nears the bed, and I stiffen.

"Had you not gotten yourself involved with the fae, you wouldn't be here."

I struggle against the restraints. "What the hell are you talking about?" My throat stings as I speak, a painful reminder of my screaming fit a few minutes ago.

Dr. Collins crosses her arms. "We would have no reason to bring you here if you had stayed human." Her tone is cold, uncaring.

"That doesn't explain *why* I'm here," I seethe, my heart throwing itself against my rib cage. I grit my teeth, dragging my gaze over her in search of her energy, the emotions she's feeling, but nothing reveals itself to me. As far as I know, humans can't hide their emotions from fae... Something must be wrong with me. My eyes go back to the IV pumping mystery fluids into me. *Is that affecting my abilities?*

"You weren't born fae. You had fae lineage, yes, but were still technically human." It's not a question, so I don't bother offering an answer. "You triggered the fae magic in your veins when you killed that fae."

*How does she know that?* I turn my face so she doesn't see my look of surprise and cough as I attempt to sit up. Failing miserably, I fall back against the bed with an angry huff. "Yep. Still no explanation." I tug on my arm, panic rising in time with my heart rate. "What the hell are you doing to me?"

She purses her lips. "We're keeping you here."

"A-plus for the vague-ass answer, doc, but that doesn't help me."

Dr. Collins almost smiles. "We don't want to harm you, Aurora; however, we have to be sure you aren't a threat to our organization while you're here."

"What organization?"

She ignores my questions and walks around the bed, checking the machines above my head. She hums under her breath, something that sounds as if it's meant to be calming, but my blood is ice cold.

"Why am I here?" I growl.

"One of you killed my daughter, Amber," she says in a voice void of emotion.

Tightness clamps down on my chest. "What?"

"Six years ago, she was out with friends and ran into a fae who made her their next meal. She was thirteen." A distant look clouds her eyes, as if she's told this story many times and is reciting a practiced version of it. "The fae didn't stop feeding until Amber's heart stopped beating."

My mind is reeling as I frown. "I'm sorry, I—"

"I don't blame you, Aurora, and I wish you no harm." Her tone is kind, an odd contrast to the dark expression on her face. "You didn't intentionally become fae. We've gathered that from our research."

I swallow hard, shaking my head. "Your research?"

"You killed an unseelie knight for putting your brother in a coma."

My chest tightens, and it becomes difficult to breathe. "How long did you know what kept Elijah from waking up?"

Her lashes lower, and she sighs. "Not as long as you, I'm sure. When I discovered that's what ailed your brother, we doubled our research to find an alternative to bring him back. Something that didn't require the fae who put him in that state."

"Did you find anything?" I ask through my teeth, not that it matters now.

She frowns. "No."

I bite back a growl, clenching my hands into fists as the restraints rub against my skin until they're raw. "Fucking hell, let me out of these!"

"You should relax, Aurora. No need to be uncomfortable. Our fight doesn't have to be with you."

I freeze. "What fight?"

Her smile fades as her expression darkens, shooting shivers down my back. "We're going to rid the earth of fae."

I blink once. Twice. My lips are glued shut and my throat is too tight to speak. "I don't understand," I finally whisper, my voice cracking.

"Myself, along with a team of scientists, doctors, and others are what's known as the Experiment. We're a group of professionals working against the fae."

"You're hunters," I mutter. "Killers."

"No," she snaps. "The fae are killers. We're the ones fighting to protect humankind. The fae are a danger to humanity and must be eliminated."

Realization hits me like a ton of bricks. The missing fae.

It wasn't the courts attacking each other at all... it was the Experiment.

"You brought me here to kill me?" I force down the panic rising in my chest with a shallow breath. "Seems like a waste of time to string me up to your concoction of drugs and lock me in here if you're just going to get rid of me."

"I'm not going to kill you." A smile touches her lips, and it makes my stomach roil. "I'm going to fix you."

My brows shoot up. "Fix me?"

"We've been researching and testing the process of turning fae human for years, long before you were even introduced to their world. Many fae before you sacrificed their lives so we could create the reversal process. Such is the reality of an experimental procedure, I'm afraid."

*How many have they killed in creating a procedure to turn fae human?*

"You're insane," I sneer. "I won't let you do this to me."

She frowns. "Oh, honey, you don't have a choice." Her tender, motherly tone makes my eyes narrow. "Look on the bright side. If it works, you'll get your life back. This is a blessing."

I cough out a brutal laugh as tears prick my eyes. I sure as hell don't subscribe to the damsel in distress narrative, but I'd give anything for Tristan to break through the door right now and take me away from this place. "You're kidding, right? Do you want me to lie here—strapped to this bed against my will—and *thank* you?"

"I expect nothing from you, Aurora." She steps away from the bed after turning a dial on a machine above me and heads toward the door. Her form gets fuzzy, and she pauses a few feet away. "If it brings you any comfort, I'm sorry you have to endure this, and I truly hope it works."

"And if it doesn't?" I snap. "You're just going to let me die?" I don't want to think about how many fae were put through whatever the fuck Collins plans to do to me and didn't survive. The more I think about it, the faster my heart pounds. Exhaustion floods through me until it's impossible to keep my eyes open. The last thing I see before the darkness pulls me under is the door closing, locking me in this prison.

---

Dr. Collins is sitting on a chair near the end of the bed when I come to sometime later. It could be hours or days, I have no idea. I choke on the dryness in my throat before I can even speak.

"Would you like something to drink?" Her tone is that of a friend asking—causal—as if she's not forcing me to be here.

My jaw clenches hard. I won't ask this woman for anything.

She sighs. "Aurora, there's no reason for you to be uncomfortable. I know you're not like the others. I met you as a human, and it will bring me great joy to give you your life back."

The thought of Dr. Collins assuming she knows anything about my life as a fae—albeit the short period I've lived as one—is cranking my pulse up. The beeping of the machines increases, measuring my heart rate. "You don't know anything about me."

She tilts her head to the side, studying my face. "You want to be fae, then?"

"I don't want to be here," I counter in a flat tone.

"I understand your anger and confusion. That will

change," she says in what I perceive as an attempt at reassurance.

"How long have you been part of this?"

She leans back. "Since just after my daughter was killed. The murder was covered up, of course. I was told some extravagant lie about her being in an accident." Her expression darkens. "That's the thing about humans. We can lie. I got no proper answers. They wouldn't even let me see her body."

I sit up by digging my heels into the mattress. "How did you know it was fae? You didn't know they existed before your daughter died."

She offers a tight-lipped smile. "Shortly after it happened, the Experiment found me and explained everything. How the fae attacked my daughter, draining her energy before she had a chance to scream for help. They told me the police covered it up, that the fae who killed her manipulated them so he'd get away with it and the humans would be none the wiser about the existence of fae. At first, I didn't believe them. I couldn't. But once they showed me one of *them* in action, I couldn't deny it. So I joined the Experiment. Amber isn't the only innocent human who's been killed by the fae. They don't care about the people they share this planet with, and considering *they* moved *here*, I'd say they should've known better than to kill our people."

I clamp my mouth shut; I can't dispute her words. So long as fae require human energy to survive, there will be a predator-prey relationship between us and them.

I've barely had enough time to adjust to life as a fae and now I'm facing the harsh reality that I'm going to be forced back into human life? This isn't—this can't be happening. I need to have a choice in this.

Would I take the chance to be human again if it was *my* decision?

*No*, a voice in my head responds before I can give it any thought. As hard as I've struggled to overcome what I am and how I have to live to survive, I want to negotiate peace between the courts, to be with my friends—with Tristan—and I want it to last forever.

"I don't want this," I say.

"I understand you're scared, but—"

"No," I snap. "I. Don't. Want. This." I shake my head. "If you do this to me—take away *my* choice—how does that make you any better than the fae?"

Dr. Collins sighs and offers me a smile. "You'll see things differently soon, Aurora. I promise."

I want to slap that smile off her face so fucking bad, but before I have the chance to attempt breaking free of my bindings, she pulls out a syringe. Walking around to the other side of the bed, she connects it to the IV attached to me and pushes liquid into the line.

My pulse spikes and my bottom lip trembles. "What is that?"

She steps back. "An elixir our team created. It's mostly harmless, aside from the iron infused oil."

"What?" I breathe as the liquid races through my veins and weakens my system almost instantly, making my limbs heavy and my head light.

"It's not a high enough concentration to be lethal. We tested it on many of your kind until we found the right ratio."

My jaw clenches. "You mean you *killed* many of my kind to find the right ratio?"

She nods without an ounce of remorse in her eyes. I've concluded that the elixir draining my energy is also somehow blocking my ability to feel her emotions, because she's still a blank canvas, no matter how deep I push.

I blink against the rush of dizziness. "Why are you doing this to me?" My voice is smaller than I want. It's scared and quiet and so unlike me.

"Consider yourself lucky, Aurora. The Experiment has spared fae instead of hunting you all."

"You're not sparing me. You're using me."

"We're *helping* you," she says, her tone so sure; she believes it. "Marisa will be along in the next few days to start the process. Until then, try to stay calm and get some rest. You'll need it."

She's gone before I can spit my venomous reply, and I'm left staring at the closed door, struggling not to burst into tears.

# CHAPTER
# FORTY-TWO

I'm not sure how long I've been here. The days blur into a haze of white lab coats, tasteless food, needles, and unanswered questions. The Experiment is keeping me weak, feeding me human food alone, and pumping me full of the iron elixir every day. I've been in and out of consciousness for so long, I've lost all sense of time.

I'm staring at the wall when Marisa walks into the room in dark purple scrubs, a dark contrast to the light gray ones I was dressed in while unconscious. My muscles lock when I catch her in my peripheral. It's the first time I've seen her since I woke up in this hellhole. Anger and betrayal go to war in my chest as I replay the moments before I was jabbed in the neck and knocked out. She tricked me. Preyed on my compassion and empathy to lure me out of the hotel, then turned me over to these fae-hating psychos.

"I thought you might be hungry," she says, closing the

door. The lock snaps shut automatically. She's holding a tray with a bowl of soup and some toast, smiling as if she's still my friend. *She never was.*

"How long did you know?" I ask in a harsh tone, attempting to ignore the way my stomach grumbles at the aroma of what I'd guess is chicken noodle soup.

She frowns, walking closer. "Know what?"

I want to roll my eyes at her ignorance, whether it's fake or not. "About the fae."

"I've known all along. Working for Tristan was part of my undercover role."

I gape at her, the knots in my stomach twisting at the mention of his name. I miss him—desperately. "You sound insane, just so you know."

She frowns. "Maybe after lunch you'll feel up to taking a shower? It'll make you feel better."

I laugh bitterly. "Better?"

Marisa sets the tray on the empty chair. "I imagine you're angry with me."

"Angry," I echo in a low voice, shaking my head in disbelief. "You betrayed me, Marisa. You let those creeps knock me out to strap me to a bed and stick me with needles."

She looks away. "I'm sorry, Aurora. I didn't have a choice."

"Bullshit," I snap. "People make choices every day. There is *always* a choice."

"My parents founded the Experiment. I didn't want to be part of it for a long time. I only joined after my best friend, Amber—Richelle's daughter—was killed by a fae. Even then, I didn't want to see anyone suffer. I want to be part of the miracle that will cure them of the need to take human energy to survive."

I blink once. Twice. "You say that as if it should be some reasonable explanation—like you expect that to convince me to forgive you for what you did to me."

"No, I—"

"Being in the fucked-up family business is a choice. You helped them take me." There's a tiny part of me that feels for Marisa, for Richelle, even. They lost someone important to them, which is their motivation for doing this. Still, I can understand and empathize without forgiving either for what's being done to me.

Marisa pulls at the hem of her shirt. "I'm really—" She stops talking and sighs before looking at me again. "Maybe after some lunch you might want to take a shower? It'll make you feel better," she repeats the words, as if saying them a second time will make me more agreeable.

Rage bubbles in me, but I don't bother saying any more. It's not worth it. Marisa won't help me. "Fine," I deadpan, shifting my gaze to the food. "You'll have to take off these restraints for me to eat unless you plan on hand feeding me." If I have to sit through another meal being fed like a child, there's a very good chance I'll lose my last shred of dignity.

She offers a nervous smile and brings the tray over. Pressing a button behind me, she adjusts the bed so I'm sitting up and sets the tray on my lap. "If you try to escape—"

"Your friends have been pumping me full of poison for days." I taste venom in my words. "They practically have to carry me to the bathroom. I'm not going anywhere."

After hesitating another moment, Marisa frees my right hand, eyeing me.

I stretch it out, flexing my fingers and making slow circular movements with my wrist to work out the kinks.

"Can you hand me a piece of toast, please?" I flick my eyes up to her, letting the desperation I feel into my voice. She used my compassion against me to get me here—it's time I return the favor. "I don't... I don't think I can lift my arm."

Pressing her lips together, she nods. "Of course."

I watch her like a hawk as she reaches over and lifts a piece of toast off the plate. "Can you put it in my hand? I can... I'll try to hold it. Please." As she lowers it, her fingers brush my palm. With all the strength I have left, I pull on her energy, swift and without caution, gripping her wrist tightly and refusing to let go as her struggles weaken.

"Aurora, stop!" Her eyes widen, but before she has the sense to shout for help, I've taken enough that she crumples to the floor and passes out.

I've never fed like that, so violently and quickly. *Desperately.* Yet I don't feel an ounce of remorse as Marisa's energy zips through me, refreshing like cold water on a hot summer day. I break the restraints, rip the IV out of my arm, and slide off the bed. My legs wobble a bit when my feet hit the floor, but after a few steps, they're steady enough I'll be able to move fast if necessary.

My muscles no longer ache; I don't feel as if I've spent countless hours strapped to a bed. In fact, I feel pretty damn close to being able to take on the world. I just have to get out of this hellhole first.

When I reach the door and find it locked from the outside, I curse. Glancing back at Marisa's still form on the floor, my eyes land on a key card sticking out of her pocket, which I swipe from her and press against the reader on the door. It beeps once and flashes green, sending my heart racing. This is it. I should prepare for what could be on the other side, but there's no time.

Opening the door, I lean my head outside the room to find an empty hallway. An all-white, bright hallway. I squint at the fluorescent track lighting along the ceiling and step forward, half expecting the movement to trigger some alarm. When nothing happens, I let out a breath and start walking. There's a chance I chose the wrong direction, but being I have no idea where I am, I don't have a plan of escape. Making this up as I go along is giving me hives; the hair at the back of my neck is standing straight.

Hurrying down the hallway, I pray I picked the right way to go as I stop at another door and press the key card against it. I poke my head through once the light flashes green and make sure the coast is clear, then step through into the next section of hallway. I'm chewing on the inside of my cheek so hard I taste blood. My head is spinning enough to make me feel nauseous, and my anxiety cranks higher with each passing second.

I pause at another door and my breathing halts when I look through the small window. The far wall is lined with shelves of test tubes, glass jars of dull blue and purple liquid, and dozens of instruments I'm certain I don't want to know the purpose of.

I need to get the hell out of here. *Now.*

Shuffling backward, I'm about to turn and keep walking when it hits me. If I'm caught, I have nothing to defend myself with besides the ability to suck these psychos' energy, and I have to get close enough to touch them. Not ideal. I glance back at the closed door. It's probably locked. Gripping the key card tighter, I step forward and tap it against the security panel, pushing my way inside.

That's when the alarm blares. A shrill, borderline deafening sound that makes me want to cup my hands over my ears and squeeze my eyes shut against it.

My heart slams against my rib cage, and I grab the first thing my fingers touch. I grip it tightly, glancing down to find a scalpel. Good. That'll do some damage.

I bounce between the only two options I have: hide in here, or make a break for it and try to find my way out.

They know where I am. I have to run—I have to fight.

"Put the knife down," a calm, borderline hypnotic voice says.

My head snaps up, and when I swallow, I choke on the dryness in my throat, then clear it. "*No.*"

The guy steps into the room and closes the door. He opens a panel in the wall, tapping on the screen a few times, and the alarm stops. When he turns to face me again, I take him in. He's eerily attractive. Dark brown hair is swept across his forehead, just short of covering his matching brown eyes. My gaze drops, and I frown. He isn't wearing a lab coat like Dr. Collins, or scrubs like Marisa. Instead, he looks casual, comfortable in dark jeans and a black V-neck.

He clears his throat. "Aurora."

My eyes fly up to his face.

He smiles. "I need you to put the knife down for me."

I narrow my eyes. "Who the hell are you?"

"I can be your friend so long as you do as I ask. I want to make sure you're safe."

An angry laugh bubbles past my lips. "You're one of *them*. Keeping me here against—"

"I'd like to help you," he cuts me off, leaning against the closed door.

"I don't want your help." *All I want is to get the hell out of here.*

He tips his head back, making the hair fall away from his face. "Ah, but you need it."

I lift my arm, pointing the scalpel at him. "You want to help? Great. Let me out of here."

He purses his lips. "I can't do that."

With great effort, I shove the panic crowding my chest down and force a shrug. "Then you can't help me."

He slides his hands into his pockets. The move makes my pulse tick faster. This guy isn't even concerned that I'm pointing a surgical knife at him.

"I won't let you experiment on me," I announce.

"You've spoken to Richelle."

"I was locked in a room and strapped to a bed while she told me about the Experiment," I correct in a bitter tone. "I didn't have a choice."

"You should get used to that," he says mildly.

My jaw clenches so tight I can't speak for several seconds. "If they sent you to talk me down, you're not doing a great job."

The corner of his mouth twitches. "They sent me to intervene, yes. It's my job to keep you here, by whatever means necessary." His eyes move across my face. "It's up to you to decide what that means for you."

I lower my arm, dropping my gaze. "Why are you doing this?"

He pushes away from the door, approaching me at an easy pace. "This is a good thing. You'll see that soon—trust me."

I swallow the lump in my throat, blinking away the dampness in my eyes before lifting my gaze to meet his. He's standing two feet away from me now. "I don't even know who you are, and you're asking me to trust you?"

He looks at me thoughtfully. "You don't remember me?"

My brows pinch closer. "Should I?"

He laughs as he plucks the scalpel out of my hand swiftly. He can't be faster than me; I must be in shock. "I suppose not." He slides the knife into his back pocket, blade down. "Nikolai stole the show the day we met. He doesn't know how *not* to be a spectacle."

As much as I want to agree with that statement, it makes my eyes widen. "You..." I trail off, my head spinning. "The fae that attacked me in the parking lot. That was *you*?" This guy looks different from the fae I remember—his hair color has changed—but taking a closer look, I recognize him now.

His cheeks flush a light pink. "*Was* me," he says. "I'm not that person anymore. I apologize for the pain I caused you." He offers a small smile. "My name is Carter."

My hands tighten into fists at my sides, a painful reminder I no longer have a weapon. "The Experiment has fae working for them? That's fucking hypocritical."

"No, they don't. That would go against everything they stand for."

"Right." I draw out the word, confusion clear in my voice. Until it hits me, knocking the air out of my lungs. "They made you human," I breathe.

He nods, and I feel a brush of his gratitude against my senses. It's soft and warm, like being wrapped in a warm towel after an afternoon of swimming. Evidently, feeding on Marisa has brought back some of my abilities. "I, like you, wasn't born fae, but turned a long time ago to be with the woman I thought was my soulmate. I was wrong. Fast forward to almost a month ago, the talented and dedicated team here helped fix my mistake and gave me my life back."

My back straightens as I pin him with a glare. "I don't want to hear your success story or whatever."

"But you should," he insists. "If you're lucky, it'll be yours, too." He comes at me without warning, but I'm fast enough to sidestep him and whirl around to slam my foot into his stomach, sending him stumbling back. He grunts in pain, coughing as his lungs struggle to fill with air.

"Aurora," he says hoarsely, "we don't have to do this."

"You've made it pretty clear we do," I shoot back, advancing once more. Grabbing the front of his shirt, I shove him back into a wall of shelves, the sound of glass bottles smashing against the floor music to my ears. I want to destroy this place on my way out.

"Listen to me," Carter says through his teeth as I keep him pinned to the shelves.

I bark out a sharp laugh, tightening my grip and leaning in as I tap into his emotions. "Hard pass."

Carter grunts, shoving me with what I imagine is his full body weight, and I give him an inch of space, dropping one arm to my side but keeping the other gripping his shoulder. I dig my fingers in, and he makes a strangled sound of pain at the back of his throat before I pull on his energy. Slowly, so Carter knows exactly what I'm doing and that he can't do a thing to stop it. "Aurora, *stop*."

All I can think is that this guy works for the people keeping me here, planning to perform a procedure that may or may not kill me. I lean in close enough my nose nearly touches his, and lower my voice. "I'm not going to let you—"

There's a sharp poke of a needle in the side of my neck, and I suck in a startled breath, my eyes widening as I reach for the shelves behind Carter. My legs go numb, the muscles struggling to keep me upright, and my grip slips off the shelves. I sway on my feet, my vision blurring and my ears ringing. Carter's arms come around me as warmth floods through my veins and my legs give out. Whatever poison he shot into me drags me into the darkness.

## CHAPTER
# FORTY-THREE

"She's waking up..." an unfamiliar voice says, the tone low, scared.

*Of me?* There's no way they fear someone strapped to a bed.

*Considering you all but drained the last person who was in the room while you were tied down, it's a possibility.* Damn that pesky little voice at the back of my head. She's almost as annoying as the voices floating around the room.

My head pounds as if I spent the night drinking cheap wine. *Is it morning? Night?* Hell, I have no idea.

"I told you she wouldn't be out long." That sounds like Dr. Collins.

I pry my eyes open and lift my head enough to peek around the room, wincing as the pain behind my eyes intensifies with each movement. Dr. Collins is standing beside the bed, with Marisa and a younger looking man behind her. Carter stands against the wall across from the bed. His expression is calm, unconcerned—the complete opposite of the guy standing near Marisa, looking at me as if I'm a monster.

*To him, you are.*

I close my eyes again, willing the stabbing pain to subside.

"Give her something for the pain," Carter instructs in a level tone.

"Go ahead, Aaron. She won't hurt you," Dr. Collins says.

I want to laugh, but it'll make the pain worse.

When Aaron doesn't move, Carter huffs out an annoyed sigh. His shoes echo on the floor as he approaches the bed.

I turn my head to the side, facing him, and narrow my eyes as he pushes something into my IV line, his hands covered by black leather gloves. *Why are you helping me?* The words are on my tongue, but my lips don't move.

"Clear the room," Carter says, keeping his eyes on me.

"Carter," Dr. Collins warns. "We don't have time to—"

"Five minutes," he says, flicking his gaze away from me.

I continue to watch him, how he handles the machines attached to me with care. Considering this is the same guy who slammed me into the side of Tristan's car, I'm confused by his actions. Maybe the Experiment screwed with him—made him nicer? Either way, he doesn't seem to mind.

Shifting my gaze, I watch the rest of the lab coats leave the room. When the door clicks shut, I turn my head to look at the ceiling.

Carter sits on the edge of the bed, as if he's comfortable with me—as if we're friends. "Aurora," he says.

I turn to him and hope the sharp look on my face tells him I'm not impressed with his proximity.

"The more you fight them, the worse it's going to be for you." He frowns. "If you work with them, let them—"

"Stop," I mutter. "What you're asking... I won't let them do to me what they did to you." The thought of allowing these people to mess with my body in an attempt to make me human again—it makes me want to hurl, and cry, and scream loud enough for someone, *anyone*, to hear me. But there's a good chance we're in the middle of nowhere, locked in some bunker underground a thousand miles away from my friends—from Tristan. My chest tightens. I've been gone a long time. Tristan must know something is wrong. I was supposed to go back to the hotel... however many nights ago that was. Hot tears burn my eyes, and I blink before Carter can see. The last thing I need is to give any of them more ammunition against me.

"I can't help you if you won't cooperate."

"How many times do I have to tell you I don't want your help before you fucking hear me?" I shake my head. "I don't know what your angle is—we aren't kindred spirits or some shit because they're trying to screw with me like they did you—so it's time for you to leave."

A muscle ticks along his jaw, and he grips the metal bed railing. "You'd be wise to allow me to show you kindness. What I'm doing is far more than what you'll see from anyone else here."

I growl at him. "Back off."

He ignores me, leaning so close I feel his breath on my face. "I was alone in here." He lowers his voice. "When they put me through countless tests and experiments until the reversal worked." He swallows hard. "It was torture. Every single day, I wished it would end—that they would make some fatal mistake and kill me, just so I wouldn't have to endure it any longer."

The tears are back, but now they're brought on by the suffocating fear clamping down on my chest. "Then why are you making me do this?" I whisper.

He steps away from the bed, his expression softening. "Because after it was over, it worked. They fixed me."

I shake my head. "You were fae, Carter. An asshole one, but from what I've seen today, that had nothing to do with your inhuman DNA. You didn't need to be *fixed*. You weren't a monster."

He offers a thin smile. "I appreciate your candor." He reaches over and releases the bindings around my wrists.

My pulse jumps. "What are you doing?"

"No offense, but you need a shower."

"Gee, thanks," I mutter, rubbing my wrists.

"Are you going to behave?" he checks, watching me carefully.

I arch a brow at him. As much as I'd like to take another shot at kicking his ass, he's right. I need a shower; I feel disgusting. Odds are, now that I've tried escaping, they have more Experiment members outside my door in the event I get out.

He walks around the bed and stands at the door. "Ready?"

I nod and stand slowly, giving myself a minute to catch my balance. I grimace as I pull the IV out of my hand, dropping it on the bed, and step toward him.

When my knees bang together, too weak to move, Carter comes to my side and slips his arm around my waist. I haven't felt this weak since I became fae and refused to feed. No... this is actually worse. They must've upped the dose of toxins they've been pumping me full of after my escape attempt.

With Carter's arm securely around me, now would be the perfect time to feed on him, but if I try it this time and fail, I may not get another chance to get out of this room. I have to be smart about this, come up with a plan before I act again.

"Lean on me," he says, and I do, because I have no choice.

*You should get used to that.* Carter's words from before echo in my ear, and the reality of them makes me want to sob. I have no control here, and they're going to use me until they get the results they want or it kills me.

Carter helps me out of the room and down the hall to a bathroom. It has a sink, toilet, and shower. No windows or mirrors—nothing I can use to escape.

"I'll stand outside," he says.

I manage a nod and grip the counter by the sink for support.

"Are you okay?"

My knuckles whiten. Of course, I'm not okay. "Get out."

He doesn't question me again. The door clicks shut behind him, no doubt locking me inside.

I stand under the warm spray of water, staring at the white tile wall in front of me. My arms are tired, and my legs are struggling to hold me up. I'm in no condition to be taking care of myself. I wash my hair and body, and by the time I finish, everything hurts and I'm crying. This situation doesn't feel real. I'm praying that I'll wake up any second, shaking and in a cold sweat from this nightmare, but the longer I stand here, it becomes apparent this is my reality, and there's a good chance I'll never see my friends and family again.

Once I get out of the shower and dress in the fresh scrubs Carter left for me, I open the door to find him leaning against the opposite wall.

"Feel better?" he asks.

I shoot him a look. "How long have I been here?"

He presses his lips together as if he's not sure he should answer.

"I deserve to know," I push.

After a moment of hesitation, he says, "Five days."

My hand flies to my mouth before I can stop it, and dread washes over me. Everyone must know I'm gone—that something happened to me. I've been stuck in this literal hell for almost a week. They've been making me feel like death for the hours I'm conscious.

"They'll kill you all," I mumble.

"They won't find us."

My gaze hardens into a glare directed at him. "They *will*," I insist. *They have to.*

"Why don't we see what we can find in the kitchen?"

"What, you're not going to tie me back to the bed?"

He gives me a look. "You should eat something."

"I need more than food, Carter," I say in a tight voice.

He shakes his head. "You'll manage without human energy until you don't need it anymore, especially considering you nearly sucked Marisa dry."

The pit in my stomach grows, making me clench my jaw. I open my mouth, but nothing comes out.

---

Sitting across from Carter at a small table in a large, industrial-looking kitchen, I poke at a piece of potato on my plate. I haven't touched the carrots or ham; my stomach clenches each time the smell wafts toward my face.

I press my tongue to the roof of my mouth, willing my stomach to settle. "How long have you been here?" I ask Carter, hoping to get out of eating.

"The Experiment found me about a week after that night you and I met. I've been here since. It took them a while to figure out the process, and you know I wasn't the first they attempted it on."

"How long has the Experiment been a thing?"

"I'm still learning the history of the organization, and Richelle knows it far better than I do. You should ask her."

"I'd rather not," I deadpan.

He exhales. "Fine. I guess it won't matter, since you'll be one of us soon."

I want to shoot back a snarky response to assure him there's no way in hell that's going to happen, but I refrain. I want answers and if this is how I have to get them, fine.

"The Experiment was founded by two families. They kept it out of the media, made sure no one knew about what they were doing. The fae were meant to be kept secret, so they were simply keeping that secret."

*And one of their own*, I want to add.

"One family, I think you already know, is Marisa's."

The muscles in my jaw throb as I clench my teeth.

"It started before you or I were born." He scratches the back of his head. "Shortly after the fae were forced to make earth their home."

*After the territory war destroyed their home.* I keep my mouth shut; Carter likely knows the story.

"Some of the fae got comfortable here pretty fast. In fact, they seemed to forget who had been here first. They walked around like they were superior."

I could attest to that from the time I spent around them during my internship at Tristan's hotel. Some of the fae *were* arrogant. "You seem to forget that *you* were one of those fae."

He nods, a solemn look passing over his face. "That's true, which is why it's important for me to make up for it now."

I roll my eyes. "Their goal is to eradicate the fae, right?" That's what Dr. Collins said the first day I was here.

"Mostly," he says. "However, they also wanted to know if they could reverse the process." He gestures to himself. "Ta da. Once they discovered that, it changed the game. Sure, they're still going after the fae who are dangerous to humans, but they're giving others—like you and me—a chance to be good again."

"If you think humans are *good*, you haven't been paying attention to the world." I shake my head. "And who the hell is the Experiment to decide which fae are good enough to give a second chance? Judge, jury, and executioner is *not* justice."

"Some of my answers won't make you feel better, Aurora, but I'm being honest with you."

I push my plate away and cross my arms. "Forget I asked. You're all out of your damn minds."

"I hope you feel differently after the procedure." His smile makes my entire body go cold, and in that moment, I've never felt so alone.

## CHAPTER
# FORTY-FOUR

I've been locked up by the Experiment for eight days now. I think.

They bring me the same plate of eggs, toast, and fruit every morning.

They inject me with iron every afternoon. I still scream. Every time.

They won't tell me anything. I've stopped asking questions.

When I'm not passed out, I'm in a drug-induced haze, left staring at the wall for hours. Time doesn't move and neither do I.

They won't let me feed. I haven't had energy since I sucked it out of Marisa a week ago—if my counting is right. I could be wrong. My body is shutting down; I feel as if I haven't slept in days. There's absolutely no chance I'd have the strength to attempt escape if given the opportunity, not that I have been. I'm clinging to the last bit of glamour I can to conceal my inhuman features, and I'm not even entirely sure why. My gut tells me these fae-hating people will treat me even worse if I *appear* as the creature they so viciously despise.

I can't take much more of this.

I thought with time I'd figure out a plan to get out of this mess, but with the profound hunger and the poison they're pumping me full of, I can't keep my thoughts straight to come up with anything viable.

*What is Tristan doing right now? Is he looking for me?*

My friends must be going just as crazy, not knowing where I am—what's happening to me.

From the moment I open my eyes, something feels off. No one has come into my room, not even to offer me food.

When the door opens and Carter steps inside, closing it behind him, the hair on the back of my neck stands straight and my stomach sinks. He's dressed in dark gray scrubs today with the same black leather gloves he wore a few days ago.

My eyes narrow as he smiles, and I force out, "What?"

"Today's the day," he says in a light voice. He's *excited* about this.

"No fucking way." My pulse is increasing as I struggle until I'm sitting upright. The restraints are gone; I'm too weak to attempt escape, anyway. It's a sobering thought that makes me want to scream and sob, of which I do neither.

Carter frowns. "This is a good thing, Aurora. When will you see that?"

"I'm leaning toward never."

He holds up his gloved hands as if he's trying to calm me down, to show me he's not a threat. But he is—they all are.

"Aurora," he says. "Please, for your own sake, don't fight them." Carter's expression is as smooth as his voice, but it doesn't ease the storm of fear raging in my chest, making my hands shake.

Tears sting my eyes, and I will them not to spill over. "Please don't," I whisper. "Don't let them do this to me." Any strength I had is gone. I'm sure he can see it in my eyes.

He drops his gaze. "Think of the bigger picture."

My throat tightens. "The bigger picture?" I echo sharply. "You are hurting people—people you used to identify with. That sounds like betrayal to me."

His gaze slices through me. "The fae are monsters. *I* was a monster."

"They really fucked with your head, didn't they? You *believe* the shit you're spewing."

His eyes narrow. "It's the truth. You're just scared to see it."

"No, you're too scared to admit what's going on here is wrong. That what was done to you was wrong, so you're covering it up with lies and pretending what's happening here is a good thing."

He shakes his head but doesn't say a word as he moves closer.

"What are you doing?" I cringe as my voice cracks, and he pulls the IV out of my arm.

"It's time," he says so casually it makes my blood run cold. He swings my legs over the side of the bed and hauls me against him.

I snap. Throwing my fists toward his face and kicking as hard as I can, I try to get him away from me. I even try to feed, but despite his hands gripping me, it doesn't work. *It doesn't work.*

The gloves. It has to be them. They must be made with iron like the restraints they've kept me in. I double my efforts in trying to break free of his grasp, but not having fed in so long has left me with the strength of a human, it seems.

"Enough," Carter shouts. "Stop fighting me."

I scream, clawing at his face until he backs off. *"Don't touch me."*

He grunts and pushes me back against the bed, staring at me hard. "I didn't want to do this," he says, pulling a syringe out of his pocket. "Unless you're willing to cooperate, you leave me no choice."

"Fuck you," I seethe.

He sighs. "Hard way it is."

"Come near me with that thing, and I'll break your fucking hand. I'm serious."

Carter gives me a doubtful look that cranks up the anger simmering in my chest.

I roll over, standing from the bed on the other side so it's between us. My eyes fly around the room in search of something I can use to protect myself. When I come to the quick conclusion there are no weapons around, though I shouldn't be surprised, my stomach drops.

I need to get out of here. *I need to shift.* It didn't work the last time I tried, but when Carter makes a move toward me, determination fuels me—I have to try again.

I force myself to concentrate on where I want to go. *Tristan's penthouse.* I repeat it over and over in my head while picturing what it looks like, how I feel when I'm there, wrapped in Tristan's arms, with his lips—

"It won't work." Carter's voice cuts into my concentration, and I lose the picture.

I glare at him.

"You can't shift in here. Iron wards," he explains, arching a brow. "Do you even know how?"

I cross my arms over my chest. "Obviously, it doesn't matter."

He laughs. "Hey, at least once you're human again, you won't have such a hard time with the lying."

I shake my head. "I'm not going to be human again." No. Tristan and I are going to be together forever. That's the way it's supposed to be. After everything we've been through, we deserve it.

Carter closes the distance between us until my back hits the wall and my panic surges. He frowns at my wide-eyed expression. "I don't want you to be scared."

My brows tug together. "Bullshit. You're doing what you're told. Congrats. You're the Experiment's bitch. Does that make you feel big and powerful?"

His anger hits me like a slap to the face, but it's gone as quick as it came, and then he smiles. "Why don't you let me know?" He grabs my arm hard and pulls me against him, jamming the needle into the side of my neck before I can react.

---

When I come to, my back hurts, my head hurts—fuck, *everything* hurts. And I'm strapped down—again.

I force my eyes open, blinking in a panic to clear my vision and find out what the hell is happening. I regret that move the moment my eyes settle on Dr. Collins and Carter standing a few feet from the table I'm restrained on. She wears the same black gloves as Carter.

"I take back what I said before." My throat stings when I speak, and I meet Carter's curious gaze. "You *are* a monster." I put as much force as I have left into those words.

He frowns, but says nothing in response. Instead, he turns to Dr. Collins and says, "I'll prepare for the transfusion."

She offers a smile and nods. "Thank you, Carter. Please notify the others we'll be starting the transition momentarily."

*Oh no. No, no, no. I need more time. I have to come up with a way out of this. This cannot happen.*

Carter leaves the room without a backwards glance, and I struggle to sit up.

Dr. Collins watches and gives me a thoughtful glance. "I'm sorry we had to do it this way, Aurora. I had to ensure the safety of my people as well as yourself."

I bark out a laugh, ignoring how it rips through my throat. "You're worried about my safety? You're about to do something that could kill me. Don't fool yourself."

She smiles. "Please don't be concerned. We've done this before and—"

"Killed plenty of fae," I cut in.

"And *saved* many, including Carter."

"You're not a hero, Richelle," I shoot back.

"Considering I could've killed you instead of giving you your life back, I think you're very wrong about that."

A man walks into the room before I can respond. His expression is strained, his shirt is wrinkled, and he's got a nasty bruise on the side of his face. The guy looks like shit.

"What is it?" Richelle asks.

He waves her off. "Nothing to worry about."

"Where are the others?"

"He's causing a bit more of a problem than we expected, so I have several of the staff staying with him as a precautionary measure."

*They're doing this to someone else?*

She nods. "All right. I'm just about ready to get started." She turns to face me. "The procedure isn't pleasant. I'm sure Carter has told you about it." She doesn't wait for me to answer. "Depending on how your body responds to the elixirs, it could take some time. And despite your recent attitude, we're going to do our best to keep you comfortable."

My mouth is too dry to respond. My entire body is shaking, and if there had been any food in my stomach, I'm sure I'd be wearing it. The idea of them waiting to do this to another fae only intensifies the nausea rolling through me. Do I know them? Were they ambushed and taken from the hotel as well? My mind immediately runs through the group of fae I know, making my panic rise higher as the list grows.

"The process is fairly involved. We're going to inject you with several DNA splicing elixirs. One to break down any fae magic in your system, another to wipe it out, and lastly, one to rebuild strands of human DNA."

My head is spinning so fast I'd fall on my ass if I weren't lying down.

"Afterwards, you'll need a blood transfusion to clear out any remaining fae magic running in your veins. This will also complete the repair needed from the elixir. It is quite potent. There's a chance it'll cause damage elsewhere, which is part of the reason for the transfusion. That, and the only way to ensure the procedure is one hundred percent effective, is if we take all of your blood, destroy it, and give you new, *human* blood. Luckily, we have connections with several nearby blood banks."

We're close enough to a city center that can have blood transported here then... I'm not sure what good that information does me now, but I hang onto it, anyway. "You're crazy," I deadpan. "Literally insane."

One of the white coats steps forward. "I have a feeling you'll change your mind once the procedure is successful." He pauses, arching a brow at me. "Unless you *want* to remain fae."

It wouldn't matter to them if I did. Their entire mission is to rid the world of fae. But if it were up to me, if it was *my* choice, I wouldn't let them do the procedure. I've already lived through the hardest part of being fae, learning *how* to live with it. Fuck, I was *just* getting to the good part, and now... I stop that train of thought before it brings me to tears in front of these monsters. "What I *want* is to not be held against my will. To have a say in what happens to *me*. To have a fucking *choice*."

He turns away from me without a word. *Coward*.

I'm forced to watch while the two of them set up a tray with a colorful lineup of glass vials and needles. My stomach churns at the sight of the purple and blue liquid. I can't even imagine what that shit is. There's a good chance I don't *want* to know, considering they're about to force it into my body. My vision blurs as my chest tightens. I swallow hard and look away, trying to breathe in through my nose and out through my mouth. It doesn't work. The anxiety has its claws in me so deep, I can't escape it.

When Dr. Collins and the man approach the table on either side of me, I use my last bit of strength to attempt escape. I get one arm free, but the bindings on my legs go from my thigh to my ankle. I struggle until I'm dry heaving and sweat is covering my forehead, damp blond strands of hair sticking to my face and neck.

Dr. Collins shakes her head and pushes my arm back

into the restraint, tightening it to the point it bites into my wrist, making me yelp at the burn of iron against my skin.

"You can't do this," I say through my teeth, my jaw locked tight. "*Please.*"

She ignores me and reaches across the table for the syringe the man is holding out to her. "Take a deep breath," she tells me in a robotically calm voice. When her eyes meet mine and I see nothing but cold, calculated focus, I know it's over.

The tears fall from the sides of my eyes as I blink. I try to swallow the lump in my throat, but it doesn't do any good. I clamp my mouth shut, keeping my sobs inside, and when she lowers the needle to my skin, I close my eyes and pray it's over quickly.

Inhaling a sharp breath through my nose when the sting comes, I try to shift away from it, but can't move. My body knows the second she pushes on the end of the needle. I can't keep my lips together as my skin ignites painfully, and I scream, hurting my own ears as my eyes fill with tears.

The chemicals racing through my veins are burning the skin off my bones, licking each part of me as the elixir makes its way through my system. Black dots cloud my vision as I slip out of consciousness, but then there's another needle and more elixir that releases a freezing into my veins. It's the complete opposite sensation to the previous cycle, but it's just as painful, if not more.

The room spins, and my throat is raw, but I'm still screaming as everything slips away into darkness. Peaceful, comfortable darkness.

## CHAPTER
# FORTY-FIVE

When I pry open my eyes, there's nothing but silence. Blinking a few times, I try to clear the fog in my head. *What the hell is going on?* I scan the room, but there's nothing to see. No windows, no furniture, just plain white walls and the bed I'm on.

I sit up in a flash, sucking in a sharp breath as memories flood through me. I'm not restrained anymore, but my whole body throbs, every muscle tight and sore, and I fall back against the pillows with a strangled whimper. The room I've been kept in fades in and out for a few minutes as I force myself to focus on my breathing, willing the pain to subside.

*The Experiment.*

My eyes bounce around the room in a panic as my pulse thrums faster. Dropping my gaze to the blankets I'm tangled in, I kick them away. I'm wearing a white long-sleeved shirt and gray sweatpants I don't remember putting on. I lick the dryness from my lips and frown at my bare feet.

My head shoots up at a loud succession of crashing noises and then shouting somewhere on the other side of the door. I bite my lip, debating if I should investigate. *Yeah, that's a good idea. Go* toward *the loud noises when you have absolutely nothing to defend yourself with.*

I slide off the bed and creep toward the door. Holding my breath, I reach for the handle and pray it's not locked. Wrapping my fingers around the cool metal, I grit my teeth and turn it. My stomach flips when the handle gives, and I open the door. The Experiment no longer sees me as a threat, it seems. *Does that mean the procedure worked?* I don't *feel* different, at least not yet. Everything just feels fuzzy.

My feet slap against the white tile floor as I bolt down the hallway, following the pain-filled screams. My heart pounds in my ears and my lungs are strained with each step I take.

I reach the end of the hall and slam my palms against the door, ignoring the flare of pain in my hands as I push it open.

My hand flies to my mouth as I cry out at the sight of Max. His face is bloody and bruised, and the rest of him—held up by cables hanging from the ceiling—doesn't look any better. My nose wrinkles at the coppery scent of blood mixed with antiseptic.

Flicking my gaze around the bright room only makes things worse. Several people in white coats stare at me with wide eyes; they weren't expecting to see me. There's a cart of metal instruments sitting next to Max and my pulse spikes at the sight of blood coating several of them. *That's where the smell came from.* It's also seeping through the material of his gray shirt and pooled on the floor at his feet, staining his shoes red.

Anger boils through me faster than I could've imagined possible. I'm out of breath and still I find the energy to scream at the top of my lungs as I charge toward the white lab coats. I launch myself at the lanky one and shove him backward, making him collide with the glass cabinet against the wall, shattering it and the vials of liquid inside. He grunts in pain but stays upright, his eyes narrowing at me as his upper lip curls into a snarl.

Two more lab coats turn to face me, while one of them hurries out of the room, most likely to call for help. *You'll be too late*, I want to shout, but I don't waste any time. I advance on the next one, a petite blond girl whose eyes widen when she sees the fury in mine.

She raises her hands in front of her. "Wait—"

I shove her hard, and she collides with the tray of instruments, collapsing as they clatter to the floor around her. My breath catches as I stare at the scalpel sticking through her stomach and the spreading red stain on her lab coat. I frown, pausing as I realize that I don't care if she dies.

They think I'm a monster, so maybe I should be.

*I want them to suffer.*

That might make me worse than these people, but I can't find the will to care after what they've done.

Only one person stands between me and Max, and I'll take great pleasure going through him.

"Aurora," Carter says in a low voice. "You shouldn't be out of bed."

My lips peel back in a snarl. "Get the fuck out of my way, or so help me, I will kill you with my bare hands." I offer an icy smile. "I'll enjoy it, too."

He frowns. "You're not listening to me."

"You think?" I shoot back. "Now move."

"I can't do that."

I shrug, grabbing a scalpel off an upright table. "Hard way it is."

Carter arches a brow. "We're going to do this again?"

"It'll go a little differently this time." My tone is snarky and cold.

Max coughs, sputtering more blood onto his shirt, and my face blanches. I have to help him. I have to get him out of those cables and out of this place so he can feed and heal.

Carter advances, and I pedal back, whipping my gaze to him. Max is going to have to hold on long enough for me to deal with Carter.

"We don't need to fight, Aurora."

I scowl. "Are you kidding? You've been torturing my friend and you think I'm going to let you walk away from that?"

He blinks. "Your friend?"

I pause, looking toward Max. He might not have started out that way. In fact, I hated him, but things are different now. He's part of my life—my family. Even though we bicker most of the time; no family is perfect.

"Blondie," Max says in a cracked voice, nodding toward Carter as his eyelids droop.

*Shit.* I have to do something. Now.

"You won't win this fight, Aurora," Carter says matter-of-factly. It makes the urge to punch him in the face much stronger.

"Why have you made this *your* fight?" I taunt. "Do you actually *want* to be human?"

He crosses his arms. "We've been over this. The Experiment saved me."

"Bullshit. They didn't give you a choice."

Offering a shrug that suggests he's indifferent to that fact, he says, "In the end, it was for the best."

It's useless. They've brainwashed him into believing this life is what he wants. That was clear from the start, but I was hoping now, faced with danger and the chance to make a choice for himself, he would choose differently.

I inch closer to him. "You don't miss being fae? The power, the possibilities?"

His facade cracks. "What you're doing won't work. I know where I belong. You won't convince me otherwise."

Max nods toward him again, and I incline my head so he knows I understand what he wants me to do.

"Fine," I say. With one more step forward, I'm close enough to touch him. Instead, I shove him toward Max. He stumbles back and whirls around to face Max.

The corner of Max's mouth curls, and then he head butts Carter, sending him to the floor in an unconscious heap.

Max gives his head a bit of a shake, blinking a few times before looking at me. "Chop, chop. We don't have all damn day, blondie."

I choke on a laugh and snatch the black gloves from Carter's hands, tugging them on as I hurry toward Max, reaching for the chains secured around his wrists.

It's ironic—I'm fighting to break the chains off the same guy who tied me up months ago. It takes several minutes—and techniques—before I loosen the restraints enough for Max to break the rest of the way out of them.

He rubs his wrists where they're swollen and bruised. "Are you—"

"I'll be fine once we get the hell out of here."

I nod, and Max steps forward and sways. I almost don't

catch him, and then struggle to keep us both upright. "Easy," I murmur. "I don't think you're fine, Max."

"You think?" he mutters, looking less than pleased to have me holding him up with his arm around my shoulder and mine around my waist.

"Sit down for a minute."

"We don't have a minute. They must know something's going on by now."

"Max," I say firmly. "Sit. Down."

He narrows his eyes. "Are you this bossy with Tristan?"

"Yep. Now, sit."

Sitting against the wall of lower cupboards, Max breathes in and coughs again. He wipes his mouth, and it comes away with blood. The sight turns my stomach, but I school my features.

"Lovely," he grumbles.

"How did you get here?" I ask.

Max stares straight ahead. "They ambushed me a few days after you were taken. Bastards. We've been looking for you. Tristan..." Max's voice trails off as his eyelids flutter again.

"Tristan, what?"

Nothing.

"Max," I say in a sharp tone. My heart races as dread fills my chest. "Max, open your eyes." I pat his cheek, but he doesn't stir. "*Max*." I slap his face.

His eyes fly open, and he grunts.

I exhale a desperate breath, grabbing his face and holding it in my hands. "Keep your damn eyes open," I snap, fighting a wave of drowsiness from out of nowhere.

Max blinks a few times, then frowns as his face clears. No cuts or bruises, and while his clothing is still shredded in places, the skin underneath is smooth, uninjured.

I gape at him. "You just... fed on me."

"Yeah." He sounds just as surprised as me. He must've needed it so badly that it was an automatic response when I touched him. "Hey," he says, reaching toward me. "You good?"

"I don't know." My brows tug together as my eyes lock with his. "Am I... *human?*"

When my eyes fill with tears, Max snaps his fingers in front of my face. "Nope. No time for that, blondie. We've got shit to do."

I struggle to pull myself together, forcing deep breaths in through my nose and out through my mouth. I can break down once we're out of this place.

Centering myself, I hurry across the room and pull the shoes off the girl on the ground. She still doesn't move—her chest is completely still. My stomach churns when I look at her face. *I think I killed her.* I should feel guilty—it should scare me that I don't.

Max says nothing as I put the shoes on, and then we leave the room without looking back.

We make it halfway down the hall before the alarms sound again.

"Goody," Max mutters, slowing to a halt to say, "Get ready to fight, blondie."

My eyes widen and whip toward him as I struggle to catch my breath. "With what weapons?"

He lifts his fists. "Put 'em up. Channel that rage you felt when you busted into the room and saw them torturing me. Very touched by that, by the way." He smirks at me.

I flip him off—with both hands. "What's the plan?" My hands clench into tight fists at the sight of at least five Experiment members turning the corner a couple hundred meters in front of us. One of them shouts when they spot us, as if they think that'll make us comply with their order to stay put.

"Get through these bastards, find the self-destruct remote, and bring this place down—preferably with us outside of it."

I almost laugh, but the dark look on his face tells me he's serious. *There's actually a self-destruct mechanism somewhere in here?* "What?" I shriek, my heart slamming against my rib cage. "What the hell are you talking about?"

"I heard one of them mention it when they thought they'd knocked me out."

"Mention what?" I say in a high-pitched voice, fighting the urge to turn and run away from the mob of white coats heading toward us.

"They have a plan in place in case their mission is compromised." He's talking so fast I can barely keep up. "They can't have the public finding out about their organization, so they have a contingency plan." He shoots me a dark grin, lowering his voice as they get close. "Bombs in the building's basement. Enough to bring the entire place to the ground."

I don't have a chance to respond. I've never been in an actual fight, but I don't hesitate, kicking out hard and catching the first woman in the gut. She doubles over, groaning.

Max makes quick work of snapping a few necks, leaving me shaking as I go head-to-head with another woman. The sound of their bones breaking so quick and easy at Max's hands echoes through the hall and around my head.

"Stop fighting us," she says to me. "You're safe now. You're not like them." She flicks a glance at Max. That's when I strike. My fist flies toward her face, and when it connects with her nose, I hear a satisfying *crunch* as her nose breaks. Blood gushes from her nostrils and she cries out, stumbling back into the last guy.

Max and I exchange a look. I nod at him, and he advances. I close my eyes, unable to watch as he snaps their necks.

"Aurora."

My eyes fly open at the sound of my actual name on Max's lips. He's standing in front of me. I blink a few times, then glance down to see his hand held out to me.

I nod once, grabbing it. "Let's bring this place down."

---

We've been running through the building for what seems like forever. Any time we run into more Experiment members, we fight through them, leaving more bodies piled on the floor in our wake. They must know we're making our way through the levels, but hopefully they don't know *what* we're doing.

Max is about to finish another member, but I grab his arm. "Wait." I pull the badge off the guy's jacket. "He has a higher security clearance than the rest of them. He might know where it is."

Max's lips twist into a smile that would turn anyone's stomach. "Wonderful." He flicks his tongue over his bottom lip and jerks the guy's face toward him, snaring his gaze. "Where's the self-destruct remote detonator?" It's a toss-up whether fae influence will work, considering feeding does but shifting doesn't.

But then the man's eyes pop wide, and he stutters, "It's... in the... control room one... level below."

"How does it work?"

"Once the button is pressed, the building locks down. The doors seal, keeping everything already inside here. Then the explosives detonate, ensuring the building and everything inside are destroyed."

My entire body feels cold and my voice trembles when I say, "Ask him if the room is protected."

Max repeats my words, using his manipulative influence over the man.

He nods. "Of course."

"How?" Max snaps.

"By guards."

Max looks as if he's struggling to keep himself from killing this guy before we get the information we need.

"How many?"

"Th-three, sometimes four. The detonator remote is locked in a cabinet. It's heavily guarded. You can't get in."

Max's responding smile is slow, wicked. It shoots goosebumps across my arms. "Thanks for your help," he says. "We'll take it from here."

I don't have time to turn my eyes away before Max snaps his neck and lets his body drop to the floor.

He wipes the sweat from his brow and settles his gaze on me. "You still breathing over there, blondie?" he checks.

"Barely."

He nods toward the stairwell. "Let's go. We're almost there."

We hurry down the stairs, trying to keep quiet in doing so. Max stops at the door, looking over at me and pressing his finger to his lips. I nod, and he opens the door a crack. He turns toward me and holds up two fingers. Two guards are standing outside the door. I'd bet at least two more are inside the room.

"What's the plan?" I whisper.

He shrugs. "Kick some ass?"

I glare at him. "Considering I can't shift at all and you can't in here, we'll have to fight through them." I sigh, leaning my head against the wall. Being human has its pitfalls. I'm about ready to collapse. All the fighting and running is knocking the energy out of me.

"You can stay here," he offers. "I'll go in, get the device, and then you and I can finally leave this place behind. What a great story we'll have to tell when we get home."

*Home.* My chest tightens. Our friends are probably looking for us.

"I can't let you go alone."

"I'll be two minutes, tops."

I bite my lip. I don't have enough fight left in me to be anything more than dead weight. "You're sure?"

He just grins at me.

I exhale hard. "Fine. But hurry."

"So bossy," he mutters, shaking his head before he throws the door open and charges toward the guards. They pull out cattle prods, zapping them to life, but Max is faster, smacking their heads together before they can touch him.

"Easy peasy," Max calls out, probably for my benefit—or his amusement.

I open the door wider and step into the hallway as Max swipes a card off the one guard's belt and taps it against the panel on the door. A light above it flashes green and the lock flips open. Max rubs his hands together, smiling like a kid in a toy store, and kicks the door open.

Another alarm goes off, and the room Max broke into is loud with what sounds like heavy objects being tossed around. I can only imagine those heavy objects are people, and Max is taking care of business in the most violent way possible.

I gasp when he steps back into the hallway two minutes later. "That was fast."

"Time to go, blondie," he says in a harsh tone, pocketing the remote detonator. "Now."

I couldn't agree more.

We return to the stairwell and continue downward. The alarms blaring everywhere have become background sound as we stomp down the stairs as fast as possible. Max is slowing down, but I don't have energy to offer him. Once we're out of here, he can go to a feeder unit and recharge.

Pushing through a set of double doors on the ground floor, we stop dead in our tracks. There, at the end of the long hallway, is a door to the outside.

Max turns to me. "Race you," he offers with a faint smirk.

"Funny," I mutter as we both start running. "Get ready to press that button," I force out in between puffs of air.

"Trust me, I've been ready since the moment I woke up here."

On that, we're the same.

A door opens halfway down the hall and three men step out, blocking our path to freedom. I slide to a stop, and Max pulls me back a few strides.

"Son of a bitch," he growls under his breath as the door we came through opens and several more guards fill the hallway.

We're surrounded.

## CHAPTER
# FORTY-SIX

The guards get closer, though they aren't moving fast. Then again, we have nowhere to go. They've got us sandwiched between them. "What now?"

"We need to get through those three before the assholes behind us catch up."

"Right, and how do you suggest we do that? Do you have the strength to take them all out?"

His eyes narrow. "I'm tempted to leave you behind for that comment alone."

I scowl. "Not the time, Max."

"Fine. Whatever. Yes, I can get through them, but you need to be right behind me so we can get out that door and hit the button to lock this place down before it crumbles."

"I can do that. Let's move."

"On three. One—"

"Now!" I push him forward and follow behind as he charges toward the guards. They pull out guns the moment we move, and I scream, fear latching deep claws in me.

"Keep moving!" Max yells.

"They have guns!"

"Which they probably won't shoot at you. You're their success story—they want you!"

Max is wrong.

We're about ten meters away when the first shot rings out. I scream again, squeezing my eyes shut at the loud sound. Pain explodes in my arm, and my hand flies up to grab it. My eyes widen at the sight of red seeping through my fingers and dripping onto the white floor. It's just a graze, but it's bleeding heavily and hurts like hell.

Max growls deep in his throat and lunges for the first guy—the one who just shot me—and tackles him into the ground, taking the second guy out.

The one remaining advances and swings his fist toward my face. I duck, but I'm not fast enough to avoid the foot he sends toward my stomach. I reel back, clutching my gut as blood continues flowing from my arm.

He grabs my injured arm and tugs hard, making me cry out as black spots dance across my eyes, then throws me into the wall. I sink to the floor, my vision blurring.

"Get up!" Max shouts, coming up behind the guy. He makes quick work of breaking his windpipe, stealing the gun out of the holster at his hip before launching him at the mob of guards coming from the other direction.

The maneuver gives him enough time to pull me up and for us to make it to the door. Max hands me the gun, which I pretend to know how to hold, and throws the side of his body into the metal industrial door. It doesn't budge.

"Don't move!" comes a loud, commanding voice.

"Shit, shit, shit," I chant as I lift the gun and struggle with it.

"Safety's off," Max hollers. "Just squeeze the fucking trigger!"

I suck in a breath, steady my wrist with my other hand, and curl my finger around the trigger. With an exhale, I start firing.

Max kicks the door over and over, but I'm out of bullets too fast, and there are still guards standing. The moment they know I'm out of ammunition, they charge.

"Don't shoot," a deep male voice shouts. "We need her alive!"

*That didn't seem to matter a minute ago.*

With one last shove, the door flies open. Sunlight bleeds into the room, and before I can turn to look, Max grabs me and throws me outside onto the pavement.

I bite back a scream, landing on my bad arm, and snap my head toward the doorway where Max still stands inside.

"Max, what are you—"

"We're even now, blondie. You saved me, now I've saved you." He slides the detonator out of his pocket.

I scream when another gunshot fills the air. My eyes go wide, flying to Max's face. His mouth is open as if he's about to scream, but no sound comes out. Two more gunshots sound, and Max stumbles forward, out of the building and to the ground.

"*No!*"

I rush to his side, grabbing the detonator from his hand. Before the guards can lift their guns, my thumb comes down on the button.

The blare of the lockdown signal drowns out their screams, and a solid metal barrier comes down, sealing the doorway closed as the ground rumbles.

"Open your damn eyes, Max! We need to move!"

His eyelids flutter until they finally open, and his distant gaze makes my blood run cold.

"Why aren't you healing?"

He groans. "Iron bullets."

"Fucking hell," I breathe. Struggling to get my arm under his shoulders, it takes several attempts to get him to his feet and start shuffling away from the building.

*BOOM.*

*BOOM.*

*BOOM.*

There go the bombs in the basement.

I force my legs to move faster, dragging us farther away.

We're still in danger of falling debris, and the building is coming down fast, getting louder the closer it gets to the ground floor.

My head shoots up at the sound of tires spinning fast on gravel, and I find a black Escalade tearing toward us. It screeches to a halt, and my breath hitches when Dr. Collins jumps out of the driver's seat.

"What did you do?" she screams, her eyes wild with devastation.

"Don't you dare," I seethe, pointing the gun at her face. It's empty now, but she doesn't know that. "Help me get him in the car, or I *will* shoot you."

She trembles, and it gives me a sick sense of satisfaction.

After we struggle to get Max into the passenger seat, Dr. Collins stumbles back, and I clock her on the back of the head with the butt of the gun. She falls against the side of the vehicle, and I hold her up while getting the trunk open. I take a deep breath and use the strength I have left to haul her inside, slamming it shut before getting behind the wheel.

Max is slumped against the door, his cheek pressed against the window.

"Hey." I shake him. "Stay awake." Shoving the key into the ignition, I turn the car on and turn around, going back the way Dr. Collins came in.

I realize that I have no idea where we are, but I figure so long as we're driving away from the building that's collapsing in the rearview, we're going in the right direction. I scan the dash, and my heart races when I see a small map icon on the display screen. Entering the address of the Westbrook Hotel, my stomach drops when I see we're almost an hour away.

"Aurora..." Max's voice is so low, so broken, it brings tears to my eyes.

"Good," I say, hitting the gas harder, "just keep talking to me."

"I need you... to make sure they know. They're my... family and... they need to know." He takes some time to get the words out, and he coughs up blood halfway through.

*Son of a bitch.*

Max might not have an hour. I need to drive faster.

I speed up again, following the GPS directions.

"Aurora," Max says through his teeth, his breathing getting shallower with each exhale.

"No," I say in a firm voice. "Whatever it is, you'll tell them yourself. We're almost there."

"Please."

That one word cleaves through my heart.

"Okay," I say hoarsely.

"They need to know... I'm not in pain. I'm not... scared, just sad I won't... be around to help... destroy these motherfuckers." He chokes on a laugh. "Skylar... is going to be angry. Let her be, but... don't allow her... to turn it inward.

She is the fiercest, most... powerful woman I've ever met, and I've... been so goddamn... lucky to have her looking... out for me all these years."

I blink back tears, sniffling as I keep my eyes on the road.

"I'm not sure... what you're going to tell Oliver... but I know you'll... make sure he's okay. He's a special one... and he deserves... the fucking world. I'm just sorry... I couldn't give it... to him."

His breathing becomes shallower, and mine gets stuck in my throat. "Max," I whisper.

"Tristan is... going to blame himself. Whatever it takes, you... need to convince him... this isn't... his fault. There... was nothing... he could... have done. Tell him... he's my brother... that I will always... admire him. I will always... love him."

I'm shaking my head and pressing the gas even harder. "Tell him yourself, Max," I say sternly.

I'm met by silence.

"Tell him yourself," I repeat louder, and my voice shakes.

More silence.

My pulse spikes, my chest rising and falling fast. I'm too scared to look at him. "Max." The crack in my voice makes my eyes fill with tears. "Say something. Please."

Nothing.

Finally, I look.

His eyes are closed, his chest is still.

Max is gone.

I press my fist against my mouth, fighting the sob that's trying to break free from my throat. Holding it in until I can't any longer, I pull the car over onto the shoulder of the country road and scream, choking on the sob. My arm hurts worse when I slam my fists into the steering wheel.

Anger radiates through me, thinking of the woman in the trunk. She might not have founded the Experiment, but she's a big part of it. She deserves to suffer for the pain she's caused; the lives lost because of her precious organization.

I shift the car into drive and pull back onto the road.

I'll let Tristan decide how to handle her.

By the time I pull into the back parking lot of the hotel, only hints of daylight still streak the sky. I park as close to the building as possible, making sure that anyone passing the mouth of the alley won't see Max in the front seat. I rummage around the back seat and find what looks like one of those useful little sleepy shots the bastards stuck me with when they took me from the hotel.

Walking to the back of the car, I open the trunk. Before Dr. Collins can scream, I stab the needle into the side of her neck. She yelps in shock, but sleep drags her under before she can put up a fight. I slam the trunk shut, toss the empty syringe on the floor of the car, and shut the door.

I do my best to run my fingers through my hair, smoothing it down, and pray I don't look half as wrecked as I feel as I round the building and walk inside through the guest entrance.

Thankfully, the lobby is quiet, not many people milling about. I catch a few worried glances as I hurry to the concierge desk, relief shimmering through me when I recognize one of the fae on Tristan's staff, who was relatively nice to me.

"Holy shit," she breathes as I approach.

I skip all formalities. "I need a badge to get to the penthouse."

She hands one over without hesitation, and I'm not sure if it's the darkness in my eyes or my disheveled appearance—or both—that stops her from asking questions, but I don't stick around long enough to consider it.

Inside the elevator, I press the button to the penthouse, smearing blood on it. It could be mine, or it could be Max's. My stomach churns as I turn away from the panel on the wall, only to catch my ghastly reflection in the mirror. I'm covered in dirt and blood—mostly mine—my hair is a gross mess of tangles, some of which are caked with blood. One side of my face is covered in bruises, probably from hitting the wall. Dried blood runs from a cut on my brow and from my nose.

Hell, I look—and certainly feel—as if I was just hit with a transport truck.

The *ding* of the elevator makes me jump. I step into the foyer and walk to Tristan's door. I swallow hard, cringing at the copper taste lingering in my mouth.

I reach for the door handle and turn the knob to find it's unlocked. Opening the door, I step inside and close it behind me.

Voices drift toward me from the living room, so I follow them.

"I have several teams scouring every inch of this city." Tristan's deep, commanding voice is a punch to the gut.

"Skylar and I are heading out as soon as team four gets back." That's Allison.

"I want to go with you." My eyes widen at the sound of Oliver's voice. What the hell is he doing here? *He knows about the fae?*

"No," Allison and Skylar say in unison.

"Come on, I can handle it. Those assholes took one of my best friends and my boyfriend."

"We'll get them back, Oliver." Nikolai's voice interjects. "We need—"

His voice cuts off the moment I step into the room. My friends stare at me as if I'm an apparition.

I lick the dryness from my lips and open my mouth to speak, but nothing comes out.

"Oh my god," Allison breathes.

My eyes travel around the room until they land on Tristan and stay there. His eyes are wide, desperate, and filled with terror. Tears blur my vision as my knees shake.

Tristan shifts in front of me just as they give out, and he catches me before I hit the floor. I cling to him, terrified to let go, as my shoulders shake with sobs.

"I didn't say it." Hot tears stream down my face, blurring my vision. "I wanted to, but I was so scared, and—I should've said it."

He guides my face away from his chest so he can look at me. "Aurora—"

"I love you, Tristan," I cry. "I fucking love you."

He smiles as if he's feeling the warmth of the sun on his face for the first time in days. "You didn't need to say it, Rory. I knew."

As happy as I am to hear that, it doesn't stop the tears. Now that I'm away from that place and my adrenaline is wearing down, everything is catching up to me.

"Aurora," Tristan murmurs. "Aurora, you're safe."

"She's human," Nikolai says, confusion clear in his voice.

"Shut up," Skylar snaps at him.

Tristan brushes his thumb along my cheek, warming the skin as he heals the cuts and bruises on my face.

"Stop," I choke out. He shouldn't be making me feel better, not while Max is...

He pulls his hand back, his eyes filled with concern. "Did I hurt you?"

"Max—" My voice cracks.

"Where is he?" Oliver asks, panicked.

I swallow hard, wanting to close my eyes and bury my face in Tristan's chest again.

"Aurora, where the hell is he?" Skylar demands, stepping forward.

Nikolai angles his body toward her, watching her out of the corner of his eye.

Tristan snags my chin gently. "What happened?"

I shake my head, tears rolling down my cheeks. "He didn't... He's gone. I'm sorry," I cry. "I'm so sorry."

Skylar stalks toward Tristan and me. She makes it a few feet before Nikolai's arm wraps around her waist and pulls her away, forcing her in the opposite direction.

"Let go of me!" she screams, pounding on his back with her fists.

He says nothing, no poorly timed witty remark or sleazy innuendo he's famous for. He just carries her away while she beats the crap out of him. A door slams in the distance, and Skylar continues to scream.

Allison guides a crying and confused Oliver out of the room as well, leaving Tristan and me alone.

"Tristan," I say, my heart breaking at the hopeless, faraway look in his eyes.

He blinks, and his gaze focuses on me. "Let me heal you."

I shake my head. "It can wait. He's... I brought him here."

Tristan's throat bobs when he swallows. He bows his head, and I don't hesitate in pulling him toward me, holding him.

Tears slip down my cheeks as Tristan's chest rises and falls awkwardly against me. "Shh," I whisper, rubbing his back to soothe him.

We stay like that for a few minutes until his breathing evens out.

"There's something else," I say.

He lifts his head until his eyes are level with mine.

"The woman who made me human again. She's also here. Alive but unconscious."

Tristan exhales heavily and nods. He traces his fingers along my arm and shoulder, healing the wounds there. I stop him before he does any more. The aches and pains I can handle.

We walk to the elevator as Tristan gets on his phone and calls security to meet us in the parking lot.

They deal with getting Dr. Collins into the building. Tristan informs them to lock her up, that she'll be dealt with later. Once they're gone, Tristan opens the passenger door, and his breathing hitches.

I watch with tears in my eyes as Tristan pushes the hair away from Max's face, and then presses his palm against his unmoving chest, over his heart.

I stand close, but give him enough space to breathe. "This isn't your fault. There was nothing you could have done."

Tristan drags in a shallow breath. "They'll pay for this." His voice is a cold, low rumble of sound.

I touch his back gently. "He wanted you to know that you'll be his brother forever. He will always admire you, always love you."

Tristan's shoulders shake, and he keeps his back to me for several moments before he slides his arms under Max's legs and arms to get him out of the front seat. He carries the body of his best friend into the building through the service entrance, and it takes everything in me not to sink to my knees and break.

---

With all the connections Tristan has in both the fae and human worlds, it isn't difficult for him to get someone to the hotel to clean Max up. After she leaves, Tristan lets the others know they can see him. They join Tristan in the guest suite on the first floor where we brought Max. I have to stand in the hall, unable to look at him again, unable to watch our friends say goodbye.

Once Tristan and I are upstairs in his bedroom, he sinks onto the end of the bed. "I don't know what to do," he admits.

"That's okay." I push my fingers gently through his hair, brushing the fallen strands away from his face. "You don't have to have all the answers."

His eyes flick to mine. "My people need me to have answers." He sighs. "They have no idea the extent of what went on in that facility."

I nod. "Neither do you... and maybe you shouldn't have to."

A dark look passes over his face, and he leans forward, resting his forehead against my collarbone. "Tell me," he says softly, "because I don't have the luxury of not knowing."

I hold him against me, rubbing my hand up and down his back for a minute. "Marisa lured me outside to the back staff entrance under the guise she was upset over something. She's always been incredibly nice to me, so I didn't hesitate to go. I wanted to make sure she was okay. Before I knew what was happening, someone jabbed me with a syringe, knocked me out, and took me to the facility where they..." My voice trails off, a shiver running through me. Flashes of all-white rooms, cold floors, and the burning scent of chemicals fill my head, and I recoil from it. *You're not there,* I chant to myself.

Tristan pulls back and stands, cupping my cheeks. "Rory, you don't have to. If it's too hard for you—"

"I'm okay," I force out, staring into his eyes and letting the deep blue waves ground me as I grip the front of his shirt. "At the facility, they kept me restrained in a bed unless I needed the bathroom. I wasn't allowed to feed and only given human food. They used an iron infused elixir to keep me weak, especially after I attacked and fed on Marisa. There wasn't a chance in hell I'd have the strength to fight them all after a week without feeding."

A muscle feathers along his jaw, his gaze darkening, though his fingers remain gentle, splayed across my cheeks. "What do you remember about the facility?"

I drag in an unsteady breath, then exhale slowly and try to focus on the feel of his thumbs stroking my skin. "It was like a medical center. Everything was white or metal, clean to the point of smelling so strongly of antiseptic it would make you sick. The room I was locked in had a bed and a chair. Besides the room where they did the procedure and where I found Max, everything else was kept behind locked doors and, of course, destroyed when we detonated the self-destruct function before we left."

Tristan nods tightly, tipping my head back to level our gazes. "You are the bravest person I know, Rory. I need you to know that. Whatever happens next, we'll figure it out. We will always figure it out."

"We'll—" My voice cracks as my hands shake against

his chest. "We'll figure it out." A sob catches in my throat and my vision blurs with hot tears.

Tristan's brows pull together, his lips falling into a frown. He slides his fingers into my hair and lowers his lips to my forehead. That simple touch breaks me. My legs give out, and Tristan catches me around my waist, cradling me against him. My heart beats like the wings of a hummingbird just trying to stay alive and my pulse jackhammers as I lose control of my thoughts, spiraling back to that nightmare I barely survived.

A strangled sound akin to a whimper-like gasp escapes my lips before I press my mouth to Tristan's. Closing my eyes, I channel every emotion flooding through me into the kiss, desperate to lose myself in him. Only if for a moment. A tiny reprieve from reliving the hell I've been through.

"Aurora," he murmurs thickly, pulling back before I can deepen the kiss.

"Please," I cry, grasping at him, "make me forget."

"I don't..." He trails off, his eyes searching mine. "Are you sure this is what you want?"

I drag his lips back to mine in response, and his grip tightens as he returns the kiss with equal intensity. He just lost his best friend; he needs this as much as I do. Our mouths move together, perfectly in-sync, and we only break apart to catch our breaths.

Taking a small step back, he reaches for the hem of the scrub shirt and lifts it over my head, revealing my bare chest. His gaze deepens as his eyes roam my body, and a shiver races up my spine. "You are the most beautiful thing I've ever seen in my decades on this earth."

Heat rushes to my cheeks, and I fight the urge to look away from the weight of his gaze. "You're not bad either, I guess," I quip, reaching for his shirt, adding it to the growing pile on the floor.

Tristan guides me back until I reach the bed, dropping onto the end of it and scooting toward the headboard. He crawls over me, kissing me slow and deep until my head spins, then pulls back and curls his fingers around the elastic waistband of the scrub pants, tugging them down to my ankles. I kick them the rest of the way off as Tristan stands and steps out of his pants, leaving us both completely naked. My gaze drops to his cock, and I lick my lips at the hardened length, its tip glistening with arousal.

He moves over me again, stealing my lips in a scorching kiss as I run my fingers up his chest, then into his hair, gripping the ends and tipping his head back to deepen the kiss. He holds himself up with a knee between my legs and his arms braced on either side of my head. His hair falls into his face as he devours my lips with his, and I push it back, moaning softly into his mouth when his erection brushes my stomach.

Breaking the kiss, Tristan drops his mouth to my chest, his tongue swirling around one breast while his fingers massage the other, wringing soft moans from me with ease. And then his mouth is traveling lower, making my skin tingle with warmth as the muscles in my stomach tighten. Gripping my thighs, he slowly spreads them open, baring my center to his hungry gaze. The first pass of his tongue over my clit has my hips arching off the bed, stealing the air from my lungs in a choked gasp. He flattens his tongue, licking along my folds before pulling my clit into his mouth, sucking gently as I writhe beneath him.

"Yes, yes, yes," I breathe, gripping the sheets on either side of me, squeezing my eyes shut as pleasure whips through me. I willingly give myself over to it, welcoming it to consume me.

Tristan moans against me, shooting vibrations straight to my core, before he pushes his tongue into me, using his fingers to hold me open. Heat floods my body, flushing my skin and making my heart rattle the cages of my ribs.

"Don't stop," I gasp.

He doubles his efforts, plunging his tongue in and out of me, while his thumb strums my clit. My thighs tighten as he picks up speed, hitting a sensitive spot deep inside me, and I clench around him, crying out my release with his name on my lips.

When he climbs back over me, sealing his mouth over mine, I taste myself on his lips. I reach between us, wrapping my fist around his cock, and he growls low in his throat, thrusting his hips forward. "I want to bury myself inside you," he says against my lips, nipping the bottom one with his teeth.

My heart trips over itself and the muscles in my stomach tense in anticipation as I guide him between my legs. The blunt head of his cock teases my entrance, rubbing back and forth as my breathing hitches.

He pushes into me slowly, inch by inch, as his lips leave mine to trail along my jaw and kiss the racing pulse at my throat. "You feel incredible," he says into my neck.

I wrap my legs around him, trying to push him deeper, and he chuckles softly, rolling his hips and thrusting deeper before pulling out almost completely. I groan before he slides in all the way, filling me to the hilt. My lips part in a silent gasp, and he gives me a few moments to adjust to the invasion before he moves. Thrusting in slow and deep, he kisses each of my cheeks, then the tip of my nose, before his lips brush mine.

Sighing contentedly, I say, "Fuck, that feels so good."

His lips curl into a soft grin, and he kisses the corner of my mouth.

I pull back enough to gaze into his eyes. "I love you, Tristan Westbrook."

He thrusts into me once more, hitting a spot that sends pleasure through me like a tidal wave. "Say it again," he murmurs, holding still inside me.

I kiss him chastely. "I." Another kiss. "Love." Kiss. "You."

His mouth descends on mine, and he swallows my surprised moan, his tongue pushing past my lips and grazing mine as his cock pulses inside me. Our bodies move together, tension crackling between us, and I careen toward the precipice of pleasure.

"Come with me," he grunts, his thrusts quickening.

"Yes," I pant, clinging to him.

"That's it," he encourages, reaching between our heated bodies to tease my clit. The overwhelming sensations launch me over the edge, and I lose myself in him as he finds his release deep inside me.

The room is filled with the combined sounds of our pleasure, and I would do anything to stay in this moment of pure bliss forever.

*Forever.*

Except, I don't have forever. Not anymore.

Tristan snags my chin, guiding my gaze to his. "Where did you go?"

I sink my teeth into my bottom lip. "I'm just having a moment," I admit. "It keeps hitting me. I'm human again. I'll grow up, aging every moment, and you... won't."

He frowns, freeing my lip with his thumb. "I wasn't sure you'd be ready to talk about that, but we can."

I lower my gaze. "What is there to talk about?"

"You should have had the choice to become fae. I want to give that to you. I'm not sure it's possible to make you fae again after you underwent the procedure to revert to your human form, but it's worth looking into—if that's what you want."

My heart beats faster at the idea of being fae again, and I'm not entirely sure how I feel about it.

"It's not something you need to decide right now," he murmurs, leaning in to press his lips to my temple.

I nod slowly. "I'll... think about it." Needing the conversation to veer away from me, I say, "I'm not sure what family Max had, but if you have phone numbers, we should get in contact with whoever we need to."

He frowns, tucking my hair behind my ear as his eyes dance over my face. Finally, he says, "He has a sister. Skylar should have her information."

"Okay." I snuggle closer as my eyelids become heavier and swallow a yawn. Now that I don't have adrenaline or endorphins racing through me, and the room is quiet, exhaustion clings to every part of me.

"Sleep now," Tristan murmurs. "We'll talk more tomorrow."

Pressing my cheek to his warm, firm chest, my eyes close, and I give myself over to the comfort of darkness, feeling safe for the first time in too long.

## CHAPTER
# FORTY-SEVEN

Despite the delicious prelude, Tristan and I both slept terribly last night.

We can't know that the Experiment was destroyed when that building was. There's a good chance our fight with them is only just beginning.

After getting dressed, I head toward the guest room where Skylar is staying. I pause when Nikolai slips out of the room, closing the door behind him. "Hey," I say, nodding toward the room. "How's she doing?"

He shakes his head. "I'm worried about her." I can see it in the lines on his face; he wants to help her, but he doesn't know how. I'm glad she has someone—even if it's the fae she often finds infuriating. Knowing firsthand how beneficial Nikolai's support can be, it makes me feel better about giving the weight of my support to Tristan.

"How are you doing?" I ask to keep the conversation off of me. Recounting what happened to me in the facility last night with Tristan was hard enough. I don't think I have the strength to talk about it again so soon.

He waves me off. "I'm fine." Dragging his hand through his hair, he flicks his eyes across my face. "What about you and Tristan?"

"He's hurting deeply. I'm doing my best to be there for him, but Max was like a brother to him."

He steps closer, lowering his voice. "I'm worried about *you*, Aurora. You've been through a lot in the last couple of weeks. You—"

"I'm alive, Nik," I cut him off.

"You've gone from being a human to being a fae to being human again. None of which was by any choice of your own."

"Thanks for the reminder." I haven't stopped thinking about it since the moment I realized I was no longer fae— that I'll die one day and Tristan won't. That alone scares the ever-living crap out of me. Even in death, the idea of not being with Tristan makes me want to sob.

I didn't even get the chance to enjoy being fae. I struggled through the beginning, *a lot*, and once I was getting the hang of it, it was taken away from me against my will.

"Talk to me," Nikolai murmurs.

"I'm scared," I admit. "I've never been through something so awful. And I know Tristan and Skylar are in pain as well, but losing someone you love is a different kind of torture than losing yourself."

"Are you sad to be human again?"

"Yes and no. I'm sad I never really got to kick ass as a fae, but I'm also relieved. The whole feeding on human energy thing... I'm not sure I'd ever be completely okay with it." And there it is. The answer I've been searching for inside myself since the conversation I had with Tristan last night. I didn't want to be fae when I changed after killing Jules, and I still don't.

"It's not for everyone," he agrees with a small smile.

"Yeah, we're not all as awesome as you," I remark in a dry tone.

He smirks. "Ain't that the truth."

I roll my eyes, but Nikolai's light, joking attitude makes me feel better.

His expression smoothes and becomes more serious. "Fae or not, I'm still here for you, gorgeous."

An unexpected smile touches my lips, and I step forward to hug him. "Thank you," I say against his shoulder before I pull away. "I'd like it if nothing changed between us. I'd miss your annoying antics too much."

"Yeah?" he checks.

"Yeah, I guess I still need you." I glance back at the door behind him. "You should get back in there."

"Okay," he says, "but you know where I am if you need anything."

"Thanks." I start to turn away before I remember what I told Tristan last night. "Nik?"

He turns back. "Yeah?"

"Can you get Max's sister's phone number and text it to me? Tristan said Skylar has it."

"You got it."

I head back to Tristan's bedroom, only to find it empty. "Seriously?" I groan as I back out of the room.

When my phone goes off, I pull it out and see Mom's name on the screen. I sigh and bite the inside of my cheek. I've barely spoken to my family in weeks. If they knew half of the shit I've been dealing with—they can never know.

Sending the call to voicemail, I type her a quick message so she doesn't worry.

> Sorry we haven't talked in a while. Things have been crazy around here. Can I call you tomorrow? Love you guys.

I make my way to Tristan's office, where I find him sitting behind the desk with a glass of amber liquid in his hand.

Setting the glass down when I walk in, he looks over at me.

"It's not even eleven in the morning, Tris," I say softly as I approach the desk. "Did you want me to make you something to eat?"

He drags his gaze up my body. "No."

I frown as I take in his appearance. He looks even worse than he did last night. His face is pasty, his eyes are bloodshot and underlined by dark circles. Not to mention the current disarray of his hair.

"Aurora." His voice makes me meet his gaze quickly, and he almost smiles. "What do you need?"

I shake my head. "I came to check on you." Walking around the desk, I take the drink and set it on the other side of me. "I'm glad I did. You don't look so good."

He reaches over and caresses my cheek. "Don't worry about me, Rory. If anything, I should worry about you." He is. I can tell by the way he hasn't taken his eyes off me since we got back to the hotel. I'm scared and hurt and angry, but I didn't just lose my best friend. He did, and taking care of him allows me to keep my mind off the fact I was just put through hell.

"I *am* worried about you. What happened to Max—Death takes a toll on a person, no matter who they are."

He drops his hand, glancing away. "I need to prepare a statement."

"It can wait. You're not well enough."

"It can't wait, Aurora. My people deserve to know the danger they face."

"Of course they do." I bite the inside of my cheek until I taste blood and cringe. "But if anyone should make a statement, it's the queen and the king."

"I'll handle it," he says firmly. "I don't want you anywhere near the royals, especially given you're human again."

"I want to help," I point out, an edge to my voice. "Tell me what I can do to help you."

He presses his fingers against his temples. "You can call the local feeding unit and have Destiny send a human over."

My brows tug closer as a flare of... what—*possessiveness?*—races through me. "You just said it—I'm human again."

He stiffens, and when I shift closer, he shakes his head. "Stop."

"Would you relax? You've saved my ass enough times."

"Aurora," he murmurs.

"Tristan, please," I say, trying to smooth his hair down. "Let me do this for you."

He lets out a slow breath, holding my gaze. "You're sure?"

"Of course."

Tristan stands, and we walk over to the couch, sitting side by side.

I reach over and take his hand. "I love you," I say in a hushed tone.

He leans down and kisses my cheek. "I love you." He closes his eyes and slides his fingers through mine. His thumb brushes soft circles across my skin as he siphons my energy into himself. It trickles out of me slowly, and I lean into him, closing my eyes as a pleasant warmth fills my veins, making me sigh.

I understand the humans in the feeder unit more now. This is... intense—in the best way. Being able to give Tristan strength, to take care of him like this, leaves me with a heady feeling and a primal need growing between my legs that has me pressing my thighs together.

Tristan pulls his hand back just as I'm feeling a little fuzzy. "Are you all right?"

I open my eyes to find him looking at me with concern, and I smile. "I'm perfectly fine." When I go to stand and the room tilts, I lean back against the couch cushion. "I think I'm going to sit here for a few more minutes."

Guilt darkens his features. "I took too much."

I shake my head. "I'm okay. Just give me a couple of minutes, and I'll be good to go." He already looks better. Brighter eyes. Straighter posture. A weird fluttering grows in my stomach; *I did that for him.*

He frowns, then sighs. "Thank you." Kissing my forehead, he says, "I should get back to work."

I grab the back of his shirt when he tries to get off the couch. "You should take it easy." I want to pull him back onto the couch and straddle him, distract him with my mouth until the tension in his muscles eases and the worry lines in his face fade.

A pang of sadness blossoms in my chest at that moment when I find myself wishing I could feel his emotions. There's a lot about being fae I won't miss, but that is one thing I definitely will.

He turns and glances down at where I have a fistful of his shirt. "You know I can't do that."

"You can take today. One day to take care of yourself.

To let *me* take care of you." I loosen my grip on his shirt. "Please."

He presses his lips together, hesitating, but finally says, "Fine."

"Good," I say, then recall the brief conversation I had with Nikolai before coming to find Tristan. "I asked Nikolai to get me Max's sister's number. I'll call her and explain what happened."

"Monica. His sister's name is Monica."

"Okay."

"Have you seen Skylar?" he asks.

"No. Nikolai is with her, though."

"You're sure about him?" he grumbles.

I hold back a smile. "Yes, and you obviously trust him to some degree." When he arches a brow, I add, "You wouldn't have left her with him last night if you thought for a second he wouldn't take care of her." His eyes narrow a fraction, and I continue, "Don't look at me like that, Westbrook. I know you, and you know I'm right."

He exhales, and it almost sounds like a ghost of a laugh. "Yeah, all right, smart mouth."

My phone dings in my pocket before I can respond. I pull it out and read the message. "Nikolai just sent Monica's number."

"I should call her," Tristan says. "She doesn't know you. It should come from me."

"You don't have to, Tris. I can do this."

He nods, holding out his hand for my phone. "I know."

I hesitate before handing it to him.

When he lifts the phone to his ear, I reach over and slip my fingers through his free hand, giving it a gentle squeeze just to remind him I'm here. I rest my shoulder against his and listen while he speaks softly to Monica, explaining what happened, his voice low and thick with grief. My eyes sting with tears, and I have to look away. He tells her to call him if she needs anything. That's after he offers to fly her here and give her a suite to stay in for however long she wants.

Once he's off the phone, I kiss his shoulder. "Is she coming?"

He clears his throat. "No. I made her promise to check in, but she doesn't want to come here. She thinks it would be too hard."

"You've done all you can do," I tell him; he has to know. He doesn't deserve the guilt eating at him; I want to take it away.

What's done is done, and now we have to find a way to live with it.

---

Three days later, we gather in a cemetery on the outskirts of town to pay our respects to Max. Tristan purchased a large plot near the back of the cemetery in a more secluded, private section that overlooks a river. It's surrounded by trees and flowers and silence—it's beautiful.

Allison stands beside Oliver, holding his hand. Tristan is next to me with his fingers entwined with mine, and Skylar stands next to Nikolai, just close enough that their shoulders are touching. I'm not sure what's going on between them, but at least she looks more put together than I've seen her lately. We're all dressed in black—the girls in knee-length dresses with stockings—under heavy coats, considering it's only the first week of March and snow still covers most of the ground—and the guys in crisp suits.

Tristan takes the lead, clearing his throat before he speaks. "I knew Max for... hell, what seems like forever. He stood by my side when my father died and again when I was knighted. He never let me down and he never questioned my intentions. Most notably, he believed in me, in my leadership, even when I didn't. Max would have you believe he didn't care about much, but that wasn't true. He cared more about the people in his life than most. He would do anything for any of us here. What he did at that facility is further proof of that. I will never forget the sacrifice he made, so I would get to see the woman I love again." He shifts his gaze toward the casket. "We won't stop until we finish what you started."

Allison steps forward next. "I didn't know Max as well as Tristan and Skylar, but I'm sad he's gone. I will do everything I can to help ensure his absence is not in vain." When she steps back and takes Oliver's hand again, I glance around the small circle, waiting for someone else to talk. No one does, so I take a deep breath and step forward.

"It's no secret Max and I weren't the best of friends. He was kind of an asshole, actually." I smile, taking the time to look at each of my friends. "Except when it mattered most. When the people he loved needed him, he was there. I will forever be grateful for his bravery. One day, when I see him again, I hope we can be friends."

Skylar's head drops slightly as she glances at the ground, hiding her face. Nikolai slips his arm around her, and she leans into him.

"Thank you, Max," I say in closing. "Rest easy." I step back, and Tristan squeezes my hand, leaning down to kiss my cheek.

"Thank you," he murmurs, so only I can hear.

I nod and smile at him.

Nikolai dips his face and whispers something to Skylar, who barely shakes her head without looking up. He frowns and looks over at Tristan and me, shaking his head.

Tristan sighs softly and closes his eyes, so the rest of us follow suit. We stand there in silence, remembering our fallen comrade and friend, and say a last goodbye.

## CHAPTER
# FORTY-EIGHT

Having a mutual enemy is what the seelie and unseelie fae courts needed to come together.

Tristan and Nikolai have been tasked with handling the logistics. The king and queen, as I've learned, are kept away from any potential danger—protected at all costs. The fae knights are ones expected to get their hands—and claws—dirty to protect their respective courts. Until now, it was from each other. Working together is something many of the fae likely couldn't fathom... until their lives were threatened by those they've been accustomed to seeing as prey for so long.

Which is why, the day after we buried Max, the ballroom of the Westbrook Hotel is currently filled with fae—from both courts. Some of them are clearly not too thrilled about it, but the near-suffocating tension is mixed with a shared emotion I don't need to be fae to sense: fear.

I walk to the front of the room where Tristan and Nikolai are waiting to address the crowd. This is the biggest group of fae I've seen. They're standing shoulder-to-shoulder with no room to move. Everyone wants to know what's going on—they're here for answers, and I don't blame them.

Nikolai whistles sharply, the shrill sound silencing the room, and Tristan steps forward to start the meeting. "Thank you for coming. I understand many of you didn't want to and are wary of standing in the same room as those you view as your enemies."

You could hear a pin drop. It's that silent. Considering the room is full of fae, *they* can hear plenty—surely the uneven ticking of my pulse as I stand off to the side with Skylar and Allison.

Nikolai scratches the back of his neck and addresses the unseelie fae. "And I understand you may be uncertain and wary of *me* representing your interests, but hey, I'm a hell of a step up from the last guy."

A few chuckles echo through the room, and I press my lips together against a smile as Skylar scowls, muttering something under her breath I don't catch.

"Let's cut to the chase," Nikolai says smoothly. "Shit is bad. I mean, I think that's a given, considering we're willing to set aside decades of distrust and utter loathing and stand together to discuss our common threat."

Tristan takes the reins of the conversation. "The Experiment is a group of humans who, through extensive research—as well as horrific trial and error—have created a way to manipulate our DNA. Their reasoning is to effectively rid the world of fae by stripping the magic from us. Many fae who have undergone the treatment during its early stages didn't survive."

"Treatment?" someone shouts. "For what?"

Tristan doesn't miss a beat. "To make fae human."

Some of the fae gasp, as others stare at Tristan with

wide eyes. Several fae turn to whoever they're with and start speaking in hushed voices, their faces pale, expressions sharp with concern. Some even glance toward the exit, as if they're considering making a break for it.

"Many of you know Aurora Marshall," Nikolai starts, and my stomach plummets as my gaze focuses back on the front of the room where Nikolai and Tristan stand. I should've guessed I'd be brought into the conversation, but evidently my nerves weren't prepared. "She was captured by the Experiment and forced to endure the treatment. As you can see, it worked."

Before I fully realize what I am doing, I step forward. "I'm the human turned fae turned human. I wish I could stand here and tell you there's nothing to worry about, that we destroyed the operation I was forced to experience, but I can't do that. Unfortunately, we have more questions than answers, and for that reason, Tristan and Nikolai—speaking on behalf of your king and queen—are going to ask you to set aside your hatred for one another and help us take these bastards down. Because the odds of that being the only location, the only group of the Experiment—it's impossible. Just like the world is filled with fae in different places, they'll have Experiment members scattered around the globe as well."

"What's going to be done?" someone shouts from the crowd.

"It's going to take time," Tristan takes over in a level voice. "I have calls out to several of my contacts in different places. Trusted members of the seelie court who take the safety of our kind seriously. I assure you of that. Until we know more, I don't suggest traveling alone. Look out for each other—everyone. At a time like this, we can't be divided," he pauses. "If we continue fighting each other, it only gives them the upper hand. We've seen this. It's the reason they inflicted so much damage unbeknownst to us. We were so quick to blame each other for the disappearing fae, we didn't consider that it could've been something else —not until it was too late. We can't allow that any longer. So, please, consider what we've said. Work with us and each other, so you can live without fear of being taken from those you love."

The room is completely silent. Fae from both courts share looks of uncertainty, anger, and fear. Some have furrowed brows and sharp jaws, their expressions filled with determination or a desire for retribution.

I inhale slowly, and before I can let it out, the room erupts in shouts of encouragement. My eyes widen as I take in the sight of a room full of fae coming together against the organization plotting against them. Goosebumps spread across my arms, and the back of my neck tingles as the hair stands straight.

My gaze lowers when Tristan slips his fingers through mine. I glance up and look into his eyes, seeing a flicker of hope there. I smile at him and nod.

*This is a start.*

---

After we spend most of the afternoon talking with the fae one-on-one in the ballroom, our group retreats to Tristan's penthouse for dinner and drinks.

Allison and I step onto the balcony attached to the guest room she's staying in, zipping up our coats. It's an unseasonably mild evening, and the air feels nice on my cheeks, already tinged with warmth from the wine we've been drinking.

Allison takes a sip of her wine and sighs. "It feels like we might've just ended the war between the courts, but only because there's a much bigger one right around the corner."

I glance down at the wine in my glass and nod. "We have little time to appreciate the fact that we're alive. We can't know when the Experiment will strike next—or even where. How are we supposed to prepare for that?"

"I think Tristan is worried about that, though he'd never let it show to the other fae."

Dread digs an even deeper hole in my chest. "I wish there was more I could do for him. I'm not even fae anymore."

"I think you do more for him than you realize, just as you are." She smiles softly. "But on that note, you haven't said much about being human again."

I shrug, lifting the glass to my lips and take a drink. "There's not much to say. We both know I wasn't all that great at being fae, and I don't *want* to become one again, but I can't help being angry. I feel... robbed. I'm not sure how else to describe it."

"Of course. You're entitled to feel anything you are. I'm just worried you're letting it hurt you."

I catch my bottom lip between my teeth, thinking about that. "You're right. I shouldn't let it consume me. I need to find a way to make peace with what happened. This is my life. I refuse to allow *them* to have any more control over it."

"Good," she says, lifting her glass to me. "Cheers to that."

I offer a smile as I clink my glass against hers and take a sip.

"Mind if I interrupt?" Tristan's voice makes my head turn, and when our eyes meet, my heart jumps.

Allison sighs dramatically. "I suppose." She wraps her arms around me and squeezes hard before heading inside, sliding the door shut.

I set my glass on the ledge, turning to face Tristan. "Hey," I murmur.

"Hey," he echoes back, the corner of his mouth curling. "How are you doing?"

"Oh, you know, living the dream."

The smile slips off his face. "Rory."

"I'm okay, Tris. It's a lot, that's all. I was just starting to adjust to being fae and then it was taken away from me. Now I need time to readjust to life as a human."

"I want to help."

I reach for him, draping my arms over his shoulders. "You're helping by being here."

He grips my waist, and my skin warms under his touch. "You are the most amazing creature I have ever met," he whispers, dipping his face to seal his lips over mine.

My eyes flutter shut as I lean into him, moving my lips with his. His fingers tighten on my hips, and blood rushes to my cheeks as I deepen the kiss, sliding my tongue into his mouth. My fingers tug at the back of his hair, and he groans, pressing his lower half into me. I gasp against his lips, and he chuckles against mine. My heart pounds against my rib cage as I fight to pull him closer, kissing him harder.

Slipping into this feeling of getting lost in each other's touch, I can't imagine living without it now that I've experienced it. I never want this feeling to end—I'll hold on to it with everything I have for as long as I have on this earth.

*He'll have longer*, a voice inside my head says, effectively ruining the moment.

I move away from Tristan, pulling my hands back and clenching them at my sides.

"What just happened?" he asks, his cheeks flushed and his hair messed up, courtesy of me.

"Nothing." I shake my head. "We should go inside. I'm not sure I trust Nikolai in your kitchen."

Tristan smirks. "As much as I agree, we aren't moving until you tell me what's going on in that beautiful head of yours."

"It's stupid," I mumble.

"Rory." He closes the distance between us again and takes my face in his hands. "Talk to me."

I press my lips together. "When we were kissing, I was thinking about how I never wanted it to end. That I wanted to feel that way forever."

Realization fills his eyes, and he nods in understanding. "We can talk about it."

I sigh. "I don't want to talk about it. Not tonight."

Tristan presses his lips to mine in a whisper of a kiss and concedes, "Not tonight."

Leaning into him, I tip my head back and kiss him fully, deeply, with absolutely every fiber of my being. He needs to know he has me—all of me.

His hands quickly move from my face to my hips, and he guides me back until I hit the frosted glass balcony wall, his body flush with mine, cranking my heart rate way up.

My gaze sweeps the surrounding space, briefly concerned we're going to be seen, until I remember the penthouse takes up the entire top floor of the hotel. We're secluded from any hotel guests, and there's a curtain-covered door between us and our friends.

That said, I'm not entirely sure I'd care at this point if anyone saw or heard us.

My nipples harden as my chest presses against his, and heat swirls low in my belly while Tristan's lips devour mine. A haze of warmth settles over me like a veil, and I gasp into his mouth when he grinds against the throbbing between my legs.

I have never been so happy to be wearing a dress. I reach for the knee-length hem, dragging it along with my jacket up my thighs, and the air feels like heaven on my heated skin. My breath catches when his fingers skim the delicate skin along my inner thigh, soft and teasing as it inches higher, closer to where I want him. I grab the solid railing behind me, my chest rising and falling faster in anticipation. His lips travel the length of my jaw, feathering light kisses, and he glides a single digit over my panties, applying just enough pressure to my aching clit to make me whimper.

"You're soaked," he murmurs in my ear, sending a shiver through me.

I press my lips together, heat filling my cheeks. "How long do you plan to torture me?"

His finger traces back and forth, circling my clit with each pass, but my panties and stockings are still on, and I need him to touch *me*. "Hmm, not as long as I'd like." He lowers his voice as he slides his hand into my panties. "Perhaps next time I'll make you beg for it." He enters me with two fingers, stretching my walls as he scissors them inside me.

"Yes," I say in a shallow voice, biting my lip. *Fuck. I'd beg if he wanted.*

"Right there?" he checks, nipping my earlobe.

"Mmm," I moan, tipping my head back and closing my eyes.

Tristan doubles his efforts, thrusting his fingers into me and teasing my clit with his thumb.

I gasp desperately, white-knuckling the railing, but it's not enough. "I want you inside me."

He pulses his fingers, moving them faster. "Whose fingers do you think are—"

"Not your fingers," I cut him off, my body flushed with heat and desire.

Tristan's lips brush the shell of my ear as he slows his thrusts. "What about our friends inside?"

"I think we can do this without them."

His chuckle stirs the hair at the nape of my neck, and his voice is low when he murmurs, "Smart mouth. They'll hear us. They probably already have with you moaning so beautifully for me."

"I don't care," I breathe, my head spinning with lust. *Let the entire fucking city hear my seelie fae knight make me come.*

"Noted." He withdraws his fingers, and my eyes snap open. I'm about to protest when he unbuckles his belt, making quick work of popping the button on his pants and tugging the zipper down. A deep sound between a groan and a growl rumbles through his chest as he pulls his cock free and pumps his hand along its thick shaft.

My mouth goes dry as I stare at it. I lick my lips, lifting my eyes to meet his gaze, and the muscles in my thighs tighten at the dark hunger in their deep blue depths.

"Turn around," he says in a gravelly voice. "Hands on the railing."

*Oh shit.*

I do as I'm told as he moves behind me, lifting my

jacket and dress, tearing my panties clean off, and leaving my stockings torn and gathered at my knees. I can't even find the will to be annoyed. That's how much I need him.

He runs his hand down my side. "Widen your stance." When I do, he adds a soft, "Good girl," that sends my pulse skyrocketing. He drags the blunt head of his cock back and forth along my folds, keeping one hand wrapped firmly around my hip. "Are you ready for me?" he whispers in my ear.

I don't miss a beat. "Always."

Between one moment and the next, Tristan thrusts into me, stealing the air from my lungs. He pushes deeper, reaching a spot that has me seeing stars as I hang on to the railing for dear life. His lips find the pulse at my neck, kissing it softly as his hand slides forward from my hip to work my throbbing clit.

I squeeze my eyes shut, chewing my bottom lip as pleasure floods through me like a tidal wave, making my skin tingle. I clench around his cock, and his name leaves my lips in a breathy moan that urges him to increase the speed of his thrusts as he rolls his hips and slams into me until my head is spinning.

I'm breathing hard, barreling toward release as I turn my head to catch his lips and kiss him hard. His tongue darts out, pushing into my mouth and grazing mine.

He swallows the sounds of my pleasure, and my heart hammers in my chest as I lose control of my body, moaning against his lips.

Everything in me tightens, and I nearly lose my grip on the railing when an orgasm rips through me. Tristan growls deep in his throat, tugging me against him as his own orgasm slams into him.

I break the kiss, panting as I fight to catch my breath

and ride the aftershocks of my climax. I fall back into his chest and swipe the sweat from my brow. "Holy shit," I breathe.

Tristan pulls out of me, sending shivers skating across my skin, and bends to kiss my cheek. "Hmm," he purrs. "Let's go have dinner. You'll need to replenish your energy for what I have planned for you." He pulls me around to face him and smoothes the front of my dress, shooting me a wicked smirk.

*Fucking hell. I want to skip dinner.*

I chuckle at the torn fabric of my panties on the patio, snatching them up and shoving them into my jacket pocket as Tristan takes my hand, then grab my wine before we walk inside and meet everyone in the dining room.

Allison sends me what she thinks is a subtle grin—it's not—and Oliver looks none the wiser, because he is. At least one person didn't hear us.

Aside from the earlier fae meeting, Oliver's been with us since we said goodbye to Max a few days ago. I pulled him aside after we left the cemetery to share what Max asked me to tell him and held him while we both cried. He's nowhere near his easygoing, teddy bear-like self, but at least he's not locking himself in his dorm. So long as I can keep an eye on him, make sure he's handling things okay and knows I'm here to talk whenever he needs, I don't have to worry so much about him.

"Oh, you decided to join us," Nikolai says with a mischievous grin.

"Watch it, Sterling," Tristan warns, and Skylar appears, punching Nikolai in the shoulder. He disappears for a moment before returning from the kitchen with his hands full.

"Bet you never thought you'd actually use this room,

did you, Westbrook?" Nikolai says with a grin, reaching to set a steaming dish on the table.

"I never thought I'd let you into my home, so crazier things have happened."

I hide my laugh behind my wineglass, taking a sip before setting it on the table and lowering myself into a chair. Tristan chooses the seat next to me, Allison and Oliver sit across from us, and Nikolai and Skylar each take an end of the table.

"He can cook," Allison announces after surveying the spread of dishes in front of her.

"Damn right, he can," Nikolai says.

I steal a look at the spread in front of us. Nikolai was in the kitchen for over an hour preparing everything, and it smells amazing. He made chicken in some sort of cream sauce, several dishes full of broccoli, asparagus, carrots, roasted potatoes, and garlic bread. My stomach grumbles, making my cheeks heat when Tristan glances over at me with a faint grin.

"I want to raise a glass," Nikolai starts, standing at the head of the table, drink in hand.

"Oh, good," Skylar mutters.

Nikolai winks at her, and she shoots him an icy glare. "As I was saying, a toast. To all the shit we've endured. We got to this point, so what the hell? Let's keep going." He lifts his glass in the air, then takes a drink.

"That was the most mediocre toast I've ever been forced to sit through," I say. "Thanks for that, Nikolai."

"Whatever," he mutters half-heartedly. "Please, enjoy the food I prepared for hours in the kitchen."

Skylar snorts.

"Something to say, kitten?" Nikolai says with an arched brow, a hint of a challenge in his voice.

Her eyes narrow on him. "Nothing complimentary." She spoons some broccoli onto her plate without breaking Nikolai's gaze.

A quick glance at Allison tells me I'm not the only one feeling the tension crackling between these two right now.

"Easy, kids," Tristan cuts in. "Some of us would like to eat dinner."

Skylar spares him a glance. "Have at it," she says with a faint smile.

He chuckles, shaking his head at her.

We all fill our plates with food and eat in silence for a while before Allison says, "Are we going to talk about the elephant in the room?"

Nikolai laughs. "Which one, Allison? There are plenty, so take your pick."

She purses her lips. "The Experiment. Do we have a plan?" She directs the question at Tristan.

He sets his drink down after taking a sip. "I'm waiting to hear from the royal court, as I'm sure Nikolai is. Until then, there's not much we can do besides look out for each other. We can't draw them out without posing a risk to our people, and I won't allow that."

"We wait for them to make themselves known, then?" Oliver asks.

I stiffen in my seat, flashes of being taken from right outside this building filling my thoughts. My pulse jumps when Tristan rests his hand on my thigh. His touch warms my skin and settles my racing heart. I clear my throat before I say, "I don't think they'll come around here, at least not for a while," I say. "The Experiment will expect us to be on high alert, so I don't see them risking an attack yet. They're likely dealing with the fallout of us destroying their facility. They must have others, and we'll find them, but it'll take time."

"Then what?" Skylar chimes in without looking up from her plate where she's pushing a potato around with her fork. "Are we going to destroy everyone we find? Sacrifice more of our people doing so?"

"No," Tristan says. "As much as within our power. Destruction and death are something the fae have experienced too much of. We need to prevent more as much as possible."

"You brought that doctor back here." Skylar lifts her head to meet his gaze. "Use her."

"I agree," I say, causing everyone to look at me. "Damn, guys, don't look so surprised."

Skylar snickers, then tries to cover it up by sticking a chunk of potato in her mouth.

"Dr. Collins has information. She may not have created the Experiment, but she made it her life after her daughter was killed. If anyone knows about other facilities, it's her."

Tristan nods. Ultimately, the decision of what to do about the Experiment belongs to the queen and king, but everyone in this room is confident Tristan and Nikolai will make a strong case.

After dinner, I'm cleaning up the kitchen, rinsing a plate when Skylar comes in and takes it from me to dry.

"Hey," I say, trying to hide my surprise that she came to help.

"I called Monica today," she says in lieu of a greeting.

"How is she?" I clean a handful of silverware and set it on the drying rack.

"Heartbroken. She won't let me visit, which I understand, but I'm worried about her."

"Does she have anyone to take care of her?"

She nods, taking the glass I hand her to dry. "She has a fiancé. He's also fae and knows what happened."

"That's good." I press my lips together, debating whether I should say what I want to. "Skylar, I know you're heartbroken, too. Max was your best friend. As much as I'm sure you wanted to strangle the guy often, you cared about him. He knew that as much as I do. And he felt the same way about you. That love isn't gone just because he is." I swallow past the lump forming in my throat. "He, um, wanted you to know that you're the fiercest, most powerful woman he'd ever met. He told me how lucky he was to have you looking out for him."

She freezes, and her eyes flick up to mine. She swallows hard, blinking as if she's fighting back tears. "Thank you."

I offer her a warm smile and nod. "You're welcome."

She goes back to drying the dish in her hand again.

"So..." I drag out the word. "What's the deal with you and Nikolai?" I cringe when she shoots me a glare. "Not looking to chat about guys. Got it."

A ghost of a smile touches her lips as she turns away to put the clean wineglass in the cupboard.

We finish the dishes, and I can't help but feel a little lighter, even with the current circumstances. Because despite them, tonight was good. I'm alive, surrounded by people I care about, and we're going to make it through whatever comes next.

## CHAPTER
# FORTY-NINE

We spend the evening sitting around Tristan's living room, chatting as flames crackle in the fireplace. It's not really cold enough for a fire, but it fills the room with a cozy warmth that makes me want to curl up in Tristan's lap and do things that wouldn't be appropriate with our friends present.

"I'm heading to bed," Allison announces around a yawn. "You coming, Ollie?" They've been staying in one of the guest rooms in the penthouse since I escaped the facility, same with Nikolai and Skylar, though they're sleeping in separate rooms.

Oliver nods, letting her pull him off the couch. "Night, guys."

"Goodnight," I mumble, leaning into Tristan's side as he runs his hand over my hair.

Nikolai and Skylar don't last much longer before they disappear too, leaving Tristan and me alone in front of the fire.

"Rory?" Tristan's smooth voice makes me open my

eyes. I hadn't even realized I'd closed them.

"Hmm?"

He gives my hip a gentle squeeze and leans down until his lips brush my ear. "Let me take you to bed."

I manage a nod as warmth spreads low in my belly. "Yes, please."

"To get some rest," he clarifies.

I offer him a sleepy pout. "But you said you had things planned for me. I want to see what they are."

"I think they'll have to wait." The corner of his mouth curls as he brushes my hair back. "Come on."

When he reaches for me, I grab his belt and fumble with the buckle. He chuckles. I ignore him, still fighting with the damn thing, until he places his hand over mine.

"Why'd you have to wear a belt?" I grumble.

His lips twitch. "You should get some sleep."

I shake my head.

Tristan sighs, his eyes flicking between mine. "This is really what you want?"

I lick my lips, grinning triumphantly. "Yes." I pull him closer, kissing his jaw. "I want *you*."

"Right here?" he whispers. "In the living room. With our friends a short distance away—again."

"I guess we'll have to be quiet," I taunt him, pressing my mouth against his bottom lip.

He sucks in a breath. "You're sure?"

Licking my lips, I shoot him a grin. "There are few things I've been more sure of."

"Thank god," he mutters, and then his lips are on mine, devouring and worshiping them simultaneously. He removes his belt as he trails his lips along my jaw, and I reach for the button on his pants, popping it open before I work the zipper down.

"Tristan," I gasp when he nips my earlobe.

"Lift your arms," he says in a deep voice that makes my skin tingle.

I comply quickly, and he slips his hand under me to unzip the back of my dress before he lifts it over my head and tosses it on the floor. He unclasps my bra and has it off before I can lower my arms. He shrugs out of his jacket, adding it to the growing pile of clothes before he lowers his mouth to my skin and makes me lightheaded with his tongue on the swell of my breast.

Tristan brings his lips back to mine as I struggle to get the buttons of his shirt open, then push it off his shoulders. He shifts his leg, pressing it to the throbbing at my core and making me moan. His gaze slams into me, warming my skin further.

"Quiet," he murmurs, fire blazing in his gaze. He trails his lips down my chest and my nipples harden in response. His tongue dips, catching my breath as he takes my breast into his mouth, swirling his tongue around the nipple and sucking hard.

I slide my hands down his taut chest and pull his pants down enough for his cock to spring free. When my fingers reach out to wrap around his thick length, he groans against my skin, sending delicious vibrations through me. "Shh," I remind him with a snicker. "You don't want Nikolai coming out to see what the noise is."

Tristan huffs out something akin to a growl. "I'll hear him or anyone else before they get anywhere near us. You don't need to worry." He shifts his attention to the other breast, driving me wild all over again as I work my hand up and down his shaft, doing the same to him. If this was a competition, it's safe to say we're both winners. The room fills with the combined sounds of our breaths, moans, and kisses. My whole body feels hot, every nerve electrified under Tristan's skillful hands.

"Aurora," he breathes against my skin, teasing my neck with his lips as he adds his pants to the collection of clothes on the floor.

"Hmm?" I murmur.

"I need you." His voice is low, gruff, filled with so much lust it makes my head spin.

"Yes," I agree, warmth pooling between my thighs at the sound of his voice.

He crawls over me, his gaze meeting mine as he splays his fingers across my cheek. "You still with me?"

I meet his gaze and smile. "I'm here."

He kisses me before leaning away. "You're sure?"

I nod. There isn't a place on earth I'd rather be.

He presses his lips together, and before I can comment on his annoying little smirk, his lips are back on mine, and he hardens against my thigh.

"Lift your hips," he instructs in a voice that would make me do just about anything.

I do as I'm told, and he slides into me in one quick, smooth motion, sealing his mouth over mine and swallowing the moan that escapes my lips.

His thrusts are slow and deep, drawing soft sounds from me with ease. He groans against my lips as he reaches between our bodies and tweaks my clit. My hips buck against him, pushing him deeper and making me clench around him.

"Fuck, Rory." His breath is hot against my cheek. He nips my bottom lip before kissing me hard.

I reach for him, sliding my fingers through his hair and tugging at the ends.

He increases the pace, and I match his thrusts, my legs

trapping him between them as my heart pounds against my rib cage. We're battling it out, in a race to see who will come apart first.

I clench around him again, holding him to me as I come hard. Only a few thrusts later, he groans, his muscles tense as his own release charges through him.

He slides out of me and peppers kisses along my jaw, against my cheek, my brow, my forehead. I giggle beneath him, trying to squirm away, but he holds me there, grinning.

"I love you," he says.

I kiss him. "I love you."

He wraps his arms around me, hugging me against his side as our breathing settles to a normal pace. Amid all the sadness and fear of what is still to come—in this moment right here—I allow myself to smile, to be happy, because after everything we've been through, we deserve it.

---

"I thought they were going to kill you," he whispers, his voice cracking as he stares at the ceiling.

We finally made it to the bedroom and have been lying next to each other in silence for half an hour, neither of us able to sleep.

My heart sinks, and I reach for his hand, sliding my fingers through his. "I'm here, Tris. I'm okay." My tone is calm, soft, but anger bubbles inside of me. I'm glad Max destroyed the Experiment's facility. I don't feel guilty over the lives I took to get out of there. If that makes me a monster, so be it. They almost took everything from me. I wasn't going to let them get away with it—I couldn't.

He squeezes my hand, but still won't look at me. His

jaw is sharp, a muscle ticking along it, and shadowed with stubble. He hasn't shaved in the six days I've been back, but the slightly unkempt look suits him.

I place my free hand against his cheek and turn his face toward me. My chest tightens at the glassiness in his eyes. His jaw is clenched against my palm, and all I want to do is take away his pain. "Breathe," I murmur.

He blinks, causing a tear to escape his eye and drip onto the pillow beside him. "I don't know what I would've done if I'd lost you." I can't imagine what's going through his head right now. He did lose someone—his best friend. The two of us were never close, but I'm mourning his loss alongside my friends.

"You didn't lose me. I'm right here." I don't know what else to say that'll ease the fear in his eyes.

He sits up, leaning against the headboard, and I follow. He pulls my hands into his, holding them in his lap. "I know this isn't exactly how you pictured your life playing out."

I offer a soft laugh. "Nothing has happened how I planned since the day I met you."

He traces slow circles over the back of my hand with his thumb. "If I could go back and change the way we met—"

I kiss him, cutting off his words. "I know," I murmur. "But you can't, and that's okay." My fingers splay across his cheek, and he turns his face to press his lips against my palm, closing his eyes.

"You're all I want," he says, opening his eyes to meet my gaze. "For the rest of whatever time we have."

I smile as tears fill my eyes. "We might not have forever, but we have each other."

He nods, pulling my hand away from his face. "I want

to show you something."

"Right now?" I ask, laughing as he slides off the bed and gets dressed. I do the same and smile when he offers me his hand. We walk out of the penthouse together, riding the elevator downstairs in silence. I'm too afraid to ask where we're going, and even if I did, I feel Tristan wouldn't tell me. He'll never tire of surprising me, it seems.

He leads me into the parking garage, and when we get in his car, I can't take it anymore. "Where are we going?"

"That took long enough," he comments with a grin.

I roll my eyes. "Smartass."

"Just give me ten minutes. No questions." He glances over at me, his eyes twinkling. "Okay?"

Huffing out a breath, I nod. "Get a move on, Westbrook. Your ten minutes start now."

---

I'm confused when he stops the car at the curb of a black brick commercial building half a dozen blocks from the hotel. The front comprises windows, but it's too dark inside to see. There are large but empty planters on either side of the door, and I immediately envision them filled with blooming spring flowers.

I turn to Tristan. "I—"

"Ah, ah, ah. I still have..."—he checks his watch—"four minutes left."

My eyes narrow. "Fine."

Tristan gets out of the car and walks around to my side, opening the door for me. I take his outstretched hand and step onto the sidewalk. We walk to the front of the building, and Tristan pulls out a key, sliding it into the lock; I still can't see what's inside.

"Don't let go of my hand," he instructs.

"We're walking into a pitch-black building." I squeeze his hand. "I'm not going anywhere."

His responding chuckle echoes off the brick alcove surrounding the door. He steps over the threshold, and I follow him, squinting at the endless darkness. Tristan closes the door and leads me a few steps farther into the room.

"You've pulled some creepy shit since I've known you, Tris, but this is—"

"Relax." He leans in and kisses the side of my head. "Wait here. I'll be right back."

My pulse skyrockets. "You just told me not to let go of your hand."

He tweaks my chin, and even in the darkness, I can see the smirk on his face. "I'll be right back," he repeats.

Biting back several snide remarks, I let go of his hand and don't move. A few moments pass, and then, without warning, the lights come to life, illuminating the entire room in a soft golden glow.

"Oh my god..."

Bookshelves stand in rows and along each wall, fully stocked with books. There's a counter set up with a Mac and a cash register, along with more stacks of books and one of those single-serve espresso machines. Strings of twinkling lights are hung along the upper shelves and across the front of the counter. There's a sitting area next to the front door with a couch, a couple of electric blue wingback chairs, and a coffee table that's covered with magazines.

This is it.

This is the bookstore I've always dreamed of owning, the one I told him about.

*He created it.*

My eyes are flying all over the room, bouncing from shelf to shelf, before they finally land on Tristan, and I am utterly speechless.

He approaches with a smile that takes my breath away and murmurs, "I love you more than anyone should even be capable of loving another person."

My brows tug closer as my pulse kicks up. "Tristan..."

His eyes flick between mine. "I want to be with you forever, Aurora. There will never be a day—hell, a *moment*—that I won't love you, respect you, cherish you. I want to heal with you, grow with you, make new memories with you. *For as long as we both shall live.*"

My heartbeat is hammering against my rib cage, threatening to burst free. "What are you—"

"You were right when you said we don't have forever," he murmurs. Silence hangs between us for several beats.

"I don't understand," I whisper, my lower lip trembling and my eyes burning.

Tristan steps forward. "What you went through those days you were locked up in that place is unimaginable. I don't condone what was done, and I'm glad those monsters are gone. But what they did..." He shakes his head. "They did the impossible, Rory. They took a fae and they made you human again."

My mouth is bone dry. I'm too afraid to speak.

"I've been thinking about it." A muscle ticks along his jaw. "They've done the procedure successfully more than once now." His expression is calm, peaceful. A stark contrast to the panic and fear etched into my features.

My heart stops and hot tears spring in my eyes. "You..." My eyes bounce all over his face. "You want to become *human?*"

His smile widens. "I want you. Forever. But I would never ask you to become fae again. If I do this, if I become human, we can grow old together. I will die satisfied, having spent my life loving you."

My knees buckle, and Tristan catches me, guiding me to the floor. He kneels in front of me, holding my face in his hands.

"This is a lot, I know. I love you with every part of me, and if you'll do me the incredible honor of spending your life with me, I will continue to love and care for you until our last day together on this earth."

Tears roll freely down my cheeks, and I don't bother wiping them away.

He reaches into his pocket and pulls out a black velvet box. He lifts his gaze to my face as he opens it. "Aurora Marshall, will you marry me?"

My eyes widen at the gorgeous diamond caged by an intricate rose gold band. I blink at it a few times to make sure my eyes aren't deceiving me before I meet his gaze, nodding as my lips curl into a smile. "Yes. Of course, I'll marry you. *Yes.*"

He pulls the ring out of the box and slips it onto my finger. We both stare at it glittering against my skin, and then at each other before we rise to our feet. His arms come around me at the same moment I lean up and brush my lips against his, letting my eyes fall shut as I melt into him and deepen the kiss. My fingers push through his hair and his hands squeeze my hips. I miss being able to hear our combined heartbeats, but as I break the kiss and hug him tight, pressing my ear against his chest, I feel it beating steadily. For me. For *us.*

*For as long as we both shall live.*

## CHAPTER FIFTY

We spend the next morning sitting with Nikolai, Skylar, Allison, and Oliver, discussing what to do with Dr. Collins. That's after Allison spots my glittering engagement ring and squeals about it for ten minutes.

Dr. Collins has been kept in a room in the hotel's basement, monitored by fae Tristan trusts, while we waited for direction from the royal courts. Tristan and Nikolai received word late last night—they've been granted discretion to handle her as they see fit.

When I brought her back to the hotel, it was so Tristan could choose how she died. It was a twisted idea, but after everything I'd been through at the facility, it felt right, even if an inherent part of me knew the whole thing was very wrong.

Tristan says nothing about his interest in becoming human; I keep my mouth shut, majorly because I'm still trying to work through it myself. The idea of living a human life with Tristan is exciting, but the chance that the procedure won't work like it didn't for many other fae has me absolutely terrified.

"Kill her," Oliver says in a low voice, tracing the rim of his coffee cup with his finger.

Skylar speaks before I process Oliver's grim suggestion. "That would be a waste. Why are you even here?"

Oliver flinches, his cheeks flushing, and says nothing more.

"Easy, Sky," Nikolai says in a soft tone.

She exhales a heavy sigh. "I'm sorry," she says to Oliver, "I get you cared about him—we all did—but we need to look at the bigger picture. Ensure Max didn't die for nothing. It's what he would've wanted."

Oliver nods, blinking away the wetness in his eyes.

"Let's use her to get some answers," Allison says. "It's a good place to start. We need to find out where the other facilities are and what their plans are. From there, we can come up with a strategy to deal with them."

That we all agree on.

Now, walking down the dim lower-level hallway toward the room Dr. Collins is being kept in—the room I was in when Max brought me here—I can't stop my hands from shaking as nervous energy crackles through me.

Tristan gives the hand he's holding a gentle squeeze. "You don't have to be here."

I swallow past the lump in my throat. "Yes, I do."

Tristan insisted on being the one to interrogate Dr. Collins, so I followed him. If he's going to talk to her about making him human, I *will* be there.

"Your heart is trying to burst from your chest." Tristan's velvet soft voice reels me back in, and I glance up at him.

"I'm fine," I lie smoothly, because I'd rather bury myself in something important than face the anxiety winding around my throat like a noose. I'm worried about what *I'm* going to do upon seeing the woman who practically tortured me.

Tristan stops at the last door at the end of the hall, and the fae guard nods at him, flipping each of the four locks open. We walk inside and the guard closes the door, relocking it.

Seeing the room brings me right back to the time I spent here. Nothing has changed, except the woman tied to a chair is no longer me.

The doctor lifts her head when she hears us come in. She glances toward the tray of food on the floor next to her, then looks at Tristan and me. The pantsuit she was wearing is wrinkled and dirty now. The rest of her appears disheveled and frail, but there isn't an inkling of guilt in my chest. She doesn't deserve comfort, not after everything she's done.

Tristan approaches at a slow pace. The lethal precision of each step he takes would make anyone nervous. Dr. Collins's fear is clear; her eyes are wide, and her hands are shaking where they're shackled at her sides.

"I'm going to make this very simple," Tristan says calmly. "You will answer my questions, do as I ask, and then you're free to leave."

My eyes swing toward him. *He's going to let her go?*

"I-I can't help you," she forces out, voice trembling.

Tristan shakes his head. "Try again."

"Why are you doing this?"

I bark out a laugh. "That sounds familiar. What is it you said to me when I asked you that very question? Oh, right. *You should consider yourself lucky.* And you should.

You've hurt many people, and instead of killing you, Tristan is giving you a chance to save yourself."

Her shoulders shake, and she sniffles. "What do you want?"

"That's better," I comment.

"We need two things from you, and then you'll be on your way."

Her eyes narrow at him. "What?"

"First, you're going to tell us everything you know about the other Experiment facilities."

"I won't. They exist to protect humans from you monsters," she seethes.

Tristan offers a dark chuckle. "You will," he says in an affable tone. "You can do it willingly or I can make you speak. It's up to you. I'm giving you a *choice*, which is more than you gave Aurora."

"There are too many operations around the world," she says. "You'll never find them all."

"We have a team of people upstairs who'd beg to differ," I say, crossing my arms.

Tristan nods. "Why don't we start with the major ones? You must have a roster of locations somewhere."

Dr. Collins looks at me. "Of course. In the building you destroyed."

"Hmm... I don't believe for a second there was only a single copy of that list. I'm sure you have databases full of useful information, so why don't you tell us about that," I suggest sharply. I'm not in the mood for this to take longer than it needs to. Dr. Collins is pushing her luck.

She says nothing.

"I'd start talking, doctor," Tristan warns, "or this is going to get very unpleasant for you, very fast." He steps closer to her, and she pulls against the restraints. "Start talking," he repeats.

After a stretch of silence, Tristan closes the distance between them and grips her chin, forcing her to look at him. She struggles in his grasp, but it's pointless.

"Where are the databases with the information on the other Experiment facilities?" His voice is a gentle, melodic caress. It tickles my mind, and he's not even directing the question at me. That's how powerful his manipulation is.

Dr. Collins's eyes are blank as she stares at him. "A backup database is kept in my off-site lab, so that in the event the facility is compromised, our work isn't lost."

"Good," Tristan murmurs. "What else is kept off-site?"

"Blood and DNA samples, old Experiment files, and the transition formula."

"Excellent. Where is this lab?"

"In the basement of an abandoned warehouse on the other side of the city."

"Does anyone else know about this place?"

She shakes her head in his grasp. "Only one member from each facility knows the location of the off-site lab for that facility."

"We're going to need an address."

She spews off an address in the warehouse district across the city, her eyes filling with tears as she betrays her precious organization.

Tristan lets go of his control on her mind and steps back. "That wasn't so hard, was it?"

She whimpers, slumping in the chair. Her chest rises and falls as she exhales a heavy breath. "You... you said there were two things. What's the second?"

The corner of Tristan's mouth curls. "You should enjoy

this part," he tells her, giving her a second to look confused. "I want you to make me human."

Her eyes widen as she stares at him. "Y-you do?" She shakes her head, glancing toward me before looking back at Tristan.

He nods. "Have you successfully performed the procedure on someone who was born fae?"

After a moment of hesitation, she nods.

"How many?" I cut in.

She casts me a glance. "I can't give you an exact number, but at least one third of the fae we've successfully made human were born fae."

"How many fae in general have you made human?"

"Again, I don't have an exact nu—"

"Ballpark it," I snap, my pulse ticking faster as my patience for this woman runs thinner.

She has the sense to look nervous. "Over the last year, over a hundred."

"What's your success rate?" I fire back. I'm asking more questions, considering the procedure is a choice for Tristan. If the risk is too high, I won't let him do it.

Pride flickers in her otherwise tired gaze. "Eighty-seven percent. We haven't lost one in nearly ten months." My eyes shift toward Tristan. Before I can say anything to him, Dr. Collins says, "So I make you human, and then you let me go?"

Tristan drags his gaze away from me, looking at the doctor again, and nods. "Once I'm human, we'll erase your memories of the fae. I may not be fae after this is over, but I'm going to protect those who are."

"No!" she shouts. "You can't do that."

"You're right. I won't be able to, but I have plenty of friends who can."

"I won't do it. I've given my life to this organization for the last six years."

I scowl, stepping forward. "Haven't you given enough?"

"I promised my daughter I wouldn't stop until humans were safe from the fae."

"Would Amber want you to die for the Experiment?"

Her eyes narrow. "You have no idea what it's like to lose—"

"I've lost plenty," I snap at her. "Don't pretend like you don't know that."

Tristan's hand rests at the small of my back. "This is happening today," he announces. "You'd better eat that food and get your energy up." He reaches for my hand and laces his fingers through mine before the two of us leave the room. The door is almost shut behind us when Dr. Collins wails.

---

"What the fuck did you just say?" Skylar demands in a vicious tone, her cheeks flushed with anger.

Tristan sighs, offering a thoughtful look despite the icy glare Skylar is shooting him.

Nikolai and I are sitting on the couch in the living room, while Tristan and Skylar stand several feet away in the space between us and the dining room.

"I understand this may seem—"

"Absolutely insane?" she snaps. "That's because it is. You can't be *human*. The seelie court needs you." She shakes her head, her brows pinching. "Fuck, *I* need you, Tristan."

He smiles, resting his hands on her shoulders. "Here's

the thing, Skylar. You don't. In the years I've known you, you've grown into one of the strongest people I've met. Which is why when Rowan sought a replacement for my position in court, I gave him your name without hesitation."

She blinks at him. "You what?"

Tristan lets his hands fall back to his sides. "You'll be summoned to appear before the king to make it official, but as of today, you are a knight of the seelie court."

Several beats of silence pass, and Nikolai and I exchange a wary glance.

Skylar finally clears her throat. "I don't know what to say."

Tristan touches her cheek. "You don't have to say anything. Just know I have the utmost confidence in you and hope you'll forgive me for this decision."

Her facade cracks, and she throws her arms around him. They stay like that for several moments, holding each other tightly, and it makes my chest ache.

Tristan is giving up everything he's ever known to be with me, and it might not even work. That thought has my stomach in painful knots and threatens to send me into a spiral if I allow myself to think about it for too long.

Tristan and Skylar finally break apart, walking over to join us in the living room.

"Guess that makes us coworkers now, huh?" Nikolai grins at Skylar.

"Fucking hell," she mutters.

---

Nikolai and Allison stay back with Oliver while we take Dr. Collins to her off-site lab across the city, but I'm glad

Skylar is with us. I'm not sure I could get through this alone.

We drive through the city in a tinted SUV. Dr. Collins is sitting in the passenger seat, giving directions to one of the seelie fae from Tristan's security team. Skylar is sitting in the seat behind her, ready to pounce if necessary. By the sharp expression on her face, she's itching for the chance.

I'm sitting next to her, while Tristan is in the row behind us with another fae. He reaches forward and slips his fingers through mine, tracing slow circles on the back of my hand with his thumb. I focus on that to keep my pulse from skyrocketing.

With traffic, we take almost an hour to get to the other side of the city. The car turns onto a long dirt road and finally comes to a stop in front of a rundown gray brick building. It's all on one level and spread out. The windows are boarded up, and ones that still have glass are mostly broken.

"Need a new investment property?" Skylar asks Tristan in a dry tone.

He chuckles.

We get out of the car, the two fae from Tristan's security team on either side of Dr. Collins as we walk into the building. If anyone were to wander into the building, they'd see nothing but an empty, dusty old warehouse. Except we're not anyone. We're here for a reason.

Dr. Collins walks in front of us toward the far side of the room. Our shoes echo off the cement floors until we come to a stop in front of a wall. Dr. Collins runs her hand along it, pausing a few times, then stops and presses her hand firmly against it.

My eyes widen as the wall moves back and to the side,

revealing a doorway to a landing and a set of stairs to a basement.

"Creepy," Skylar mutters. She's not wrong.

The group of us descend the stairs until we're at the bottom. Dr. Collins leans over and turns on the light, bathing the room in harsh overhead fluorescence. The room looks the same as the one I found Max in. White floors and walls and glass cabinets against the far wall, filled with vials of blood and other colored liquids that turn my stomach. The counters are metal and there's a sink in the middle. Off to one side is a row of black filing cabinets, no doubt filled with research and information on the fae, and beside that is a desk covered with stacks of paper and a computer.

Tristan tells the other fae to pack up the computer and files. We'll take it back to the hotel and go through everything there.

When he tells Dr. Collins to prepare for the transition, my entire body goes rigid. I wrap my arms around him, leaning up to kiss just below his ear. "Are you sure about this?" I whisper.

He turns his face to meet my gaze. "One hundred percent. I want a human life with you, Aurora."

His words make my heart skip a beat, but the fear still consumes me. "What if it doesn't work?" Shaking my head, I say, "I can't lose you."

"It's a risk," he agrees. "There's a chance it won't work, but my gut is telling me it will. For you, for me, and for us."

*Anything as important as love is worth the risk.*

I take a deep breath and let it out. "Damn it. You better not die."

Tristan chuckles, leaning in to brush his lips across

mine. "You won't get rid of me that easily." He leans back, murmuring, "Eighty-seven percent."

I cling to the success rate of the procedure he's about to put himself through, recalling how terribly agonizing it is.

"It's ready." Dr. Collins's voice makes my stomach drop and kicks my pulse into overdrive.

"Breathe, Rory," Tristan murmurs, his lips brushing my ear.

I force myself to take slow breaths until my heartbeat calms, but my nerves are still jumping like a kid on a trampoline.

Skylar walks over to Tristan. "I don't like this."

"I'm aware," he says gently.

Her eyes narrow. "Don't die." She lowers her voice. "I can't lose you, too."

I swallow my tears and step to the side.

Tristan wraps his arms around her, whispering something before he leans back and kisses her cheek.

"Okay," he says, taking my hand as we walk toward the table Dr. Collins has set up. "Let's get this over with."

Skylar moves with inhuman speed, grabbing the front of the doctor's shirt and glaring into her eyes. "You will not pull any shady shit or sabotage this procedure. You will do everything in your power to make this work and keep Tristan alive. Understand?" Her manipulation grips Dr. Collins completely, making her back go ramrod straight.

"I understand," she replies in a monotone voice.

"Good." Skylar lets her go and moves away from her.

Skylar and I sit on either side of Tristan, holding each of his hands. His security is nearby, but gives us some space. Dr. Collins stands at Tristan's head, looking over the vials of purple and blue liquid she has on the tray beside her, as well as several syringes lined up next to them.

Skylar and I strapped Tristan to the padded table; he could hurt himself or fall off if he thrashes all over the place—and once the process starts, he probably will.

"This will differ from when you underwent the procedure," Dr. Collins says, looking at me. "With you, we injected each serum one at a time, but according to our research, for a fae-born, because their magic is so attached, the serums must be injected simultaneously."

Tristan stares hard at the ceiling, and I squeeze his hand, leaning down to kiss his shoulder as Dr. Collins fills two of the syringes—one with the purple mixture and one with the blue.

"This is going to hurt worse than any pain you've ever felt," she warns, bringing the needle toward his neck.

Skylar growls, but she stops to look down at her hand when Tristan grips it tighter.

"Do it," Tristan says. His tone is deep, harsh.

I keep my eyes on his face as he stares upward. He doesn't flinch when the needle pierces his skin, but his hand is shaking in mine. "Breathe," I remind him, just as he's done for me so many times.

He takes a deep breath in, but before he can release it, a scream tears its way up his throat and past his lips. The sound of his pain fills the room, and he tries to press his lips together to stop it, but he can't. In the midst of his agony, he's unable to keep his glamour in place. I find it impossible to look away when his teeth sharpen to points as his eyes glow and his skin takes on a bluish, near-translucent hue. His ears become pointed, poking through his hair, and his fingernails transform into claws. I don't remember this happening to me, though I was entirely delirious from the pain, so it's quite possible it did.

Skylar's face pales, and I clench my jaw hard, wincing

at the grip Tristan has on my hand, his razor-sharp claws scratching my skin.

"This is a normal response," Dr. Collins says, then pushes the rest of the serum into him and pulls the needle out, setting it on the tray before picking up the next one.

Tristan's screams only get louder.

He's in agony for almost an hour. I prayed he would black out at some point, but it didn't happen. He's too damn stubborn.

Once his screams finally turn into grunts and heavy breathing, he slips into unconsciousness.

I press my ear against his chest to make sure he's still breathing. "What now?" I ask Dr. Collins. "How long before he's awake?"

"It ranges from person to person," she says, wheeling the tray away from the table. "He survived the procedure, but it could be another hour before he regains consciousness."

I push the hair away from his face and brush my hand over his cheek. "Wake up," I murmur to him, and press my lips to his in a whisper of a kiss. "Please." I won't be able to breathe normally until he opens his eyes, until I know for certain it worked and he's okay.

Another hour later, Skylar and I are pacing the room while the fae who came with us sit on either side of Dr. Collins, making sure she stays put. Tristan still hasn't stirred. His chest is rising and falling evenly, but he hasn't opened his eyes.

Skylar sighs. "We should check in at the hotel. I'm sure—"

She's cut off by a loud gasp. We whip around to find Tristan's eyes open, blinking rapidly as if the light above hurts.

My heart slams against my chest as I rush to his side, cupping his face in my hands. "Tristan," I murmur through my tears, relief flooding through me so strongly it nearly brings me to my knees. "I'm here," I cry, moving one hand to his chest to feel his heart beating steadily against my palm. "You're okay." I kiss him deeply, the panic in my chest finally easing when his mouth moves against mine. I pull back reluctantly to allow us both to drag in a breath.

"Holy shit," Skylar breathes, staring at him in disbelief. "You're fucking human."

Tristan goes to chuckle, but winces in pain, and starts coughing. Skylar and I help him into a sitting position, and I rub his back until the coughing stops.

"How do you feel?" Dr. Collins asks, walking over to look at him.

He blinks at her, then says in a low, hoarse voice, "Everything hurts, but I'm alive so I won't complain."

I glance over at Skylar. "Think you could help him out with that?"

She nods, pressing her hand against his chest. "Already on it."

"You don't have to—"

"Hush," Skylar cuts him off.

This time when he laughs, it's lighter, stronger. "Thank you," he says after she pulls her hand away.

"Take it easy," she directs. "You've never lived as a human."

Tristan shoots me a wink. "I think I'll manage." He swings his legs over the edge of the table, and Skylar and I help him stand. He takes a few steps, testing his strength, and nods. "I'm all right," he assures me.

Dr. Collins takes a few steps back, glancing nervously between us and Skylar. "I... I did what you asked."

Tristan tilts his head to the side, flicking a glance at her. "You did. And once Skylar adjusts your memories, you can go home."

Unbridled panic fills her eyes, as if she forgot that was part of the deal. Dr. Collins whirls around and bolts toward the door we came in through, whimpering desperately when the fae who'd been guarding her move faster, blocking her exit.

Skylar scowls and prowls closer, shaking her head. "You don't deserve a shred of mercy," she hisses at her. Dr. Collins's eyes widen as Skylar grabs her by the throat. "Tristan said he would let you go." She digs her nails into the doctor's skin, making her cry out. "I, however, promised no such thing."

"Sky—" Tristan starts.

It's too late. Skylar snaps her neck and drops her lifeless body on the floor like it's nothing. My mouth drops open as I stare at her face, her eyes wide and vacant.

Tristan sighs, his brows furrowed. "Was that necessary?"

She whirls on him and says one word: "Max."

His eyes soften, and he nods, wrapping his arm around my shoulders and guiding me toward the door while the team of fae who followed us here come in and prepare to destroy this facility too. "Let's go home."

## CHAPTER
# FIFTY-ONE

"You're what?" Mom shrieks, her eyes wide as she stands in front of me.

A few days after Tristan became human, I meet my parents at an Italian restaurant downtown for lunch to share the news of my engagement.

Tristan stayed at the hotel with Skylar, who's meeting with the seelie king later today to make her knight position official. Elijah is with our grandparents, and as much as I miss him, I'm happy to have some time with my parents.

Dad swallows hard, his eyes glassy. "Congratulations, kiddo."

Mom turns to him. "You're too calm. Why aren't you freaking out? Our daughter is getting married!"

He smiles, wrapping his arm around Mom's shoulders, and leans in to kiss her cheek. "Because I already knew." Dad laughs at my wide-eyed expression. "I spoke to Tristan on the phone before he bought the ring."

*Holy shit.*

I blink, trying to force back the tears. Just when I thought I couldn't love Tristan any more.

Mom reaches for my hand and lifts it so she can look at the ring. She sucks in a breath. "Oh, honey, it's beautiful."

"I'm in love with it," I say with a smile, staring at it myself. I've barely taken my eyes off it since Tristan slid it onto my finger.

We haven't set a date for the wedding yet, deciding it best to wait until we have a better handle on the situation with the Experiment and Tristan adapts to being human. He still owns and operates the Westbrook Hotel, considering it's always been a mostly human business, and—on paper—my bookstore that will be open for business next month, once I graduate.

That said, there's an ongoing battle with the Experiment to deal with before I can think about dresses and flowers. That's not to say Allison hasn't been sending wedding idea photos since we told her we were engaged, because she hasn't stopped.

She and Oliver, along with Skylar and Nikolai, are no longer staying in Tristan's guest rooms since we announced our engagement. I've barely spent any time at the dorm, which has worked out so that Oliver can stay with Allison to finish out the semester. For someone who knew nothing about the fae not too long ago, he's handling that part exceptionally well. The grief surrounding Max's death is another story, but Allison assures me each day is a little easier for him. It probably helps that exams are looming, giving him plenty of distraction in the form of final assignments and studying.

Needing a slight distraction of my own, I spend the afternoon with my parents, allowing myself not to think about the fae, and enjoy seeing them for the first time in too long. Today, I'm going to breathe, smile, and just be human.

After lunch, the three of us walk along the downtown shopping district.

Mom squeals when she spots a bridal shop. "Let's go in!"

I press my lips together, shaking my head. "Mom, no. Come on, we haven't even set a date yet."

She waves me off. "It's never too early to look."

I look to Dad for help, but he just shrugs, laughing at Mom's sparkle-eyed excitement. "Humor your poor mother, kiddo. She won't give up until you do, and we both know it."

I glance back and forth between them and sigh. "All right, fine."

Mom's eyes light up immediately, and we walk into the store, being greeted by an employee who asks if she can help us find 'something special.'

Mom nods. "Our daughter just got engaged," she says, beaming. "We're looking for the perfect dress."

The store clerk smiles and leads us deeper into the store. "Can I offer anyone champagne?"

"That would be lovely," Mom answers before Dad or I have a chance to say anything. We exchange amused glances and say nothing, letting Mom have her excited mother-of-the-bride moment.

The store clerk ushers me into a more private part of the changing room. "When's your big day?"

I bite my lip. "We haven't set the date yet. I wasn't looking to go dress shopping for a while, but my mom saw your store and insisted we come in."

"How nice," she says politely. She takes my measurements and asks me what kind of dress I'm looking for.

"Something simple but elegant," I say, a tinge of uncertainty in my voice. I haven't given it much thought, regardless of the number of photos Allison has sent me. "I like lace," I offer.

She nods. "Okay, good. And you're wanting to go with the traditional white?"

"I think so," I answer, then think about it for a few seconds. "Yes, white."

She smiles at me. "Gotcha. Give me a few minutes, and I'll bring you some options."

I tap my fingers against my thigh until she comes back, knocking before bringing in a handful of dresses. She hangs them in a row on the rack attached to the wall.

"Take your time and let me know when you're ready to zip it up."

"Thanks," I say, my tone absent as I stare at the dress in the middle. I blink and glance around, noticing that she left the room.

Without even touching it, trying it on, my heart is sure. *It's the one.*

Oh my god. It's my wedding dress.

There's going to be a wedding.

I'm getting *married*.

Holy fuck, I'm going to be Aurora Westbrook.

The room suddenly feels too warm. I sink onto the cushion and try to take a deep breath, but it catches in my throat.

"Breathe, blondie," I mutter to myself. My heart skips. *Blondie.* I laugh, my voice cracking as my eyes burn. "Damn it, Max. You couldn't let me enjoy this panic-filled moment alone, could you?" I wipe away the unshed tears and focus on slowing my breathing. Once I don't feel like my heart is going to burst from my chest or my stomach is going to jump up my throat, I stand and walk over to the wall of dresses. I trail my fingers along the lace bodice of the middle one, and before I realize it, I'm pulling it off the hanger and putting it on. I keep my eyes closed as I approach the mirror, and the second they open, I suck in a breath.

I peek my head out and find the clerk standing there, waiting. She steps forward and does the dress up, offering me a bright smile.

"Would you like a moment?"

I wet my lips, nodding. "Please."

Once she's gone, I walk toward the mirror, unable to peel my eyes away.

"This is it," I whisper to no one.

The dress is perfect. It's a traditional floor-length gown with a V-shaped open back, layers of fabric all around my waist, and long, open sleeves. It hugs my waist and molds my chest with a high neck. I can't stop looking at it—at how I look wearing it.

I don't want to wait. I want to be married to Tristan *now*.

"Come out!" Mom shouts. "We want to see!"

I smile at my reflection before stepping out and approach where they're sitting.

Mom gasps, shooting up from her seat. "Oh, Aurora." She chokes on her words. "It's beautiful."

"I know," I say in a daze. My eyes shift to Dad and stay there. He's smiling at me, his eyes filled with tears.

The clerk bounces over. "You look stunning. What do you think?"

I flatten my hands down the front of the dress. "This is it," I announce, unable to hold back a grin.

"Congratulations!" the clerk says with a kind smile.

I press my lips together, exhaling a shaky, excited breath. "Thank you." Buying a dress doesn't mean the ceremony has to be right around the corner. It's just a dress. The most stunning, breathtaking dress I've ever seen.

Dad stands and walks over to me, kissing my cheek. "Your mom and I would like to buy the dress."

I shake my head. "Thank you, but I can't let you do that." My chest tightens. Hell, I don't even know how much this dress is. It was so meant for me, I didn't even look.

He offers me a smile. "That's too bad, because I gave the clerk my credit card while you were in the dressing room."

"Dad!" I slap his shoulder. "I don't want you spending your money."

"Please let us do this for you," Mom cuts in, moving to stand beside Dad. She reaches for my hands and squeezes them. "We are so proud of everything you've accomplished. Please let us help make your special day everything you want it to be."

This isn't a battle I'm going to win.

I sigh. "Okay."

They pull me into a hug and kiss my cheeks. "We love you so much."

"I love you, too."

Back in the dressing room, I reluctantly take the dress off. I'm putting my shirt back on when my phone buzzes. I pull it out and smile, my stomach giving a healthy flutter.

"Hey, you," I murmur.

"How's it going with your parents?"

"Good. They're thrilled for us." I hold the phone to my

ear with my shoulder as I tug my pants back on. "I'll be home soon."

"There's no need to rush."

I laugh softly. "Want to try that again? I'm not entirely convinced you meant it."

"I'm a patient man, Aurora." The deep melodic sound of his voice sends a shiver through me, and I close my eyes as heat gathers between my thighs.

"I miss you," I murmur.

"I miss you," he echoes. "Okay, maybe rush a little."

A grin curls my lips. "I'll see you soon."

---

I walk into the penthouse, pausing when my eyes land on where Tristan, Nikolai, Skylar, and Allison are sitting around the living room. None of them appear distressed, so I don't let myself panic about their meeting.

"Nice of you to join us," Nikolai says with a wry grin.

I flip him off as I approach. "Sorry, I was—" I cut myself off before I slip up and tell them I bought a wedding dress. "What's going on?" I ask, directing the question at Tristan.

"We've been discussing how things are going to work." Skylar's voice is commanding. She looks so much better than the last time I saw her, filled with concern for Tristan and a literal murderous rage toward Dr. Collins. Her hair is neatly curled down her back, with perfect makeup like I'm used to seeing it, and her outfit is sleek and sharp. I missed this Skylar. As much as she still kind of intimidates me, she is also admirable as hell. "The Experiment remains a very real and dangerous threat to our people. Since Tristan stepped down, I've taken the reins when it comes to meeting with the royals and our contacts around the globe.

I spoke to several of them last night who have located facilities they believe to be run by the Experiment."

"The king and queen have agreed to a ceasefire to focus on putting a stop to them."

My chest tightens as I nod. I'm not fae anymore, nor was I for very long, but the weight of a truce between the fae courts isn't lost on me. "What's the plan?"

"We're gathering more information," Skylar explains. "We aren't going to make a move yet. It's too risky."

"We're just going to sit and wait?"

Tristan shifts closer to me, wrapping his arm around my waist and tucking me against his side. "We fought our fight, Rory. It's time to let others help, and these things take time."

I look up at him, my eyes traveling across his face, drinking in the sight of him. Alive. Safe. *Human.* "Okay," I whisper.

"Now that we've got that business out of the way, why don't we whip out the champagne?" Allison chimes in with a grin. "We might still be at war, but we also have plenty to celebrate."

I wave her off. "I already had a glass today." I realize my mistake once it's too late.

"You drank champagne at lunch?" she asks.

I bite my lip, looking away. "Well..."

Tristan chuckles. "What are you hiding?" he murmurs, his lips brushing my ear.

I hesitate, pressing my lips together against a smile until I can't hold it in any longer. "I found my wedding dress."

His face lights up. "You did?" When I nod, he dips his face and seals his lips over mine, kissing me.

I giggle when he pulls back. "Sorry. I know we haven't

set a date yet, but my mom begged me to check out this bridal store today, and it sort of just happened."

"Are you happy?" he asks, holding my gaze.

I nod.

"Then don't apologize." He kisses my forehead.

Allison squeals, clapping her hands together. "I need to see it! I'll forgive you for finding it without me as long as I get to pick out my maid of honor dress." She jerks her thumb toward Tristan. "And he's paying for it."

I shake my head at her display, but grin all the same. I steal a quick glance at Tristan, who nods, smiling. "Deal," I say, turning back to Allison. "You can find one when we go to pick mine up."

"Excellent," she beams.

Skylar rolls her eyes at the whole thing, but I smile when I see her standing with Nikolai's arm draped around her shoulders, looking rather comfortable.

Tristan slips away and returns with two bottles of champagne and glasses. Nikolai helps him hand them out, and once we each have a glass, we clink them together and drink.

"Does this mean we get to start wedding planning?" Allison asks.

I shrug. "Now doesn't exactly seem like the best time. Maybe we should wait?"

Tristan slips his fingers through mine. "I want to marry you just as soon as you'll have me."

"But I thought—"

"Fuck it," he says with a little smirk. "Let's do what's going to make us happy."

"Yay!" Allison cheers. "This is awesome. How soon are you thinking?"

"Considering I thought this was a far-off thing I could think about later, I really have no idea."

"Maybe you should give her some time to enjoy being engaged?" Nikolai suggests.

She waves him off. "Oh, please. Girl bought her dress. She's ready."

Heat rushes to my cheeks, and I lower my gaze. It's true. I came to that realization today at the bridal store. I meant it—I want to marry Tristan *now*.

"Aurora?" Tristan's voice is soft, calming. It's quick to ease the weight on my chest.

I look up, smiling at him, before I turn my gaze to Allison. "How fast can you plan a wedding?"

## CHAPTER
# FIFTY-TWO

One week. It took us one week to plan our wedding. A number of strings were pulled to make it happen, but we figured it out—we always do.

My parents were shocked at the sped-up timeline but happy all the same. Elijah, too, who's excited to gain a brother in Tristan.

Luckily, Oliver's cousin was ordained a few months ago to officiate a friend's wedding, and Oliver could convince him to do ours. Skylar handles the location, finding us a stunning venue just outside the city, with vaulted ceilings and beautiful white French windows and doors.

Allison and Skylar spend the morning doing my hair and makeup before helping me into my dress, while Nikolai and Oliver get ready with Tristan.

Once everything is ready and all the guests are in their seats, it's time to start the ceremony.

What I've always imagined would be one of the most anxiety-inducing moments of my life is actually what's making my pulse steady, my steps sure, and my heart happy.

Allison and Oliver walk down the aisle first, followed by Skylar and Nikolai, and then Elijah, our ring bearer in a very dapper suit he proudly picked out himself.

Mom stands on one side of me and Dad on the other, both with their arms linked through mine. Supporting me, loving me, and delivering me to the only person on this earth I want to spend my life with.

The moment the double doors open and we step into the room, everyone rises. The space glows with the soft strings of lights and candles all around the room. All eyes are on me, but the only ones that matter are waiting for me at the end of the aisle, surrounded by our friends and gorgeous white and purple calla lilies like the ones I'm holding. The sight of him knocks the air out of me, and I stop walking for a second, taking him in, waiting there for me. Tristan has always looked incredible in a suit, but today is special. Today is the only day that counts; everything—every moment we shared was practice for today—for what the rest of our life together will be.

Dad squeezes my hand in the same moment Tristan smiles, sending my heart racing. *I'll never tire of that.* I take a step forward, then another, until we're standing at the front of the room. Mom leans over and kisses my cheek before letting go of my arm. Dad does the same before sitting beside Mom in the front row.

Tristan guides me up the few steps, his eyes never leaving mine. His expression matches mine: pure bliss. Today is the best day of our lives, and I can't wait to share the rest of mine with him.

Standing behind me in matching rose gold dresses are Allison and Skylar, and flanking Tristan is Oliver and Nikolai. It makes my heart heavy that Max isn't standing with them as the best man, but something tells me he's here.

The officiant speaks, but I can't focus on his words. All I can do is stare at the man in front of me and smile—smile because he's mine and I'm his.

"Do you, Tristan Westbrook, take this woman to be your wife, your best friend, your partner in life and love, for as long as you both shall live?"

Tristan doesn't miss a beat. "I do."

"Do you, Aurora Marshall, take this man to be your husband, your best friend, your partner in life and love, for as long as you both shall live?"

Blinking back tears, I smile. I've never been so sure. "I do."

We exchange rings, unable to stop staring and smiling at each other as though there isn't an entire room full of people watching us.

"By the power vested in me, I now pronounce you husband and wife. Tristan, you may kiss your bride."

He exhales. "Finally." His lips are on mine before I can laugh at his response, and the room fills with clapping and celebratory shouts. Tristan slips his arm around my waist and dips me low, kissing me until my head spins and my world is nothing but the two of us.

When he lets me back up, he kisses me again, and again, until Nikolai cuts in and says, "Easy, Westbrook. There are children present."

I laugh and kiss Tristan's cheek, whispering, "Later."

"Later," he agrees with a devilishly handsome grin.

Once we move over to the ballroom at the Westbrook Hotel, the proper party begins. An open bar and a huge buffet of food was the easiest decision I made for this wedding, aside from the man I chose to marry.

Call me weirdly sentimental, but I wanted to have the reception here—in the place Tristan and I met—even though it wasn't under the best of circumstances. It was still our start.

Allison and Skylar spent the last few days ordering hotel staff around getting the place ready for this night. Everything is perfect—they wouldn't accept anything less.

Tristan and I stand in the hotel lobby, waiting to make our entrance.

I take a deep breath and let it out slowly. "We got married," I say, grinning.

He gazes down at me. "We did."

"I own a bookstore."

"You do."

"Holy shit," I breathe.

He chuckles, bending to kiss the side of my head. "You still with me?"

I smile up at him. "Always."

The doors open, and we step forward, walking into the room with a slow, melodic song playing. The guests stand from their seats around the room, clapping, whistling, and cheering as we enter to the party as a married couple.

The place looks amazing. White material is hung like streamers from the high ceilings, flowing down the walls, and the round tables are set up with dishes and wine-glasses and the same calla lilies from the ceremony. Each table is glowing with soft light from candles, and the buffet tables are off to the side, near the bar. There's a dance floor at the front of the room, complete with a small riser where Nikolai is manning the DJ set up.

Not having had the chance to dedicate much time to music since that night I saw him sing at the pub, Nikolai requested to be in charge of it tonight. It almost surprised me when Tristan agreed without hesitation.

Nikolai taps the mic, turning the music down a bit. "It is my great honor to introduce to you, for the first time, Mr. and Mrs. Westbrook!"

The cheering gets louder, all but drowning out the music, so Nikolai turns it up as we get closer to the dance floor to share our first public moment as husband and wife.

We stop in the middle of the dance floor, and Tristan turns to me, resting his hand on my hip. I lift my free hand and rest it on his shoulder as we sway in time to Ruelle's "I Get to Love You."

"I know how you feel about making plans," Tristan murmurs after a few moments of silence. "I didn't choose anywhere for us to go."

A smile touches my lips. "Like a honeymoon?"

Tristan nods. "Wherever you want to go, name it, and I'll get us on the next flight."

"Are you sure it's a good time for us to leave?"

"We just got married, Rory. I'm going to take my beautiful wife wherever she wants to go. Any issues will exist when we get back."

"Can I think about it?"

"Take as much time as you need," he whispers, resting his forehead against mine and closing his eyes.

By the end of the song, other couples have joined us and are dancing. We stay for a couple more songs before Tristan leads me away. He introduces me to some of his distant family, cousins mostly, who are fae, some of whom don't seem thrilled he isn't anymore. He seems unaffected by it, which I admire so much.

Tristan introduces me to an endless line of colleagues and other fae and human friends who traveled here from all over the world.

At one point, I have to stifle a yawn, turning my face away from the couple we've been talking to for what seems like forever.

"Boring your bride on her wedding night, Westbrook?" an unfamiliar voice chimes in with a musical laugh that makes me turn to look at him. My eyes widen, and I immediately feel embarrassed.

"Do you have any unattractive friends?" I mutter.

The stranger laughs, flashing a perfect set of teeth as his eyes sparkle. "She's lovely *and* charming. How wonderful."

Tristan apologizes to the couple, and they smile before walking away. He slips his arm around my waist and sticks his other hand out to the man, who shakes it.

"Jae," Tristan says, offering a grin. "I'm surprised you made it."

"I heard rumblings that the legendary Tristan Westbrook was human. I had to see for myself."

"It's true," he says, shifting his gaze to meet mine. "And I've never been happier."

Allison chooses that moment to join us. "Damn, who's this?" she jerks her thumb in Jae's direction.

"Jae," Tristan says, though Allison hasn't looked at any of us since her eyes landed on him. "He's a friend from out of town."

I roll my eyes. "Wipe your drool away, Allison. It's not very becoming."

He offers her his hand. "Lovely to meet you," he murmurs in a silky voice.

She blushes, shaking his hand.

"Hey, Al?" I cut in.

"Huh?" she mumbles.

"Where's Oliver?" They came together; I'm hoping she didn't ditch him.

"Hmm? Oh!" She pulls her hand back and finally looks at me. "He's with Skylar at the bar. I think they're having some sort of drinking contest."

"That's my cue," Jae says with a smirk, turning to Tristan and me. "Congratulations. May you enjoy your life together."

"Thank you," I smile. "Maybe we'll see you again?"

"If you happen to be so lucky." He winks before walking away, and even that looks catlike and graceful.

Allison whistles under her breath before following him.

---

We spend the rest of the night and into the early morning celebrating the best day of our lives with the people we love.

I share a dance with my father, making half the guests cry, and Tristan guides my mom around the dance floor, the two of them smiling and laughing as they talk and dance.

Nikolai steps away from manning the music and offers me a dance. "How does it feel to be a married woman?" he asks, spinning me around with a wicked grin. He pulls me back in, and I wrap my arms around his neck.

"Pretty epic," I say.

"Have you decided where you'll go on your honeymoon? Tristan told me he's waiting for you to decide."

I press my lips together. "It sounds weird, but I kind of want to stay here."

"You just married probably the richest man in the city and you want to have a local honeymoon? How drunk are you?"

I slap his shoulder. "Shut up, I'm not drunk." I glance away and see Tristan dancing and chatting with Skylar. I smile and face Nikolai again. "It doesn't matter where we go."

"Let me guess, *as long as you're together?*"

"Yeah, pretty much." I laugh when he rolls his eyes. "Oh, quit being so bitter. You could have the happiness I feel right now." I nod toward Skylar and Tristan. "You know it, too."

He laughs. "Yeah, I don't think happiness like what you and Tristan have is in the cards for her and I. Sex, *definitely*. But romance? I don't think so."

I frown. "She'd want you to be happy," I whisper. "Layla would want you to love again."

His eyes widen, flicking back and forth between mine, and a small smile touches his lips. "Thanks, Aurora."

The song ends, and Tristan steals me away. We say goodbye to our friends and family and head upstairs. Once we're alone in the penthouse, Tristan wraps his arms around me and breathes deeply.

"Have you decided where you want to go?"

"We're already here."

He raises a brow. "Here, as in the hotel?"

I nod. "It's where we met. I think it's fitting we spend our first night as husband and wife here."

"You will never cease to amaze me."

I kiss the corner of his mouth and kick off my heels.

"That's good." I pat his chest. "Because you just signed up for a lifetime of this."

He smiles as he catches my hand and draws me closer, his breath warm against my cheek. "A lifetime will never be enough. I'll never have enough time with you."

"I know," I murmur. "Let's just start with right now." My fingers trail across his cheek, running along the stubble shadowing his jaw.

"Right now," he agrees.

---

We spend the next three days locked away in the penthouse. We barely leave the bedroom, unless we're eating or showering, and even then, we spend most of that time attached to each other. Our friends don't contact us. Everyone knows we're here, but they're giving us time to enjoy being together.

Finally leaving the suite, we stop by the bookstore—*my* bookstore—where we sit inside and plan an official launch. Excitement floods through me. I'm opening my bookstore.

"There's something else," I say after we've finished the business discussion.

"I'm listening."

"All of your stuff is at the hotel and most of my stuff is still at the dorm. We're already living together, but we still have our separate spaces."

"Tell me what you want, Rory."

"I want a place that's just ours. Not yours or mine. I want us to live away from the hotel and the apartment. Hell, I want us to get a house outside of the city with a porch and bay window with a reading nook and a pond in the backyard." I take a second to catch my breath. "Is that too much?"

He chuckles, brushing the hair away from my face and tucking it behind my ear. "That sounds perfect."

"Perfect," I echo with a sigh. "It can't be, not until we're safe from the Experiment. If they used Carter, what's to say they won't try to come after us to showcase their *success stories*?"

He frowns. "We'll find a way to keep them out of our lives. I promise."

We head to The Iron Lounge for lunch after Allison texts me, asking us to meet her there, and when we pull into the parking lot, I'm surprised to find it empty. We walk inside and find our friends—save for Oliver—eating and chatting at the bar.

"Where is everyone?" I ask as Tristan and I join them.

Nikolai takes a drink of his beer. "We closed the pub for the afternoon."

"Why?"

Allison licks her fingers and tosses a napkin onto the empty plate in front of her before she spins around to face us. "Because we need to talk to you about something."

"I guess the honeymoon's over," Tristan comments, and my pulse ticks faster.

"It doesn't have to be," Skylar says, sliding off her stool. "You have taken care of your people for as long as I can remember, Tristan. It's time you let *us* take care of *you*."

"What are you talking about?" I ask, the tension of this conversation already making my temple fill with uncomfortable pressure.

Nikolai moves to stand next to Skylar and hands me a large manila envelope. "Just hear us out, please."

My brows tug together as I open it and pull out the

contents—passports and driver's licenses. "Nikolai..."

"Almost a week ago, the two of you started your life together. It's time you *really* got to start that life."

I flip open one passport and see my face, but it isn't my name. I open the other and see Tristan's photo, but again a different name. "Very confused here," I say, glancing up from the passports to look at our friends.

Tristan puts his hand on my shoulder. "They want us to start over."

My eyes widen. "Start over, *how?*" There's an edge to my voice.

Allison answers, "We'd give you new identities and put a block on your memories of the fae world and all that entails. It'll give you a real chance at a happy *human* life together."

I shake my head. "What about the people who know us? What about my parents? They already almost lost one child because of the fae. What's to say they'd be safe once Tristan and I are no longer part of the fae world?" Jules put Elijah in a coma to get to me; my family's lack of knowledge of the fae world by no means protects them from it.

"I understand your concern," Allison says, tucking her hair behind her ear. The blond has faded since the start of the school year and it's grown past her shoulders. "We'd keep tabs on them and make sure they're safe. There are plenty of fae in the area, many of which respect Tristan and Skylar—Nikolai, even—and would happily agree to monitor and protect your family for as long as necessary."

"We'd also have to block their memories of you," Skylar adds, "and give them new ones so there aren't unexplainable blanks."

I rub my palms against my thighs, wiping the dampness from them. "I don't know if I can do this to them."

Unease blossoms in my chest, and for a split second, I consider the idea of telling them the truth. I quickly shove that away—it's too dangerous, especially now with the Experiment's involvement. "How would it work?"

Skylar and Allison exchange a glance before the latter fae says, "It'll be a process. Once we block their memories of you, using fae manipulation to make them forget you until we allow them to remember."

When my breath catches, Tristan slides his fingers through mine, and my eyes shift between our friends. "What about all of you? Are you going to make us forget you?"

"That was the plan," Skylar comments in a low voice, leaning against the bar and taking a drink of what appears to be whiskey.

I look at Nikolai, my mind racing. As much as I want a real shot at a life with Tristan, what they're proposing terrifies me. "There has to be another way."

"I don't know—"

"Find one," I demand desperately. I sound selfish when I should be grateful our friends are trying to give us the chance at happiness while they fight the enemy.

"We're doing this for you," Skylar snaps.

"It wouldn't be permanent, Ro," Allison chimes in, her eyes almost glassy. "It's to give you a chance at a normal, human life while we deal with the Experiment."

"Are you sure it'll work?" I ask.

Nikolai shrugs. "We won't know until we try it. Blocking your memories will be the easy part. It's the unblocking when the time comes we're not entirely certain about. I imagine it would depend on how much time had passed. Tristan?"

"That's right. I've seen it done a couple of times. Of

course, it's easier to remove if the period the memories are blocked is relatively short." He turns to me. "Should we consider it?"

Panic wraps like thorny vines around my chest, and my grip on his hand tightens. "I don't know." My voice is tight and uneven. I take a deep breath and let it out.

*... a normal, human life...*

"This would be *temporary*, right?" I check. "After the Experiment is no longer a threat, you'll give us our memories back?"

Allison nods. "If that's what you want."

A muscle in my jaw twitches from clenching so tight. "I don't want any of this, Al. I don't want to lose my friends. What if something happens to one of you during this entire battle, and we never get to see you again?"

"Freedom from the fae world comes at a price," Skylar says. "We've all had to make sacrifices—some bigger than others."

Nikolai frowns at her before turning to me. "We won't force this on you, but you should consider it. You're human. You no longer have any obligation to fight for the fae, though we know you would."

"Of course we would," Tristan says.

Nikolai nods. "You've helped just by bringing the courts together. We couldn't fight this battle without that union—even if it only lasts until the Experiment is stopped."

I bite the inside of my cheek, cringing when I taste copper. "This seems extreme. Why can't we keep our memories?"

Nikolai arches a brow. "You're telling me if you kept your memories of the fae and the Experiment, you wouldn't try to rush into battle with us?"

I stare at him, but he doesn't blink. Finally, I roll my eyes, scowling. "Whatever," I mutter.

"What exactly would you have us forget?" Tristan asks.

"Not so much forget, but we'd implant false memories. You'd believe you were different people, that the life you'll be living is the one you always have."

My brows tug together. "Tristan wasn't able to erase my memories when I found out about the fae. What makes you sure you can now?"

"We're not sure," Allison comments, reaching for her water glass on top of the bar, and gulps down a mouthful. "It's something we'd have to try."

"With everything the Experiment did to make you human, maybe you're susceptible to fae influence now," Nikolai adds.

My stomach drops; he could be right. "What about Tristan? It could be different for him as well, right? Because he was born fae?"

"Again," Allison offers, "we won't know until we try."

Tristan places his hands on my shoulders, turning me to face him. "It has to be our choice. We're not going to do this if it's not what you want."

I nod slowly, wishing I could read his emotions right now. "What do you want?" I ask in a quiet tone.

His eyes flick between mine. "I only want you."

Tristan took a tremendous risk and became human for me, to live a life with *me*, because he knew I was no longer immortal, and the idea of us not being together wasn't an option. He took a chance to be with me. It's time I take a chance to be with him.

"Okay," I say after what feels like an eternity of silence. "Let's start our life together."

# EPILOGUE

*Two Years Later...*

Sunday mornings are my favorite.
    I wake to the sound of cartoons on the television and the smell of French toast wafting through the house.

We've lived here for almost two years. It's a quaint country farmhouse on the outskirts of a one-stoplight town—the perfect environment for a new family, for *our* family.

I get out of bed and slide my feet into my slippers, pulling on my robe as I head down the hall into the kitchen.

"Morning," I murmur in a sleepy voice.

He glances up from the stove and grins at me. "Hmm... Good morning."

I walk around the kitchen island and slide my arms around him from behind, pressing my cheek into his back. "Breakfast smells amazing." I shift around and lean against his side, stealing a strawberry out of the basket and biting into it.

He leans down and kisses me. "It'll be ready soon."

I glance at the TV mounted to the wall above the fireplace in the living room. "He's still set on this one, huh?"

"I don't get it either, but the kid loves that talking cartoon sponge."

I lean up on my tiptoes and kiss him again before I walk into the living room and sit next to our son on the couch. He was born just over a year ago. Maxwell Donovan. He's absolutely perfect.

We watch cartoons until breakfast is ready, then I turn the TV off and carry Max to the table, sitting him in the highchair before I take the seat across from his father.

We eat breakfast, chatting about our upcoming week. I get up to clear the table just as the doorbell rings. I frown. "Are we expecting someone?"

He shakes his head, rising from his chair and kissing my cheek on his way past. "I'll get it."

I finish clearing the table and let Max go back to watching cartoons while I tidy up. Muffled voices sound from the front hallway as I load the dishwasher, and I offer a polite smile when my husband comes into the kitchen a few minutes later with a man and woman I've never seen before.

I look at my husband, drying my hands quickly and tossing the dish towel onto the counter beside me. "Are these friends from work?"

His jaw is set tight, his deep blue eyes filled with an unfamiliar darkness. "You should sit down."

My brows tug together as my stomach sinks. "What's wrong?"

He holds out his hand, and I take it automatically,

letting him guide me to a chair at the dining room table. The black-haired Asian woman with impeccable style and flawless makeup stands against the wall, watching me while the other man with dark hair and stubble and striking green eyes sits in the chair closest to me.

"I don't understand what's going on," I say, panic creeping into my voice. "Who—"

"Aurora," the man says, catching my attention.

"What?" I shake my head. "My name is—"

"Aurora," he repeats, ensnaring my gaze. "It's time to remember."

I run those words through my head a few times, and then the world goes dark. Photos flash across the backs of my eyes. Scenes at a hotel with the man and woman who are currently in our dining room, scenes of people I've never seen before but feel as though I *know*. I'm not sure how long it goes on for, but the longer the photos dance across my eyes, the more I remember.

Oh my god. This can't be real...

We're not these people we've been living as for two years.

We're Aurora and Tristan Westbrook.

My eyes snap open, and I gasp, covering my mouth with my hand as I look frantically between Nikolai, Skylar, and Tristan.

"It's okay, Rory," Tristan squeezes my shoulder.

*Rory*. My eyes fill with tears, and I throw myself at Nikolai, wrapping my arms around him. When I pull back, sniffling, he grins at me.

"Hey there. Long time no see."

"It's been two years," I say, glancing at Skylar. "What happened?"

"We did what we said we were going to," she says with

a hint of a smile.

"The Experiment?"

"Is gone," Nikolai says, "and that's all you need to know for now."

"Holy shit," I breathe. "Wait. Where's Allison?" My chest tightens with panic. "Why isn't she here?"

"Relax, she's fine." Skylar walks around the table and sits across from me. "She's been running your bookstore for the past two years. Right now, she and Oliver are visiting your parents and brother."

"How are they?"

"We've been checking in on them lots, don't worry." Nikolai pats my knee. "They're doing well. Elijah's on his high school football team."

I let out a breath, my lips curling into a smile as I wipe away my tears. "Good." My mind is still going a million miles an hour. "We can go back to our life?" I finally ask.

"It looks like you're enjoying your new one," Skylar comments mildly.

"Sure, but it's not really ours." I glance over at where Max has fallen asleep on the couch. Well, some of it is. I reach for Tristan's hand. "What do we do about the people who know us here?"

Nikolai shrugs. "Tell them you changed your names."

I shoot him a dry look. "Both of us? Because that doesn't look weird."

"There are too many people to manipulate their minds," Skylar says. "You don't have another option."

I glance up at Tristan, and he shrugs. "We'll make it work." There are so many obstacles, but the certainty in his voice and the way he's looking at me calms my nerves. He's right. We've come this far together—we'll figure this out too.

Nikolai glances down and grins at Max, who is tugging on his pant leg.

I scoop him up. "This," I say to Max with a smile, "is uncle Nikolai."

Nikolai snorts at the same moment Tristan scowls.

I rest Max on my lap. "Hey, buddy. Do you want to meet more of Mommy and Daddy's friends?"

Tristan chuckles behind me. "Allison is going to go nuts over him. Are you prepared to share your son with your best friend?"

My lips curl into a smile. "I can't wait. She's going to be the best aunt ever."

Skylar rolls her eyes, but she's smiling too. "If you decide you want to tell your family the truth about everything, it's safe enough now. And something tells me your parents would very much want to meet their grandson."

I keep my eyes on Max, uncertainty swirling in my stomach. The Experiment aside, I'm not sure I want my family to know about the fae. Not when it has the potential to open a door to the past that'll be impossible to close.

"Let's talk about it before we decide," Tristan says, his fingers sliding along the back of my neck, massaging it gently.

I nod in agreement, standing and passing our son to Nikolai.

After Tristan and I get dressed and Max is ready to go, the five of us get into Nikolai's car and head toward the city.

As I stare out the window, my fingers laced through Tristan's, I've never felt so at peace.

*Our family is going home.*

## THE END

# THESE WICKED DELIGHTS SNEAK PEEK
## CHAPTER ONE

Spending my eighteenth birthday working late on a school project is hopefully not a sneak peek into what my year is going to look like.

Stifling a yawn, I reach for my peppermint tea and take a sip, wrinkling my nose at its lukewarm temperature.

"We're almost done," Lana says with a sympathetic smile as she ties back her red wine-colored hair.

I wave her off and move to push my tea aside. My fingers hover around the outside of the paper cup, and I frown. It's radiating heat. *What the—*

"Emery?" Jessa says, pulling my attention away from the cup.

I shake my head, flipping the page in my notebook. *I need sleep.* "It's fine. We need to get it done." The assignment is due in a few days, and with the girls' opposite work schedules, tonight was the only time we were all available to finish it.

"We should be out partying, not stuck in this musty library," Jessa whines, picking at her chipped manicure.

I shrug, glancing around to find we're the only ones left in the building.

We finish the assignment an hour later. As we walk out of the school, Lana and Jessa link their arms through mine, the wind whipping around us, shaking leaves off the trees lining the lot. It's already dark, and the temperature has dropped. It's only the second week of November, but it feels more like the middle of December.

"Come on," Jessa says with a grin, "let's grab some food."

"Can't," I say. "I need to get home."

Lana pouts. "We have to do something to celebrate you getting old. Where do you want to go?" When I open my mouth, she quickly adds, "I'm not taking 'no' for an answer. Holly can scold me later." As if my mom would ever yell at her.

"Old?" I laugh, elbowing her side. "Fine. Let's go to Bread and Butter. But only for a little while." As much as I'd rather go home, I can't deny the desire for a latte and a massive piece of chocolate cake.

I send Mom a text to let her know I'll be a little late.

"Excellent choice," Jessa says, tugging us along toward Lana's car, where we pile in and head for the café.

---

Lana drops Jessa off before we head to my place. We take a right onto my road and drive for a while, gravel crunching under the car until Lana slows to a stop in front of my two-story farmhouse. The lights on either side of the door cast a warm glow on the covered porch where I've spent many summer afternoons reading until dark. The black shutters on the windows are a stark contrast to the white siding, but it gives the place character. Most of the house is obscured from view by massive trees anyway, which makes it feel private and secluded. The house belonged to my dad's parents and their parents before that. I often picture myself living here for the rest of my life and passing it down to my own child someday.

"Thanks for the ride," I say, shooting Lana a wink, "and the cake."

She grins at me, her pale green eyes glimmering. "Of course. Hey, before I forget, I'm going shopping in Augusta this weekend. You want to come?"

I grab my bag off the floor. I've lived in Covington my entire life; I've never been anywhere. My heart longs for the adventure of getting away from this town, but I've never been able to bring myself to leave. Even for a day of shopping a couple hours away. "Let me make sure my mom doesn't have anything planned. I'll text you later."

"Perfect." She glances toward the house and arches a brow. "Whose car is that?"

"Huh?" I turn to look, and excitement bubbles in my chest. I'm grinning like a kid on Christmas morning when I say, "Nova's here."

"This a secret boyfriend of yours I don't know about?"

I smack her arm. "No. Gross. I've told you about him. He was my dad's best friend. He comes around a few times a year and always visits on my birthday. Has for as long as I can remember."

"Oh yeah! The silver fox that brings you presents. Huh. He's kinda like a sexy Santa, but for your birthday."

I roll my eyes, shaking my head. "Are you done?"

"Yeah, yeah. Happy birthday, Em."

"Thanks." I shoulder my bag before closing the door, then hurry up the gravel driveway and the steps, the harsh wind making my hair fly in every direction. A hurricane of burnt orange curls obscures my view as I fumble to get my key in the lock.

Lana honks before backing out of the driveway and disappearing down the dark road.

Once inside, I drop my bag onto the bench and flip the lock over before hanging my key on the little hook next to the door. Then I kick off my shoes and toss them into the coat closet. The scent of cinnamon and apples tickles my nose; Mom always has at least one candle burning in the house, and she tries to coordinate them with the seasons.

Muffled voices float through the warm house, and I follow the sound down the hall, the old wood floors creaking under my stocking feet. I run my fingers through my hair, attempting to untangle it as I step into the kitchen and find Mom at the stove. My eyes quickly land on Donovan—or Nova as I've called him since I was old enough to talk—who is sitting at the kitchen table. His brown hair is a bit grayer than when I saw him over the summer; longer, too, curling slightly at the ends.

"Hey, Nova." A grin spreads across my lips as he gets up, opening his arms just in time for me to run into them.

"Happy birthday, Emery," he says, wrapping his arms around me. There's a fondness in his tone that makes my heart swell.

Donovan is the closest thing I've ever had to a father. My dad died a few months after I was born from a brain aneurysm. Mom says it was completely random. He was fit and healthy, but none of that mattered. For eighteen years, I've missed someone I never really knew, someone I have no memory of. It's a weirdly unexplainable grief that I'm still learning to live with.

Nova made it a point to become a part of my life after his death, and I look forward to each visit. Maybe it helps me feel connected to my dad, and maybe that's weird, but I don't care.

And when my birth mom died in a car accident while on a business trip in Savannah when I was five, her sister Holly took me in and raised me. She never married or had kids, but from the moment she adopted me, we became the only family the other needed.

"Hi, honey." Mom smiles once I detach myself from Nova, who leans against the table. She pushes the pin-straight light brown hair away from her face with the back of her hand and wipes her palms on her worn jeans. "Did you have a good day?"

I take a seat at the table. "Same old." I look to Nova. "What have you been up to?"

"Same old," he says with a smile. It's the kind of smile that makes the skin around his eyes crinkle.

"I ordered burgers from that barbecue place you love." Mom glances at the silver watch on her wrist; I gave it to her for her fortieth birthday a few months ago. "Should be here soon."

I try to catch her gaze, but her eyes won't meet mine. "Did you get fries?"

She finally looks at me for a brief moment, forcing a smile. "And onion rings."

I nod along because I'm not sure what else to do. If something is wrong, I don't want to bring it up in front of Nova. "Great," I say instead.

"I'll be right back," Nova chimes in. "I left Emery's gift in the car."

That catches my attention. "You didn't have to get me anything."

He waves me off, grabbing his navy jacket from the back of the chair and shrugging it on as he leaves the kitchen.

"Is everything okay?" I ask after hearing the front door shut. We don't have long before Nova comes back, but I need to know what's going on. Maybe she had a bad day at work. She's a nurse at one of the hospitals in Atlanta, and as she's told me on more than one occasion, some days are harder than others.

Mom nods, again forcing a smile.

I can't help but frown. "Why don't I believe you?"

She presses her lips into a firm line. "It's your birthday, Em—"

"I don't care. Talk to me." I want to be there for her like she's always been there for me.

There's a moment of heavy silence, then she sighs. "There's a lot you don't know about this family, and I'm not sure how to tell you."

*Uh, where did* that *come from?*

I cross my arms. "Wait, what?" That is *not* the direction I was expecting this conversation to go. "What are you talking about?"

"Oh, Emery, I—"

The front door opens and closes. "Food's here," Nova hollers, coming back into the kitchen with a brown paper bag in one hand and a purple gift bag in the other. He glances between us. "Everything okay?" He sets the gift bag on the counter and the food on the table.

"Of course," Mom says as she turns to the cupboard and pulls out plates. "Let's eat while it's hot."

We sit around the table. I chew and swallow, but my burger tastes like dust. My stomach is twisted in knots and my mind is racing. Mom didn't have a chance to elaborate before Nova came back, so my brain has resorted to coming up with impossible answers. I have a long lost sibling. Mom was in the CIA, which is why she was always away on business trips. My inheritance was stolen and now I have no way to pay for college.

*This is ridiculous.* I shove those thoughts away. *I need real answers.*

I glance up from my plate at the exact moment Nova and Mom seem to be exchanging a worried glance. I drop the fry in my hand and exhale a heavy breath. "Okay, that's it. Someone needs to tell me what's going on. You're both acting super weird, and I'm freaking out over here." I shove my plate away and turn to my mom. "What were you going to tell me?"

Her face pales as her bright blue eyes go wide, and she looks at Nova as she wraps her beige cardigan tighter around herself.

"Emery," he starts, his voice level and calm, which only makes my pulse race.

My attention snaps to him. "You know something about this?"

He nods. "It's why I'm here."

For some reason, my stomach sinks. Something like betrayal flickers through me, but I don't have time to question it. "I don't understand," I whisper. Nova comes every year on my birthday.

"There are things you need to know." There's a subtle urgency in his tone that I definitely don't like. "You're eighteen now," he continues. "Things are going to change quickly. You need to be prepared for that, or it could be very dangerous for you and those around you."

The food in my stomach feels like concrete. "What are you talking about?"

He hesitates before saying, "I understand what I'm about to say is going to sound crazy. You've known me forever, so I hope you can trust that I want to make sure you're safe. It's what your parents wanted."

My vision blurs as tears gather in my eyes. I swallow hard, but can't bring myself to speak.

Donovan's face is filled with a gut-wrenching mix of concern and guilt. "You're a Wielder, Emery. Someone with the ability to call on the elements of nature and use them. And now that you're of age, your magic has been awakened. You may not sense it now, but you will soon. It could take days, or weeks ... even months for some Wielders, but it's important you start learning how to use and control it early on."

I stare at the man I've known my entire life who suddenly feels like a stranger. I open and close my mouth twice before turning to Mom and shaking my head. "Is this some sort of joke? Because it's not funny." It sounds absolutely ridiculous. *Wielder. Magic. Awakened.* What the hell am I supposed to do with that?

She glances down, exhaling a shaky breath. "It's not a joke, honey." She lifts her head and meets my gaze, her eyes glassy with unshed tears. "He's telling the truth. Your father's family ... they had power—"

"No," I snap. "I don't believe any of this." And I don't want to hear about it.

"I'm so sorry, Emery," she says. "I wanted to tell you. I should have years ago, to prepare you for what's coming.

But I was scared. I didn't know how to tell you or how'd you react."

I'm waiting for one of them to laugh, to let me in on the joke, but their expressions remain serious.

My head spins as I try to rationalize what I've been told. Nope. It's not happening. This is crazy. It's not... This isn't real.

I push my chair back, and it scrapes across the linoleum floor. "You're lying." I'm not sure which of them I'm directing the accusation at. Both, I guess. Hot tears burn my eyes, and I try to blink them away. "Why are you doing this?"

"I know this is a lot to take in," Nova says, his voice soft and filled with sympathy. "I'm here to help you, Emery. I have a place you can stay. It's a safe environment where you can learn and explore what abilities you have. There are other Wielders who live there. Spending time with them will help you adjust as your magic grows stronger."

He's insane. I need to get out of here. No. *He* does.

"Stop." My voice cracks as I back away from the table. "You need to leave." I press my hand against my chest as if that will help stop my heart from cracking in two. I've looked up to this man my entire life, and now... I don't even know what's happening, or *why*.

"Emery, please," Mom says, getting up and coming toward me.

"No," I say through the tears. "He's lying. He has to be. My dad—"

"Was one of the strongest Wielders in history," Nova says, still sitting at the table.

Mom reaches for me, but I pull my arm back and retreat another few steps until I bump into the counter.

"Mom..." My voice is thick with tears.

Her expression crumbles. "Your father didn't die from what you think he did," she says.

I freeze. "What?"

Nova gets up now. "His magic consumed him. He pushed his power away, refused to work with it. He wanted to live a normal life, to be a normal husband. Simon didn't want his magic, so he pretended it didn't exist. And it worked for a while—until it didn't. His power went unchecked and it destroyed him, Emery, and if you don't come with me and let me help you, the same thing will happen to you."

My vision blurs with tears, and my throat feels so tight I don't think I can speak.

"Honey—" Mom starts.

"Get. Out." I manage those venom-filled words and swallow past the lump in my throat.

Mom shakes her head, panic flashing across her features. "Nova—"

"It's all right, Holly," he assures her in a soft tone.

"Get out!" I scream until my throat is raw.

Mom closes her eyes, tears rolling down her cheeks. "You need to go with him, Emery." Her voice is steady.

I shake my head. "You can't be serious. Mom, he's crazy. There's no—"

She sniffles, opening her eyes to meet my gaze. "I started packing your bag while you were at school."

Betrayal whips through me like a smack to the face. "What?"

She wipes under her eyes, but tears continue to fall. "I can't help you with this, but Nova can. Please, *please* let him." She reaches for me again, and this time I let her wrap her fingers around my wrists. "Because I-I can't lose you too."

"I can't just leave. I'm in school. I have a life." It sounds like a weak argument even to me, but it's all I can come up with. I don't believe anything I've been told. I can't. Because if it's true—if I somehow have magical abilities—everything I've ever known about my family, my life, it all comes into question. And I'm not sure how to live with that.

# ACKNOWLEDGMENTS

I published the first edition of this book in 2018 with an incredible team of support behind me. It's equal parts crazy and amazing that so many of you are still here, cheering me on as loudly as you did five years ago.

To my early readers, Allison Alexander, Bethany Atazadeh, and Katie Wismer, for your helpful feedback and encouragement to make this book epic.

To my cover designer, Keylin Rivers, for your amazing eye for design. It is always an absolute pleasure to work with you.

To my proofreader, Mackenzie Letson of Nice Girl, Naughty Edits, for your attention to detail while polishing this book.

As always, thank you to my friends and family, for your continued support of my creative passions.

# About the Author

Jessi Elliott is a paranormal and fantasy romance author. She lives in Ontario, Canada with her adorable calico cat, Phoebe.

When she's not working on her next book, she likes to hang out with friends and family, get lost in a steamy romance novel, watch *Friends*, and drink coffee.

Find Jessi at www.jessielliott.com and on social media. You can join her newsletter to stay up to date on book news and upcoming releases, and her Facebook reader lounge for exclusive news, promos, review opportunities, and giveaways!

- instagram.com/authorjessielliott
- amazon.com/Jessi-Elliott/e/B079X3RDSJ
- bookbub.com/authors/jessi-elliott
- goodreads.com/authorjessielliott
- facebook.com/authorjessielliott
- tiktok.com/@authorjessielliott

Manufactured by Amazon.ca
Bolton, ON

33134473R00365